STAR TREK®
TYPHON PACT

PLAGUES OF NIGHT

DAVID R. GEORGE III

Based upon *Star Trek* and
Star Trek: The Next Generation®
created by Gene Roddenberry
and
Star Trek: Deep Space Nine®
created by Rick Berman & Michael Piller

POCKET BOOKS
New York   London   Toronto   Sydney   New Delhi   Adarak

Pocket Books
A Division of Simon & Schuster, Inc.
1230 Avenue of the Americas
New York, NY 10020

This book is a work of fiction. Names, characters, places, and incidents either are products of the author's imagination or are used fictitiously. Any resemblance to actual events or locales or persons, living or dead, is entirely coincidental.

™, ® and © 2012 by CBS Studios Inc. STAR TREK and related marks are trademarks of CBS Studios Inc. All Rights Reserved.

This book is published by Pocket Books, a division of Simon & Schuster, Inc., under exclusive license from CBS Studios Inc.

All rights reserved, including the right to reproduce this book or portions thereof in any form whatsoever. For information, address Pocket Books Subsidiary Rights Department, 1230 Avenue of the Americas, New York, NY 10020.

First Pocket Books paperback edition June 2012

POCKET and colophon are registered trademarks of Simon & Schuster, Inc.

For information about special discounts for bulk purchases, please contact Simon & Schuster Special Sales at 1-866-506-1949 or business@simonandschuster.com.

The Simon & Schuster Speakers Bureau can bring authors to your live event. For more information or to book an event, contact the Simon & Schuster Speakers Bureau at 1-866-248-3049 or visit our website at www.simonspeakers.com.

Manufactured in the United States of America

10 9 8 7 6 5 4 3 2 1

ISBN 978-1-4516-4955-0
ISBN 978-1-4516-4957-4 (ebook)

To Colleen Genevieve Ragan,
Friend, sister, native, spirit,
A woman who brings love and laughter with her,
Forever the benevolent queen of all she surveys

MacBeth: Do you not hope your children shall be kings,
When those that gave [a noble title] to me
Promis'd no less to them?

Banquo: That, trusted home,
Might yet enkindle you unto the crown,
. . . . But 'tis strange;
And oftentimes, to win us to our harm,
The instruments of darkness tell us truths,
Win us with honest trifles, to betray 's
In deepest consequence.

—William Shakespeare,
The Tragedy of MacBeth, Act I, Scene 3

And each day brings a new darkness—
A deception, a betrayal,
Or some simpler brutality—
Strung together like plagues of night.

—K. C. Hunter,
Cycles in the Sky, "Nyx and Eos"

Ab Initio

A river of fire flooded the corridor. Visible through ports in the outer bulkhead, uniformed Starfleet officers raced before the wave of the explosion, but not fast enough. Overtaken and engulfed by the flames, they surely could not have survived.

Subcommander Orventa T'Jul stood before the main viewscreen on the bridge of the Romulan vessel *Dekkona,* aboard which she served as second-in-command. Alongside the ship's commander, Marius, she peered at the drama playing out aboard Starfleet's Utopia Planitia command facility. The space station orbited the fourth planet in the Sol system, located in the very heart of the Federation. A shallow arc of the rust-colored, largely desert world curved across the bottom of the viewer, the night-shrouded portion of the surface flecked here and there with the lights of cities. Above Sol IV, scattered in space about the station, a score or more of starships in various stages of construction hung suspended in docking scaffolds. The sizable number of vessels marked Starfleet's ongoing efforts to recover from the devastation wrought by the previous year's Borg invasion. T'Jul wondered how many of those ships would carry the revolutionary quantum slipstream drive, and just how long it would take the UFP to press its tactical advantage against Romulus. The thought reinforced the importance of the mission upon which Commander Marius currently led them.

"They're venting atmosphere," reported Centurion Kozik from his tactical board. A green tinge suffused the dim lighting on the bridge, indicating to the crew that the ship's cloak remained engaged and functional.

"Very good," Marius said beside T'Jul. "The first crack in the dam."

T'Jul studied the viewscreen, her gaze tracing along the narrow conduit that joined one of the station's four outer, hemispherical modules to the tall cylinder that formed its core. Two-thirds of the way out on the connecting arm, a tattered gash had opened the structure to space, a jet of vapor streaming out into the void. The subcommander assumed that emergency bulkheads would automatically gird into place inside the station and halt the loss of air, but even before they could do so, a blue-white flash of energy cut across the compromised section of the hull, the telltale sign of a force field activating to seal the breach.

Anticipating the commander's next order, T'Jul looked to Marius, who nodded once. "Take us into position," T'Jul said, turning to address Lieutenant Torlanta, whose pilot console stood on the starboard side of the bridge, angled toward the main viewer.

"Yes, Subcommander," said Torlanta, immediately moving her hands across her control panel.

T'Jul looked back at the viewscreen, where the image shifted as the ship began to move. She imagined that she could perceive *Dekkona* springing to life about her, that she could feel the thrusters firing, pushing the great hawklike vessel closer to the Utopia Planitia station. She craved those sensations, wanting a command of her own, a starship that would function as an extension of herself, her orders translated into action by its crew in the same way that her central nervous system converted her thoughts into movement.

On the viewer, the space station grew larger and slipped downward as *Dekkona* neared it, rising up along its cylindrical core. The ship approached the second, upper row of structures that extended from the central body of the station on slender arms, a quartet of circular assemblies. A pair of large, dome-shaped constructs at either end of the core completed the facility.

Beside T'Jul, Marius turned and climbed the steps to the command chair. He took his seat, then told her, "Prepare for extraction."

"At once," replied T'Jul, knowing that the most critical moment of their assignment drew close. She quickly moved to the console she crewed on the port side of the bridge and keyed in a signal to Lieutenant Rixora.

Sparing another glance at the space station, she hoped that the Breen operative would succeed in carrying out his segment of the mission. The explosion aboard Utopia Planitia signaled that he'd begun implementing his endgame. It would soon require precise coordination between Kazren and the *Dekkona* crew to complete it.

T'Jul spun crisply on her heel and headed for one of the bridge's aft doors. As it glided open before her, Lieutenant Korvess spoke up from her communications console, which adjoined the tactical board off to port. "Commander, internal comm traffic within the space station suggests that they're closing in on the operative."

As concern rose within T'Jul, she turned to see Marius face the stout, aging officer. Korvess stood with a hand raised to the side of her head, one fingertip extended to the earpiece protruding from beneath her graying hair. Before Marius could respond to her, Kozik said, "The Starfleet patrol ship is energizing its tractor beam."

"Have they detected us?" Marius demanded.

T'Jul's gut tightened. She knew that the latest generation of cloaking device should have rendered *Dekkona* largely undetectable to Federation technology, but until now, no Romulan vessel had deployed the improved practical-invisibility apparatus in the field. For all the subcommander knew, the ship could be trailing positrons or some other particles that would lead Utopia Planitia's patrol vessel—identified as *U.S.S. Sparrow*—directly to the ship and its crew.

Kozik worked his tactical panel. "I don't think so," he said. "The patrol ship isn't mov—"

A bright light bloomed on the main viewscreen, halting Kozik in mid-sentence. T'Jul looked to the viewer and saw a huge fireball erupting from the station's lower core. A mass of broken hull and burning atmosphere surged toward *Sparrow,* reaching it in seconds. T'Jul watched as the vessel quaked beneath the assault, though it did not appear to sustain much damage.

She could not say the same for the space station. A great, gaping hole had been blasted through the lower quarter of its cylindrical core, the large dome at that end nearly severed from the rest of the facility. Lights visible through the station's many ports all went dark, then flickered back on above the wrecked area, though not below it.

"Utopia Planitia's shields are down," Kozik said.

"Go. Now," said Commander Marius. "Get us to the rendezvous."

Without waiting to hear an acknowledgment of the order, but knowing that the command crew would follow it, T'Jul rushed out. Past the open blast doors that allowed *Dekkona's* bridge to function as its own escape pod, one of two parallel corridors extended the length of the ventral conduit that connected to the main, aft body of the ship. Doors lined either side of the passage, all the way to the hatch that sealed off the forward third of the conduit from the middle third. With the crew on high alert, the passage stood empty.

T'Jul hastened forward. As she bypassed the turbolift, she broke into a sprint. She passed conference rooms, engineering substations, equipment junctions, two weapons caches, transporter rooms. Her long legs easily devoured the decking, her footfalls thudding along the matte gray carpet that padded the space.

The second explosion shouldn't have followed the first so quickly, she thought as she ran. Kazren's plan had called for the first blast to cover his theft from Utopia Planitia's computer system, and for the second to bring down the station's shields once he'd reached the extraction point. The interval between the two actions should have required more than a few moments. *He's in trouble,* she concluded, and that put the success of the mission at risk.

The large hatch between the forward and middle sections of the corridor split along an angle and opened at T'Jul's approach, the two panels retracting into the bulkheads. She cleared the raised threshold and immediately eyed her destination. A broad set of closed double doors on the left side of the corridor shielded the latest upgrade to *Dekkona,* the ship possessing the most advanced technology in the Romulan Imperial Fleet.

When T'Jul reached the doors, she flattened her hand against a security plate. The scanner glowed yellow as it read the details of her flesh, and then the adjacent screen displayed some of the particulars of her service record: rank, serial number, posting, clearance level. She gazed at the image of her face that accompanied the facts of her life in the fleet. Her brunette hair and green eyes set her outside the norm of Romulan physicality, and the style in which she wore her hair—not quite so closely cropped or rigidly shaped as that of most of her fellow citizens—extended her individuality. Such distinguishing features had brought her both praise and disapprobation inside the military. As she had numerous times before, T'Jul wondered if she would need to bow to convention in order to receive a command. She had climbed to the brink of being given her own starship, but honestly didn't know what more she might need to do in order to pull herself up the final rung.

The hard, metallic sound of locks releasing reached T'Jul, and the doors divided to allow her entry. She quickly stepped into the phase-transition control room, the doors sealing loudly behind her. Directly ahead, a large platform filled most of the deck space within the compartment. Mounted atop it, an elaborate latticework of thin silver piping put her in mind of one of the Tholians' energy webs. At the center of the mechanism, she spied six pieces of black mesh, paired along the height, width, and depth axes, each of them bordered and supported by four of the silver tubes.

Along the right bulkhead, a viewscreen showed a portion of the Utopia Planitia station. A small crate sat on the deck below it, one side covered with minuscule, unreadable text, with a keypad set into the top. In the left-hand portion of the compartment, two officers—a man and a woman, Lieutenants Diveln and Rixora—crewed a long, freestanding control console. Without preamble, T'Jul pointed to the viewer and said, "Display the ship."

"Yes, Subcommander," said Diveln. On-screen, a simulated image of the cloaked *Dekkona* appeared, superimposed onto the live view of Utopia Planitia. The perspective, fixed from beneath the aft hull of the Romulan vessel, showed the underside of the ship's long neck stretching away at the top of the picture; at the bottom, one of the space station's connectors that branched off the core filled the screen from left to right, becoming larger as *Dekkona* eased nearer. As T'Jul watched, the apparent forward motion of the ship ceased.

"We're in position, Subcommander," Rixora said. "But we're no longer reading the operative's homing beacon."

"Resort to secondary protocol," T'Jul ordered, snapping her head around toward the officers behind the control panel. "Employ passive sensors, restricted to the section of the space station containing the extraction point." Kazren's physical parameters had been recorded for just such a circumstance.

"Yes, Subcommander," Rixora said. "Initiating scan."

If they couldn't pinpoint Kazren, T'Jul knew that Commander Marius would not risk attempting to retrieve him blindly, nor would he resort to employing active sensors. While the success of the mission would provide great rewards for the Empire, recklessness could result in the destruction of *Dekkona* and the death of its crew—or worse, the capture of both. Before Marius would permit the chance of that to increase, he would allow the mission to fail. When Praetor Tal'Aura had approved the plan some time ago, she—

"Subcommander, I've located the operative," Rixora said. "He's alive, near the extraction point, but stationary."

They must be closing in on him, T'Jul thought. "Is he alone?"

Rixora worked her controls. "Yes. For now."

T'Jul wanted to order a wider sensor scan, an active scan, so that she could better understand Kazren's situation. But she knew that Marius would not want her to chance giving up the location of *Dekkona*. Nor did they have the luxury of time; the sooner the ship and its crew could depart the Sol system, the better their chances of escaping Federation space safely.

"Take us in," she ordered.

"Signaling the bridge that we're taking over piloting control," Diveln said. "Firing thrusters."

T'Jul peered back at the viewscreen, where the representation of the cloaked vessel slowly approached the Federation space station once more. Diveln recited the dwindling distance between the two, counting down from one hundred in increments of ten. As he reached fifty, the bridge of *Dekkona* passed above Utopia Planitia's connecting arm. At twenty, Rixora reconfirmed Kazren's location and status. At ten, the midpoint of *Dekkona*'s long neck—which housed the phase-transition control room where T'Jul presently stood—hovered above the station's connector. At that point, the procedures that Commander Marius had put in place required her to issue the final order.

"Is Kazren still motionless?" she asked. "And still alone?"

Rixora consulted her panel. "Yes, Commander."

"Then proceed with extraction," T'Jul said.

"Proceeding with extraction," Rixora replied.

On the platform, the silver rods began to move. T'Jul watched the frames that bordered the black, metal mesh shift, stretching and condensing the material. When the repositioning achieved the necessary dimensions, the pieces moved together to form a rectangular parallelepiped at the center of the platform— essentially a box roughly large enough to contain a standing humanoid.

When Diveln began to count backward from ten, T'Jul again looked to the viewer. There, the depiction of *Dekkona* slowly descended toward the connecting arm of the station. Not completely confident in the new technology, T'Jul braced herself for what seemed like the collision to come. Instead, as planned, the neck of the starship appeared to pass through the station's arm, stopping at the moment of greatest intersection.

"Extraction point achieved," said Rixora. "Initiating phase transition."

The new Romulan cloak achieved more than practical invisibility. It altered the structure of matter in the objects it enveloped, allowing those objects to pass through normal matter. At the moment, the mesh enclosure surrounded the space the Breen operative occupied aboard the Utopia Planitia station, in unphased space.

The base of the platform glowed a brilliant white. Within the mesh box, T'Jul saw, the air began to shimmer and pulse. Amorphous splashes of blue-green slowly resolved themselves into the shape of a man, and then into the man himself. As the radiance of the platform faded, the mesh planes withdrew to reveal Kazren—the structure of the matter composing his body newly modified to a phased state.

To Diveln and Rixora, T'Jul said, "Disengage *Dekkona* from the station, then signal Commander Marius that we can proceed to the delivery point."

"Yes, Subcommander," said Rixora.

Kazren stepped off the platform and approached T'Jul. In contrast to the subcommander's tall, lean form, the Breen operative possessed a stocky build, short but solid. He had wide, cloudy green eyes, and his bronze-colored skin contrasted dramatically with the thin carpet of white hair that crowned his head. "Subcommander," he said, and he pulled a Federation isolinear optical chip from a pocket in the blue engineering jumpsuit he wore. "We have our objective."

T'Jul felt a rush of energy inside her, satisfied at the accomplishment of the most perilous part of their mission, but also excited at what that accomplishment would mean for the Romulan Empire. She reached for the data-storage device Kazren held up before her, but he let the isolinear chip slip into the curled fingers of his fist. "Our orders are to deliver the schematics directly to Salavat," he said, naming a world within the Breen Confederacy.

"Of course," T'Jul said, containing her frustration; she knew that Commander Marius wanted the stolen data for the Romulan Empire. While he in general supported the alliance of Romulus with the five other Typhon Pact nations, he had often stated how difficult he found it to trust anybody outside the Empire. T'Jul fought back her impulse to seize Kazren's wrist, forcibly peel his fingers from around the isolinear chip, and take custody of the data-storage device for Marius. She would content herself with the knowledge that, while the Breen operative retained possession of the stolen quantum slipstream drive schematics, Commander Marius retained possession of Kazren.

"With your permission, Subcommander," the operative said, gesturing toward the crate below the viewscreen.

"By all means," T'Jul offered, nodding with what she meant to appear as magnanimity.

Kazren slipped the isolinear chip back inside a pocket of his jumpsuit, then paced over to the crate. He keyed a code into its locking mechanism, which emitted a series of trills at his touch. Then he opened the top of the crate and pulled out a Breen full-body environmental suit. T'Jul had only ever heard the suits referred to as refrigeration units, a means of re-creating the frozen climate of the Breen homeworld. But Kazren clearly had required no such environmental adjustments to survive the more than two hundred days he'd spent posing as a civilian engineer aboard the Utopia Planitia facility, calling into question what little T'Jul thought she knew about the Breen.

Kazren pulled on the layered tan suit, then slipped on the distinctive snout-nosed helmet his people unaccountably wore. The complete outfit produced a slimming effect on the operative, who appeared not simply thinner, but also taller. A burst of electronic noise issued from his helmet, which T'Jul's universal translator rendered as, *"Thank you, Subcommander."*

T'Jul nodded in response, looking at the horizontal green light above the pronounced muzzle of Kazren's helmet, roughly where his eyes would be.

"Have quarters been assigned to me?" he asked via his electronic garble. *"I am fatigued."*

T'Jul raised her hand in the direction of the control console on the opposite side of the room. "Lieutenant Diveln will escort you there." Kazren bowed his head in reply, then headed for the doors after Diveln.

"Trop Kazren," said T'Jul, employing the Breen's title, though she had no clear idea of what the designation meant. He stopped and turned back to face her. "Once you are settled into your quarters, but before you lay your head down, Commander Marius would appreciate the opportunity to debrief you." It occurred to T'Jul that she did not even know if Breen actually slept lying down—or if they slept at all.

"Of course," Kazren said. *"I'll expect him shortly."* He then followed Diveln into the corridor.

T'Jul looked over at Rixora, who busily secured the phase-transition console. The subcommander then glanced back at the viewscreen, where an empty field of stars had replaced the Starfleet space station. *Dekkona* and its crew had spent too long a time in enemy territory for her liking, and it pleased her that, at last, the ship headed, if not for the Romulan Empire, then at least for the friendly provinces of an ally.

Exiting into the corridor, T'Jul headed back to the bridge. She would provide Commander Marius with a status report. After an appropriate interval, T'Jul knew, she would accompany Marius to Kazren's guest quarters, where the commander would insist on a full description of the Breen's leg of the mission. As she considered the acquisition of the slipstream schematics, T'Jul again felt energized.

She had no appetite for war, but she respected the balance of power. It unsettled her to know that, even with the Romulan fleet's development of the phasing cloak, the quantum slipstream drive provided the Federation with a first-strike capability. Once Commander Marius delivered Kazren to the Breen Confederacy, once the operative delivered the schematics to their engineers, and once those engineers turned those technical specs into reality, everything would change.

No, T'Jul did not want war. If it came, though, she wanted her side to achieve a decisive victory. And so she would do everything she could to ensure the military superiority of the Romulan Star Empire and the Typhon Pact.

I

Fears and Scruples

Banquo: Fears and scruples shake us.
   In the great hand of God I stand, and thence
   Against the undivulg'd pretence I fight
   Of treasonous malice.
      —William Shakespeare,
       The Tragedy of MacBeth, Act II, Scene 3

April 2382

1

Kasidy Yates watched as a seething sea of fire cascaded toward her. Within the roiling flames, she spied sections of hull plating hurtling forward, end over end, the conflagration feasting on the lost atmosphere and fractured fragments of the wounded space station. The blaze grew until it filled the screen on her companel, and then the image changed to a view of the aftermath of the explosion. From above, with the red globe of Mars in the background, Utopia Planitia floated in orbit with a substantial chunk of its main cylinder ripped away. The great dome at that end of the station, dark and seemingly abandoned, barely remained attached to the structure.

Tension gripped Kasidy's chest, as though a cold hand had reached in and seized her heart. According to the news feed, some sort of industrial accident had befallen Utopia Planitia. Starfleet had yet to offer casualty figures, but she had no doubt that lives—many lives—had been lost.

Kasidy reached up and stabbed at the controls of the companel to deactivate it, then pushed herself away from the wall-mounted device. The wheels of her chair rolled smoothly on the hardwood floor, and she stood up as though propelled from her seat. She stalked across the room that served primarily as a home office, but doubled as a guest room for any visitors who stayed overnight. Framed photographs of family, friends, and special places adorned the walls, and a sofa to her left converted into a comfortable bed.

The heels of Kasidy's shoes clocked against the floor as she crossed the room and over to the window. Pushing aside the wine-colored drapes, she glanced out the back of the house. She slid open the window, and a warm drift of air greeted her, carrying with it the bittersweet scents of autumn. In the distance, atop the rolling hills of Kendra Province, the skeletal forms of denuded trees marched along a base of yellowing grass, the groundcover partially veiled by the vibrant crimsons, ochers, and golds of fallen leaves. Just three weeks earlier, the sky had grown pale, and a cold snap had attested to the impending arrival of winter. Over the previous few days, though, the cerulean expanse of summer seemed to return, with higher temperatures bringing a temporary reprieve from the snows that would eventually blanket the land.

Kasidy concentrated on the vista before her, attempting to put thoughts of the Utopia Planitia calamity out of her mind. Away to the right, she could just make out a short arc of the Yolja River as it bent southward, to where it twined through valley plains and dense forests until it spilled into the turquoise waters of the Korvale Ocean. To the left of the house stood an outbuilding that Kasidy had built during the past six months, a constructive outlet for her anxious energy. The oversized shed lodged the escape pod that Nog had long ago modified for planet-based emergency use. A good friend, Nog had worried about her when she'd been pregnant and alone back then, and he hadn't wanted her to have to walk the couple of kilometers into Adarak if the town's local transporter went off line for maintenance or some other reason. At the time, six years earlier, Ben had yet to return from his mysterious sojourn in the Bajoran wormhole.

Ben.

Just thinking about him hurt.

Except that it didn't *just* hurt. Even more than a year after her husband had gone, thoughts of him dredged up a complex mix of emotions. Kasidy recalled vividly the last time he had been home—and how she had pulled open the front door and told him to leave. In retrospect, that night had not brought an end to their marital troubles, nor had it truly been the beginning of their separation. Emotionally, they had parted ways months prior to that, perhaps even years.

No, not years, Kasidy thought. She had waited for Ben through her pregnancy, choosing to believe the veracity of the vision she'd experienced just after the end of the Dominion War. In it, her husband spoke to her from within the wormhole—

what Ben and the Bajoran faithful called the Celestial Temple—
and told her that he would someday return to her.

And he had. Just a moment after Kasidy gave birth to
Rebecca, Ben walked through a doorway in the Shikina Monastery, as though he'd simply been away on some ordinary excur-
sion. The three of them—mother, daughter, father—went back
to the house outside Adarak, to the land that Ben had secured,
to the house that he had planned and that Kasidy and Jake had
built during his absence.

For years, all had been well. Rebecca grew up healthy and
happy, and despite her status among adherents of the Ohalu religious sect as the Avatar—a harbinger of a new age of awareness
and understanding for the people of Bajor—the Bajorans for the
most part respected the family's privacy. Kasidy and Ben settled
into a relatively quiet life centered around raising their daughter.

Starfleet had wanted Ben back, of course. They offered him
an admiralty, which he declined, preferring instead to step away
from active duty. Kasidy, too, distanced herself from her vocation; though she continued to remotely oversee the operations of
her freighter, *Xhosa,* she turned over the actual day-to-day running of the ship to her first mate, Wayne Sheppard.

Those days at home in Kendra had brought simple but deeply
abiding joys. With Ben's attentions not continually given over to
the responsibilities and vagaries of command, and with Kasidy
not away for weeks at a time on cargo runs, she felt closer to
her husband than ever. And the emotions engendered in her by
their daughter filled her so completely, she could scarcely believe
it; Kasidy never before knew anything like the bond she shared
with Rebecca.

As though summoned by Kasidy's thoughts, a high-pitched
peal rang out. In the instant before she recognized her daughter's
laughter, her brain processed the sound as a scream. A sensation
like an electric charge flowed through Kasidy's body. Two years
prior, such shrieks had haunted her dreams. A religious zealot
had kidnapped Rebecca, and in the nights before they safely
recovered her, Kasidy's nightmares frequently woke her with the
echoes of Rebecca's shrill cries for help still seemingly in her ears.

Kasidy watched as her daughter came racing around the corner of the house, dressed in her pink jumper. Her thin little legs carried her confidently past the once-colorful flowerbeds that mother and daughter had planted in the spring. Behind Rebecca followed Jasmine Tey, the young Malaysian woman she and Ben had retained after their daughter's abduction. While Tey nominally helped around the house a few days a week, her advanced security training provided peace of mind with respect to Rebecca's safety. Kasidy and Ben—and now just Kasidy—felt sure in their ability to protect their daughter, but when Rebecca went to school, or when they sometimes needed to focus their attentions elsewhere, they brought in Tey. That morning, Kasidy had required a few hours to plan out *Xhosa*'s manifest and itinerary for the next month, and in the afternoon, she'd wanted to go into Adarak, so Tey had agreed to spend the day there.

Rebecca ran with abandon along the back of the house, her wide smile exposing the gap where she'd recently lost her two upper front teeth. A bit small for her age, she otherwise tested normal for a five-and-a-half-year-old human girl. She favored neither of her parents particularly, her features seeming to blend the best of both of them. Rebecca possessed her father's rich, dark coloring, but with the smooth texture of Kasidy's own complexion; she had Ben's penetrating eyes and self-assured bearing, but Kasidy's high cheekbones and slender nose; she smiled with her father's lips, but expressed amusement with her mother's laugh.

As Rebecca darted past the window, she waved a hand in Kasidy's direction without looking. "Hi, Mommy," she yipped, and kept running.

Kasidy had not seen her daughter take notice of her standing at the window. Kasidy dismissed the odd moment, but not quite as easily as once she would have. Such episodes—Rebecca perceiving some detail she had apparently neither seen nor heard, knowing some fact that seemed beyond her knowledge and experience—had occurred from time to time, even all the way back to her infancy. How often in the middle of the night had she stopped crying the moment Kasidy opened her eyes, as though Rebecca somehow sensed that she would soon receive food or a diaper change or whatever would satisfy the need that had caused her tears?

Tey chased along after Rebecca, looking up at the window, also waving and offering a "Hi, Ms. Yates" as she passed. With a slim figure and a personable demeanor, the young woman, just turned thirty, did not appear especially formidable. Her extensive law-enforcement training and experience told a different story, though. Skilled in the implementation of protective techniques, in the use of numerous weapons, and in myriad forms of hand-to-hand combat—including the rigors of Klingon martial arts—Jasmine Tey constituted an impressive one-woman security force. At the time Rebecca had been seized by the Ohalu extremist, Tey had just stepped down after a five-year tour on the detail safeguarding Bajor's first minister, Asarem Wadeen. At Asarem's suggestion, Tey had been brought in to assist in safely recovering Rebecca, and she had been instrumental in those efforts.

From the first time Rebecca had met her, she'd loved "Auntie Jasmine." For her part, Tey seemed to return that affection. On days when she came out to the house, the two spent all their time together, sometimes playing, sometimes reading, sometimes staying outdoors.

As Kasidy looked on, Tey caught up to Rebecca, reached down, and grabbed her around the waist. Rebecca let out a loud burst of laughter, and the two tumbled to the ground together. Kasidy could not help but smile at her daughter's unbridled delight.

Kasidy turned from the window, intending to return to her work on *Xhosa*'s upcoming schedule. Instead, she felt the smile melt away from her face as she saw the shattered form of the Utopia Planitia station still on her companel; she had meant to switch off the device, but evidently had only paused the news feed. She quickly paced back across the room and punched with a finger at the proper control. Mercifully, the screen went blank.

You're being foolish, Kasidy told herself. Under normal circumstances, she simply would have grieved for those who had lost their lives in the accident, but the ache that once more rose within her stemmed from a cause more specific than the accidental deaths of people she didn't know. *All roads lead back to Ben,* she thought. Fifteen or so years before, after the destruction by the Borg of *U.S.S. Saratoga,* the ship on which Ben served as first officer, Starfleet assigned him to Utopia Planitia. He spent nearly three years there before his transfer to the command of Deep Space 9.

Kasidy peered at the empty screen of the companel, but in her mind's eye, she still saw the battered hulk of the Utopia Planitia station. The fact that Ben had served there more than a decade earlier should not have troubled her. When he left Bajor last year and returned to Starfleet, he took command of *U.S.S. Robinson,* and the last she knew, the *Galaxy*-class starship patrolled the Romulan border in the Sierra Sector, far from Mars and Utopia Planitia.

Still, it's possible he could have been there, she thought. The news feed had not identified the ship that had recorded the explosion on the station and had then been struck by the resultant debris, and so the prospect at least existed that it could have been *Robinson.* Even as Kasidy set aside the notion, recognizing the irrationality of her fear, she could not as easily set aside the emotion that had taken hold of her.

She reached behind her and pulled the chair back to the companel, where she again sat down. She worked the controls to call up a message she had stored in memory for the past two months, though she had many times considered deleting it. Just as often, she played it back, searching for understanding and acceptance even as the words devastated her anew.

Ben appeared on the screen, a thin cover of black hair atop his head, his face freshly shaven. As many times as she'd viewed his message, Kasidy still couldn't quite get used to seeing him without his goatee. He'd had the beard the day she'd first met him more than ten years earlier, and he'd continued wearing it at least until the day he'd walked out of the house for the last time.

"Kasidy, it's Ben," he said. Kasidy could see a dimly lighted room behind him, presumably his cabin aboard *Robinson.* Just visible on the left side of the screen, tall ports showed the elon-

gated streaks of starlight that indicated a ship traveling at warp. *"I know that in a few weeks it'll be a year since I left. I know that I've hurt you, and I've done so in a way that's probably unforgivable."*

Probably unforgivable, Kasidy thought, echoing the phrase that had provided her a measure of hope over the past two months. Probably *unforgivable.* If Ben considered forgiveness possible at all, then didn't that indicate that he aspired to reconciliation? What other need would he have for her absolution?

"No," Kasidy said aloud, speaking over the recording of Ben as his message continued to play. For several months after her husband had walked out, Kasidy had judged their rift as an argument—clearly a major argument, but one that she believed they would eventually talk through so that they could work out their differences. At no time in those first three months did she think that their marriage had come to an end. Beyond that, for perhaps as long as half a year, even as the depth and severity of their separation became clear, she still expected Ben to one day walk through the front door of their home and take her in his arms.

"And I do love you still, Kasidy," Ben's message continued, *"and I imagine that I always will. And it's because I love you, and our beautiful Rebecca, that I had to leave."*

The words sounded suspiciously like an excuse. *I love you so I have to leave you.* Didn't irresponsible parents who abandoned their families often make the same claim? *You'll be better off without me.* Anger welled within her.

"Kas, I know that you don't believe in the Bajoran Prophets," Ben went on, *"at least not in the way that I do. But I have conversed with them, I have communed with them, and they have guided me on a journey that allowed me to help, and even save, the people of Bajor. I don't regret that. I* can't *regret that.*

"But I do regret how my relationship with the Prophets has impacted us . . . how it has impacted you and Rebecca. I told you before we got married that the Prophets had let me know that if I spent my life with you, I would know nothing but sorrow. And you said that it sounded like a threat. But it wasn't.

"It was a gift."

Before she consciously knew that she meant to do so, Kasidy brought the side of her fist down hard onto a control on the panel. The playback of Ben's message paused, and Kasidy felt a strong urge to thrust her knuckles into the companel screen. "'A gift,'" she spat at the image of her husband, as though he could hear her.

Kasidy understood Ben's justification for categorizing the statement of the wormhole aliens as something positive; she had listened to him numerous times as he explained it in his message. She understood it, not because of his words, but because she had *lived* it, and not just once. Ben's decision to leave her and Rebecca a year earlier had not been the first time that he'd done as the wormhole aliens had bade him, to the detriment of their family.

There had been the shock of his disappearance from the surface of Bajor after the end of the war, and then his materializing before her in a vision to announce that he could not go home with her just then, or at any specific time in the future. He vowed to return at some point, but he also reaffirmed his status as the Emissary of the Prophets, and asserted that they still had much for him to do. Kasidy accepted the situation because she had feared him dead, and because she could do little else, but the eight months of her pregnancy that she spent without her husband had been difficult.

There had also been the time that Ben had heeded his own visions from the wormhole aliens and prevented Bajor from joining the Federation. Worse than that, Ben willfully declined medical care when those visions threatened his life. In an obsessive attempt to fully understand the tapestry of the aliens' plans for the Bajoran people, he plainly demonstrated that he considered the seeking of that knowledge more important than his continued presence in the lives of Kasidy and Jake. Although his death would have left a gaping emotional void for both of them, Ben never relented on his dangerous quest; only when he'd fallen unconscious and Jake intervened had his approaching death been prevented.

Ben had also been willing to risk his son's own life for what he deemed the greater good. When one of the wormhole aliens forcibly took possession of Kira Nerys's body, and one of their adversaries invaded Jake's, the two engaged in a battle that threatened the lives of both combatants, as well as the existence of DS9 itself. Ben had a ready means of averting or ending the conflict, but even as he hoped for a victory that might well mean the death of his son, he allowed it to continue. After Kai Winn took steps to bring the battle to a premature and inconclusive close, likely saving Jake or Nerys or both, Jake forgave his father. Kasidy also found a way to let it go, but it occurred to her at that moment that Ben need never *proclaim* his position as the Emissary of the Prophets; over the years, his actions left no doubt as to his priorities.

Over time, the presence of the wormhole aliens in Ben's life did not alone drive his actions; so too did their absence. Eight years earlier, when Jadzia died and the wormhole collapsed, cutting Ben off from the aliens, he took Jake and went back to Earth. He abandoned Deep Space 9, his Starfleet obligations, his friends—and Kasidy. She had been away from the station at the time, making a cargo run aboard *Xhosa,* and when she returned to DS9, she learned that he had gone. He'd left a brief message for her—Kasidy thought she still probably had it stored on an isolinear optical chip somewhere—apologizing and trying to explain his actions, but also imploring her not to contact him until he came back to the Bajoran system—*if* he came back to the Bajoran system. That quickly and that impersonally, she discovered that her serious romantic relationship with the man she loved might be at an end, and she could do nothing about it.

"I *am* a fool," Kasidy said, as though speaking to the image of her husband. How could she be surprised that he hadn't come back to their house on Bajor, when clearly he didn't value his family more than he did "the will of the Prophets"?

"I should've been expecting it."

Kasidy let herself fall against the back of the chair as a heavy sigh escaped her lips. As so often happened, her thoughts and feelings whirled in a dizzying array of confusion. She felt angry with Ben, but also with herself. A sense of deep sadness suffused her, and her mind worked overtime to formulate some means of repairing the damage done to her family.

Looking at the companel screen, at the frozen mask of Ben's face there, Kasidy also felt something she seemed powerless to keep herself from feeling: love. She had known Ben for more than a decade, had been romantically involved with him for most of that time, and she remembered well all the reasons she had fallen for him. She had never met anybody else with his strength of will, with his sense of right and wrong, with his resolve. He overcame the terrible loss of Jennifer, his first wife, to open up to Kasidy, to laugh with her, to delight her with his cooking, to share a passion for baseball, to entwine their lives in ways that brought both of them profound happiness. They spent a great deal of time together, particularly after his return from the wormhole, and most of it had been wholly joyful.

Most of it, Kasidy thought, *but not all of it.* Events beyond their marriage had intruded, pulling Ben away from their home and involving him in troubling, sometimes dangerous situations. In hindsight, she could see that, bit by bit, those affairs eroded something inside of him. The residents of the small village of Sidau suffered a brutal massacre. The Ascendants and the insane Iliana Ghemor confronted Deep Space 9 and the people of Bajor. Endalla became the scene of a terrifying threat to local space.

More recently, events had struck closer to home. Their close friends Audj and Calan perished in a fire in their home almost three years earlier. During the Borg invasion, Elias Vaughn suffered a traumatic brain injury, and he remained in a coma. Ben's father died.

And there had been Rebecca's kidnapping. Kasidy couldn't trace all of her marital troubles with Ben to that time, but the threat to their daughter had exacerbated Ben's growing isolation. That in turn concretized Kasidy's feeling of disconnection from him. When he went back to Starfleet to aid in the efforts against the Borg—a decision she understood but did not favor—she hoped that they could essentially make a new start when he returned home. Though she feared for his well-being while he was away, it never truly occurred to her that he would never come back to her.

Kasidy sat forward in her chair and reached for the playback control. Ben's lips began moving again, and he said the words that she had heard so often that she could probably recite them from memory. Still, she found that she needed to hear them again.

"The Prophets do not exist in time the way that we do," he said. *"And neither did I in the time that I spent with them in the Celestial Temple, so I have some firsthand understanding of this. The Prophets live a nonlinear existence, but more than that, they live a continuous existence. It's how they can generate accurate prophecies, how they can know the future: they live in what we call the future, the past, and in the present. They are aware of every moment in their lives at all times. And they also see potential moments in uncountable possible timelines."*

As they always had, the ideas seemed fantastical to Kasidy. She could not quite conceive of the existence Ben described. At the same time, she did not disbelieve him.

"I don't think I can explain it any better," he continued. *"But I lived that way, and even though I can't remember the details of it, of a future that was the same as my present and my past, I do remember how overwhelming it was. And I recall the nature of it . . . the* reality *of it.*

"My point is that when the Prophets told me that I would know only sorrow if I spent my life with you, they weren't threatening me. They were telling me what they had already seen . . . what they were seeing at that instant. They saw me marry you, and they saw my life inundated by sorrow. They also saw an existence where I did not *spend my life with you, and where I was* not *inundated by sorrow."*

For a moment, Kasidy's vision blurred. Tears formed in her eyes. She knew the words about to come.

"For you, Kasidy, for your love and because I love you, I could suffer many things. But this isn't about making things better for me; it's about saving you. *And Rebecca. If I stayed with you, I would know nothing but sorrow, and at some point, that sorrow would include something terrible happening to you, and something terrible happening to Rebecca. That would be my greatest sorrow."*

As Ben listed some of those awful things that had happened around them and to them before he'd left, Kasidy's tears spilled from her eyes and down her cheeks. She didn't believe in Bajoran prophecy, or in the divinity of the aliens that resided in the wormhole, but despite all that had happened, she believed in her husband. She believed that he still loved her.

"The sorrow was getting closer, and deeper," he told her. *"I couldn't let something happen to you and Rebecca. It was hard enough when we almost lost her the first time.*

"I didn't tell you all of this before I left because I know that you don't believe in the Prophets, and I knew you wouldn't believe in the truth of their prophecy. But that's what this is: a prophecy. And unless I heed their advice, it will continue to come true.

"I love you, Kasidy. And despite what I've put you through, I suspect that you still love me too. I think it's okay for you to love me, at least in the way that I still love Jennifer. But I was eventually able to let go of Jennifer enough to fall in love with you. I think it's okay for you to let go of me in that way. When you're able, I want you to be open to love again.

"I'm sending this message to you because I think it will help you—today, and I hope, tomorrow. I hope you'll let it help Rebecca too, when she's ready to know all of this."

Kasidy's hand hovered over the playback control, ready to halt the recording. She did not want to hear what would come next, but she also knew that she *needed* to hear it again. If she wanted to move forward, she would have to hear it all.

"Right before I started recording this message, I transmitted a petition to the courthouse in Adarak to dissolve our marriage. It might have been the hardest thing I've ever done. But it will be the best thing for you.

"I love you. And I'm sorry."

On the companel screen, Ben reached forward and touched a control. The message winked off, replaced by the Starfleet emblem. Kasidy's tears flowed freely, and for a few minutes, she let them. She loved Ben, and she resented him. He genuinely believed the warning—or threat—given him by the wormhole aliens, but had he taken any actions to beat back that warning?

Had he entreated the aliens to do something to alter their prediction? Had he done everything he could possibly do to keep his family intact?

Kasidy deactivated the companel. Not for the first time, she pondered the dilemma Ben thought he faced: stay with his wife and daughter, and in so doing, risk their deaths, or leave them. Faced with the same dreadful choices, what would she do?

And what do I do now? she asked herself. After receiving Ben's message two months earlier, she had checked with the courthouse in Adarak. The administrators there did indeed receive a petition for the dissolution of Kasidy's marriage to Ben. She had yet to endorse the document.

"Maybe it's time I signed the petition," Kasidy said, allowing herself for the first time to consider granting her husband the termination of their marriage that he'd requested. For so long, she had expected Ben to come home to her, and when he hadn't, she'd then spent countless hours attempting to figure out how she could convince him to return. "But maybe I just finally need to let go."

Kasidy nodded to herself, tentatively trying on the idea of agreeing to end her marriage. Could she find the strength within herself to accept the loss of her relationship with the love of her life? Whether she could or not, she realized, she found something else: the determination to refuse to accept one of the consequences of Ben's leaving.

For fourteen months, Kasidy had withheld the truth from their daughter. After having already explained to Rebecca about her father captaining a starship in order to help protect the Federation from the Borg, Kasidy transformed that reality into a convenient explanation for Ben's subsequent absence. She told Rebecca that Starfleet needed him to continue to command a starship—not entirely a lie—but she also led her daughter to believe that Ben would one day return to them. Kasidy often sat down with Rebecca and watched family holovids, all of which included Ben; Kasidy did not want her daughter to forget her father, or to think that he no longer cared about her.

Kasidy reached forward and reactivated the companel. She

would grant Ben the end to their marriage that he had set in motion, but in exchange, he would also have to give something to her—to Rebecca. According to Ben, the wormhole aliens' prophecy involved his life with Kasidy, but she realized that it said nothing at all about his relationship with their daughter. If Ben wanted to cease being Kasidy's husband, so be it, but she would not allow him to stop being Rebecca's father.

Kasidy worked the controls of the companel. She still wished to make certain that Ben had not been present at Utopia Planitia at the time of the accident there, but she also wanted to enlist the assistance of a friend who could get through to Ben, who could remind him of his responsibilities as a parent and urge him to reestablish a relationship with Rebecca. Kasidy thought she knew somebody who could help her on both counts.

The insignia of the Bajoran comnet appeared on the companel display. "Releketh Province, Vanadwan Monastery," she said. "I'd like to speak with Vedek Kira Nerys."

2

Captain Benjamin Sisko looked up from his personal access display device as the door chime fluttered through his quarters. Seated on the sofa beneath the tall ports in the outer bulkhead, he felt the impulse to stay quiet, to keep still and not respond. Though he had yet to change out of his uniform, the evening had grown long, he had dimmed the lighting in his cabin, and his browsing of the padd in his hands had left him feeling isolated. Like a man in an escape pod, the lone survivor of some remote starship catastrophe, he endured, but he remained adrift.

Except that as the captain of *U.S.S. Robinson,* he could not drift, he could not hide. For the better part of a year, he had tried to do just that, keeping himself aloof from his crew. His reasons had been manifold. Having been forced by circumstances to abandon his wife and young daughter, Sisko felt no desire at all to befriend anybody new—nor even to communicate with anybody outside the ship whom he already counted as a friend.

Beyond the bitterness permeating his everyday existence, which made even the most basic personal interaction with others difficult, he also sought to avoid putting anybody else at risk by getting close to them. More than a year on, he finally understood the folly of such thinking, recognizing that the warning the Prophets issued to him spoke only of the dangers of his spending his life with Kasidy, and not with anyone else.

Along with those motivations, Sisko had also recently come to realize that an element of abnegation, perhaps even of self-punishment, played a part in his social detachment. To his surprise, his sessions with Counselor Althouse had yielded positive results, not only for Sisko himself, but for his crew, who served under a commanding officer who over the past couple of months had become, by degrees, more forthcoming and more approachable. With his change in demeanor, the morale aboard ship had improved noticeably.

Which is all Anxo wanted, Sisko thought. The ship's exec, Anxo Rogeiro, had come aboard *Robinson* at the same time as Sisko, the two men replacing officers lost during the Borg invasion. Rogeiro seemed to acclimate to the new crew quickly, while Sisko willfully held himself apart from the ship's complement. After seven or eight months, the first officer confronted his captain, essentially challenging Sisko to tear down the impregnable wall he'd put up between himself and the people who served with him. Eventually, that challenge transformed into a demand that the captain speak with one of the ship's counselors—a demand that Rogeiro promised to formalize if necessary. Not wanting to have to explain himself to Starfleet Command, Sisko relented.

And Anxo was right to do what he did, Sisko thought. Counselor Althouse had helped—and continued to help—the captain face the actions he'd taken in leaving his wife and child, and to understand how the course he'd chosen related to the reclusiveness he'd developed. Sisko couldn't do anything about the former without putting at risk the lives of the people he loved most, but he discovered that he could do something about the latter.

The door chime beckoned a second time, and Sisko shook off his reverie. "Come in," he called across the main room of his quarters. Out in space, beyond the ports, stars appeared to hurtle past as *Robinson* warped along its patrol route beside the Romulan border.

The doors parted, revealing the man of whom Sisko had just been thinking. Dressed in civilian clothes—beige slacks and a violet, long-sleeved shirt—Commander Rogeiro stepped forward into the captain's cabin. A bit taller than Sisko, he had a swarthy complexion, with black, wavy hair and dark eyes. At that late hour of the ship's artificial day, his face showed the heavy shadow of his potential beard.

"Mister Rogeiro," Sisko said. "You're up late." The time had just passed midnight, well into the ship's gamma shift.

"I'm not the only one," Rogeiro said, indicating the captain himself. The first officer crossed the room until he stood opposite Sisko over the long, low table in front of the sofa. Behind Rogeiro, the doors slid closed with a whisper. He pointed toward the padd in Sisko's hands. "Business or pleasure?"

Sisko held up the padd, but kept its display facing away from his exec. "Neither," he said, and he reached to deactivate the device. On the screen, a photograph of Sisko and his daughter vanished. Although his professional relationship with Rogeiro had improved considerably over the past few months, and even though the two men had begun to develop something of a friendship, they had yet to discuss Sisko's home life on Bajor, and what he'd left behind—though not for want of trying on Rogeiro's part. "So what can I do for you, Commander?" Sisko leaned forward and casually set his padd down on the table, wanting to invite no further questions about what he'd been doing.

"I just couldn't sleep," Rogeiro said, "so I thought maybe I'd try to tire myself out." He spoke with a slight accent, a shibboleth that identified him as a native of Portugal.

"What did you have in mind?" Sisko asked, though he suspected he already knew.

"I thought maybe you might like to spar," Rogeiro said. He hiked a thumb up over his shoulder, apparently motioning in the general direction of the ship's gymnasium.

Sisko smiled. "Feel like hitting your captain in the face and not standing court-martial?" Over the past month or so, Sisko had taken to accepting Rogeiro's invitations to join him in the ring for some light boxing. At first, he wondered if his first officer cleverly sought to use the cover of athletics to directly take out his frustrations with Sisko, but a quick review of Rogeiro's records showed that he'd taken up the sport years earlier, at Starfleet Academy.

"Punching my commanding officer with impunity isn't the main reason," Rogeiro said, also smiling. "That's just a bonus."

"I bet it is," Sisko agreed. He leaned back on the sofa. "The problem is, I *am* tired. I don't think I'd be able to give you much of a fight."

"Even better," Rogeiro said. "If you can't defend yourself or hit me, then I'll really get exhausted landing all my punches."

Sisko let out a short burst of sound: *"Hah!"* As he'd begun to get to know Rogeiro, he'd come to appreciate his wry sense of humor. "You're not exactly selling me on your invitation, Commander."

"Oh, well," Rogeiro said, shrugging and taking one of the two comfortable chairs in front of the table. "How about some good conversation over a nightcap then?"

"Now that sounds like a much better idea to me," Sisko said. He rose from the sofa and started across the room toward the replicator. "What can I get for you?"

"Actually, maybe we should go down to the Black."

Sisko stopped and turned back to face his first officer. The captain wanted to decline, wanted to stay in his quarters rather than accompany Rogeiro down to Tavern on the Black. Situated on Deck 11 in the forward section of *Robinson*'s saucer, the ship's lounge served as the primary social venue for the crew. Although less reticent than when he'd first come aboard, Sisko still didn't feel entirely comfortable among the people with whom he served, particularly in social settings. Still, Rogeiro continued to push him in that direction, as did Counselor Althouse and, often enough, Sisko himself. "All right," he finally said.

"Fantástico," said Rogeiro, offering up his satisfaction in what Sisko assumed to be Portuguese. He rose, and the two men

headed for the door. "I hear that Lejuris has created another of her amazing concoctions, this one with Siluvian bubble—"

"Bridge to Captain Sisko," came the voice of Ensign Radickey over the comm system.

Sisko and Rogeiro stopped immediately. Radickey, the captain knew, currently crewed the ship's primary communications console. "Go ahead, Ensign."

"Captain, we've received a transmission from Starfleet Command," Radickey said. *"It's designated priority one."*

Rogeiro glanced at Sisko, the amused expression the first officer had worn just seconds earlier replaced by one of concern. "Route it to my quarters, Ensign," said the captain, already moving toward his desk on the other side of the room. He gestured for Rogeiro to follow.

"Aye, sir," said Radickey.

"Sisko out." He sat down at his desk, and saw that the emblem of Starfleet Command had already appeared on the computer interface there. Rogeiro remained standing to one side, peering at the display over the captain's shoulder. Sisko tapped a control, and the message began to play. Where the logo had been, a familiar face materialized, its narrow shape and sharp features softened somewhat by the blond tresses that framed it. Sisko noticed that since he had last seen the admiral, strands of silver had begun to weave their way through her hair.

"Captain Sisko, this is Admiral Nechayev," she said. *"This morning, a pair of explosions ripped through Utopia Planitia. Casualties are thirty-one dead, nearly a hundred injured."*

Sisko glanced up at his first officer, whose expression hardened at the news. Sisko himself momentarily felt the horrible burden of responsibility, as if his posting to Utopia Planitia a decade and a half ago contributed directly to the disaster. The Prophets' warning to him and their nonlinear existence—and for a time, his own nonlinear existence—occurred to him, but he shook off his feeling of culpability as illogical.

"Starfleet Command reported the incident to the news services as an industrial accident," the admiral continued. *"It wasn't."*

Again, a shared look of concern passed between captain and first officer.

"*The first explosion was triggered in order to hide the theft of sensitive data from the station's main computer by an apparent spy, while the second masked his escape,*" Nechayev explained. "*Sensor scans of the region lead us to believe that a cloaked vessel retrieved the spy and is now trying to flee Federation space.*" The admiral paused, as though her words to that point had been only pre-amble to what would come next. "*Captain, the spy stole schematics for the quantum slipstream drive, and we believe he's making his escape aboard a Romulan vessel. I don't have to tell you that, since Starfleet's devastating losses during the Borg invasion, the only thing that's allowed us to maintain the balance of power with the Typhon Pact has been the slipstream drive. If we lose that tactical advantage, the Federation becomes vulnerable.*"

Vulnerable, Sisko thought, not without bitterness. Whatever primitive compulsions he might have had to take up arms had been well sated during his years in Starfleet: the last Tzenkethi War, the Battle of Wolf 359, the Dominion War, the Borg assault. If continually forced to fight, would the day finally come when the Federation would not prevail?

"*With* Robinson*'s position at the Romulan border, your orders are to actively search for the vessel carrying the stolen plans and prevent it from leaving Federation space with those plans,*" said Nechayev. "*But that ship was able to penetrate our defenses because we believe it's utilizing a new type of cloak, a phasing cloak. Phase alteration technology not only provides for better concealment, but also allows a ship to pass through normal, unphased matter. This is obviously a recent advancement by the Romulans, and one we need to learn how to detect in real time. I'm including the sensor readings we took at Utopia Planitia; have your engineers begin working on the problem at once.*"

Again, Nechayev paused, and Sisko anticipated what her final orders would be. "*Captain, you are not authorized to enter the Neutral Zone, which would constitute an act of war and could lead us into a conflict we're not prepared to fight. But as long as you remain in Federation space, Starfleet Command approves the use of whatever means necessary to stop that Romulan ship.*

"I want a status report every three hours," the admiral concluded. *"Good luck, Captain."* The message ended with the reappearance of the Starfleet logo.

"'Whatever means necessary,'" Rogeiro quoted. "That doesn't sound good."

"It isn't," Sisko said.

"I thought the new praetor—Kamemor?—didn't hate the Federation," Rogeiro said. "I thought she was supposed to be more of a moderate."

"I don't know," Sisko said, thinking of his encounter with Donatra. Fifteen or so months earlier, the self-styled empress had forced a schism in the Romulan Star Empire, taking control of many of the breadbasket worlds and calling it the Imperial Romulan State. Empress Donatra clashed with Praetor Tal'Aura, and when their struggles for supremacy finally ended, both wound up dead, with the Empire reunited under the leadership of doyenne Gell Kamemor. "The notion of a moderate Romulan might be an oxymoron," Sisko said, "but even if it's not, there's always the Typhon Pact to consider."

"Right," said Rogeiro. "It's not as though we don't have adversaries there." Along with the Romulans, the year-old alliance included the Breen, the Gorn, the Kinshaya, the Tholians, and the Tzenkethi—most of whom the Federation had come into armed conflict with in the past.

Sisko stood up. "I'm heading up to the bridge to initiate a search grid," he told his first officer. "Take the admiral's sensor readings down to engineering. I want Commander Relkdahz to start working immediately on detecting the new cloak."

"Yes, sir."

Sisko strode to the door of his cabin, Rogeiro falling in beside him. Out in the corridor, they moved off in separate directions. Sisko had only taken a few steps before his first officer called after him. "Captain?" he said, his tone uncertain.

Sisko stopped and turned. Rogeiro moved back over to face him directly. "Sir, we don't even know that the Romulan vessel is heading back to the Empire. It could be making its way to any of the Typhon Pact states. And even if it is headed for the Empire, how are we supposed to find a lone vessel out here, especially one that's hiding behind a new type of cloak, one we don't even know how to detect?"

"I don't know how we're supposed to find it, Anxo," Sisko said, fully aware of the enormously difficult nature of the tasks he and his crew had been handed, "but we're sure as hell going to try."

3

From across the chamber, Praetor Gell Kamemor studied what she could only regard as her throne. Ornately carved from rich, textured wood, its tall back clad in gold filigree, it sat atop a high platform, elevating it above the lustrous black floor. It directly faced a set of massive wooden doors that allowed visitors admission into the audience chamber, ensuring that callers would see it—and presumably its occupant—immediately upon entry. As with the throne, elaborate scrollwork embellished the doors, though they had not been decorated with gold, but rather inlaid with green-traced ruatinite.

Her back to the doors, the leader of the Romulan people drew in a long breath in the comfortably warm room, then exhaled slowly, preparing herself for whatever news would shortly arrive. After the death of Tal'Aura not even a hundred days earlier, the Senate had elevated Kamemor to the praetorship from among their ranks. She accepted the position reluctantly, just as she had when her clan, the Ortikant, appointed her to replace their prior representative in the Senate, Xarian Dor, after he succumbed to a fatal disease. When Tal'Aura later died from that same virulent illness, many drew the obvious conclusion that the two—the younger senator and the older praetor—had been involved in a clandestine relationship. Kamemor remained unconvinced, though the isolated and specific casualties of the lethal disease did give her pause.

Several decades past her centenary, deep into a full life pervaded by service to the Empire—as a university instructor, military liaison, stateswoman, metropolitan administrator, and territorial governor—Kamemor had previously retired to a life that mixed peaceful contemplation and robust activity. When the calls came for her to return to politics, first as a senator and then as praetor, she thought each time to demur. In both cases, under the familial pressures of the Ortikant, and out of her own sense of civic obligation and her strong desire to bring much-needed calm to the Empire, she relented. With her wife and son long since perished, little would have prevented her from once again engaging in the affairs of state, other than her own disinclination to do so.

And this, she thought, still looking at the throne, *is what makes me averse to politics.* She found it objectionable enough that the collective Romulan psyche included a chauvinism that had too many times made enemies out of other species. For so many Romulan politicians, though, holding governmental office exacerbated their natural patriotic bias into a sense of overblown self-importance. Kamemor understood the argument that the ruling class needed to exalt itself in order to inspire confidence among the masses, and to convince them that the best of their race led them. Too often, though, the self-aggrandizement of administrators and governors, of senators and praetors, resulted in those leaders making choices that indulged their own egos or inflated their personal wealth, rather than promoting the general welfare of the people. How many times had the praetor and the Senate marched Romulan citizens off to a war not absolutely necessary to the continuation of the Empire?

Kamemor pulled her gaze from the throne and peered around the rest of the circular chamber that she had inherited from her predecessor. Its opulence bespoke her lofty station. Braces of royal blue columns circumnavigated the periphery of the space, the alcoves between them set deep into walls of gleaming volcanic stone. Ancient and celebrated works of art dressed the recesses, all of them evoking a nationalistic theme. High above, tying them together, a spectacular mural filled the ceiling. An expertly rendered copy of Dorin Zhagan's famed *Nascence,* it depicted a powerful raptor ascending from a dark wood and into the sky, where it soared above a pair of towering peaks. As a woman with a great appreciation for art, Kamemor recognized the skill of the painter, but its theme failed to impress her, instead reminding her once more of the too-common belief of her people in Romulan exceptionalism. As long as she served as praetor, she vowed to battle that low form of communal egomania.

In her own way, Kamemor had sought to diminish the lavishness of the praetorial audience chamber. Though not entirely comfortable removing the artwork long ensconced there, she chose to add her own touches to the decor. Off to one side stood a small, circular table, surrounded by four decidedly plain chairs. Of greater impact to the interior design of the space, a large, conference-style table consumed a significant portion of the room's open center. As well, Kamemor kept the lighting bright, banishing the impressions of mystery and grandeur brought by shadows and instead contributing an air of workmanlike starkness to the environs.

A midrange chime suddenly resounded through the chamber. Kamemor stepped away from the doors and turned to await the entrance of her visitors. After a moment, the doors swung effortlessly open, and two men stepped into the room, accompanied by a pair of armed sentries, a man and a woman, both *uhlan*s by rank. The two officers scanned the room, then withdrew back to their posts, pulling the doors closed behind them. The men waited for the praetor to speak.

In the short time that Kamemor had held her high office, the work seemed to rejuvenate her sister's grandson, whom she had appointed proconsul. Though several decades her junior, Anlikar Ventel's mop of gray hair and his wizened face always made him appear older than she. They shared a vague family resemblance, most noticeably in the gray hue of their eyes. When Kamemor approached him about joining her in the upper stratum of government, he accepted with vigor, noting his excitement about the new praetor's personal tendency to seek out all opinions when deciding an issue. So far, in a small sample size, Ventel had disagreed with Kamemor on a number of issues, and he'd already succeeded on one occasion in convincing her to adopt his position over her initial stance.

The second man appeared somewhat younger than Ventel, though he cut a similarly tall, lean figure. Unlike Kamemor's grandnephew, who wore semiformal but understated attire, Tomalak chose to wear a tailored, black-and-gray suit echoic of an Imperial Fleet uniform, undoubtedly intended to underscore his lengthy military record. The former starship commander clearly believed in political opportunism, and it seemed to Kamemor that he sought to impress the relatively new leader of the Tal Shiar, with whom the praetor had called the meeting about to take place.

"Gentlemen," said Kamemor, "thank you for coming." Her manners might have appeared deferential to some, perhaps even beneath her station, but she had learned such civility at her father's knee. It proved a valuable asset during her extensive career in the diplomatic arena, though in truth, she wielded her courtesy less as a tool than simply as a habit of long standing.

Ventel bowed his head in acknowledgment, while Tomalak proffered an unctuous smile. "It is always a privilege to provide counsel," said the latter.

Kamemor did not hold Tomalak in particularly high regard. Before his selection by Tal'Aura as her proconsul, he spent decades in the Imperial Fleet, his time there marked by steady, if plodding, advancement. While hardly a dullard, he did not impress her with his mental faculties. Still, he had demonstrated his skills in developing and implementing broad strategies for the military, even as he pursued a personal agenda.

When Kamemor had accepted the praetorship, she had met with Tomalak, who immediately and expectedly offered his resignation as proconsul. He spoke of his desire to return to his life in the Imperial Fleet, and Kamemor's subsequent public statement about his stepping down reflected that. Later, though, she reconsidered. She genuinely believed that in order for her to lead well, she needed to consider a divergence of viewpoints, especially those of people with whom she did not typically concur. She also trusted in the old aphorism: *A well-fed serpent at home threatens less than a hungry one in the wild.* So, she had reversed course and invited Tomalak to stay on in her cabinet as an advisor, as a second proconsul to serve alongside Ventel.

Kamemor moved to the center of the room and paced the length of the conference table. As Ventel and Tomalak followed, she asked, "Have you learned anything more about the incident?" She stopped at the far end of the table and turned to face them.

"Starfleet is reporting to the news agencies that the explosions at their Utopia Planitia facility occurred as the result of an industrial accident," Ventel said.

"An industrial accident?" Kamemor repeated. She gestured to the chairs to her left and right, and the two men sat down. The praetor took the seat at the head of the table, placing the throne at her back, and thus out of her line of vision, which pleased her. "Do we believe them?"

"It's difficult to know what to believe," Ventel said. "The Federation is offering few details about what took place, beyond citing more than a hundred dead and injured. But Starfleet has little history of accidents like this."

"Not recently, no," Kamemor said, thinking of an event that had transpired nearly three-quarters of a century earlier. On that occasion, Starfleet's flight testing of a new type of starship drive had ended in disaster, with the destruction of the test bed and its entire crew. But that had happened decades ago. She turned her gaze toward Tomalak.

"I've reviewed the recent reports of all our vessels along the Federation borders," he said. "There's no indication that any neighboring powers, within or without the Typhon Pact, have penetrated into their space."

"So you believe that it *was* an accident," Kamemor said, aware that she sought confirmation of what she hoped to be true.

"I neither believe nor disbelieve," said Tomalak. "The Federation cannot be trusted, either in their assertion of alleged facts or with respect to their motives for doing so. The wisest course is to proceed as you've ordered: find out and verify as much as we can for ourselves."

"So what precisely do we know with certainty?" Kamemor asked, looking to both of her proconsuls.

"Not much, really," Ventel said. "We—"

The door chime interrupted the meeting, a few moments

earlier than expected. Kamemor rose from her chair, and Ventel and Tomalak followed suit. The doors opened, and Uhlans Preget and T'Lesk escorted in the chairwoman of the Tal Shiar. This time, the two guards remained inside the room when they closed the doors. In light of the political turmoil of the recent past, the Continuing Committee had ordered that only members of the praetor's cabinet could meet with Kamemor without the presence of at least two armed guards.

The chairwoman strode purposefully into the room. She wore the standard uniform of the Romulan intelligence agency: a light gray, simply patterned top with squared shoulders, with slacks and boots shaded a darker gray. A strap rose from her belt and up her torso, splitting at her chest and angling across her shoulders, the right-hand branch doubled. In one hand, she carried a data tablet. She did not stop at the far end of the table, but continued on toward the praetor and her advisors. Shorter by ten or so centimeters than either Ventel or Tomalak, Sela nevertheless projected an air of confidence and strength.

She'd have to, Kamemor thought. Despite ears that tapered upward to Romulan tips, Sela's countenance more resembled that of a human. Though she wore her hair in a traditional Romulan style, her blond locks fell well outside the color norm. Her lack of upswept eyebrows and forehead ridges also marked her mixed parentage. *And yet she's succeeded on Romulus, within a deeply insular culture,* Kamemor thought. In some ways, Sela's rise to power reminded her of Shinzon, a full-blooded human who'd managed to enthrall enough followers to stage a bloody overthrow of the Imperial Senate and Praetor Hiren, and then to launch an attack on the Federation. While Sela's personal record demonstrated her own antipathy for the UFP, though, she had also proven herself loyal to the Romulan government.

"Chairwoman Sela," Kamemor said as the head of the Tal Shiar stopped beside Ventel. "Thank you for your prompt response to my request for a meeting."

"Of course, Praetor," Sela said. "I am always at your disposal."

"Please," Kamemor said, indicating the chairs. Once everybody sat, she said, "What can you tell us about the incident in the Federation?"

Sela set her data tablet down on the table, its display blank. "First, that there *was* an incident," she said. "We have observers and contacts within the Federation, and we've obtained independent corroboration of the two explosions at the Starfleet construction installation."

"And what of Starfleet's characterization of the event as an industrial accident?" Kamemor wanted to know.

"The truth of that is less clear," Sela said.

Kamemor had anticipated that news. "I am troubled by that."

Ventel tilted his head to one side. "May I ask what in particular troubles you?"

"My primary concern," Kamemor said, "lies with Starfleet's quantum slipstream drive."

"You worry that they are attempting to transform their engine technology into a weapon," said Tomalak, forming an inference from the praetor's words, and perhaps divulging his own suspicions.

"No," Kamemor said. She had dealt with the Federation enough in her life to know that, while they practiced their own insidious brand of political and social imperialism, they did not spark to war without just cause, nor did they seek to disturb the delicate equilibrium that maintained peace among the powers of the Alpha and Beta Quadrants. What she suspected, though, would almost certainly meet with resistance among those she'd assembled. She folded her hands together on the table. "I am concerned about the slipstream drive," she said, "but *not* about the Federation."

Tomalak looked confused—almost comically so. He glanced over at Ventel and Sela in turn, then back at the praetor. "I don't understand."

"Another power," Sela said, more statement than question. "You think that some other power may have been trying to steal the slipstream plans."

"Yes," Kamemor said, impressed but not surprised by the chairwoman's easy acumen. "The Federation has been utilizing their advanced drive technology for some time now without employing it to threaten the Empire or the Typhon Pact. We can therefore draw a positive conclusion about *their* motives."

"I'm not certain that the Tzenkethi would agree," Tomalak interjected before the praetor could complete her thought. "I'm not sure that *I* agree."

"The Tzenkethi complain about virtually everything the Federation does," Ventel said. "Believe me, if the autarch thought that Starfleet's slipstream-equipped vessels endangered his people, he'd be demanding that the rest of the Pact launch a preemptive offensive."

"Or," Sela said, deftly returning the conversation to the point Kamemor sought to make, "Autarch Korzenten would attempt to acquire the slipstream drive for the Tzenkethi Coalition."

"That is one of my concerns," Kamemor said. "Not necessarily that the Tzenkethi mounted an espionage mission, but that some nation did."

Ventel nodded. "If one of the powerful independent states, such as the Watraii or the Gottar or the Patriarchy, obtain the slipstream technology, it could destabilize the region."

"It could," Tomalak agreed. "And that could cause problems for the Empire. But with the combined resources of the Typhon Pact, isn't such a threat one that we could effectively contain?"

"What if it's not one of the independent states," Kamemor asked, "but one of our own allies? What if it *was* the Tzenkethi?"

Tomalak's eyebrows rose in evident surprise. Through a smug smile, he said, "That would be a boon, of course."

"Would it?" Kamemor said. She pushed back from the table and stood up. "It would prove that one or more of our allies is willing to commit an act of war without even notifying us, let alone seeking our consultation and approval."

"We could be facing destabilization not only in the region," Ventel said, "but within our own alliance."

"Yes," Kamemor said, "but even that is not what most

concerns me." She turned from the table and paced away. Her gaze passed once more over the throne. She hoped that what she viewed as a symbol of Romulan hubris would not mirror what had actually transpired at Utopia Planitia. Turning back toward the proconsuls and the Tal Shiar chairwoman, she said, "Starfleet reported explosions and an industrial accident, and nothing more. That means that whatever truly happened, nothing took place that they couldn't hide."

"What . . . ?" Tomalak started, clearly missing the implication of Kamemor's words. Sela apparently did not.

"No one saw an alien vessel there," said the chairwoman. "Which means that if this wasn't an accident, if it was an attempt to steal plans for the slipstream drive and there was a ship, then it was cloaked."

"The Klingons?" Tomalak asked, his inability to follow the thread of the argument seeming almost willful.

"Not the Klingons," Kamemor said, walking back over to the head of the conference table. The tips of her fingers brushed its polished surface. "The Klingons are allies with the Federation, and their cloaks are primitive enough that, with the proper effort, Starfleet can detect their vessels."

"Besides," Ventel noted, "whether the Klingons appropriate the slipstream drive or the Federation hands it to them, it would not alter the balance of power."

Silence descended in the chamber, and Kamemor hoped that the group she'd gathered together followed the chain of reasoning she'd put forth. She did not want to be the one to utter the conclusion she had reached. Sela did not disappoint her.

"You're concerned about Romulan involvement," she said.

Kamemor locked eyes with the Tal Shiar chairwoman. "I am unaware of any such involvement," said the praetor, "and so, yes, the possibility concerns me greatly." She slowly sat back down.

Ventel peered over at her, his expression grave. "The Empire did provide cloaking devices to the other members of the Typhon Pact," he said.

"Most of whom have been unable to adapt the technology

effectively to their space fleets," Sela said. "And if I understand correctly, Praetor Tal'Aura waited to share the cloak with our allies until our engineers had achieved for ourselves the next step in its development."

"So while the Breen and the Gorn and the other powers now possess the ability to cloak their ships, at least in theory," Kamemor said, "the Empire retains the most advanced cloak, one far less likely to be detected by the Federation."

"Has the new cloak even been deployed?" Ventel asked.

"On a moderate number of ships, yes," Tomalak said. "But the Imperial Fleet's standing orders are not to use the new technology. Praetor Tal'Aura wanted the tactical advantage available if needed, but did not wish to risk revealing even its existence unless absolutely necessary."

"A policy I have continued," Kamemor said.

"Are you suggesting that a Romulan commander violated orders and used the new cloak to commit an unsanctioned act of espionage against the Federation?" Tomalak asked. His tone conveyed his skepticism.

"I am suggesting that is one possibility among several," Kamemor said. "And that's the point: we don't know much for certain. It's possible that Starfleet really did suffer an industrial accident. It's even possible that the explosions occurred as the result of an attempt to create a new, powerful weapon." Kamemor remembered well a similar claim levied against the Federation by the Klingons decades earlier—a claim politically motivated and false, but not entirely without justification. "We need to identify more than possibilities. Whatever happened at Utopia Planitia could have implications for the Empire."

"As I said, we have assets within Federation space," offered Sela. "I'll make full use of them."

"Do so," Kamemor said, "but I want no deeds that could be considered an act of aggression against the Federation."

"Just having operatives within their territory could be considered aggressive," said Tomalak.

"I think not," Kamemor said. "Not only does our Empire host Federation citizens within our borders, but we allow them to openly dissent. The UFP's former ambassador, Spock, continues to foment the idea of reunification between Romulus and Vulcan." The praetor stood from her chair. "Chairwoman Sela, pursue whatever leads you can find among our assets inside the Federation. Proconsul Tomalak, I want you to use your contacts within the military to see if you can confirm or refute Romulan participation in what took place. I will meet with Fleet Admiral Devix to gather what information I can from him." Kamemor did not relish conferring with Devix, a hard man who had risen to command the Romulan military after the failures of its previous head. "Proconsul Ventel, you will collate all of the information we gather until we have a complete picture of what occurred at Utopia Planitia."

Ventel, Tomalak, and Sela all acknowledged their assignments. Kamemor stood up again, this time to signal an end to the meeting. "Thank you, all," she said. The three visitors rose from their chairs, Sela scooping up the data tablet she'd brought with her, but which had gone unused. They made their way back along the conference table to the other side of the chamber. Uhlans Preget and T'Lesk pulled open the doors, allowing them to exit. Once Ventel, Tomalak, and Sela had gone, the two security officers turned back toward Kamemor.

"Will there be anything more, Praetor?" T'Lesk asked.

"No," Kamemor said. "You may return to your posts."

The two uhlans left the chamber, closing the doors behind them.

Kamemor stepped away from the table and headed around the platform upon which the throne sat, toward the door hidden behind it that led to her personal office. She could not prevent herself from regarding the ostentatious display of authority exhibited by the great chair. The idea of such obvious power, so distasteful to her in the way that it for so long had been applied in Romulan society, seemed to mock her. Though she did not crave leadership, neither did she wish to be deposed. Having risen to the office of praetor, she wished to fashion her government into a tool that would help all the people of the Empire, and not merely its elite. Under the best of circumstances, she faced a difficult task, but if her suspicions proved correct—if members of the Romulan Imperial Fleet had attacked a Federation facility without her knowledge or approval—she might soon be facing a coup.

In that case, Kamemor knew, she might not even be able to help herself.

June 2382

4

Sisko delivered his report directly to the commander of Starbase 39-Sierra. The stone-faced Admiral Philip Herthum seemed to listen intently, his hands out before him, palms lying flat on the surface of his desk. Crafted of a rough-hewn, tightly grained wood, the large piece of furniture fit well with the nature-inspired design of the office, Sisko thought. Slate flooring and paneled walls also tied into the theme. Set into a side wall, a mammoth picture window, easily the room's dominant feature, looked out toward the vast span of the Ravingian Mountains in the west. Still early in the day, the morning sun illuminated the impressive range, from its snowcapped peaks to the timberline running along its base.

For forty minutes, Sisko had detailed the efforts of his crew over the course of the previous two months. Since the theft of the slipstream drive schematics from Utopia Planitia, *Robinson* had pursued an interlacing path across the sector, the crew hunting for any indication of Romulan vessels on the Federation side of the Neutral Zone. Using modified probes and marker buoys, they expanded and enhanced Starfleet's existing mechanisms—gravitic sensors, subspace listening stations, and tachyon detection grids—for unmasking Romulan ships veiled by their standard cloak.

In addition, *Robinson*'s lead science officer, Corallavellis sh'Vrane, guided her department through numerous attempts to devise a means of detecting the Romulans' suspected new phasing cloak. Correspondingly, Lieutenant Commander Relkdahz led his engineering team in their labors to translate the scientists' theories into practice. Starfleet Command had provided some additional information acquired from a research project carried out a quarter of a century earlier, but while that had helped the efforts of the *Robinson* crew, it had not provided the desired result. Without the specifications of the actual phasing cloak, nor even definitive sensor readings of a ship concealed by the device, all efforts essentially amounted to searching for a black pinpoint in an unlighted room.

Sisko concluded his report by summarizing the most positive aspects of his crew's mission. Although they had failed to produce a method for penetrating a phasing cloak, their preliminary work in that area would provide a foundation on which other Starfleet research-and-development personnel could build. And though they hadn't located any vessels absconding from Federation space, they had within the past week recorded anomalous readings within the Neutral Zone that might have resulted from the recent passage of a phase-cloaked ship.

"You've done good work here, Captain," Herthum said. "Your crew's earned their five days."

"Thank you, sir." Starfleet Command had authorized Sisko's request for a layover at the starbase, allowing *Robinson*'s complement a well-deserved respite. "Do you have our orders going forward?"

"You should receive official notification aboard the *Robinson* this afternoon," Herthum said, "but it'll be a return to your patrol route."

Sisko felt an expression of disappointment waver across his face before he could prevent it. For more than a year, he and his crew had traveled the Romulan border, protecting the Federation against unwanted incursions. *For all the good that's done,* he thought cynically, the incident at Utopia Planitia foremost in his mind.

"Is there a problem?" Herthum asked. The question seemed obligatory; the admiral's tone suggested that he not only understood Sisko's frustration, but empathized with the captain.

"Not a problem, no, sir," Sisko said, prevaricating to some extent. He knew that the tedious task of keeping vigil along the Neutral Zone had taken its toll on his crew—and on himself—over the past fifteen months. At first, the nature of the duty suited Sisko, who after leaving Bajor wanted to find something to usefully occupy his time—something that would still allow him to sequester himself away. The repetitive and relatively undemanding charge of watching over the Federation's boundary with the Romulan Empire satisfied his needs, but it also severely underutilized the abilities and neglected the desires of a crew trained for, and aspiring to, much more.

Eventually, as Sisko dealt with his emotional challenges, he too began to yearn for something more rewarding than mere guard duty. "It's just that functioning solely as a sentry seems like a waste of resources for a *Galaxy*-class starship and crew," he told Admiral Herthum. Though equipped with powerful weapons and strong defenses, *Robinson* and its sister ships had been conceived and constructed as instruments of long-term exploration, with matériel aboard to accommodate civilian personnel, including family members of the crew.

"I understand your point, Captain, and I concur with it," Herthum said. "But Starfleet lost more than ships and personnel during the Borg invasion; the Salazaar Shipyards suffered massive damage, and the Beta Antares and Tri-Rho Nautica facilities were completely destroyed. We're not only having to construct new starships and train new crews to staff them, we're having to rebuild our infrastructure. Yes, it's been sixteen months, but it's a deep hole, and it's been a long, slow climb."

"I know, Admiral, I know," Sisko said, raising a hand to signal that Herthum needn't justify to him *Robinson*'s continuing assignment. Maintaining the solidity of the Federation's borders, and thus the safety of its citizens, had always counted as one of Starfleet's uppermost priorities. The recent reintegration of the Romulan Empire and the advent of the Typhon Pact made that responsibility even more important, and in light of the theft of the slipstream blueprints, critically so.

"You're hardly the only *Galaxy*-class patrolling our borders," said Herthum. "Hell, we've got the *First Minister* and the *President* out on the Tholian frontier." Sisko recognized the names of the two vessels, both of which belonged to the *Sovereign* class, a generation of exploratory starships more advanced than the *Galaxy*. "Plus other *Galaxy*s and other *Sovereign*s on other borders," Herthum continued. The admiral pulled his hands from atop his desk, then leaned forward toward Sisko. "Believe me, Captain, many of us in

Starfleet Command are pushing for a return to missions of discovery," he said earnestly. "We've managed to send a handful of vessels out to unexplored space, but we need to bolster the fleet even more before we'll be able to add to that number."

"I understand," Sisko said, and he did. But he also felt something he never really had: wanderlust. He'd entered Starfleet as an engineer, had been pushed into various command positions by his superiors, and then had become a religious icon during his time in the Bajoran system. He had never truly hungered to travel the galaxy and explore the unknown in the way that, say, Elias Vaughn had. Suddenly, though, the idea of such an undertaking intrigued him.

"I'm sorry, Captain," Herthum said. "Right now, we need the *Robinson* right where it's been." The admiral stood up and extended his hand. "Hopefully, shore leave will reinvigorate you and your crew."

Sisko stood and shook Herthum's hand. "I'm sure it will, Admiral," he said. He gathered up the padd he'd brought with him from the ship, which he'd set down on the edge of Herthum's desk. He headed for the door, then made his way through the outer office. He acknowledged Lieutenant McKeown, the admiral's aide, as he passed his desk.

Outside, Sisko started across the white-marble plaza that separated the starbase's administration building from its transporter facility. A light breeze spilled down from the mountains and through the sparsely traversed space. Sisko welcomed the bracing feel of the cool air on his face, a reprieve from the claustrophobic sense induced by a long—and soon to be longer—patrol assignment. As he walked, his bootheels drawing a metronomic lane through the square, he wondered how long it would take Starfleet to fully recover. They'd been rebuilding shipyards and constructing new vessels for more than a year, and still only a small number of ships traveled out beyond the frontiers of the Federation. Would it require another year of such efforts before more crews could rejoin in the exploration of the universe? Two years? More? Perhaps if the Klingon Empire could—

A figure moved into Sisko's path in the plaza, and he quickly stepped around it. Still thinking about the future of Starfleet, he did not register the calling of his name until he heard it a second time.

"Benjamin."

A woman's voice—a voice out of place here at Starbase 39-Sierra, but one he nevertheless recognized. It belonged to somebody who'd resented him on sight when first they'd met, but who had later become a trusted colleague and a good friend.

Sisko stopped and turned.

Kira Nerys strolled beside the Emissary along the hard-packed dirt path. The well-worn trail meandered through the lush valley that nestled in the foothills of the Ravingian range. They had walked there together from the starbase, where Kira had located her old friend and erstwhile commanding officer. They hadn't seen each other in person in more than a year, since Benjamin had left Bajor, though they'd spoken over subspace several times during that period.

Kira inhaled the sweet scents of the surrounding vegetation, dense shrubbery speckled liberally with flowering plants. She wondered just how she would broach the subject she had come to the starbase to discuss. She'd considered and reconsidered her options for some time, ever since Kasidy had visited her at the Vanadwan Monastery. Given the circumstances, she thought it would be difficult to approach any friend, but Benjamin's status as the Emissary of the Prophets complicated matters for her even further.

She peered over at him. He walked with his hands clasped behind his back, his head tilted downward. When she'd called after him in the plaza at the base, he'd seemed sincerely happy to see her. They exchanged pleasantries, then talked easily as they agreed to take a walk down into the valley after he contacted his ship. He asked about her presence at Starbase 39-Sierra, and she spoke at length about her mission of mercy to aid the survivors of the Borg attack on the Velestral Colony. Kira acted on behalf of Bajoran relief efforts to bring nutritional and medicinal aid to populations in need.

After that, she and Benjamin had fallen into silence. It didn't strike her as uncomfortable, but her companion seemed preoccupied. Kira could only surmise that her sudden appearance had something to do with that—perhaps as an unanticipated reminder of the life he had left before returning to Starfleet.

"I'm still not sure that I'm used to you being back in uniform," she said with a smile, trying to find the right tone to reopen their conversation. "I'd become accustomed to seeing you in civilian clothes." She hoped that the obvious references to Benjamin's time as the commander of Deep Space 9, and to his subsequent days at home with Kasidy in Kendra Province, wouldn't upset him.

As she awaited his reply, she studied his face. He looked better to her—healthier—than he had in some time. No dark circles hung beneath his eyes, he did not move as though he carried his burdens around with him on his shoulders, and earlier, when he'd spoken, his words had come with an animation he had for a while lacked. Still, as she gazed at him in his pensive state, she thought that she could sense something in him that remained unsettled. *Frustration? Guilt? Loneliness?* When he finally glanced down at Kira, though, whatever haunted him slipped away, like the shadow cast by a cloud that has glided past the sun.

"I'd gotten used to seeing *you* in robes," Benjamin said, and then something seemed to occur to him. "You're still . . . did something happen?"

For a moment, Kira didn't understand Benjamin's apparent concern, but then she put his question in the context of the russet slacks and dark brown jacket she wore. "I'm still a vedek," she said. "I wear my robe when I'm at the monastery in Releketh, or when I'm conducting myself in a spiritual role." She spied an opening and decided to take it. "Besides, I came here to speak with you not as a vedek, but as a friend."

"Wait," Benjamin said, evidently gleaning her implication. "You came here *specifically* to see me? I thought you were on your way back to Bajor from the Velestral Colony."

"Actually, the survivors of the Velestral Colony weren't able to revive their croplands," Kira explained, "and so they were recently relocated to Corat Three. I'm on my way home from there."

"Corat Three's not in this sector," he said. "In fact, it's not even in Federation space."

"No, but it's a lot closer than Bajor is to Starbase Thirty-nine-Sierra," Kira said. "When I learned that the *Robinson* would be here now, I decided to extend my journey."

Sisko nodded slowly, as though carefully weighing Kira's words. He began walking again, dirt crunching beneath his boots. Kira fell in alongside him.

"You *knew* that the *Robinson* would be here?" he asked.

Kira offered him another smile. "Believe it or not, I still have some contacts in Starfleet who'll talk to me," she said. "I might not always have done everything by the book, but some people saw that as a virtue, not a vice." She waited for him to respond, but once again, he seemed lost in his own thoughts. "Right, Captain?" she prodded.

"Oh," Sisko said, as though roused from a daze. "Right, Captain."

Kira couldn't tell if he intentionally alluded to her rank when last she'd commanded DS9, or if he simply echoed her last words. For the second time, Benjamin stopped walking and moved around to face her.

"Nerys, why did you make a special trip to see me?" he asked. "Is everything all right? Has something happened to . . . ?" He didn't seem able to complete the question, and Kira understood the conclusion to which he'd jumped.

"No, no, nothing's happened," she said quickly. "Everybody's fine—Kasidy, Rebecca, Jake, Korena—they're all fine." Benjamin exhaled deeply, and he seemed to unwind, as though releasing the sudden tension that had built within him at the prospect of harm having come to his family. Kira felt bad for accidentally worrying him, and she wanted to say more to ease his mind. But she had traveled to Starbase 39-Sierra to have a particular conversation, and so she hesitated before adding anything more. Throughout her life, she'd had few qualms about providing unsolicited advice to friends, but the idea of doing so with the Emissary of the Prophets discomfited her. At last, she said, "Kasidy asked me to speak with you."

Benjamin did not appear surprised—nor, to Kira's relief, angry. He began walking again, and Kira followed beside him. "How is she?" he asked. "And how's Rebecca?"

Before Benjamin had left Bajor, he'd asked Kira to visit Kasidy, to try to comfort her about his leaving. She would have done so anyway; she and Kasidy had grown close during the Emissary's time away in the Celestial Temple. "The last time I was out at the house," Kira said, "Rebecca was a bundle of energy, laughing, singing, running from room to room. She also insisted that I read her a book. According to Kasidy, she's got quite a few favorite stories."

Benjamin smiled—a deep, natural expression that reached all the way to his eyes. The fullness of his emotion, of his apparent joy, lasted only a moment before being mitigated by the pain he obviously carried with him. "Kasidy and I started reading to her when she was just an infant," he said. "She's always been very verbal, but even as a baby, she'd quiet down when we read her a story."

Kira chuckled at the memory of her last visit out to Kendra Province. "Rebecca also insisted that I quiz her with flashcards," she said. "She knows the alphabet, and she's got quite a vocabulary for a girl who's not even six yet."

Benjamin's smile faltered. "I miss her," he said, his voice nearly a whisper.

"She misses you," Kira said gently.

Benjamin shook his head, his features a mixture of love and regret. "How can she?" he said. "After so much time, she probably can't even remember me."

"She knows," Kira said. "Kasidy hasn't let her forget."

Again, Sisko shook his head. "Kasidy must hate me by now."

"She doesn't hate you," Kira said, her tone definite. "She's frustrated and upset . . . she's angry . . . but she doesn't hate you. In fact, she misses you. She told me that herself."

"Is that why she sent you here?" Sisko asked. "To tell me that? To try to convince me that I've made a terrible mistake?"

"That's not why she asked me to see you," Kira said. "But she does believe you've made a terrible mistake."

"And what about you, Nerys?" Sisko asked. "What do you think?"

Kira blanched, feeling her face grow cold as the blood drained from it. More than almost anything else, perhaps even more than the idea of lecturing the Emissary about his responsibilities, Kira dreaded facing that question. "I . . . I can't answer that," she said.

"No?" Sisko said, halting in his tracks and snapping his head toward her. "Because as I recall, you thought that I was doing the right thing when I decided *not* to marry Kasidy based upon the Prophets' warning. So now that I'm doing what they told me to do and *not* spending my life with her, don't you think I'm doing the right thing?"

"Benjamin," Kira started, but she didn't know what to say. She looked away. "It doesn't matter what I think," she finally managed to utter. "It's not my business."

"No?" Sisko said, his voice rising. "You seem to think it's enough of your business to come talk to me about it."

"I . . . I'm . . ." Kira faltered. She tried again. "Emissary—"

"I'm *not* the Emissary!" Sisko roared, his voice bounding down the valley. He turned and stalked away, his long strides carrying him quickly back along the dirt path. Kira thought that he didn't intend to stop until he reached the starbase, but then he did. He stood silently, his back to her, perhaps attempting to compose himself.

"I'm sorry," Kira called after him.

Benjamin turned and walked back to face her. "I'm sorry too," he said quietly once he'd reached her. "What I've done isn't a mistake, but it is terrible. It's still difficult to deal with."

"I understand."

Benjamin seemed to harden further at the words, and she thought that he would challenge her assertion. Instead, he dropped his gaze to the ground and shrugged. "Why are you here, Nerys? Kasidy won't agree to legally end our marriage, or at least she hasn't yet. Does she want you to try to talk me out of making our separation permanent?"

"No," Kira said. "Kasidy loves you and she misses you, but she doesn't want you coming back to her, or staying married to her, other than of your own volition."

Benjamin looked up and into Kira's eyes. He held her gaze for what seemed like a long time, as though searching there for the truth. "Then why?" he finally asked.

"For Rebecca," Kira said. "She needs her father in her life."

Sisko raised his arms, then dropped them to his sides, the padd he carried in one hand slapping against his thigh. "I'm a danger to her," he said. "The Prophets said so."

"The Prophets warned you about spending your life with Kasidy," Kira said. "They didn't caution you against having time with your daughter."

"If I go back to Bajor, Kasidy will push for us to be together," Benjamin said. "That can't happen. It's too dangerous—not for me, but for Kasidy and Rebecca."

"Kasidy doesn't believe that—" Kira started, but before she could finish, Benjamin turned and started away from her again. "Kasidy doesn't believe that, but she knows that *you* do," she called after him. "If you'll spend time with Rebecca, see her regularly, Kasidy will endorse the papers you submitted to the courthouse in Adarak." Sisko stopped and peered back over his shoulder. "She doesn't want to, but she'll agree to end your marriage for the sake of your daughter."

"Kasidy wants me to resign from Starfleet?" he asked. "Return full-time to Bajor?"

"She wants you to be a part of Rebecca's life," Kira said. "You don't have to live on Bajor. You don't even have to leave Starfleet or even the *Robinson*. You just need to take regular leave to spend time with Rebecca."

Slowly, Benjamin made his way back over to Kira. "Even so, it will be difficult because of my situation with Kasidy."

For the first time since they'd begun speaking, Kira did not feel sympathy for her friend. "Since when did—" She'd wanted to say *the Emissary,* but successfully fought the impulse to do so. "—you shy away from difficult circumstances? Especially when it involved the welfare of someone you love?"

Benjamin said nothing, but Kira could see him considering her words.

"This is for your daughter," Kira pressed. "She's doing well, but she needs her father."

"I know," Benjamin said, his voice almost inaudible.

They stood that way, in hushed tableau, for drawn-out moments. Kira heard the rasp of insects nearby, and the twitter of birds. She watched the Emissary closely, waiting to see if her words had reached their mark.

"Thank you," Benjamin finally said. "Tell Kasidy . . . tell her we'll talk."

Kira didn't know if that meant that he would agree to his wife's proposal or not. She wanted to know, wanted to ask, but she felt as though she'd already tested the bounds of her friendship with Benjamin. Instead, she simply said, "I will." She regarded the man who, despite becoming a religious icon to her, also remained her friend, a man she loved and admired apart from his role as the Emissary.

Less out of habit and more from a desire to confirm that her friend would be all right, Kira reached for Benjamin's ear. He stepped back quickly, almost as though he thought she meant to slap him. Her hand frozen in the air, Kira said, "I'm sorry. I was just going to assay your *pagh.*" The last time she had done so, back on Bajor more than a year earlier, Kira had come away with the assessment that Benjamin's essence had been deeply wounded. She hoped now to find that he had begun to heal.

"I know what you meant to do," he said evenly. "But I've played my part as the Bajoran Emissary. I'm done now."

She lowered her arm. "Benjamin—" she began, but he interrupted.

"Thank you for coming to see me, Nerys," he said. "It was good to see you." He turned again and strode back along the path the way they had come.

This time, he didn't stop.

5

Filled to capacity, the Cailax Auditorium hummed with animated conversation. From the wings, Spock listened, satisfied with the attendance at the event, as well as with the reception that the first four speakers of the evening had received. As he watched Corthin pace across the stage toward the lectern at its center, he took note of an increase in both the amount and the volume of the chatter in the hall. It reconfirmed for him an observation he'd first made a month earlier: the stately schoolteacher had become a recognized and popular face for the cause of Vulcan-Romulan reunification.

Clothed conservatively in dark brown slacks, emerald blouse, and black dress jacket, Corthin approached the podium. A thread of applause began to weave its way through the audience, then quickly spread to the full house of more than a thousand. For longer than a year, ever since Praetor Tal'Aura had agreed to allow the Movement to conduct itself openly and without fear of reprisal, Spock and the other leading proponents of reunification had taken their cause directly to the Romulan people. That the praetor had exploited the Movement, using it as a drumbeat to stir up sentiment to unite the sundered Empire, did not matter. After Tal'Aura dissolved the runaway Imperial Romulan State and made the Romulan Star Empire whole again, she suffered her own demise, but Vulcan-Romulan reunification continued as a viable cause—and thanks to the new praetor, Kamemor, championing that cause publicly remained safe and legal.

On the stage, Corthin waited for the clapping to fade away. In early middle age, she stood out in no particular way. Of average height and weight, with a physiognomy that did not rate a second look, she might have generated interest in the Movement by essentially standing as the epitome of the average Romulan citizen. Certainly her role as an educator of young students, rather than as somebody in a position of political or military power, appealed to many who had begun paying attention to the public debate in which she participated.

"To those of you here in the Cailax Auditorium," she started as the applause sputtered into silence, "to the residents here in Villera'trel, to the inhabitants of Romulus, to people throughout the Empire, and to Romulans everywhere, good evening." Though not broadcast live, the recorded rally would later appear on the comnets.

As always, Corthin carried no prepared text with her, nor had she committed any specific words to memory. Where Spock preferred to orate from a carefully crafted discourse, segueing from one point to the next in a manner designed to compel, Corthin contended that it served her to make her case not simply out of facts and sheer logic, but from the weaving together of opinion and passion. Spock could not dispute that the juxtaposition of her Romulan style and his Vulcan methodology worked well to underscore their overall message that a marriage of the two cultures would enhance both, creating a whole greater than the sum of its parts.

"My name is Corthin, and I am an educator," she continued. "I was born here on Romulus, in Ki Baratan, back in one of those heady periods when the capital had been redubbed with one of its ancient names, Val'danadex Trel. During my childhood, the designation of the city changed several times. The various names always harked back to an earlier time, and it continually intrigued me to discover why a particular name had been restored, and why it had been used—and then disposed of—in the first place."

D'Tan stepped up beside Spock and peered from backstage at Corthin. "What is she talking about tonight?" he asked in a hushed voice.

Without turning toward D'Tan—still a young man even after spending nearly a decade and a half associated with the Movement—Spock replied quietly. "I believe Corthin is speaking, as she always does, of her personal reasons for supporting reunification."

"Yes, of course," D'Tan said. "But I mean that I've never heard this story."

"The variations with which Corthin elucidates her consistent thoughts about reunification are notable," Spock said. More than anybody else he had met within the Movement, and perhaps even more than Spock himself, Corthin persistently found new approaches to voice the belief that bringing the Vulcan and Romulan cultures back together would redound to the benefit of both. In Spock's estimation, her overall method of advocating for reunification spoke to the broadest number of people, which likely accounted for the recent and significant increase in her popularity.

"As a child," Corthin continued, "I often wondered about the residents of the original Val'danadex Trel, and how they differed from the people who dwelled in the modern city. What similarities did the inhabitants of the first Dartha share with those of the most recent version of the city? What would be lost or gained if the Ki Baratan of antiquity could coexist with the Ki Baratan of today?

"Millennia ago, the Angol'rey first established a settlement that, after growing across many generations and a war-torn history, would eventually become the beating heart of the Romulan Star Empire. Back then, the colonizers recognized the value of the land, situated in temperate climes on the Apnex Sea, with abundant fresh water available from the two great rivers that ran nearby. Centuries later, the Five Great Clans created the Imperial Assembly, the precursor of our Senate.

"Often, I think, when we consider our forebears, we gauge them as primitive, as something less than our society of today. Technologically, that's true, and in terms of magnitude: the Empire comprises not merely a single world, nor two, but many. And our political influence and military might reach far beyond that, into spheres populated by Gorn and Tzenkethi, by Breen and Tholian, and even by Klingon and Terran. But in terms of who we are as a people, are we so dissimilar to those who came before us? Are we not, in some meaningful sense, just a slightly modified form of our antecedents?"

Spock glanced away from Corthin and over at a bank of displays that observed the auditorium. Three of them presented views of the stage, one of them from close range, two from farther away, while several others showed various locations behind the scenes. Spock checked the remaining screens, which monitored different sections of the crowd. It did not surprise him to see the audience sitting rapt, their attention unwaveringly on Corthin. Indeed, the beginning of her speech had easily captured his own notice.

"In my youth, during my early school years," Corthin continued, "I first became aware of the historical connection between our people and the Vulcans. It fascinated me to learn that we had come from somewhere else, from some*body* else, and that the place and the people from which we sprang still existed in the universe. I immediately wished to—"

Footsteps quickly neared, and a hand fell on Spock's shoulder. He turned to see the short but muscular form of Venaster, a former military officer and a longtime supporter of reunification. Together with a man named Dorlok, he supervised the security needs of the Movement. "I'm sorry to disturb you just before your address," Venaster said, "but I thought you'd want to know that we've had an incident."

"What's happened?" asked D'Tan, ever excitable, despite his seemingly paradoxical commitment to the Vulcan way of life.

Spock reached up and guided Venaster by the elbow, moving him away from D'Tan and into an empty corner of the offstage area. "Tell me," Spock said.

"Protesters interrupted the event in Vela'Setora," Venaster said. "There was an altercation."

"Involving our people?" Spock wanted to know. Even with the new praetor's willingness to allow the open discussion and even the promotion of reunification, the entire concept of free speech within the Empire lived a fragile existence. Spock and his comrades strived never to provide any justification for the praetor or the Senate to criminalize their advocacy.

"No, not directly," Venaster said, not hiding his relief at being able to truthfully report the news. "But some of those who attended the event to listen to our people confronted the protesters." He held up a data tablet. "We have a record of what transpired."

"Show me," Spock said. Venaster positioned the tablet so that both men could view its display. The security officer touched a control, and a still image of Corvalet Sharana appeared. An older woman, her hair shot through with streaks of gray, she nevertheless practiced a fiery brand of oratory. On the screen, she stood on an outdoor proscenium before a large crowd. Venaster worked the data tablet, and the recording began to play, a symbol in the upper right-hand corner indicating that the sound had been muted. In silence, Sharana moved across the stage, addressing her audience, her gesticulations broad. It intrigued Spock that some of the most emotional Romulans he'd ever met sought reunification, and a mix of Vulcan calm with their Romulan passion.

After a few seconds, the view on the tablet changed, swinging around to focus on the audience. Among arcs of concentric benches, perhaps twenty rows from the stage, a man and a woman stood in an aisle with their arms raised above their heads, each of them holding up a data canvas. Both electronic placards displayed the rounded, blockish characters of the Romulan language. One, presented in a font clearly designed to appear handwritten, read ROMULANS FOR ROMULUS in large letters, and below that, smaller, IT'S LOGICAL! The other carried the sentiment, WE EVOLVED FROM VULCANS—WHY GO BACK?

Although no sound accompanied the playback, Spock could see the mouths of the protesters opening wide, obviously voicing their dissent in loud tones. He also saw several members of the audience clearly yelling back at them. After a few moments, a number of individuals left their seats and advanced on the protesters. The two sides appeared to exchange heated words, until finally one of the men from the audience threw a punch at the male protester. A couple of people attempted to break up the physical conflict, but in just seconds, several other scuffles erupted.

The irony of the episode—taking place as it did at a pro-reunification event—did not escape Spock. At least in part, the goals of melding back together the Vulcan and Romulan cultures included bringing the ideals and the practice of emotional restraint to the Empire. On Vulcan, such a brawl would never have taken place.

On the display, Spock saw Romulan security officers descending on the scene, disruptors at the ready. He knew that their presence at the rally had nothing specifically to do with reunification; they conspicuously attended all large public events, expressly for the purpose of preventing—or in this case, stopping—violent activity. It did not take them long to do so in Vela'Setora, fortunately without having to resort to discharging their weapons.

Venaster deactivated the data tablet and lowered it to his side. He looked up at Spock with an expression of concern. "If the praetor or the Senate or the Tal Shiar are looking for a credible reason to shut down our rallies," Venaster said, "they might use this incident as justification."

"If any portion of the government is searching for a rationale to recriminalize the Movement," Spock said, "they might well have provoked, or even staged, this incident."

Venaster nodded slowly. "I hadn't considered that."

"Obviously, we must consider all possibilities," Spock said. "Were any arrests made?"

"I don't know," Venaster said. "This happened just a short time ago."

"We need to determine the identities of the protesters, and of the individuals in the audience who confronted them," Spock said. "Perhaps even of the Romulan Security personnel involved. Learn what you can about all of those people so that we can evaluate whether or not this altercation occurred organically. I'd also like eyewitness accounts from our people."

Again, Venaster nodded. "I'll begin immediately," he said. "I also think we should increase our own security measures at the rallies."

"Agreed," Spock said. Behind him, he heard sustained applause in the auditorium, a sure indication that Corthin had concluded her remarks. He began walking back toward the stage, Venaster following along. "Keep me informed of any other unusual occurrences at reunification events, particularly those that could undermine our cause. If necessary, I will seek an audience with the praetor to reassure her of the intentions of the

Movement, and to request her guidance, and possibly even her protection." Four months earlier, not long after Gell Kamemor had ascended to the highest office in the land, Spock had met with her in order to gauge her judgments about reunification, and to appeal to her to keep public discourse about it legal. He'd found her reasonable and open, a much different Romulan leader than many of those who had preceded her in recent years—Tal'Aura, Shinzon, Hiren, Neral.

"I'll solicit and coordinate reports from all of our rallies immediately," Venaster said.

"Very good." As Spock continued toward the wings of the stage, to where D'Tan still stood, Venaster headed off in the other direction. Spock knew that the security officer had assigned several of his lieutenants to that evening's detail, which under normal circumstances allowed Venaster to manage security needs across multiple Movement events.

The audience continued to clap as Corthin left her position at the lectern and made her way offstage. Her face a mask of calm, she betrayed nothing of any emotions she felt in the wake of her speech. When she reached D'Tan, the young man congratulated her enthusiastically on her presentation, praise which she accepted with equanimity.

"You seem to have captivated the audience," Spock said.

"I believe they are receptive to our message," Corthin said.

Spock allowed Corthin to pass through the narrow space, then started for the stage himself. "*Vornta vel,*" offered D'Tan; the phrase literally translated as *fortunes many,* and in essence carried the same meaning as the human phrase *good luck.* Spock did not respond directly to the words, but acknowledged his young comrade with a nod. Then he stepped out onto the stage and headed toward the lectern.

The ovation that had accompanied Corthin offstage had drifted away, but the audience began to clap again when Spock appeared—though not, as best he could tell, with quite as much enthusiasm. By the time he reached the podium, the applause had already begun to fade, and as he stood waiting to commence his remarks, it quickly ended. He took a moment to gaze out over the audience. He saw many faces peering back at him, though, unexpectedly, not all of them.

"I am Spock of Vulcan," he said, his voice carrying out across the midsized hall. "I am a citizen of the United Federation of Planets, but I am also a legal visitor to Romulus." He started each of his reunification addresses with such words, wanting to identify himself to the crowd. While many might know his name from the comnets, fewer would recognize him on sight, particularly since the stock video many of the news feeds often showed featured him in Vulcan ceremonial robes; that night, he wore beige slacks and a dark-blue tunic.

"As the speakers preceding me this evening have explained," Spock said, "the aspirations of those of us within the Reunification Movement are to promote mutual understanding between Romulans and Vulcans, to cultivate peace and friendship between the two cultures, to find the best that both have to offer, and to advance toward the time when the two societies can again become that which once they were: a single, unified people."

As Spock paused and regarded the audience, movement caught his attention. On the left side of the auditorium, halfway to the rear of the hall, two people had risen from their seats. Spock anticipated a vocal protest, expecting the pair to wield placards with opposition sentiments emblazoned across them. Instead, they simply made their way to one of the exits and departed the event.

Spock continued his speech. He highlighted some of the primary distinctions between the Vulcan and Romulan societies, and posited how they could benefit from the interaction of one with the other, and ultimately from the commingling of the two. He expressed his ideas easily, and in a manner that Romulan audiences had received well during the period that he and the others in the Movement had been speaking publicly. That evening, though, he had a different experience.

As Spock addressed the crowd, more of their number followed the lead of the first two who had exited the rally. He willed himself past the distraction of individuals moving about in the auditorium, but he remained keenly aware of the exodus. By the end of his half-hour oration, a tenth or so of the audience had left—approximately a hundred people.

When he concluded his remarks, Spock received a round of applause, seemingly genuine, but tepid when compared with the ovation granted Corthin. As the other speakers joined him onstage to take questions, he considered whether the mass departure during his address could have been a coordinated effort aimed at weakening the Movement. Perhaps a group from the government, or some other faction opposed to reunification, attended the rally in order to prevent more citizens from doing so. Or their exiting when they did could have been designed as a message to the Movement, or as an attempt to undermine Spock's perceived value as a spokesperson and leader. Coupled with the appearance of protesters at the event in Vela'Setora earlier, and the subsequent violence, any or all of Spock's suspicions could be accurate.

But he didn't think so.

Praetor Kamemor and the Imperial Senate needn't resort to such deception to effectively shut down the Movement. Spock and his comrades had not grown so popular that their disappearance from the public discourse would merit anything more than limited notice, much less any sort of social uprising. And while the Tal Shiar certainly had a penchant for subterfuge, and its chairwoman a genuine animus for Spock, such efforts at their behest would have seemed . . . clumsy.

No, Spock thought. *Not the actions of the praetor, the Senate, or the Tal Shiar.* He would allow Venaster and Dorlok and their security team to investigate those possibilities, but he knew that they would find nothing. Rather, Spock thought it far more likely that the audience in the Cailax Auditorium had delivered its own message, and a much simpler truth: his own status as the de facto standard-bearer and driving force of the Reunification Movement had plateaued, even as the status and reputation of Corthin—and of some other of Spock's comrades—continued to grow.

In the auditorium, about a quarter of the audience remained in their seats as several of their number asked questions of the six individuals onstage. As Spock expected, based upon the reactions of the crowd throughout the evening, Corthin received the bulk of the attention. No one directed a single query to Spock.

For the first time in fourteen years, since embarking on his quest to see his people reunited with their ancestral cousins, since taking over a leadership role in the Movement from the corrupt Senator Pardek, Spock realized that his days championing reunification might be nearing their natural end.

6

Korzenten Rej Tov-AA, autarch of the Tzenkethi Coalition, strode through his personal corridor in the Anwol Kaht, the great, sprawling edifice that housed the offices of the national government. His footsteps whispered along the black, velvety fabric that swathed every surface. The passage connected from the autarch's own suite of offices—which included workspaces for him and his advisors—to the Ministerial Gallery. Over time, Korzenten had ornamented the corridor with selections from his extensive art collection, creating an elegant display designed neither to parade his vast wealth nor to shrink from it.

Ahead loomed a large door, a rondure composed of curved, burnished strips of wood, fitted together in a complex and eye-catching pattern. The sigil of the office of the autarch—a slender, silvern triangle set base upward atop a circular yellow background—adorned its center. A narrow lighting ribbon ringed the door; illuminated a deep scarlet, the ribbon indicated that the Tzelnira had all arrived for their session, and that they awaited the appearance of their head of state.

As Korzenten neared the door, it irised open, its arced slats sliding around in an intricate motion. From beyond the open doorway, the autarch heard the bell-like tones of Tzenkethi voices, drowned out a moment later by a series of chimes that automatically announced his entrance. The ringing faded as he stepped across the threshold of the Ministerial Gallery.

Without breaking his gait, Korzenten headed across the empty space toward its center, toward its only feature: a low, circular wall that surrounded the dais from which he presided over the Tzelnira. Looking directly forward, he did not see the Tzenkethi ministers, though he heard the lyrical notes of their muted conversations. As he made his way across the chamber, those voices quieted.

At the low wall, a panel slid aside, allowing Korzenten to mount the dais. A cylindrical block of polished black stone sat at its center, and he eased himself down onto it. Only after pulling his legs up and wrapping them around the lower portion of his torso did he raise his head.

Above him—at least from his perspective on the Gallery's superior floor—he saw the Tzelnira. They sat arrayed in a concentric configuration on the inferior floor, at long, solid slabs of stone that formed circular tables. A single path cut through each of the tables, from the outer section of the Gallery to its center, allowing each of the ministers access to their positions.

Korzenten surveyed the ranks of the eighty-one officials who formed the Tzelnira. They all gazed at him with large pupils, the colors of their eyes as varied as that of their flesh. The skin tones of the ministers ran mostly from a dusky orange to a deep, ocean green, all of them radiating a gentle glow. The autarch could see a few reds scattered throughout the chamber, though none as brightly hued as himself, nor any of those with his highly contrasting golden eyes.

"Ministers of the Tzenkethi Coalition," he intoned, "I call this session of the Tzelnira to order." An audio pickup amplified his words and carried them throughout the Gallery. Unlike the high-pitched voices of many Tzenkethi, Korzenten spoke in deep, low tones. "We are gathered today to discuss an issue involving worlds proximate to our borders."

Technically, as autarch, Korzenten wielded absolute power. The ministers and their staffs for the most part managed the day-to-day and longer-term needs and operations of individual localities, coordinating with each other on national matters as circumstances dictated, but any of their decisions could be overridden by the autarch. As a matter of law, he required no authorization from the Tzelnira or anybody else to take any action he deemed advisable. From the standpoint of practicality, however, he believed that it made sense for him to seek out information, opinion, and advice. With his genetic disposition placing him firmly in the Tov classification—the echelon of governmental leaders—his valuation as one of the few AA levels in Tzenkethi society left him as one of the very few eligible to serve as Rej—as autarch of the Coalition. But even as the most qualified for the position, and even after his long experience serving in that capacity—he had succeeded the previous autarch upon her death during the last Tzenkethi-Federation War—he still found benefit in consulting the Tzelnira. Korzenten's superior DNA had gone unsurpassed during the time of his rule, but he understood that made him neither omniscient nor infallible.

At the same time, he had already decided on a course of action with respect to the issue he would raise before the Tzelnira.

Korzenten scanned the inferior floor for his aides, and saw two of them situated in a corner, apart from the ministers. Velenez Bel Gar-A and Zelent Bel Gar-A formed a useful tandem, providing the autarch a great deal of support. Both glowed a pale yellow, one with yellow eyes, the other with orange.

"My aides have prepared a brief presentation about the issue," Korzenten told the Tzelnira.

On his cue, the lighting dimmed, although the natural luminescence of all the Tzenkethi present prevented the chamber from darkening completely. The autarch lowered his gaze from the Tzelnira and peered to the side, at the lateral floor that connected the superior and inferior floors. There, on the curved surface, a large display activated. On it appeared the image of a blue-and-white world hanging in space.

"This is the planet Laskitor Three," said Velenez, his voice amplified and transmitted throughout the chamber. "It is on the Coalition frontier, and it was first mapped three generations ago by the astronomer Corliad Ank Zon-B, and later surveyed by the crew of the vessel *Seyer*." On the display, the planet vanished, replaced by a pastoral scene of tall grasses swaying atop rolling hills. "Its atmosphere, surface temperature, and gravity make

Laskitor suitable for Tzenkethi life. It possesses an abundance of natural, though by no means exotic or particularly valuable, resources. It is uninhabited." Velenez paused, and the image of the world reappeared. This time, a starship orbited above it, but not one of Tzenkethi design.

"At least, it was uninhabited."

A peal of voices immediately rang out in the Gallery. Korzenten appreciated the dramatic timing of the presentation. As he watched the display, the picture on it changed to a closer view of the ship. It featured a roughly triangular forward hull, with two separate, parallel beams protruding aft, from which flanged wings supported warp nacelles. There could be no mistaking the origin of the grayish vessel.

"This is the Federation vessel *Mjolnir*," said Velenez. "Two hundred days ago, *Mjolnir* and other Starfleet ships began ferrying Federation citizens from their colony world of Entelior Four to Laskitor." The image changed again, to an aerial view of numerous artificial structures. "All indications are that the Federation is bent on colonizing Laskitor."

Again, the jingling sound of Tzenkethi voices rose in the Gallery. Korzenten heard one minister exclaim, "Imperialists!" The autarch agreed completely.

On the display, a map of the stars appeared. A shading of green clearly identified the territory of the Tzenkethi Coalition, while blue distinguished Federation space. Between the two, three pinpoints of light stood out. As Korzenten watched, names materialized one by one beside each.

"This is Laskitor," said Velenez. "And this is Ergol, and this is Corat. Since first transporting colonists to Laskitor, the Federation has also claimed worlds in these systems." Velenez waited for a few moments before saying anything more, presumably to allow the enormity of what had taken place to impress itself upon the ministers. "Right now, we don't know which worlds they will take next."

As the display blinked off and the lighting returned to a normal level, the excited voices of the ministers became a tumult. Korzenten looked up to see many of the Tzelnira gesturing demonstratively as they spoke with each other, responding to what they had just seen. The autarch waited. Slowly, voices quieted, until one of the ministers triggered his request signal; others followed. Set into the desk of each Tzelnira, the light shined indigo when activated, indicating that its owner sought permission to address the autarch and the Gallery.

When all of the ministers had stopped speaking, Korzenten selected one from among their number. He reached forward to a panel set into the wall enclosing his dais. Touching a control, he disengaged the request signal for all but one of the Tzelnira, simultaneously activating the minister's audio input. "Minister Vonar," Korzenten said.

The chosen Tzelnira, with yellow skin and green eyes, unwrapped his legs from around his midsection, set them on the floor, and stood up. Vonar Tzel Tov-A hailed from a planet on the opposite side of the Coalition from the Federation. While hardly an apologist for the UFP, he could typically be counted upon to eschew a call to arms. Korzenten had recognized him first in order to dispense with such talk. The autarch might not have needed the backing of the Tzelnira, but gaining their support certainly simplified his efforts in accomplishing a particular goal.

"My Rej," Vonar said, his voice transmitted throughout the Gallery by the audio system, "was not the world of Entelior Four one of those savagely attacked by the Borg during their invasion of Federation space?"

"It was," Korzenten said, pleased with the minister's predictability.

"And what of the other worlds from which the populations were displaced to Ergol and Corat?" Vonar asked. "Were these also devastated by the Borg?"

"They were," said Korzenten.

"Does it not stand to reason, then, that the Federation is merely and reasonably finding whatever means they can to rescue their citizens in the wake of the invasion?" Vonar said. "Have we detected any advanced weaponry being installed on these planets?"

"The settlements have been equipped with standard defenses," Korzenten said. Then, measuring his words, he added, "At least, as far as we've been able to determine."

"Then it seems unnecessary," Vonar said, "to infer from the available information that they have chosen these worlds in order that they might more readily attack us."

"It was not suggested that the Federation intends to attack," Korzenten said. He operated his controls to switch off Vonar's request signal and audio input, then watched as numerous other Tzelnira vied for a chance to speak. The autarch decided on one from the world on which they stood, Ab-Tzenketh, the capital of the Coalition, located directly in its heart. "Minister Aztral."

The pink-skinned, blue-eyed Aztral Tzel Tov-B leaped to her feet, which she had already planted on the floor beside her chair. Among the Tzelnira, she had a well-deserved reputation for favoring military solutions over diplomacy. "My Rej," she said, "Minister Vonar speaks of what we can infer from 'available information.' I will point out that such information includes the facts that the United Federation of Planets has consistently been at odds politically with the Tzenkethi Coalition, and that they have pressured us into several costly military engagements. They have also pursued an expansionist policy without surcease, even now, at a time when they have been dramatically weakened by the Borg."

"All of what you say is true," Korzenten acknowledged. "So what would you have the Coalition do?" In sessions of the Tzelnira, the autarch disliked asking questions to which he did not already know the answer. Aztral did not disappoint him.

"Attack," she said. "While they are still in the process of restoring their forces."

"Starfleet may not be at its fullest strength," Korzenten said, "but they do have starships equipped with quantum slipstream drive." The autarch also knew that the Typhon Pact, and therefore the Coalition, might soon have the slipstream drive for themselves. A Breen operative had stolen the plans for the advanced propulsion system from Starfleet not long ago, and Breen engineers presently worked to construct a functioning prototype of the hyper-warp engine. But Korzenten did not yet wish to reveal that information, both because a Pact version of the drive had yet to be made a reality, and because it would not serve his purposes in eliciting the full support of the Tzelnira.

"They have slipstream," Aztral said, "and we have the Typhon Pact. Surely an equalizer."

"Nothing is sure in war," Korzenten said. He deactivated Aztral's request signal and audio input, her use to him in the current session at an end. "And if we launch a war, would we not want our forces and those of our allies to be more than equal to those of our enemy and their allies?" The autarch selected another Tzelnira to speak. "Minister Zeleer."

"My Rej," Zeleer Tzel Tov-A said, rising to his feet. Green skin, and eyes of a lighter green. "While not espousing war, I do think it seems unwise to allow the Federation a beachhead on the threshold of our territory."

"Would you have us attack the populations on Laskitor, Ergol, and Corat?" Korzenten asked, permitting a note of disgust to tinge his voice. "These are innocent refugees resettling from decimated worlds."

"My Rej," Zeleer said haltingly, likely indicating that he intended to disagree with the autarch. "I would suggest that no Federation citizen is innocent. It is they who choose their leaders, and it is their leaders who provoked the Borg, who brought destruction down upon themselves."

"That is true," Korzenten agreed, "but it is not specifically the refugees on these three worlds that threaten the Coalition."

"Then we must take the fight to those who do threaten us," Zeleer insisted.

That quickly, Korzenten had maneuvered the Tzelnira to his point of view. It did not matter that he did not require their approval, but it simplified his life when he received it. He would allow their dialogue with him to continue, let more of the ministers voice their opinions, but he felt confident that he would generate a consensus among them to do as Zeleer had proposed: take the fight to the recovering Starfleet. The autarch did not want war with the Federation, not yet, but they needed to be reminded that they could not encroach on Coalition territory with impunity.

Harrowing Starfleet and the Federation satisfied Korzenten in the same way that manipulating the Tzelnira did: both made for interesting sport.

7

"I do not have to kill you to change the shape of your life."

The words terrorized, even though they came delivered without inflection, without nuance, cold syllables electronically pronounced and secondarily translated into Federation Standard so that Sarina Douglas could understand her Breen inquisitor. A chill seized Sarina, clad only in her undergarments, even as a hot spotlight blinded her to her surroundings. Metal restraints bound her limbs to the hard chair in which she sat, her feet feeling frozen atop the unyielding concrete surface beneath them.

Sarina had traveled to the Breen Confederacy, to the world of Salavat, to try to find where the Typhon Pact had begun constructing a starship equipped with quantum slipstream drive. Starfleet Intelligence had assigned her to locate and destroy the concealed shipyard, as well as to eradicate the purloined schematics and any backup copies of them—and the man assigned to interrogate her already knew that. He sought other information.

He wanted to know where Sarina had acquired her Breen armor and mask, which had been stripped from her body and lay in a heap on the floor in front of her. He wanted to know how Starfleet had learned about the secret operation headquartered beneath the barren surface of Salavat, and how she had penetrated the territory of the Confederacy to reach the icy planet. But mostly he wanted to know about her collaborator.

"Tell me about your partner," the inquisitor demanded. The harsh, computerized speech burst from his snout-faced mask like the discharge of an energy weapon. *"The one named Bashir."*

Julian, Sarina thought, with no small degree of anxiety.

Seven years before, Jack, Lauren, and Patrick—the genetically enhanced but socially maladjusted humans institutionalized along with Sarina—had essentially abducted her from the psychiatric facility and made their way to Deep Space 9. They hoped that Doctor Bashir could treat her, that he could free her from the prison of her own altered mind. Her senses too slow to keep up with her brain, the variance between the two had left her mute and unfocused. Doctor Bashir—Julian—thought he could modify her condition; he thought he could *fix* her. But she'd been afraid that any changes to her body might hurt her.

"It won't hurt," Julian assured her, leaning over her in the bare room on Salavat, his handsome face in shadows as his head momentarily blocked the light shining into her eyes. "I promise."

"And I can promise that it will *hurt,"* said the inquisitor, unseen, from somewhere behind Sarina. *"I promise the only thing to make it stop hurting will be death."*

Fear washed over her like a wave, forcing her down beneath its relentless onslaught, threatening to drown her. Death did not frighten her, but absence did. If she lost her life, she would no longer have a chance to finish what she'd started with Julian. Once, he had saved her, and once, he had loved her. On their mission to the Breen Confederacy, he had divulged the continuing emotions he felt for her, and she had walked into his arms.

"I love you," he told her, his face just centimeters from hers, but still backlit and impossible to discern in the bleak torture chamber. Sarina could feel his warm breath on her lips. She wanted to lean forward and kiss him, but her head had been restrained too. Her eyes sought his in the darkness as she labored to make out his features, to gain strength from his visage.

"Is that what will save you?" asked the inquisitor, the buzzing, mechanical tones of his transmitted voice no longer menacing, but merely curious. *"Or is that what will defeat you?"*

Sarina heard the sharp rap of the Breen's footsteps as he walked out from behind her. In her peripheral vision, she saw him, saw the layered armor that wrapped his body, saw the canine-like helmet hiding not only his face, but the identity of his very species. He reached for something, but the silhouette of Julian's face filled most of her gaze and she could not see.

And then the shadows quivered. Sarina realized that her inquisitor had taken hold of the standard supporting the spotlight. The room seemed to waver as the Breen carried it forward. As he brought it abreast of her, and then past her so that it shined from just over her shoulder, Julian's face became visible, the light sweeping across his features like the surface of a moon emerging from an eclipse.

Except that it wasn't Julian.

The mature woman peered at Sarina with brilliant, dispassionate eyes. The pointed tips of her ears peeked through her shoulder-length black hair. "I told you I would return," said L'Haan. "You *will* escape your captivity."

Sarina struggled against her restraints, to no avail.

"You broke from the confinement of your own mind," L'Haan said. "You found your voice and your life. And you finally found a necessary outlet for your intellect."

Four years earlier, Starfleet Intelligence had recruited Sarina into its ranks, making the compelling case that not only did her enhanced assets make her particularly suited to field operations, but that such work would *fulfill* her capabilities—that it would fulfill *her*.

And for most of the intervening years, it had. But then one day not long before, L'Haan had appeared on behalf of Section 31. The Vulcan operative presented a different argument than Starfleet Intelligence had, contending that while SI did make good use of her abilities, it also placed limits on her by virtue of its licit nature. The extralegal Section 31, L'Haan insisted, would provide her a broader canvas on which to draw the story of her life.

"You set your mind free once, from the prison of your genetic engineering," said L'Haan, her face bathed in the indifferent light the inquisitor still held in his hand. "Then you set yourself free by enlisting in Starfleet Intelligence, and then again by joining Section 31. Surely this situation—" L'Haan gestured toward the steel bands binding her arms to those of the chair in which she sat. "—can be no match for you."

Awareness dawned on Sarina. She stared deep into L'Haan's eyes, and the covert agent took two steps backward. Sarina slowly rose to her feet, the restraints around her limbs falling to the concrete floor with a clatter.

She remembered the inquisitor, and she turned to face him.

He stood behind the straight-backed wooden chair. He carried the tall stand supporting the spotlight in his left hand, illuminating that side of his body while leaving the other side in darkness. In his right hand, he held a neural truncheon, a favored Breen tool for controlling and incapacitating prisoners.

"You're no match for me," Sarina said.

"No?" said the inquisitor, his skepticism evident even in the single electronic word. He dropped the spotlight to the floor, where it teetered on its stand for a few seconds, causing light and shadow to dance about the featureless walls. Then he reached up and pulled off his mask.

Julian stared back at her.

Sarina could only gape as he lifted the truncheon and brandished it in her direction. He skirted the chair and thrust the weapon into her midsection. Her brain screamed in agony as the device overloaded her synapses, triggering terrible waves of pain. She doubled over, her arms wrapping around her body. She cried out—

And awoke. Sitting upright, her arms enfolding her abdomen, she felt the clammy sensation of perspiration cooling on her skin. Her heart raced, and her breathing came in heavy rasps.

For a moment, Sarina had no idea where she was. "Lights up one-quarter," she said around mouthfuls of air. She half-expected the darkness to remain, and to find herself still a prisoner of the Breen—or a ward of Starfleet Medical. But a quick tone answered her, and her surroundings brightened to reveal Julian's quarters aboard Deep Space 9. Her locale did little to ease her discomfort.

Seemingly constructed of hard edges, awkward angles, an inordinate amount of grillwork, and a host of shadowy corners, the old Cardassian station struck Sarina as a sinister version of the institutions in which she had spent most of her life. Certainly it embodied the worst aspects of those facilities. Though she knew it recycled, the atmosphere seemed stagnant, absent of any scent. Metal surfaces abounded, along with computer interfaces. The place felt confining, even claustrophobic.

Although most of the substance of her dream, and even its general outlines, had begun to fade as soon as she woke, her unease remained. As her pulse rate slowed and her respiration returned to normal, Sarina wanted nothing more than to walk in the open air, to feel grass beneath her feet and the soothing rays of some star on her face. Short of that, she thought she'd settle for a warm embrace.

Sarina looked to her side, confirming what she already knew: Julian did not lie beside her. She moved her hand across the surface of the bed, to the place he would eventually occupy when he completed his shift in the infirmary. She briefly considered climbing out of bed, dressing, and paying him an impromptu visit, but she decided against it. She still had so many things to think about, so many choices to make.

It had been two weeks since Captain Dax and the *Aventine* crew had recovered her and Julian from open space in Breen territory. In the end, they succeeded in finding and destroying a prototype Breen vessel equipped with slipstream drive, while also eliminating the stolen plans that allowed the construction of the experimental starship in the first place. They also managed to do so without igniting an interstellar war—although on that count, Sarina and Bashir and Dax came close to the brink.

It had taken some time for *Aventine* to make its way from the Confederacy to DS9. While en route, Sarina and Julian spent time in sickbay, the ship's medical staff tending to the wounds the pair had suffered during the carrying out of their mission. The two also underwent complete physicals—an ordeal Sarina would have preferred to skip—and then, mercifully, they had a few days to do little but rest.

As soon as they had been rescued by the *Aventine* crew, even before they had exited the transporter room to which they'd been beamed, Julian had looked ahead. During their time together in Breen space, they had rekindled the brief but intense romance they'd shared after he'd successfully treated her catatonia years earlier. Still in each other's arms on the transporter pad, considerately left alone there by the operators on duty, Julian rushed to talk with her.

"Now that this is over," he'd said, referring to their mission, "what's next? For us, I mean?" He wanted to know if she intended to continue serving with Starfleet Intelligence, and if so, whether or not she wanted him to join her there. His words spilled from him quickly, almost desperately. He doubtless would have asked more questions had they not been interrupted by the entrance of the ship's chief medical officer and a nurse.

The intrusion, though, had given Sarina a few moments to think. On the way to *Aventine*'s sickbay, walking side by side, she took Julian's hand in hers and squeezed it tightly. "In answer to your question," she told him, *"I go where you go."* He smiled, as widely and naturally as she'd ever seen.

A pang of guilt had risen within Sarina when she'd seen that smile. Julian didn't know about her involvement with Section 31, or their ongoing plans with respect to him. Nor did she think he suspected what she did: that they would not wait indefinitely for him, and that at some point, they would discontinue their classification of him as a promising prospective agent, and instead catalog him as an enemy combatant. From what she knew of his past dealings with 31, he surely would have understood the danger of being labeled by the organization as an adversary.

Sarina stood up from the bed, her rumpled nightshirt falling to her knees. She paced across the small room to the oval port in the outer bulkhead, which she'd rendered opaque prior to retiring for the night. "Computer," she said, "set the window to transparent." As with the lights, a brief note answered her, and then the environmental system complied with her command. The stars became visible, though not B'hava'el—Bajor's sun. Deep Space 9's slow rotation would carry it past within the hour—it did so for a few minutes within every hour—and she couldn't imagine being able to fall asleep again before it reappeared. She had such important questions to answer for herself that it surprised her that she'd been able to slumber in the first place.

After the completion of the Breen operation and their time in *Aventine*'s sickbay, Sarina and Julian had done little beyond compiling their individual reports of events, which they had then submitted to Starfleet Command and Starfleet Intelligence. Still recovering and decompressing from their ordeal, they remained off duty upon their arrival at DS9, at least until that night, when Julian agreed to take a late shift for Doctor Boudreaux, whose husband had apparently suffered a bad fall at an archeological dig on Bajor. Spending the evening alone had finally allowed Sarina the freedom to seriously consider what she would do next. Unfortunately, she hadn't decided on a course of action by the time fatigue had overcome her.

Tomorrow, she knew, Commander Erdona of Starfleet Intelligence would arrive at Deep Space 9. Among other duties, he would personally debrief Sarina and Julian on the details of their mission. He also might attempt to recruit Julian into SI, and he almost assuredly would inform Sarina of her next assignment. That meant that she had little time left to her before she needed to reach some significant decisions.

Sighing in frustration, Sarina peered out at the stars. Reflected in the port, she suddenly saw movement behind her. She whirled around, upset that somebody could so easily enter the room without her hearing. But when she turned, she found herself still alone.

She closed her eyes and shook her head. "Now you're getting paranoid," she told herself. Except that she truly had more than enough good reasons to maintain a suspicious nature. Just the previous night, when she'd woken from a dream, she'd decided to rise and spend some time by herself. She left Julian in bed and slipped into the living area of his quarters, where she ordered up a hot cup of herbal tea. When she turned from the replicator, L'Haan regarded her from a chair across the room.

Clad wholly in black, the Section 31 operative had noted that an acoustic-dampening field protected their conversation from being overheard, and that a mild sedative introduced into Julian's dinner would ensure that he slept soundly through the meeting. L'Haan commended Sarina on the success of her primary mission—to thwart the attempt of the Typhon Pact to develop quantum slipstream drive—as well as of her secondary mission—to begin the final push to enlist Doctor Bashir as an asset. To accomplish that, L'Haan wanted Sarina to continue her romantic relationship with Julian, to make it as intense and intimate as possible. "Make him *love* you," she'd said, "and then we will *have* him."

"A sound plan," Sarina said aloud in Julian's empty bedroom. She turned back to the port. B'hava'el had just come into view, she saw, a yellowish speck of light just slightly larger and brighter than the other stars she could see from her vantage. It occurred to her to make a wish upon it—she half-recalled an ancient tradition of doing so—but simply wishing would not help her make the choices she needed to make.

Feeling a touch of self-pity, Sarina said, "Maybe it would have been better if I'd never returned from the Breen mission." But she knew that her death wouldn't have solved anything. And then she remembered the words of her inquisitor on Salavat, and a chill raced down her spine.

"I do not have to kill you to change the shape of your life."

Doctor Julian Bashir sat at the long, narrow conference table in the wardroom, battling the urge to fold his arms together before him and lay his head down. The long hours of his debriefing— of his *two* debriefings—had exhausted him, both mentally and emotionally. Fortunately, an end at last seemed in sight.

Bashir glanced to his side at Sarina, who appeared more anxious than fatigued. Then he peered across the short width of the table at Commander Aldo Erdona, who sat with a collection of padds amassed before him. The tall, dark-haired man had arrived at Deep Space 9 that day from Starfleet Intelligence. Although he claimed that he'd already read through the after-action reports that Sarina and Bashir had submitted to SI, the rigorousness of his questioning raised doubts about that in the doctor's mind.

Erdona had initially interviewed the two of them separately—first Sarina and then Bashir. After taking a break, presumably to collate the information he'd gathered, the commander asked to speak with them together. Bashir assumed that Erdona intended only to clarify some minor inconsistencies that might have arisen—the result of mere differences in perspective and memory—but he instead wanted to hear a shared account of their time in Breen space.

Listening to Sarina describe what had happened to her on Salavat after they'd separated during the mission had been more than difficult for Bashir; it had been wrenching. In the time since their recovery by the crew of *Aventine,* she had told him about her capture and detention. But Sarina spoke to him only in general terms about her experience, a truth he came to realize as she recounted for Erdona her brutal interrogation by an inquisitor from the Breen Intelligence Directorate.

Bashir wondered again, as he had numerous times throughout the previous two weeks, if he had failed the woman he loved beyond any chance of redemption. During the mission, Sarina made the tactical decision that they should split up. He protested, to no avail, but he also knew that he could have said and done more to ensure that they stay together. Instead, Sarina ended up alone, surrounded by Breen military forces, and delivered into the hands of a torturer. Although she managed to escape her captivity and the mission subsequently succeeded, how much had she suffered? As he sat beside her in the wardroom, Bashir asked himself whether his love could possibly overcome the terrible agonies that she'd endured at least in part because of his actions.

Across the table, he saw Erdona continuing to speak, but Bashir's own thoughts superseded the commander's words. The doctor absently reached up and passed his hand over his close-cropped beard. He could not help but dwell on the two questions to which he so desperately needed answers: Could Sarina possibly forgive him for failing to keep her safe? And even if she could, would he ever be able to forgive himself?

Since their return to DS9, things had not been quite right between them, although their lives had become far more intertwined. They had yet to truly discuss their relationship or their potential future together, but Sarina had stayed with Bashir in his quarters. Their many hours together allowed them to reacquaint themselves with each other in a way that hadn't been possible during the execution of their mission. They each revealed the details of their lives in the years since they'd last been together, and more than that, they shared who they'd been and what they'd experienced even before they'd met. They took long walks on the Promenade, talked over drinks at Quark's, and made love back in his quarters. But for all of that, Sarina seemed to keep a part of herself in reserve, and perhaps he did too. They connected, but not completely—not in the way they had that one night on Salavat, holed up at one point on their mission in a one-room residential unit. Bashir became convinced that something stood between them, and he kept coming back to his failure on Salavat, to his not being there with Sarina to prevent the inquisitor from—

"Doctor?" said a voice. "Doctor Bashir?"

Bashir blinked, and saw the commander looking across the conference table at him. Past Erdona, through the wide oval windows lining the wardroom, the doctor saw a Frunalian science vessel departing the station. Bashir had no idea how long he hadn't been paying attention.

"Julian?" Sarina put a hand on the forearm of his uniform. "Are you all right?"

"Yes," he said instinctively, though not truthfully. "No . . . I mean, yes, I'm fine." He shook his head, as though that would clear the dour thoughts from his mind. "I'm sorry, Commander, I guess I'm just a little tired after all this." He waved one hand above the table, vaguely meant to include their long day of discussion.

"I'm sorry about that," Erdona said with apparent sincerity. "We're usually pretty thorough about this sort of thing anyway, but in this case, considering the gravity of your mission and the continuing potential for catastrophic fallout, we want to make doubly sure that we're aware of every detail of what took place."

"In order to prevent a war from being waged because of the actions we took," Bashir said, more cynically than he'd intended.

Erdona offered a small nod in agreement. "President Bacco has been delaying a meeting with the Typhon Pact ambassador expressly so that she can be absolutely certain of her facts."

"It won't come to war," Sarina said quietly, her hand still on Bashir's arm. "The Federation hasn't divulged the Typhon Pact's illegal intrusion into our space, or their violent theft of the slip-stream schematics, and the Pact hasn't divulged our violations of their territory or our assault on their secret shipyard. That means that neither side is prepared to go to war."

"For now," said Bashir, acutely aware of his continuing pessimism.

Sarina withdrew her hand from his forearm and gazed at him with what seemed like a measure of sadness. "Julian," she said, "*everything* is temporary."

Her body language wounded him, her words formed a dagger to his heart. *Everything* included their relationship. Had Sarina meant her truism about the evanescence of life to be an augury of her intention to leave Deep Space 9—to leave *him*?

Bashir tried to divine the answer in Sarina's eyes, but instead felt the unwelcome presence of whatever stood between them—which in itself provided an answer. He had to look away from Sarina, and so he turned to Commander Erdona. "So what happens the next time a phase-cloaked Romulan warbird penetrates Federation space all the way to Utopia Planitia or Gavor or some other Starfleet shipyard? Or when a squadron of such vessels ambushes the *Aventine* or some other *Vesta*-class starship so that they can seize it and reverse-engineer its slipstream drive?" He could hear the sense of defeat in his own voice.

Erdona raised one shoulder in a half-shrug. "I believe the conventional wisdom is that military secrets are the most fleeting of all."

"So we keep fighting the good fight, is that what you're saying?" Bashir snapped back.

"Yes, Doctor," Erdona said. "We keep fighting the good fight. Each day that we can keep the peace with the Typhon Pact is a good day—and a day closer to the lasting peace we're all working toward."

Lasting peace, Bashir thought skeptically. Suddenly, it all seemed so pointless. As long as the Federation enjoyed a technological advantage over the nations of the Typhon Pact, those nations would do whatever they needed to do in order to undermine that advantage, and thereby secure the safety of their own people. From their perspective, it seemed completely reasonable. Under the same circumstances, wouldn't the Federation do the same? In fact, hadn't his mission to Salavat with Sarina been an example of that? And their attempt to preserve the current balance of power—which tilted in the UFP's favor—did not by any reckoning mark the first such actions taken by Starfleet. Bashir recalled an incident from a century earlier, when a Federation starship illegally violated Romulan space so that its crew could steal a cloaking device.

For an uncomfortable moment, Bashir saw no difference between the two sides. The nations of the Typhon Pact feared the Federation, and the Federation feared them, and each faction conducted their foreign policy on that basis. But then Bashir drew the distinction: the United Federation of Planets did not wage preemptive war with their adversaries, did not eschew diplomacy for hostility, did not seek to usurp the territory and resources of others.

"You're right, of course," Bashir said. He really wanted very much to close his eyes. Instead, he said, "Okay, so I guess I'm in."

Erdona regarded him for a few seconds without replying, as though attempting to parse Bashir's words. "Pardon me, Doctor?"

"What are you talking about, Julian?" Sarina asked, in a way that suggested she already knew what he meant.

"I've been thinking of making a change," he explained, keeping his gaze fixed on Erdona. "I may as well transfer permanently to Starfleet Intelligence."

"Please understand that I've been in no way pressuring you to join us," the commander said. "But we would consider having a man of your abilities a tremendous asset."

"Julian?" Sarina said quietly.

He turned to face her. "We can be together," he said. He had perceived that Sarina didn't wish to stay with him, but he needed to know why. If she could not forgive him for his transgression on Salavat, he could understand that, and he would have little choice but to accept it. But if she simply wanted to remain with Starfleet Intelligence, Bashir would not allow that to stand in their way.

"But you don't want this," Sarina said.

Bashir reached over and placed his hand on hers. "I know of only one thing in this universe that I want," he told her.

Sarina glanced sidelong at Commander Erdona as a flush rose across her features. Then she looked back at Bashir. "I know," she said, and she reached for his other hand. "There's only one thing I want too."

Bashir opened his mouth to respond, but he couldn't find his voice. He loved Sarina, but as they'd stayed together on DS9, he'd felt something between them, something holding them back. But as he looked into her eyes, all of that had fallen away. Once, a long time ago, Bashir had described Sarina as the woman for whom he'd been waiting all his life. In that moment, finally, he stopped waiting.

The woman of his dreams had arrived.

Sarina met his loving gaze with her own before turning to look over at Erdona. "Commander," she said, "would you mind giving us a few moments?"

"Of course," he said. He stood and began gathering up his padds. "We were done here anyway, other than that I wanted to speak with you, Ms. Douglas, about your return to active duty with Starfleet Intelligence. If you wish to join us as well, Doctor, we should be able to process your transfer relatively quickly."

"We'll let you know," Sarina said.

Erdona picked up his padds, came around the table, and headed for the nearer set of doors. The instant they closed behind him, Bashir said, "We're going to stay together." He couldn't take his eyes from Sarina's beautiful face.

"Yes, Julian, yes," she said. "But not at Starfleet Intelligence. That's not right for you."

"It can be," he said. "As long as I'm with you."

"No," she insisted. She let go of Bashir's hands, stood up, and paced away from him. When she turned back to him, she said, "Before we left for Salavat, you spoke with me about all the good things you'd accomplished here on Deep Space Nine."

"And you spoke about your intelligence work," he reminded her. "About helping to prevent wars, to end political oppression, to—"

"What we were both talking about was working to make the universe a better place," Sarina said. "We can do that here."

"I agree with your point," Bashir said, "but I don't want you to give up on your ambitions for me. Even before you came back into my life, Sarina, I was thinking of making a change."

"Were you?" she said, taking a step closer to him. "Why?"

Bashir looked away, easily recalling the despair he'd felt not that long ago. He remembered sitting at a table in Quark's, alone in the middle of the station's most popular social space. His closest friend, Miles O'Brien, had left DS9 with his wife and children years earlier. Garak, Odo, Jake Sisko, Thirishar ch'Thane, even Worf had departed to pursue other directions in their lives. Captain Sisko had eventually returned from his time apparently spent with the wormhole aliens, but had then left Starfleet for his home on Bajor. More recently, Elias Vaughn, Kira Nerys, and Nog had left the station—though Vaughn had ultimately returned: injured during the Borg invasion, he lay in DS9's infirmary, brain-dead, his once vital body an empty shell.

Peering across the conference table and out through the ports at the cold stars, Bashir said, "So many of my friends have moved on from this place."

"And you can't make new friends?" Sarina asked, though not unkindly.

He looked over at her. "Well, yes, but . . . it's just that I've been here for thirteen years."

"And that's too long?"

"Yes," he said, the uncertainty in his voice plain. "Maybe . . . I don't know."

Sarina smiled at him and walked back over to the conference table. She sat down, leaned forward, and once more took his hands in hers. "Julian, if you want to leave Deep Space Nine, that's fine with me. I told you on the *Aventine*: where you go, I go. So if you want to transfer to some other Starfleet posting, I'll find a place there. If you want to retire from Starfleet and practice medicine on some remote planet, I'll be there. If you want to resign your commission and go peddle Spican flame gems . . . or mine Spican flame gems . . . or, I don't know, create works of art out of them . . . I'll be there.

"But Starfleet Intelligence? No. It's too dangerous. There would be too great a chance of losing you."

"There are dangers everywhere in the universe," Bashir said. "Including here at DS-Nine."

"I know," Sarina said. "But living aboard this station isn't quite as risky a venture as two humans waltzing into the Breen Confederacy, posing as citizens, and destroying an experimental starship and the top-secret facility that constructed it. We both ended up drifting without a vessel in open space. We were fortunate to survive."

"I know," he said. "You're right."

"Look, you've been here for thirteen years," Sarina said. "You've achieved a great deal, you've made good friends, and you've watched them pick up and move on. Now, if you're truly prepared to move on too, then we'll move." She paused and squeezed his hands. "But do you know what this place sounds like to me?"

"What?"

"It sounds like it's your home."

"Sarina," Bashir said, "*you* are my home."

Again, she smiled. "Then it doesn't matter where we go. It's your choice."

"It's *our* choice."

Sarina leaned farther forward and pressed her mouth against his. Soft and warm, her lips tasted sweet.

When she sat back, she said, "Then how about this? How about we stay here for right now? I'm going to resign from Starfleet Intelligence, and I'll see what I can find to do, either on the station or on Bajor." She raised her head and looked all around the wardroom, as though seeing it for the first time. "This has been your home, Julian. Share it with me."

"But what if you don't like it?" he asked. "What if I really am ready to move on?"

"Then we'll move on," Sarina said. "It doesn't matter where or when, as long as we're together."

Bashir could not keep himself from matching Sarina's smile with his own.

8

Ben Sisko hesitated. He had no idea what he would say—had no idea what more he *could* say. But he did know that delaying any longer would not suddenly allow him to find the words.

Sisko reached up and pressed a fingertip to the touchpad set beside the door. Inside, chimes announced his arrival. A few seconds later, he heard footsteps approaching—footsteps he still recognized.

Kasidy opened the front door. It had been nearly a year and a half since he'd last seen his wife in person, and in that time, he thought that he had, at least to some degree, inured himself to missing her. When he laid eyes on Kasidy, though, he felt a strong impulse to toss his duffel onto the porch, step across the threshold, and take her in his arms. She wore black slacks and a ruby-colored wraparound blouse. She'd let her dark hair grow longer, and it cascaded past her shoulders. Kasidy looked as beautiful as the day he'd met her . . . as the day he'd married her . . . as the day he'd left her.

"Hello, Ben," she said evenly. Her voice carried neither bitterness nor warmth. The same had been the case in the messages they'd exchanged during the past couple of months, once Sisko had reestablished contact with her.

After Nerys had tracked him down at Starbase 39-Sierra, it had not taken him long to see the merit in what she'd said to him—in the perspective that Kasidy had asked her to pass along to him. He sent Kasidy a message telling her so, which opened up a dialogue between them about how best to reintegrate Sisko into Rebecca's life. As part of that process, he wanted simply to tell his daughter the truth of their situation, but Kasidy resisted.

"It's good to see you," Sisko said, almost nonsensically after all that had transpired.

Kasidy did not respond to his words. Instead, she said, "Come in, it's cold out there."

Sisko glanced upward, where dark clouds spilled across the sky, threatening snow. Then he walked forward and through the door, into the home that he had planned so long ago, in what seemed like an entirely different existence. Behind him, Kasidy closed the front door on the brittle winter air that had descended on Kendra Province.

The interior of the house looked much as Sisko remembered it. To his right, beneath a vaulted ceiling, the great room spread to a comfortable sitting area, with a sofa and several easy chairs arranged before large picture windows that afforded ample views of the Kendra Valley. He peered out at the landscape, where bare *moba* trees stood guard over grasses that had grown brown with the season. In the distance, the dark twist of the Yolja River flowed along the base of the mountains.

Looking to his left, Sisko saw two wing chairs facing the hearth, sitting on either side of a small, triangular table. Red flames crackled in the firebox, effectively keeping the day's chill at bay. Above, an assortment of framed family photographs lined the mantel. While Sisko saw a number of new additions, mostly featuring Rebecca, none of the pictures he knew seemed to be missing—not even those that included him. He saw an image taken on the day he and Kasidy had first brought their daughter home, another from their wedding, a portrait of him wearing his Starfleet dress uniform. That Kasidy hadn't taken the photos down and packed them away, or even rid herself of them entirely, surprised him. He suspected that it demonstrated her avowed attempts to keep Sisko familiar to Rebecca even without him there.

It did not surprise him, though, that from above the mantel she had removed his canvas reproduction of *City of B'hala,* a historic Bajoran icon painting. Years earlier, Sisko's study of the work of art had coincided with unusual activity in his brain. He experienced visions, which directly led to his unearthing the ruins of the actual city of B'hala, previously lost for twenty millennia. He also felt on the cusp of completely seeing the complex tapestry of Bajor's past, present, and future, of understanding the Prophets' plans for the people, the meaning and structure

of the Celestial Temple, the role of the Cardassians in all of it—
only to have it all taken away when Doctor Bashir operated on
him. Sisko initially refused the surgery that would have restored
his brain to a normal, healthy state, instead choosing to risk his
life for the chance to comprehend the deep reality surrounding Bajor and its people. But when he lost consciousness and
faced impending death, Jake authorized the doctor to perform
the procedure.

As a result of its nearly fatal effect on Sisko, Kasidy had never
liked *City of B'hala,* although she did claim that she'd come to
appreciate its artistry. Once he'd left, apparently, that had not
persuaded her to keep the painting on display. In its place hung a
pointillist work, a bucolic scene of a mother and daughter walking through the countryside. Sisko recognized the signature of
the artist, Galoren Sen, as one of Kasidy's favorites. He suspected
that she'd acquired the painting from Rozahn Kit's gallery in
Adarak.

Sisko walked past the front rooms to the dining area, where
an arrangement of dried flowers garnished the table. To the
right, an open doorway led into the kitchen. Sisko unslung the
duffel from his shoulder and set it down on the table.

"You're not planning on staying," Kasidy said, gesturing
toward the duffel. Her tone had gained an edge.

"No, no, I'll be with Jake and Korena for the two weeks," he
said. "As we planned."

Once Sisko and Kasidy had decided on the length and fre-
quency of his visits, they'd also agreed that his sleeping at the
house, even in the guest room, would be too difficult. Depending on what they chose to tell Rebecca, such an arrangement
might also confuse her too much. Fortunately, Jake and his wife
welcomed the opportunity for him to stay with them.

After leaving Bajor and returning to Starfleet the previous
year, Sisko had kept in touch with his son and daughter-in-law.
In recorded messages and written letters, Jake often told his
father how much he missed him, and also found different ways
of suggesting that he should return home to his wife and child,
who also suffered from his absence. Meanwhile, it eased Sisko's

mind to know that Jake and Korena often visited Kasidy and Rebecca, providing whatever support they could.

Placing his hand on the duffel, Sisko said, "This isn't an overnight bag; I just brought a couple of things for Rebecca." To her credit, Kasidy did not ask what he intended to give to their daughter.

"Can I take your coat?" she said.

"Yes, of course." Sisko walked back across the room. He shrugged out of his long, black coat, revealing the black-and-gold dashiki he wore over brown pants. Kasidy took his coat and hung it on the rack beside the front door.

"Rebecca will be home from school in a few minutes," she said when she turned back to face him. Her manner appeared stilted, as though, under the circumstances, she too struggled with what to say and how to act. She motioned to the sitting area before the windows, and Sisko took a seat on the sofa. Kasidy followed and moved to one of the chairs, but she did not immediately sit down.

"How does she like first grade?" Sisko asked.

"She just started, so it's hard to know," Kasidy said. "But she loved kindergarten, and even though it's only been a couple of days, I think she's taken a shine to her new teacher."

"Nerys tells me that Rebecca's doing very well learning to read."

"Well, you remember how much she loved us reading to her." Kasidy's voice trailed off toward the end of her statement, as though she wished she hadn't alluded to happier family times. She paced over to one of the windows and gazed out, as though looking for Rebecca.

"Is Ms. Tey bringing her home?" Sisko asked.

"After what happened," Kasidy said, turning to glare down at him, "Rebecca doesn't go *anywhere* without me, Jasmine, Jake, or Rena."

Sisko understood at once that Kasidy referred to the terrible ordeal they had lived through nearly two and a half years earlier, when a delusional, mentally ill fanatic had abducted Rebecca. "Of course," he said. "I'm sorry."

"Sorry for what?" Kasidy snapped at him. "For questioning my abilities as a good parent? You better not look in the mirror then." She closed her eyes, clearly attempting to bring her emotions under control. She stalked back across the room, away from him, but then spun around once more to face him. "Or maybe you're sorry for choosing to raise your daughter in a place where she's revered as a religious icon by one subset of the planet's population, and considered suspect by another group? Or maybe you're just sorry for abandoning your family."

"I'm sorry for everything," Sisko told her.

Kasidy regarded him, and as she did so, she seemed to deflate. After a moment, she moved to the nearest chair and sank into it. "Ben, I'm sorry," she said. "I didn't mean to ambush you. I honestly didn't plan to get angry or argue with you."

"You've got every right to be angry," Sisko said.

"And I am, though maybe not as much as I was when you first left," she said. "Mostly, I'm hurt."

Again, as Sisko peered at her from across the room, he wanted to go to her, wanted to enfold her in his arms. He also knew that he couldn't . . . that he *mustn't*. "I never wanted to hurt you," he said. "In fact, I left specifically to prevent that from happening."

"But why didn't you tell me that?" Kasidy asked, almost pleading for an answer to a question that obviously continued to vex her. "Why didn't you at least discuss it with me?"

"And say what, Kasidy?" Sisko said. "That I was going to follow the will of the Prophets, that I was going to heed their warning? That wouldn't have convinced you to agree with what I had to do. You're *still* not convinced."

"But it would have given *me* the chance to convince *you* that you didn't have to leave," Kasidy said. "Maybe I could have shown you how the right thing would have been for you to stay."

Sisko leaned forward on the sofa, resting his forearms atop his thighs. "Don't you see?" he said. "That's what I feared most: that you *would* convince me to stay. I was worried that I wouldn't be strong enough to leave, and that you and Rebecca would ultimately pay the price for my weakness . . . for my spending my life with you."

Kasidy threw her hands in the air. "But you can't know with certainty that would have happened." She stood up and turned to the window, hands on hips, her back to Sisko.

"I know you don't understand," he said, moving back on the sofa. "I'm not sure I really do either. But everything else I learned from the Prophets turned out to be true. I defied their warning by marrying you, and we started to suffer for it."

Kasidy turned toward him. "But not right away. And not in any way I can see that's connected to our being together."

"The Prophets didn't tell me that if I spent my life with you, sorrow would manifest the next day, or the next month, or the next year," Sisko said. "They simply said that it would happen. And just because we can't see the connections doesn't mean they're not there. I'm not even sure that it's about connections in the way you mean. I only know that the Prophets saw my future with and without you, and they warned me about the dangerous consequences—or the dangerous *concurrences*—of us being together."

"Ben, bad things happen in life," Kasidy said. "Do you think that your father wouldn't have died if we hadn't been together? Or that Elias wouldn't have gotten injured in the Borg invasion? Or that Audj and Calan wouldn't have died in the fire? Our marriage didn't have anything to do with any of those things."

"I know that's how it seems," Sisko said. "But I also know what the Prophets told me. And I know what I feel. I cannot risk your safety."

Kasidy's features softened. She walked over and sat on the sofa beside him. "Isn't every day a risk?" she asked. "Ben, you're the man who stood up to the Cardassians for the sake of the Bajoran people. You led an overmatched, outgunned squadron into battle against the Borg in order to save the Alonis. You fought the Dominion and the Founders in an attempt to preserve the Federation itself." She reached forward and placed her hands on his. "Why can't you fight for Rebecca and me? For our family?"

Sisko stared down at their hands, at her light, caramel-colored skin against his darker complexion. Kasidy's simple touch had sent a shockwave through him. He felt a yearning that went far beyond the physical. His heart, his mind, his . . . *pagh* . . . ached for Kasidy, craved a return to the shared life they'd created together, and that had brought them the marvel of Rebecca, a blend of the two of them with her own unique life force.

Under the guise of responding to her question, Sisko stood up, breaking their physical contact. As he padded across the room, a sensation of loss overwhelmed him. He felt as though he had been emptied somehow, that his flesh and bones had become tattered rags and hollow supports, devoid of spirit. *This is why I couldn't talk to Kasidy about the situation,* he thought. He wanted so badly to stay with her.

"Why can't you fight for us, Ben?" she asked behind him again.

He turned. "Fight who? Fight what? How can I combat existence, how can I battle the natural forces of the universe?"

"I'm talking about the Prophets."

"The Prophets?" Sisko said. "They're not doing this to me, to us. They only warned me about it."

"I'm not as convinced as you are of their part in this, or of their motives," Kasidy said. "But even if you can't fight them, why can't you seek clarification? Why can't you find out what will happen, and when and how. Maybe if we knew the dangers, we could prevent them, or at least avoid them."

"You know it doesn't work like that."

"No, I don't know that," Kasidy said, her voice rising in evident frustration. "And I don't know why, if Rebecca and I are so important to you, why you can't just try to talk with the Prophets about this."

"What makes you think I haven't?" Sisko asked. He sat down in one of the chairs, keeping some distance between him and Kasidy. He felt defeated. "I did try," he said. "Literally for years, I tried. I'm *still* trying, but . . . they won't respond. I think . . . they're done with me."

"Oh, Ben," Kasidy said. "I won't pretend I know how difficult that obviously must be for you, but . . ." She paused, seemingly giving consideration to what she would next say. "I can't pretend I'm disappointed if the Prophets are no longer a part of your life."

Emotion welled up within Sisko. Some days, the loss of the Prophets from his life struck him as a liberation, as freedom from a long period of forced servitude. At other times, he mourned the loss of an ongoing experience that for so long had shaped the course of his days. After the death of his first wife, the Prophets had in some regard brought purpose back into his existence, allowing him a hand in a great endeavor well beyond the compass of most people's lives: the caretaking of an entire race.

"It is difficult," he said. "It marks a significant change to my life, and a loss about which I have no say." Sisko knew well that his own actions had affected Kasidy in the same ways. "But mostly it troubles me because it leaves me—because it leaves *us*—with no possibility of recourse."

Kasidy gazed across the room at him with a longing he easily recognized, because he also felt it. Before he could stop himself, before he even knew the words would come out of his mouth, he said, "I still love you, Kasidy."

Tears immediately welled in her eyes. As they spilled down her cheeks in glistening trails, Sisko again wanted to go to Kasidy and embrace her. He feared that if he did, he would never be able to leave again.

"Ben . . . don't," she said, almost as though she could read his thoughts.

"No," he said, "you're right." He knew that she dreaded not that he would stay, but that after staying, he would go again.

Sisko looked at Kasidy, at the mother of his daughter, at the woman who had returned to him an important aspect of his life he thought had forever perished with his first wife. When Jennifer died at the hands of the Borg during the Battle of Wolf 359, so much changed for Sisko. He never knew that his heart could ache so much and continue to beat. If not for the love he felt for his son, and his responsibilities as a parent, he didn't know what he would have done.

He had remained in Starfleet because of its familiarity, and because he had needed to do something. But his ambitions to one day command a ship of his own—born several years earlier when Captain Leyton had plucked him from *Okinawa*'s engineering section and deposited him on the bridge—washed away like rain down a windowpane. Nor did his technical background provide him with any desire to return to the roots of his training as an engineer. He took a posting at Utopia Planitia only because it opened up and Starfleet wanted him there.

During those years, the idea of romance had never even occurred to Sisko. After Jennifer, how could it? He had loved her so thoroughly that her death had broken something inside of him. He took care of his son, he did his job, and he accepted that life had little more to offer than that. For a long while, that sufficed, until Sisko's assignment to Deep Space 9 thrust him into the role of the Bajoran emissary. Even then, though his life grew fuller, it took meeting Kasidy Yates to open him up to the possibility of loving again.

And he had loved her . . . and loved her still. But if her safety depended on Sisko's not spending his life with her, then how could he possibly stay? He understood Kasidy's antipathy to the Prophets; he felt it himself.

They sat together in silence. Sisko wanted to say more, but what more could he say? What more could either of them say?

On the far side of the room, the fire danced and popped as it consumed the wood that fueled it. Outside, in counterpoint, a wind picked up and whistled intermittently through the eaves. The moment swelled, as though growing in import, and Sisko feared that it would crush his fragile concord with Kasidy, or worse, that it would weigh him down so greatly that he would not be able to leave, which would eventually crush them both.

"Ben . . ."

The single word, though spoken softly, shattered the equilibrium in the room. Sisko dreaded what would follow. But instead of Kasidy's voice, he heard footfalls. Sisko looked over at his wife, who rubbed her eyes and quickly wiped away the tracks of her tears. They both rose as the front door swung open.

Jasmine Tey stepped inside with Rebecca, the little girl's arm raised so that she could hold the hand of her protector. Both wore coats buttoned up to their necks. Each of them looked to Kasidy first, and then over at Sisko.

Coming out from the sitting area and squatting down, Sisko peered across the width of the room at his daughter. She couldn't have been much more than a hundred centimeters tall. She looked delicate and beautiful. *And so much more like Kasidy now,* he thought. "Hello, Rebecca," he said in a light singsong.

Rebecca pulled her hand from Tey's and raced around the other end of the sofa into the sitting area. Kasidy crouched just quickly enough to allow Rebecca to throw herself into her mother's arms. "Hi, sweetie," Kasidy said. Rebecca responded by trying to burrow deeper into Kasidy's embrace. Kasidy asked Tey, "Did something happen, or is Miss Rebecca just being shy?"

"I think she's just being shy," Tey said.

Rising from his haunches, Sisko said, "Hello, Ms. Tey. It's good to see you again."

"And you as well, Mister Sisko," Tey said. "You're looking well." Sisko replied with a nod, and Tey looked back over at Kasidy. "You won't be needing me for the rest of the day, then, Ms. Yates?"

Over Rebecca's shoulder, Kasidy said, "No, thank you, Jasmine. We'll see you in the morning for school."

"Very good. Have a lovely rest of the day." To Sisko, she said, "Enjoy your stay." Then she opened the door and headed back out into the chilly afternoon.

Once Tey had gone, Kasidy peeled Rebecca's arms from around her neck and stood up. "What's going on with you today?" she asked. "You knew that your father would be here when you got home from school."

"I forgot," Rebecca whispered. She kept her back to Sisko and did not look around at him.

"Well, now you remember," Kasidy told her, "so why don't you go give him a hug and say hello."

In reply, Rebecca wrapped her arms around her mother's waist. "Come on now," Kasidy urged. "Let's get your coat off." Kasidy pulled Rebecca's arms away, then helped her out of her coat. Beneath it, she wore dark pants and a striped, multicolored pullover. "Now go give Daddy a hug."

Rebecca refused even to look around at Sisko, instead just shaking her head mutely.

"Would it help if I told you that I brought you something, Rebecca?" Sisko coaxed.

"Did you hear that?" Kasidy asked their daughter. "Daddy brought you a present."

"What present?" Rebecca asked in her tiny voice.

"Well, I don't know," Kasidy said. "Why don't you go over and ask him."

Cautiously, Rebecca peeked back over her shoulder. Sisko moved to the table and grabbed his duffel. He kneeled down and set it on the hardwood floor before him. "Come take a look," he said, unfastening the cylindrical carryall.

"Go on," Kasidy urged.

Slowly, with steps that seemed far too long for her little legs, Rebecca made her way over to Sisko, her gaze firmly on the duffel. "Hello, Rebecca," Sisko said.

"Hello." She dropped to her knees without looking up from Sisko's carryall. "What did you brought me?" she asked.

"*Bring* me, Rebecca," Kasidy said from across the room. "What did you *bring* me?"

"Bring me," Rebecca echoed. "What did you bring me?"

"Let's find out," Sisko said. He opened the bag, but shielded its contents from Rebecca. He reached in and pulled out a lightweight, metal model, about fifteen centimeters long. He handed it to Rebecca.

"What is it?" she asked.

"That's a replica of my starship, the *Robinson*," he said. "I'm the captain."

"Mommy's a captain too," Rebecca said.

"I know she is," Sisko said. "That's why I brought you this too." He went into his duffel again, this time extracting a similarly sized model of an *Antares*-class freighter. "This is the *Xhosa*. It's Mommy's ship."

Rebecca put down the *Robinson* model on the floor and took the *Xhosa*. Kasidy hung Rebecca's coat on the rack, then walked over to Sisko and their daughter. "What do you say, Rebecca?" she asked.

Rebecca set down the second model. "Thank you," she said

in her small voice. Then, looking up at Kasidy, she asked, "Can I go to my room?"

"Sweetie, your father came here to visit you," Kasidy said.

"Don't you like the spaceships?" Sisko asked.

"Yes, thank you," Rebecca said, though she made no move to pick up either one of them from the floor.

"I do have one other gift for you," he said. From his duffel, Sisko retrieved a hardcover book. On its cover, a young, red-haired girl sat amid some farm animals, all of whom watched as a spider spun a web in the air above them.

"A book!" Rebecca said with great enthusiasm. She reached for it, and Sisko handed it to her. "Can I read it, Mommy?"

"Yes, of course," Kasidy said. "If you want, we—" Rebecca immediately scampered to her feet and raced down the hall that led deeper into the house, opposite the doorway to the kitchen. "Rebecca Jae Sisko!" Kasidy called after her. Rebecca stopped in her tracks, the book clutched to her chest. "Come back here this instant," Kasidy said, pointing to a spot directly before her. Sisko collected the duffel, stood up, and placed it back on the table.

Clearly feeling chastened, Rebecca dutifully marched slowly back to Kasidy, again taking longer steps than seemed appropriate for her size. "You said I could read it," she said quietly, looking down at her shoes.

"Did you thank your father for the book?" Kasidy asked.

"Thank you, Daddy," she said without looking up.

Sisko squatted back down. "You're welcome, Rebecca," he said. "Maybe it would be okay with Mommy if you went to your room to look at your new book, and then let me come read it with you a little later."

For the first time, Rebecca peered directly at Sisko. "Okay," she said.

Sisko got back up. "Is that all right with you, Kasidy?" he asked.

"It is if Miss Rebecca promises to mind her manners," Kasidy said.

"I promise."

"All right then," Kasidy said. "You may go to your room."

Still clutching her new book as though she feared it might fly away if she didn't, Rebecca headed back down the hall. Kasidy bent to pick up the two starship models, which she placed on the table beside the duffel. "I'm sorry," she said.

"Don't be," Sisko said. "It's my fault for staying away so long."

"I know," she said, and motioned toward the chairs in front of the fireplace. Sisko followed her over and they both sat down. "But it's not as though you left when Rebecca was an infant. She remembers you, and I make sure that we talk about you often. We look at family pictures and recordings, and I've shown her your last couple of messages. She knew you were coming home, and she was genuinely excited about it."

"It'll be fine, I'm sure," Sisko said, though in truth, Rebecca's reaction concerned him. More than anything, he thought, it underscored the impact of his departure on his daughter and their relationship. He also wondered how he could continue being parted from Kasidy, but still keep a good, positive presence in Rebecca's life. "We just need to get reacquainted."

"I hope so."

Kasidy offered Sisko something to eat or drink, which he declined. They sat quietly in front of the fire for a while, the silence between them feeling neither particularly unnatural nor unbearably awkward. Finally, Sisko said, "We need to tell Rebecca what's going on."

"We can't do that," Kasidy said at once. "Don't you think I've had to deal with this question of what to tell our daughter and what to keep from her? I face it every day."

"We can't continue to lie to her," Sisko maintained. "It's not right."

"And it wouldn't be right to tell her that her father left because he worried that, if he stayed, something terrible would happen to her and her mother."

"We don't have to put it quite like that," Sisko said.

"However we put it," Kasidy said, "if we tell her your reason for leaving, it will scare her when you do come to visit. And Rebecca would also likely interpret the situation as somehow being *her* fault."

"I understand your point," Sisko said. "But can we really justify continuing to lie to our daughter?"

"We're not lying," Kasidy insisted. "When you left, and since you've been gone, I've told her that Starfleet needs experienced starship captains to help protect the Federation. None of that is untrue."

"It's a lie of omission."

"For right now, Ben, I can live with that," Kasidy said. "And since I'm the one raising Rebecca right now, you need to respect my decision."

Sisko didn't say anything for a few moments. He considered all that Kasidy had said, in relation to his own feelings about the situation. "All right," he said at last. "But at some point, we need to tell Rebecca everything."

"At some point, yes," Kasidy agreed. "But not now. She's not even six years old yet."

Reminded of Rebecca's age, he said, "Soon. I wish I could be here for her birthday." Rebecca would turn six just a few days after he returned to *Robinson*.

"You should record a message before you go back to Starfleet," Kasidy said. "That way, she'll be sure to have it on—"

Kasidy stopped and looked past Sisko. He turned to follow her gaze and saw their daughter standing just inside the hallway. When she saw him look at her, she held out to him the book he'd earlier given her. "Daddy, are you going to read to me?"

Sisko smiled. He looked to Kasidy, who smiled back at him and nodded. "I would love to, honey." He walked over to Rebecca, and she immediately led him off toward her bedroom.

Despite doing what he needed to do in order to protect his wife and daughter, Sisko knew that he had made life difficult for his family. But as he sat down on Rebecca's bed and she nestled against him, as she handed him the book and waited for him to read to her, he thought maybe things would work out after all.

Only later, when he stood on the bridge of the *Robinson* and saw Kasidy's ship exploding in space, would he realize just how wrong that assessment had been.

9

Proconsul Anlikar Ventel sat at the conference table, between two of the six spiral arms that extended outward from its large, round center. As he listened to the reports of the individual representatives of the Typhon Pact member states, he grew progressively more perturbed. In the two hundred days since the Romulan Senate had voted to elevate Gell Kamemor to the praetorship as Tal'Aura's successor, the new leader of the Empire had worked tirelessly to stabilize the political state of affairs in the Alpha and Beta Quadrants. She set the welfare of the Romulan people—as opposed to military superiority, or the acquisition of space or resources—as her top priority, and Ventel agreed with her assessment that pinpointed the primary component of that welfare as interstellar peace.

But as each of the Typhon Pact representatives spoke, their accounts of information relevant to the alliance included actions their people had taken detrimental to continued amity with their spacefaring neighbors. Ventel had hoped for, and had actually anticipated, a far more positive experience when he'd agreed to replace Tomalak as the Empire's envoy to Typhon I, the space station jointly constructed and maintained by the six Pact nations. Praetor Kamemor judged Tomalak better suited than Ventel as a liaison to both the Romulan Imperial Fleet and the Tal Shiar. As a former, longtime member of the Imperial Fleet, and one who had risen to positions of considerable authority within it, Tomalak retained numerous high-level military contacts. And though he had clashed with Rehaek, the previous chairman of the Tal Shiar, he shared a mutual respect with Sela, the secretive organization's current head.

Directly across the table from Ventel, the Gorn ambassador detailed a recent clash between Hegemony forces and a Federation starship. As though on cue, a Gorn warship became visible behind Skorn, rising into view through a circular port in the outer bulkhead. The formidable-looking vessel featured a long, tapering primary hull, with slightly curved warp nacelles on either side, mounted asymmetrically to it on short, wide struts. Ventel had first seen the ship when he'd arrived at Typhon I.

An impressive sight in its own right, the space station symbolized in three dimensions what the conference table did in two. A central sphere formed the main body of Typhon I, with six spiral arms projecting from it at its equator. The entire structure evoked the form of the galaxy. Each arm denoted one of the founding members of the Pact, with an internal environment specific to that species, and with external docking ports made to accommodate their vessels. The main sphere blended various features of the different settings in an attempt to provide the best generic space for all the member species. Just as Tomalak had warned him, the temperature of the communal areas dipped below the comfort level for Romulans, but not unbearably so. It pleased Ventel that, unlike the Breen and Tholian diplomats, he did not need to wear an environmental suit.

The proconsul listened as Skorn's comments drew to a close. Although Ventel's automated translator interpreted the speech of the reptilian Gorn ambassador, he could still hear the original vocalizations. To him, the hiss of Skorn's words sounded less like a language and more like a slow atmospheric leak—or like the sibilant warning of a wild animal. The latter characterization matched the content of his remarks, which mostly told of a confrontation between Gorn forces and a Starfleet vessel—a tense encounter that only served to heighten the friction between the Federation and the Hegemony, and worse, between the Federation and the Pact.

Skorn's address followed one made by the representative of the Holy Order of the Kinshaya, Patriarch Radrigi, and before that, one by that of the Tzenkethi Coalition, Speaker Alizome Vik Tov-A. Radrigi sat perched atop a low disk, his four legs splayed out around it, his two arms at his sides, his wings remaining tucked on his back. He had spoken at length of the seemingly unending skirmishes being fought by the Order with the Klingon Empire. The two powers had warred for centuries, but the recent increase in activity suggested that it might be difficult to preserve the current status quo, with hostilities possibly intensifying to include the Klingons' Khitomer Accords ally, the Federation, and the Kinshaya's Pact partners.

Speaker Alizome had delivered a similar report on behalf of the Tzenkethi. A tall woman of beautiful proportions and exquisite features, she moved with elegance and poise. Her green pupils filled her eyes, and her golden flesh glowed with an internal radiance that had an almost mesmerizing effect on those around her. Though a bipedal humanoid, she too sat on one of the low disks at the conference table, her legs pulled up and wrapped around the base of her torso, making her appear as though the bottom half of her body had gone missing.

Alizome had articulated her words with a voice that sounded like the gentle ringing of wind chimes, though the content of her report possessed a harshness Ventel didn't appreciate. She related accounts of the Federation relocating several populations from worlds attacked by the Borg to planets located beyond UFP borders. Demonstrating at least a modicum of restraint, the Coalition did not adopt a war footing, nor did they petition the Pact to make any declarations or take any actions against the Federation. Still, it troubled Ventel to hear that the Tzenkethi had chosen to menace the new settlements. The autarch wanted to send the message to the UFP that it could not encroach upon Tzenkethi territory with no fear of reprisal. He also hoped to drive the displaced populations back into Federation space.

Once the Gorn ambassador had finished his report and responded to questions, the Breen representative, Vart, issued an account of recent Confederacy matters. The muzzled helmet of the standard Breen environmental suit converted Vart's voice into an electronic garble almost unrecognizable as speech. As Ventel's translator decrypted the ambassador's words, the pro-consul realized that he didn't actually know Vart's gender, but had assumed male because of the harsh sound of the vocoder.

"I regret to inform this assembly that our attempt to construct a starship with a functioning quantum slipstream drive has failed," Vart said.

The news appeared to surprise everybody present, including Ventel, though he guessed that he alone did not count the information as disappointing. After the supposed industrial accident at Starfleet's Utopia Planitia facility, Praetor Kamemor, suspecting a different reality and fearing Romulan involvement, had set several members of her government the task of learning what truly occurred at Sol IV. Tal Shiar Chairwoman Sela uncovered a secret proposal by her predecessor to employ a Breen operative and a Romulan starship equipped with the new phasing cloak to steal the quantum slipstream schematics from the Federation. The praetor's own predecessor, Tal'Aura, approved the plan. Tomalak managed to confirm the actual theft via his contacts aboard the Imperial Fleet vessel *Dekkona,* although when Kamemor spoke with Fleet Admiral Devix, he denied any knowledge of the operation. Pending his own investigation, Devix removed *Dekkona*'s commander, Marius, from active duty.

The praetor believed the Federation's characterizing the theft of the slipstream plans as an industrial accident was a clear indication that the UFP sought peace in the region—or at least that they wished to avoid a shooting war. Ventel concurred. And the fact that the Breen had not succeeded meant a continuation of the current balance of power, a state that, to this point, had not led to open warfare.

"A slipstream engine had been completed and installed on a test bed," Ambassador Vart continued, *"but two humans, likely working for Starfleet, infiltrated one of our worlds and sabotaged the prototype. The engine, the vessel, and the shipyard were all destroyed."*

"Surely that could not have been the only attempt being made to deliver slipstream technology to the Pact," said Alizome, the Tzenkethi speaker, not waiting for Vart to finish his report. "I presume that a secondary effort has now been started."

"For the sake of security, our engineers limited the scope of the project to a single facility," Vart said.

"Which would have been effective," hissed Skorn, "if you had actually been able to keep that shipyard secure."

Vart rose to his feet and leaned in over the table, the green glow of his wide eyepiece shining in the direction of Ambassador Skorn. *If Breen even have eyes,* thought Ventel. He had never seen a member of the species out of an environmental suit.

"I did not notice any Gorn willing to travel into Federation space, to conduct an espionage operation at a Starfleet site, or to steal their most advanced technology," Vart said, Then he turned his gaze on Alizome before continuing. *"Indeed, other than the Romulans, it seems none of our Pact allies has much of a backbone."*

Ventel construed the comment as a pointed slight against the Tzenkethi, whose internal anatomy contained bones only along their spines.

"But we do have brains," Alizome said, the lyrical sound of her voice unable to mask the venom in her words. "And mine would have told me to maintain a secure backup for the slipstream plans. Surely you made this minimal effort."

Vart lifted his hands from the tabletop and stood back for a moment before taking his seat once more. *"We did make backups,"* he said. *"They were all held at the shipyard. Prior to the destruction of the facility, one of our engineers packaged them in an emergency transmission to the Confederate Information Bureau."* He paused, apparently not pleased with what he next needed to reveal. *"Somehow, the backups became corrupted."*

"'Somehow,'" Alizome echoed. "With the loss of this opportunity, the Breen have allowed the Federation to maintain their capacity to launch a first strike."

"Pardon me," Ventel said, "but if the Federation intended to attack preemptively, wouldn't they have done so already?"

For the first time since Vart had begun his report, the Tholian ambassador spoke up. Like her Breen counterpart, Corskene wore an environmental suit. Black and angular, it showed off her white, polygonal eyes, which shined brightly through her faceplate. "The Federation Starfleet is still recovering from the Borg invasion, so they are hardly equipped to conduct a war at this juncture," she said. The electronic transmission of her words sounded far less abrasive than that of the Breen. "But that does not belie Starfleet's technological superiority, nor does it obviate the Typhon Pact's need to meet their capabilities in order to keep our own people safe."

A general murmur of agreement filtered through the conference room. Ventel wanted to argue the reverse, that matching the technological advancement of the Federation's starships would disturb the flimsy stability of the Alpha and Beta Quadrants in a dangerous way. Though Kamemor meant to lead a new, enlightened Romulus into the future, there remained hawkish factions within her government, and the same held true for the Empire's allies. If the Pact could exceed, or perhaps even simply equal, the military might of the Federation, the possibility of war would increase dramatically. But because of his newness to the proceedings, and his lack of familiarity with the participants, Ventel chose to hold his tongue.

When everybody had quieted, Corskene spoke into the stillness. "There may be another means of disrupting the Federation," she said. All eyes turned toward the Tholian ambassador. "As you may know, the people of Andor are facing a health crisis. For centuries, their four-sex reproductive configuration has led them toward the path of extinction. In recent times, decreases in fertility have hastened this process." Corskene paused, apparently for effect. "The Tholian Assembly has chosen to help them solve their dilemma."

Patriarch Radrigi peered at the Tholian ambassador with a quizzical expression on his face. "How does helping the Andorians disrupt the Federation?" he asked.

"UFP and Starfleet scientists have been hard at work for some time now attempting to find a genetic solution for the Andorians, including the possibility of introducing alien DNA into their gene pool," Corskene said. "The people of Andor are divided on whether or not this would be a viable answer or a pollution of their race. There are those on Andor who would banish members of Starfleet from their world, and even some who advocate closing their borders to non-Andorians."

"But why would the Andorians accept a solution from the Tholians," Ventel asked, "if they're unwilling to accept one from the Federation, of which they are a founding member?"

"The Andorians are mostly not averse to a scientific answer to their problem, only one that would corrupt their unique genetic composition," Corskene said. "A century ago, the Tholian Assembly and the Federation both came into possession of a complex library of scientific information that could be readily employed to resolve the Andorian crisis without resorting to the introduction of foreign DNA into their genetic structure. But that data remains classified within the Federation, and its leaders have chosen *not* to avail themselves of it, even to help the people of Andor.

"So we did."

"You did . . . what?" asked Skorn.

"Through an intermediary," Corskene explained, "we provided Andor's leading scientist working on the genetic crisis with enough data to make significant advancements in her research. When the time is right, we will make it known that, while the leaders of the Federation willfully chose to withhold from the Andorians a means of averting their prospective extinction, the leaders of the Tholian Assembly—and by extension, those of the Typhon Pact—have chosen to help them step away from the precipice."

"What do you hope to accomplish by this?" Ventel asked, working to keep the anxiety out of his voice. "I mean, other than compassionately offering aid to a population in need?" Corskene had already suggested the goal of the Tholians in taking the action they had, but Ventel wanted to hear it spelled out.

"We believe that this could broaden the call for the expulsion of non-Andorians from their planet," Corskene said, "as well as lead to a mass exodus of Andorian officers from Starfleet as they return to their homeworld."

"The percentage of Andorians serving in Starfleet is significant?" Skorn asked.

"Yes," Corskene replied. "Enough, at least, to have an impact."

The idea met with general consent around the table. Ventel stayed silent. He could not tell with certainty which of the representatives present sought military superiority over the Federation for the sake of maintaining the peace, and which saw war and conquest as an ultimate goal. But it seemed clear that most, if not all, of them favored might over diplomacy in dealing with the UFP.

Ventel also took note of Corskene's mention of the Tholians' possession of a "complex library of scientific information," which clearly originated beyond the borders of the Assembly. To the best of the proconsul's knowledge, no such repository of advanced technical data had been made available by Tholia to Romulus. Even from their allies, it seemed, the Tholians kept secrets. So too, Ventel suspected, did every other member of the Typhon Pact—including, he knew, the Romulan Star Empire. Praetor Tal'Aura had provided cloaking technology to each of its Pact allies, but she had done so only after Romulan engineers had developed the next generation of such technology, to which Tal'Aura had zealously clung. Even though the existence of the phasing cloak no longer remained a secret, Praetor Kamemor had continued Tal'Aura's policy. That had not become an issue since the other Pact members had yet to perfect the implementation of even standard cloaking technology on their ships.

After Ambassador Corskene finished speaking, the time came for Ventel to address the gathering. He did so by conveying a relatively innocuous report on the status of Romulan affairs. After the dissolution of Empress Donatra's Imperial Romulan State, the reintegration of the Romulan breadbasket worlds into the Empire had allowed the praetor to slow the distribution to the people of medicines and foodstuffs from other Typhon Pact nations. Ventel provided a timetable to completely halt the transfer of such emergency provisions within the next fifty days. He also spoke about a recent decrease made to the number of Romulan forces built up along their borders with both the Federation and the Klingons. Seemingly as a direct result of Kamemor's reductions, the Romulan Imperial Fleet had seen a commensurate drop in the activity on the other sides of the Neutral Zones.

After the meeting, as Ventel made his way toward the Romulan arm of the space station and *Khenn Onahj,* the vessel that would carry him home, he studied the new problem that faced

Praetor Kamemor. As she strived to keep order among the various spacefaring powers, many of those powers worked essentially for the reverse. Although the reduction in Romulan forces along the Empire's borders had seemed like an important and momentous action when she'd ordered it, Proconsul Ventel realized that it would require a great deal more than that to lead the Typhon Pact along the path to peace.

October 2382

10

Having completed her inspection of *Defiant*, Captain Ro Laren paced through the vessel's main starboard corridor, headed for the airlock at the bow. Around her, the ship had stilled, its powerful warp drive shut down, its impulse engines likewise laid low. The reduced lighting of *Defiant*'s standby mode brought shadows and silence descending around her.

In such moments, alone on the ship after an extended mission, *Defiant* simultaneously soothed Ro and scared her. Freed from the rush of impossible velocities, from the pulsing rhythms of the almost tameless energy that drove it, *Defiant* at rest reminded Ro of the promise of simpler times, of the peace of mind that repose could afford. At the same time, the inactivity felt like a decline of defenses, felt like an invitation to peril.

Especially now, Ro thought, unsettled. Although she had commanded Deep Space 9 for three and a half years, it had been just two months earlier that she'd received her promotion to captain. Somehow, the simple advancement in rank seemed to weigh her down. Virtually none of her duties changed, and yet much of what she had learned over time to do as a matter of course suddenly burdened her. For one thing, she took a good deal longer to discharge many responsibilities that she previously completed with ease. *Such as inspecting the* Defiant.

Technically, regulations did not require Ro to tour the ship immediately upon its return to the station unless it had sustained damage while in the field. She had picked up the habit from Captain Vaughn, whom she'd seen doing it when he commanded DS9 and she served as his executive officer. Once he transferred to *U.S.S. James T. Kirk* to better pursue his aspirations to explore the universe, Ro took up the practice herself. Since becoming *Captain* Ro, though, she spent twice as much time doing so—though less that night, after having consulted with the station's counselor about the change in behavior. Lieutenant Commander Matthias had explained the psychological underpinnings of Ro's lengthier, more onerous approach to many of her tasks, and that understanding had already allowed Ro to begin adjusting her outlook and returning to a healthier way of conducting herself in her duties.

As the captain neared the airlock, she heard the tread of somebody approaching from the opposite direction. Up ahead, Lieutenant Prynn Tenmei emerged from a connecting corridor. She saw Ro and stopped, obviously waiting for the captain to reach her.

"Good evening, Prynn," Ro said, choosing familiarity over ceremony. The duty shifts of both officers had ended two hours earlier, when *Defiant* had returned to DS9 from the Gamma Quadrant. "I didn't think I would see anybody here so long after the ship's arrival at the station."

"I could say the same thing to you, Captain," said Tenmei.

Ro noted the wry smile on the lieutenant's face. Since the captain had used Tenmei's given name, she normally would have expected her friend to reply in kind. Ever since Ro's promotion, though, Tenmei appeared to enjoy employing the captain's new rank, even in casual conversation.

"So why are *you* still here?" Ro asked. "Thinking of commandeering the *Defiant* and taking it out for a little jaunt of your own?" The crew of DS9 knew well Tenmei's penchants for high speed and piloting starships—or, for that matter, piloting any sort of vehicle.

"I wish," Tenmei said. "Actually, do you remember that lag I detected between helm control and the impulse-power readings?"

"I do," Ro said. The captain and her crew had taken *Defiant* into the Gamma Quadrant, where they had spent the past ten days mapping star systems and performing preliminary planetary scans, all in anticipation of Starfleet's future exploratory efforts. "You reported the lag as an insignificant concern. I've got it on my task list for Chief Chao to take a look at." Lieutenant Commander Jeannette Chao served on Deep Space 9 as its chief engineer.

"Well, it was definitely a minor issue, but it still bothered me," Tenmei said. "So I spent some time executing diagnostics on the flight-control systems. It turned out there was a minute misalignment in one of the conn relays. It wouldn't have caused us any real problems, and it wouldn't have gotten any worse, but I still wanted to repair it."

"Excellent. I'll have the chief verify the fix and take it off my list," Ro said. "So are you headed for the station then?" Tenmei nodded, and Ro motioned ahead. They started forward together.

During her first couple of years aboard DS9, Ro had grown close to Tenmei's father, Elias Vaughn, though not particularly to Tenmei herself. But once Captain Vaughn's broken, inert body had been relocated from his mangled starship to the station's infirmary after the Borg invasion, the two women had found common ground. Tenmei had been estranged from her father for many years, but over the course of their mutual posting to Deep Space 9, they'd found a deeper understanding of themselves and each other, which ultimately had allowed them to permanently renew their family ties.

For Ro, Vaughn had also provided a father figure, albeit that of a surrogate. She supposed that during the time Tenmei shunned his presence in her life, he had latched onto Ro as something of a substitute daughter. Eventually, after Tenmei and Vaughn had reestablished their relationship, the two women had developed their own friendship, which had flourished in the wake of Vaughn's devastating injury.

As she and Tenmei got to the bow of the ship, Ro reached up and keyed a control pad. They passed through an airlock aboard *Defiant,* and then through a similar chamber aboard the station. They crossed the main corridor of DS9's docking ring, headed toward the nearest lift. "Any plans for the evening?" Ro asked, though much of the evening had already passed, with station time nearing 2200 hours. "I was thinking of heading to the Promenade." She'd actually first thought about going to her office, but she realized that she needed to stop pushing herself harder than necessary—harder than would be productive—just because she'd been granted the title of captain. Upon *Defiant's* arrival at DS9, she'd immediately checked in with her first officer, Colonel Cenn Desca, so no need existed for her to visit ops.

"I'm pretty tired," Tenmei said. "I thought I'd stop by the infirmary for a few minutes before turning in."

"Of course," Ro said softly, a note of tenderness entering her voice. In the year and a half since Vaughn had been wounded in battle at Alonis, he had shown no indications of higher brain function. Six months into his stay in the infirmary, Tenmei reluctantly authorized the removal of her father's respirator. To the surprise of Doctor Bashir and the rest of the medical staff, Vaughn continued breathing on his own. Despite that, the physical trauma to his brain made recovery impossible. Tenmei understood that, but so far, she had been unable to bring herself to take the final step and have Vaughn's feeding and hydration tubes disconnected. When aboard the station, Tenmei visited her father every day.

Ro wanted to offer words of condolence to her friend, but she didn't know what more she could say than she already had in the previous eighteen months. After so much time, expressions of sympathy seemed only to add to Tenmei's already terrible burden. Ro chose silence instead, which Tenmei matched.

They reached the lift and entered it. Ro specified their destination as the infirmary. The cab accelerated smoothly, traveling horizontally along one of the station's three crossover bridges, past the habitat ring, and then up through the central core to the Promenade. They alighted beside the DS9 medical facilities, and Ro accompanied Tenmei to the entrance. Just inside, Nurse Etana Kol sat at a workstation.

"Sleep well," Ro told Tenmei.

"You too, Captain." Even in her ongoing grief, Tenmei managed a smile.

Once alone, Ro turned her attention farther on down the Promenade. At that time of night, she did not expect to find it quiet, and indeed, as she neared the entryway to Quark's, she heard a dense mix of many voices, punctuated with bursts of laughter. *Quark must be happy,* she thought, which in turn pushed up the sides of her lips into a smile.

Inside, Ro didn't see an empty seat. She spied a few familiar faces scattered about, starting with the waitstaff: Broik, Frool, and Grimp bounded between tables and the bar, serving trays balanced on their outstretched hands, while Aluura and Hetik worked the dabo wheel, surrounded, as usual, by the most boisterous patrons in the room. She spotted Lieutenant Commander Wheeler Stinson, her second officer, who captained *Defiant* when Ro did not. She also saw the station's lead science officer, John Candlewood, and Ensign Rahendervakell th'Shant, one of the engineering team. At the far side of the room, Lieutenant Commander Jefferson Blackmer roamed through the crowd, apparently keeping a watchful eye on the proceedings. *And who's keeping an eye on Blackmer?* Ro thought, still unsure about DS9's new security chief.

Mostly, though, Ro saw crew members of *U.S.S. Gryphon.* The *Akira*-class starship had arrived at Deep Space 9 nearly two weeks ago to provide its complement a period of rest and relaxation. The vessel's presence at the station also allowed Ro to take *Defiant* safely away from DS9 and Bajor for the extended mission in the Gamma Quadrant.

Ro made her way through the throng to the far side of the bar, where she tucked herself into the corner, trying to keep herself unnoticed. For a few moments, she watched as Treir and Quark took orders at the bar, mixed drinks, and gathered empty glasses. The two moved quickly but smoothly, easily keeping up with the clientele. It didn't take long, though, before Quark threw a lingering look in Ro's direction. Somehow, he almost always seemed to sense her presence. She hadn't opened her mouth since entering the place, so he couldn't have heard her.

You never know, Ro thought. *Maybe he heard and recognized my footsteps. After all, those are* really *big ears.*

As Ro chuckled to herself, Quark sauntered over, sporting one of the tailored, varicolored jackets he preferred. He carried with him a tall bottle in the shape of an obelisk, which appeared to contain liquids of two different colors side by side. Despite filling the same container, the green and red fluids remained unmixed.

"Captain Ro," Quark said, offering her a toothy smile. "I didn't know you were back on the station."

"If you're going to lie to me, Quark," she said without hesitation, "I may as well not even stay."

"Lie to *you*?" he said. "Where's the profit in that?"

Ro arched an eyebrow. "Make sure you don't forget that," she told him. "And don't try to tell me you didn't know that the *Defiant* got back two hours ago. You've got better tracking software than Starfleet Intelligence."

"Well, I might have heard something about the *Defiant* returning to the station," Quark admitted with a shrug. "But that didn't mean that the crew didn't discover some new, highly intelligent civilization in the Gamma Quadrant who decided to keep you around as their queen."

Ro leaned in over the bar to respond. Before she did, she noticed that Quark wore another new scent—something Bajoran, she thought. She liked it, and she appreciated his effort as well. "So you think I should be treated like a queen, do you?"

"I absolutely do, and I say that—" Quark set down the unusual bottle, spread his arms, and bowed his head. "—as your most loyal subject."

"Oh, really?" Ro said, feeling herself relax, and thoroughly enjoying the playful banter. Through her years on DS9, she'd certainly enjoyed that and more with Quark. When Ro had first come aboard, she and the Ferengi barkeep had realized that they had a great deal in common—not the least of which included their feeling like outcasts no matter where they went. They ended up spending time together and getting to know each other, both finding pleasure in the other's company.

At one point, when Bajor stood poised to join the Federation, both Ro and Quark came to believe that their time on Deep Space 9 had come to an end. A moneyless economy would undermine Quark's business, and Starfleet's absorption of the Bajoran Militia would put a halt to Ro's career; her record during a previous stint in Starfleet included disobeying orders, a court-martial, imprisonment in the stockade, and desertion. And so, knowing that they would no longer have a place on DS9, they considered leaving the station together. But then Quark's brother, Rom—who also happened to be the Grand Nagus of the Ferengi Alliance—added another function to Quark's Bar, Grill, Gaming House, and Holosuite Arcade: Ferengi Embassy to Bajor. And Ro's former commanding officer, Captain Jean-Luc Picard, not only persuaded Ro with a simple gesture to consider rejoining Starfleet, he also managed to convince Starfleet Command to offer her that opportunity.

In the years since deciding to remain on the station, Ro and Quark had shared a solid friendship, as well as an intermittent flirtation that occasionally moved beyond mere playfulness. That relationship contributed significantly to Ro's feeling something on Deep Space 9 that she had seldom, if ever, felt before: a sense of home. She felt that still.

"So you're willing to cast yourself in the role of my most loyal subject?" Ro teased, still leaning in over the bar, her voice low. "So what if I asked you to come over to my quarters and do whatever I told you to do?"

Quark reached up and errantly tugged at his right earlobe. "I'll leave Treir in charge," he said anxiously. He started to turn away, but Ro reached across the bar and caught him by the upper arm.

"Wait," she said. "Don't you want to know what I'm going to tell you to do?"

"Oh, I think I know," Quark said with a roguish tilt of his head, his mouthful of sharp, skewed teeth encompassed by a broad smile.

"Good," Ro said. "Because I really need somebody to clean my quarters."

Quark's smile evaporated like dew on a hot summer's day. He began to pull away from Ro, but with her hand still on his arm, she pulled him closer, bringing the side of his head up beside her face. "But when you clean," she whispered, "maybe you don't need to wear any clothes." Then she pursed her lips and blew a quick, warm breath directly into the center of his ear, into his external auditory canal—lacking a feather, an otherwise perfectly executed tympanic tickle.

Ro released her hold on Quark's arm, then sat back on her barstool. She savored the look of surprise that blossomed on his face. It lasted only a moment, replaced in the next instant by a devilish grin.

Out of the side of his mouth, quietly enough that she could barely hear him, Quark said, "It is definitely worth it to be your loyal subject." He turned and surveyed the bar. "I can leave Treir in charge," he said, "but it's a pretty large crowd tonight—"

"You don't have to do that," Ro said. "But if you want to, come by after you close up."

"I look forward to it," Quark said, his tone matter-of-fact. He'd really gotten much better at controlling his lascivious demeanor in public when they flirted with each other. "Until then, is there something I can offer the station's captain?"

The idea of a drink before she headed to her quarters appealed to Ro, but nothing in particular came to mind. Pointing at the bottle Quark had carried over with him, she asked, "What's this?"

"This," Quark said dramatically as he grabbed the bottle and hefted it up from the bar, "is my newest concoction." He set the bottle back down and pointed to it. "The green liquid is Aldebaran whiskey, and the red is a Tzenkethi spice called *leskit*."

"Tzenkethi?"

"Don't worry, it's not illegal," Quark said. "There's no Federation embargo against the Coalition."

"I'm not concerned about it being illegal," Ro said. "I'm concerned about it being poisonous."

Quark raised his shoulders in an exaggerated shrug. "So far, it's killed fewer than a quarter of the customers who've tried it."

Ro could not suppress her own grin. Quark's sense of humor rarely failed to amuse her. "All right," she said. "Let's see what you've got there."

Quark reached under the bar and produced a large snifter, which he placed in front of Ro. He twisted off the pyramidal cap of the bottle, then poured two fingers of the potion into the glass. The green and red liquids mingled briefly, then quickly separated out into their distinct selves. Quark then retrieved the bottle's transparent cap, which Ro saw contained a white powder, something she hadn't noticed earlier.

"What's that?" she asked.

"Magic." Quark upended the cap and shook it once, sending a quick shower of the white granules into the glass. The contents of the snifter immediately reacted, roiling furiously as the two different liquids appeared to combine. In just a few seconds, the solution settled down, leaving behind a bright-yellow drink.

"Wow," Ro said. "I didn't realize I'd be getting a drink *and* a show."

"I love chemistry," Quark said. "Give it a try."

Ro curled her fingers beneath the glass's large bowl and brought it to her lips. A bit warm, the drink glided silkily down her throat, slightly sweet, and actually finished with a cooling sensation. "Very nice," Ro said. "What do you call it?"

"A Tzenkethi cauldron."

"And you invented this?" she asked, impressed.

"Well, I imported it," Quark said.

Ro took another sip. "You made a good find," she told him. "This should be popular—"

A loud but indistinct voice coming from the other side of the room startled Ro. Both she and Quark looked around, seeking its source. Before she could determine who had spoken, a tide of agitation rippled through the bar. Here and there, Ro spotted anxious expressions, and then she saw somebody holding up a padd, presumably so others could watch something on its display.

Ro quickly looked back at Quark to ask him to activate the Bajoran comnet. He must have seen the same thing she had and drawn the same conclusion, though, because he'd already turned to the companel behind the bar. He expertly worked its controls, and the image of a Bajoran man appeared.

"—*cited the deciding reason as the discovery that the Federation, for more than a century, has held in secret a cache of advanced genetic knowledge that could have been employed to treat the Andorian reproductive crisis*," said the reporter.

What? Ro thought. She knew that the Andorian people faced

a mounting problem with their ability to successfully procreate at a rate that would sustain their society, but she also understood that scientists on Andor and throughout the Federation were searching for a long-term solution. It seemed absurd to think somebody would hide information that could prove useful in resolving such a serious situation.

The reporter continued. *"The head of the government, Presider Iravothra sh'Thalis, suffered a vote of no confidence by Parliament Andoria because of her close ties with Federation and Starfleet authorities. After the deputy presider, Ledanyi ch'Foruta, took office as the new leader, a worldwide referendum was conducted over four days, and then acted upon today by Parliament."*

A referendum? Ro wondered. *A head of government removed from office? Doesn't the Federation have enough to worry about without this sort of political theater?*

"The results of the referendum," the reporter went on, *"while not unanimous, were nevertheless decisive. The Andorian ambassador, Gilmesheid ch'Pavarzi, delivered the news directly to Federation President Nanietta Bacco earlier today. The new presider will speak before Parliament Andoria shortly, in an address that will be broadcast via the Federation News Service. In his remarks, he will formally declare the secession of Andor from the United Federation of Planets."*

"What?!" Ro heard herself say through the uproar that rose in the bar. She looked at Quark and saw his mouth agape, his eyes wide. Ro felt her own mouth hanging open and realized that the expression on her face must match his. As she heard the reporter saying that President Bacco would speak to the Federation Council in her own broadcast address immediately after the Andorian declaration, Ro hopped to her feet from her barstool. On the heels of such a momentous announcement, she felt that she needed to do something, that she should take action, though she didn't know precisely what sort of action.

In the bar, she heard Security Chief Blackmer's voice as he moved through the crowd, attempting to calm the patrons. Ro looked for him, but instead her gaze fell on one of the station's engineers: Vakell th'Shant. Even across the room, Ro could see that his blue face had gone pale. He sat motionless, looking stunned.

They all must be stunned, Ro realized, thinking of the several dozen Andorians who served aboard Deep Space 9. She started across the room toward th'Shant, but Quark called after her.

"Captain." She looked back. "Good luck," he said. "If you need anything . . ."

"Thanks, Quark," she said. Then she headed for Ensign th'Shant, uncertain of what he would need or what she would say to him—or to any of the Andorians under her command. But she would do whatever she could.

11

The tall stone doors—one engraved with the cobralike symbol of the Cardassian Union and the other with a stylized representation of Cardassia Prime—parted at President Nanietta Bacco's approach. She entered the room alone, with neither aide, nor escort, nor security detail. She considered her unaccompanied status a luxury, one typically reserved for her home and office in Paris, though even in those places, she often found herself attended by members of the Federation's or another power's government.

Bacco knew that she would not remain alone for long, so she spent a few moments taking in her unfamiliar surroundings and reveling in her transitory solitude. As the doors closed behind her with a noticeable thump, she resisted the temptation to continue straight ahead, to where bright sunlight streamed into the large room through a wide opening in the far wall. Beyond it, she could see a low, ornamental railing bounding a richly tiled deck.

Instead, Bacco stood in place and turned. Beneath her lay a woven rug, its material matted down from long use, one of three such pieces in the room. But for the doors through which she'd entered, the opening to the balcony, and a large fireplace off to one side, shelves lined the walls from floor to ceiling. Thousands of books marched along those shelves, interspersed in numerous places by works of art and history: paintings, sculptures, flags, the ancient-looking fragments of a carved panel of striated wood. On each wall, Bacco saw, a movable ladder allowed access to the higher shelves, which reached upward perhaps six or seven meters. Above, a lattice of aged timbers formed the ceiling.

On one side of the room sat a massive wooden desk. Books and papers cluttered its surface, though Bacco saw no padds or computer interfaces. She wondered if the castellan actually used this room in her residence as a workspace, or if the desktop had been arranged just for show.

On the other side of the room, the fireplace stood surrounded by sofas. Fresh wood had been assembled within the firebox, but not set alight, no doubt because of the warm temperatures outside. Above the unpolished granite mantel hung a framed painting, not of the current castellan or any of her predecessors, but of the ancient fortress that had long been a second home to the leader of the Cardassian government.

Bacco finished a complete turn and decided to walk out onto the balcony after all. She hadn't noticed from afar, but up close, she saw that the balusters supporting the railing tapered upward, resembling the webbed appearance of Cardassian necks. Out beyond the balcony stretched a grassy courtyard. Bacco heard birds chirping and saw several flitting about the grounds. Past the outer wall, the green-blue waters of a beautiful lake filled the near vista, while a line of jagged peaks ran across the distant horizon.

Placing her hands on the railing, Bacco took some time to appreciate the view. A light breeze ruffled her short, white hair, which she wore pulled back from her face. She closed her eyes and looked skyward, allowing the rays of the Cardassian sun to warm her.

She stood that way for several minutes, until she heard the sound of the library's stone doors closing. Bacco did not move at first, preferring to wait for the castellan to come to her. The Federation president had traveled a great distance to meet with the Cardassian leader, in the hope that Rakena Garan would in turn travel politically. Bacco would let the castellan's first few steps of their meeting symbolize that.

At the sound of shoe heels on the balcony tiles, Bacco remained still. The footfalls stopped briefly, then continued on until the castellan stepped up beside her. Neither woman took her gaze from the view of the countryside.

"It is a lovely land," said the castellan. "It pleases me to have visitors here with whom I can share it."

"Thank you," Bacco said. "This is my first time on Cardassia."

"Really?" Garan asked, turning toward Bacco. "I was not aware of that. As the head of your government, I just assumed that you had been here at some point."

"I've only been in office for three years," Bacco said, finally turning to regard her counterpart, "and it's a very big galaxy."

"So it is," agreed Garan. "Though it seems to be growing smaller all the time."

Bacco laughed, though it sounded more like a grunt of disgust. "A hundred thousand light-years in diameter, a few hundred billion stars, fifty billion planets, maybe five hundred million *habitable* planets . . . you'd think there would be enough to sate even the most avaricious desires."

"Indeed," agreed Garan. "Not even the Ferengi Alliance seeks to expand indefinitely." She stepped away from the railing and pointed toward one end of the balcony. There, two chairs sat next to two of three sides of a triangular table. "Would you care to sit, Madam President?"

"Thank you, Castellan."

The two women moved to the table. It almost always surprised Bacco when she saw Garan. For a woman with such a streak of iron in her, she had a slight figure, her height barely topping a meter and a half. Still, she carried herself with an air of resolution and strength.

At the table, three covered, pewter-colored ewers filled a tray, along with matching cups. As Bacco sat down, Garan offered her a choice of beverages. "I've had my aide replicate Terran coffee and tea for you," she said, indicating two of the pitchers. "We also have *ravat,* a sweet nectar squeezed from the fruit of the *ravala* tree."

Bacco craved a cup of coffee, but she wanted to be able to sleep on the first leg of the journey back to Earth. She also doubted the quality of Cardassian replicators. "I'll try the ravat, thank you." She reached for the pitcher to serve herself, but Garan lifted it and poured them each a cup. The beverage came out pink and thick, and looked as though it might taste cloyingly sweet. When Bacco tried a sip, though, it had a delicate, agreeable flavor.

Once Garan had sipped at her own cup, Bacco said, "It's interesting that you should bring up the Ferengi Alliance. I've just come from there."

"Are you touring prospective allies?" Garan asked. The castellan spoke, as she often did, with an informal tone that made it difficult to assess her intentions.

"Not merely 'prospective' allies," Bacco said. "Grand Nagus Rom has agreed to have the Alliance join the Federation and the Klingon Empire as a signatory in the Khitomer Accords. The Congress of Economic Advisors has already ratified his proposal of membership."

"I'm sure that is welcome news for the Federation," Garan said. "The Treasury Guard has a serviceable number of vessels and officers."

"Not as many or as impressive as does Cardassia," Bacco said, aware of how much the Union had rebuilt its forces since the war. "The addition of Ferenginar *is* welcome news, though. It is also overdue." A year and a half earlier, still in the throes of the immediate aftermath of the Borg invasion, the president had first learned of the formation of the Typhon Pact. Fearing that the alliance of such powerful states could pose a threat to the Federation, Bacco sought an expansion of the Khitomer Accords as a means of tamping down any possible aggression. She and the Klingon chancellor, Martok, invited the leaders of several neighboring nations to a summit on Zalda to explore that possibility; many of them agreed immediately to meet and consider such a proposition. Castellan Garan had been among the last heads of state to consent to the gathering, though she did attend that and several subsequent meetings.

"The defining of such allegiances can be complicated and require time," Garan said.

"So it can," Bacco allowed. As talks with the Cardassian Union and other nations had continued, a steady, if uneasy, peace had emerged with the Typhon Pact. The urgency for strengthening the Khitomer alliance decreased across the span of a year, until the Breen and Romulans conspired to conduct an espionage mission and steal the plans for the Federation's quantum slipstream drive. Bacco then called for renewed discussions to swell the ranks of the Khitomer Accords, though when Starfleet operatives destroyed the Breen's prototype vessel and their copies of the slipstream schematics, the political situation in the Alpha and Beta Quadrants again appeared to stabilize. Within the past few weeks, though, the peace once more had become threatened. "It is my opinion—as well as that of Chancellor Martok and Grand Nagus Rom—that we may be running out of time."

"Such a dramatic pronouncement," Garan said. She drank from her cup, then set it down on the table. "I assume that your call for exigency derives from Andor's secession from the Federation."

"It is not just the loss of a founding member of our union that concerns me," Bacco said. "It is also the role that the Tholian Assembly played in bringing about that turn of events. It is quite clear that the Typhon Pact intends to continue working to weaken the Federation. Considering the natural inclinations of any nation or alliance to protect itself, and therefore to fear those that they deem adversaries, such efforts are understandable; in a vacuum, they might even be acceptable. But the fact is that, over time, several of the Typhon Pact states have demonstrated their continuing antipathy for the Federation in the form of open hostilities. If the scales of power tip too far in favor of the Pact, I fear that our region of the galaxy will again be plunged into war."

"Again, very dramatic, Madam President," Garan said. "Am I to gather, then, that you are here to rekindle your attempt to persuade me that the Cardassian Union should join the Khitomer Accords?"

"I am here for your signature on a treaty," Bacco said. "I

am here for you to expedite endorsement of that treaty by the Detapa Council."

Garan smiled. She lifted her cup from the table, considered it for a moment, then set it back down without drinking. She stood up and walked to the near corner of the balcony, to where two railings met at an odd angle. Peering out over the countryside, she said, "My world is a beautiful world, Madam President. My people are a beautiful people." She paused, and then said, "I imagine that all leaders must believe that—all *true* leaders." She turned back to face Bacco. "Regardless, it is what *I* believe. And as the leader of this beautiful world and these beautiful people, I am responsible for their safety and happiness."

"And the Federation supports you in those endeavors," Bacco said, likely interrupting, since it seemed that Garan wished to say more. "After all, how much aid have we sent to the Cardassian Union since the end of the Dominion War?"

Garan's teeth clenched and her jaw hardened. "And are you suggesting that my people owe your people a debt?" she asked coldly. "Are you trying to tell me that because of the Federation's munificence, I should agree to place my people at the heart of an unstable and dangerous political situation?" She stalked back over to the table, her diminutive frame unable to mitigate the fervor she projected. "Are you saying that the loss of more than eight hundred million Cardassian lives in the war wasn't enough? That we should willingly march into the line of fire and *hope* that you can keep the peace?"

Slowly and with the utmost care, Nanietta Bacco rose to her feet. Somewhere, she suspected, a surveillance team monitored the castellan, and considering the nature of the Cardassian culture, it would not have surprised Bacco to find out that a security squad had the Federation president targeted in the sights of their weapons. She had no interest in challenging Rakena Garan, but she also had little time to waste.

"I'm saying none of that," Bacco told the castellan. "I was not in charge of our government when the Federation fought the Dominion and the Breen and the Cardassians, but I do know that we didn't start the war. And yet when hostilities finally concluded, we demonstrated our principles by helping to elevate the very people who made war against us. We strived not only to heal the physical and emotional wounds of the Cardassian Union, but to befriend its people so that nothing like this could ever happen again."

Garan glared at Bacco. "And yet you would place us squarely in the middle of your confrontation with the Typhon Pact," said the castellan. She turned and paced away, as though barely containing her indignation.

"Garan," Bacco said, softening her tone. "Rakena. Please. I do not intend an alliance between the Cardassian Union and the Federation to be an empty one, or one that unnecessarily endangers your people, or anybody else's. I am desperately trying to maintain the peace, to fortify and extend it, to ensure that there will be no new war."

"That may well be," Garan said, looking back, "but what you intend and what will be may be two quite different things." Despite her words, Bacco could see that the castellan's anger had subsided.

"Make no mistake, Castellan," Bacco said. "Even without a treaty between Cardassia and the Khitomer Accords, if the Typhon Pact ever does go to war with the Federation, they will not differentiate you from us. But even if they do, this section of the galaxy will be devastated. Your eight hundred million dead in the Dominion War, and even the sixty-three billion killed by the Borg, will pale in comparison, because an interstellar battle between the Typhon Pact and the Khitomer Accords will last far longer, and destruction and misery and death will be brought down upon *all* of us. Even if you do not participate in the war, you will have assets that will attract conflict to your shores: planets strategically located, worlds abundant in natural resources, power plants, starships, soldiers."

Garan's eyes narrowed. "That sounds like a threat, Madam President."

"It *is* a threat, Madam Castellan, a threat to you and your people," Bacco said. "But not from me, and not from the Federation. It is a threat leveled by the Typhon Pact, made plain by the actions they have taken and the course they have pursued since their establishment." She waited for Garan to respond, but the Cardassian leader said nothing. Finally, Bacco added, "I am here to implore you to help me end that threat before it becomes reality. I'm trying to avert a war."

Garan walked back over to Bacco until only centimeters separated them. In a low voice, she said, "Why should I believe you? Why should I trust you?"

"Why *shouldn't* you?" Bacco asked. "The Cardassian Union sided with the Dominion and launched a war against the Federation. And when it was done, we came to your rescue."

Garan took a step back, but kept peering at Bacco. "As I recall, it was Cardassia who came to the rescue of the Federation."

"Yes," Bacco said. "The Cardassian Guard changed allegiances at the end of the war and helped defeat the Dominion. But it should never have come to that point; it *wouldn't* have come to that point if the Cardassian Union hadn't thrown in with the Dominion in the first place. And still, afterward, we sent you food and medicine for your ravaged population, we sent doctors and nurses to treat the injured, we sent engineers and architects to help rebuild your civilization. Is that not the mark of a friend? Or at the very least, is that not the action of a people who can be trusted?"

Garan looked at Bacco for a moment, then shook her head and turned away again. She walked to the balcony railing, and, as Bacco had earlier, she placed her hands on it and gazed outward.

Bacco waited. She felt that she dared not say anything more, that she dared not move, for fear of interrupting Garan's train of thought. Bacco deemed it a positive sign that she had not been summarily escorted from the castellan's home.

At last, over her shoulder, Garan said, "I will consider your proposal, President Bacco."

Bacco inhaled deeply before voicing her next thought. "I'm afraid that's not good enough, Castellan," she said.

Garan spun around as though Bacco had commenced a physical attack on her.

"The time for action on this alliance is now," Bacco insisted.

"I understand that is your opinion," Garan said. "It is not necessarily mine."

"Then make it yours," Bacco said icily. She sat back down in her chair, grabbed her cup, and took a drink of ravat. After placing the cup back on the table, she met Garan's gaze and said, "I'm not leaving Cardassia without an agreement."

For the first time, the castellan smiled. "Then you may be in for a long stay with us," she said. "Even if the Cardassian Union is to accede to your wishes, it will take time. There are many details to consider, and our nation is most assuredly no longer run by the military or the Obsidian Order."

"With respect, Castellan, you already know the details of an alliance with the Federation and Klingon Empire," Bacco said. "How many times have our officials met with yours to discuss those issues? How many communications on the subject have you and I personally exchanged? How many times have we stood in the same room and discussed it?"

As she had at the beginning of their meeting, Bacco waited for Garan to come to her. It required two full minutes of silence, but then the castellan walked back over to the table, her heels clicking on the tiled balcony. "You are . . . indefatigable, Madam President."

"I am tired, Castellan Garan," Bacco said. "And more than a bit concerned about what might happen if we do not come together at this time for the purpose of protecting us all."

Garan sighed, then leaned forward and took hold of her cup. She upended it into her mouth, then offered a knowing smile. "I think I need something stronger than fruit juice," she said.

Bacco smiled back. "I think we both do."

12

Although they barely contrasted with their surroundings, the spartan concrete walls still appeared out of place where they climbed upward from the shifting snows. Having walked some distance from the redoubt just so that he could view its completed form, Trok saw that drifts had already begun to fill the trail he'd left. He peered around in all directions, and for as far as he could see, the icy tundra stretched to the horizon. Wintry gales drove the snow in thick panes across the boreal landscape. Visibility fluctuated, clear in one direction and impenetrable in another, but then changing in the next moment.

Trok heard a rush of random sound as particles of ice and snow pelted his armor, though they did not penetrate its closed environment. Still, his suit struggled to keep him warm in the frozen wasteland of Goventu V. Once more, he cursed the Special Research Division of the Breen Militia for not sending an Amoniri in his stead, considering that members of that bloodless species originated in such a climate, and actually required low temperatures for their survival. Trok knew well why the SRD had sent him to such a bitter world, though, and he would have requested the assignment had they not, but still, he hated the cold. He swore aloud against it, and then said, *"Such places are not fit for Vironat."* He guessed that the gelid winds carried away the electronically encoded output of his helmet before his attendant even knew that he had spoken.

Trok gestured to the security officer, indicating his intent to return to the recently completed redoubt. Knowing that the guard would trail him back to the structure to ensure his safety, Trok started for the fortification's only entrance, a single-paneled door in the center of the nearest wall. Once there, he pressed the snout of his helmet against an audio receiver and articulated the long password assigned specifically to him. The panel shot upward, and he quickly stepped inside amid a swirl of snow, leaving the guard behind as a part of the perimeter patrol.

The door sliced down behind Trok, leaving him alone in an empty, featureless anteroom. Though he saw no indication of it, he knew that standard Breen surveillance equipment worked to scan him and verify his identity. In only a moment, the single panel at the far end of the space darted upward. He paced forward and through the doorway, out into the main portion of the hastily erected facility.

Trok moved between the two security officers who guarded

the inner door and over to the railing directly ahead, which lined the catwalk that ran continuously along the four sides of the rectangular structure. He peered down into the pit about which the redoubt had been constructed. There, a squad of Breen teemed over the ground, working to excavate the object recently discovered on Goventu V.

The hole in the glaciated soil had deepened, Trok saw, and a rounded tip of starship hull rose into open air, exposed. He noted the matte texture and the purplish gray color of the metal, both of which confirmed what he already knew. Although the general mass of the vessel remained hidden from view, rudimentary scans had confirmed its origin as Jem'Hadar.

This is why the Research Division sent me, Trok thought with satisfaction, *and not some arbitrary Amoniri.* He turned to his left and paced along the railing toward the inner corner of the redoubt, to where the catwalk skirted the enclosed space that served as his office for the project. *This is why they sent me and not anybody else.*

For scores and scores of days, Trok had worked not on Goventu V, but in the Alrakis system, under Keer. An engineer of considerable intellect and ability, Keer held the rank of *thot* in the Breen military. In the Alrakis system, he led a secret, fast-track program to design and assemble an attack cruiser equipped with quantum slipstream drive. Utilizing plans somehow acquired from the United Federation of Planets, the development team made significant progress, producing a prototype vessel in a covert shipyard buried in the Alrakis system's asteroid belt.

As they'd neared completion of the prototype, Trok had been dispatched to the Breen homeworld. There, he reported the program's status to Domo Brex, the appointed political leader of the Confederacy. During Trok's time away, Starfleet operatives had sabotaged the new vessel, destroying both it and the clandestine shipyard, as well as corrupting all recorded data regarding the slipstream drive.

All data recorded in our computers and communications networks, Trok thought, *but not the information I carried in my mind.*

On Goventu V, Trok reached his office, took one more glance over his shoulder into the excavation pit, then entered his private area. Inside the small room, hard-copy printouts dominated the space, pinned up on the walls and spread out across his desk. Some displayed re-created drawings of Keer's slipstream-enabled prototype ship; others, renderings of Jem'Hadar vessels; and still others, holographic images of Jem'Hadar starships in flight. Trok leaned his gloved hands on his desk and started poring over Keer's schematics.

Throughout his time on the slipstream project, Trok had witnessed Keer's frustrations over the incessant demands that he accelerate the production of a prototype vessel. In the end, though Keer managed to build such a craft, Trok wondered whether the flight trials would have resulted in triumph or disaster. Since the new technology utilized deflectors to focus a quantum field about the ship, that meant that the ship's physical profile, its defensive-screen geometry, and its capacity to maintain structural integrity impacted not merely the performance of the advanced drive, but also its ability to function safely. That made the simple installation of a slipstream engine in existing starships problematic at best. Early slipstream simulations employing existing Breen vessels generated mostly failed, and often catastrophic, outcomes. That necessitated Keer's design of an entirely new class of ship, one that Trok had never been convinced would actually prove successful.

He swept the blueprints for the old prototype off to the side of his desktop, uncovering various three-dimensional views of Jem'Hadar vessels under power in space. As the lone survivor of the destruction of the Alrakis shipyard, Trok endured as the only link to Thot Keer's slipstream program. He therefore ranked as a vital asset to the program's continuation, and became the obvious choice to carry on with those efforts. Although Trok had never overseen a venture of such magnitude, the domo and the director of the Special Research Division had leaned heavily on him to accept the assignment. With equal measures of enthusiasm, anxiety, and fear, he had taken on that leadership role, knowing that the Breen Confederacy and the Typhon Pact needed it to succeed in order to achieve at least an equal military footing with the Federation and its Khitomer Accords allies.

During his tenure under Thot Keer, Trok had given a great deal of thought to the deflector and structural integrity aspects of slipstream technology. Somewhere along the way, it occurred to him that he knew of two spacefaring fleets that boasted ships with impressive maneuverability: those of the Tzenkethi and those of the Dominion. Such agility implied the generation of powerful deflectors and strong structural integrity fields. When appointed the task of making the slipstream drive a reality, Trok immediately obtained as much information as he could about the starships of the Confederacy's Typhon Pact ally, the Tzenkethi Coalition. Unfortunately, he ultimately concluded that, with the smooth contours of Tzenkethi vessels—teardrop-shaped starships and helical harriers—their equipment could not functionally pair with the slipstream drive.

With additional research, though, Trok became convinced that he could make use of Jem'Hadar technology. He believed that doing so would allow him not only to create a new fleet outfitted with slipstream, but to adapt existing vessels in the fleet of the Breen Militia—and in the fleets of the other Typhon Pact worlds as well. But in order to begin his work, he needed to study an actual Dominion ship.

The Special Research Division had sent out a call to the Breen military. They began a search of the Alpha Quadrant for the remains of Jem'Hadar vessels. During the Dominion-Federation War, numerous such ships had been incapacitated, some of them downed on planets, moons, and asteroids. Breen scouts located forty-six such crash sites before the one on Goventu V, but none of those debris fields surrendered Jem'Hadar ships undamaged enough to allow analysis of their deflector and structural integrity grids and field generators.

But that's about to change, Trok thought.

The Breen Militia officers who had located the Jem'Hadar ship on Goventu V theorized that the heat of its entry into the atmosphere had softened the frozen ground, perhaps even liquefied it. The vessel then sank into the muck, which eventually resolidified around it. Magnesite deposits in the soil interfered with both sensors and transporters, but basic sounding scans showed a hull mostly intact, which represented a tremendous opportunity for Trok.

Once the excavation uncovered enough of the Jem'Hadar ship, he and his lead assistant, Keln, would take their hand-picked team of engineers inside to examine its systems directly, and if necessary, repair them. Trok would analyze the Jem'Hadar systems in operation, expecting to confirm the adaptability of the Dominion technology to his slipstream drive efforts. If he corroborated his convictions, he would be able to integrate the Jem'Hadar systems with a new quantum slipstream drive. After that, the Breen Confederacy and the Typhon Pact would not only draw level with the Federation and the Khitomer Accords in terms of might, but would surpass them.

Eager for the events of the coming days, despite whatever challenges they might bring, Trok stepped away from his desk and exited his office. Outside, he turned left and followed along the side wall, his boots beating a metallic rhythm against the grating of the catwalk. He headed for the midpoint of the walkway, where a ladder descended to the surface of the planet. He would climb down so that he could observe the crews carrying out the dig.

Trok suspected that it would take an act of will to keep himself from joining in the excavation. At the moment, with the way he felt, he would gladly drop to his knees on the icy ground and carve it out by hand if he thought that would appreciably hasten the opening of the Jem'Hadar ship. He did not want to wait to contribute to the rise of the Breen Confederacy.

Soon, Trok told himself, trying to tamp down his anticipation. *Soon.*

Gell Kamemor liked the feel of the pavement passing beneath her feet, her heels drumming against the ground as her long strides carried her quickly along the pedestrian thoroughfare. More than those sensations, though, she appreciated her proximity to the residents of Ki Baratan. Since her elevation to the office of praetor, rarely did the security dictates of her position allow her outside the physical confines of her political life. Rank certainly provided her with room to move around at her praetorial residence and the Hall of State, and she could travel almost anywhere she chose as long as her security forces had time to clear the place beforehand. But none of that alleviated her disconnection from the everyday citizens of Romulus—of whom she counted herself as one, despite her lofty role among them.

Up ahead, dispersed amid the pedestrians of Avenue Renak, a segment of the security detail assigned to protect the praetor traveled incognito. To Kamemor, they stood out collectively, moving stiffly and constantly scanning their surroundings for threats, but she doubted that anybody else on the thoroughfare noticed them. She knew that another group of guards trailed her through the city, further ensuring her safety.

It had taken nothing less than her absolute sense of urgency *and* a fit of temper to convince Ranos Malikan, her security director, to permit her outside among the general public. She wore a traditional Romulan robe of a crimson hue, with a decorative silver-and-black sash draped over one shoulder, and a baggy hood that obscured her features. Clad similarly—though in a robe of deep green—Proconsul Anlikar Ventel walked beside her. They had traveled via secure transporter from the Hall of State to a hub not far from their destination, to which they would make their way on foot.

As she walked, Kamemor saw on her left the broad expanse of natural growth that defined Cor'Lavet Park. The slightly sweet scent of grass and flowers reached her and immediately carried her away. Years earlier, back on her homeworld of Glintara, she and her wife had often brought their young son to a similar greensward to play and enjoy the outdoors. Later, once Sorilk left home for the military academy, Gell and Ravent resumed their visits to the park, indulging in romantic evenings there, often stretching out on a blanket together, sharing a bottle of wine beneath a candy-colored sunset.

The memories struck Kamemor with unexpected force. She had lived half a century since her son had perished; ironically, after surviving for more than a decade serving in the Imperial Fleet, he'd lost his life in the collapse of a scaffold in a chemical plant. Even after so lengthy a time, she still missed her boy, though the pain had eased over the thousands of days since losing him, her agony dulling to an ache. Eventually, time provided Kamemor with the ability *not* to constantly feel the gaping hole her son's death had carved out of her. Throwing herself into her various roles as a public servant had helped.

Having Ravent by her side had helped even more. Kamemor knew that marriages did not always endure the loss of a child, but she doubted that *she* could have endured without her wife. Their son's death struck both of them hard, but somehow they each found a way to be strong when the other needed it most. They leaned heavily on each other, and loved each other, and came out the other side of their ordeal with their relationship not only intact, but stronger than ever.

The loss of Ravent, Gell still felt daily.

As Cor'Lavet Park slipped past and the Orventis Arena loomed into view up ahead, Kamemor tried to push those recollections away. She had spent almost all of her adult life with a woman she respected and admired, counted upon and trusted, laughed with and loved, and she could cope with those memories, no matter the poignancy they evoked. But she struggled to escape the thoughts of the hundreds upon hundreds of days during which Tuvan Syndrome inexorably stole her beloved from her. The neurological disease first robbed Ravent of her motor skills, and then ravaged her mind. At some point, she grew incapable of even recognizing Gell, much less remembering and understanding the depth of their love. Over the torturous course of a decade, the relentless malady diluted Ravent's essence to nothingness, leaving behind only the barest wisp of identity.

During those terrible days, Kamemor had withdrawn from civil service—and everything else in her life—to concentrate on battling Ravent's illness. When the implacability of the faceless enemy became clear, Kamemor shifted her efforts to rendering her wife's days as comfortable as possible. Eventually, even that became an impossibility. When the end had finally come,

Kamemor had welcomed it, for in truth, she'd already lost the woman she loved.

The praetor followed her security throng past the front of the Orventis Arena. Often utilized to stage theatrical productions, musical concerts, and other forms of entertainment, the facility could accommodate an audience of up to fifteen thousand. Instantly recognizable to citizens not only of Ki Baratan, but throughout the Empire, it featured a parabolic roof, its sloping entrance façade lined with elliptical stained-glass windows. Kamemor and her escorts continued along one side, headed, she knew, for a rear entryway typically used by performers and closed to the public.

A sense of anticipation formed within Kamemor, and she wondered about the course of action on which she planned to embark, about its chances for success. She doubted that the Breen or the Gorn or the Kinshaya would have chosen a similar path, and she understood that neither the Tholians nor the Tzenkethi ever would have done so. In fact, Kamemor had run into opposition within her own government, though she enjoyed at least a modicum of support as well. Still, she felt profoundly alone, even with Ventel, her sister's grandson, walking beside her. But she had felt alone for a long time.

After Ravent's death, Kamemor had fallen into solitude. She elected not to pursue a return to her position as territorial governor of Alva't'kresh, not merely because it would have proven problematic after so much time away, but also because interacting with others pained her. Instead, she spent long days and sleepless nights attempting to make sense of the senseless. She shunned family and friends, sequestering herself away in a fog of loss.

One day, she recalled, she had picked up a stylus and written about what she felt. Kamemor intended her words for no one— not even for herself, really, since she did not expect ever to read them. She simply needed the act of writing as an outlet for her deep emotions and fevered remembrances.

To her surprise, that had led Kamemor to composing poetry. She initially did it without consciously choosing to do so. It seemed that, more than just trying to organize itself, her mind sought to create something—to create *any*thing—out of her pain. In time, it succeeded enough for her days to return to a semblance of normality, and for her to allow the people who cared about her back into her life.

Although she had decided to remain essentially retired from government work, she'd still wanted to contribute to society. She took on various projects suited to her abilities, such as overseeing the modernization of a solar power plant in the Ar'hael Desert, and leading a soil reclamation project in Venat'atrix Territory. Perhaps because of such activities, when her great-grandfather, Gorelt, passed away, the Ortikant called upon her to assume the mantle of clan elder. When Praetor Tal'Aura reconstituted the Imperial Senate after the madman Shinzon had assassinated most of its members, Kamemor presided over the gathering that selected Xarian Dor as the family's representative in the re-formed legislative body. The dreaded disease *Velderix Riehn'va* then felled Dor, however, and the clan turned to Kamemor as his replacement. So too had the Senate itself looked to her when Tal'Aura had died of the same disease.

For the last decade, she realized, *the path of my life has been defined almost entirely by death.* Maybe a desire to break from that pattern drove her to take her current course of action. Well beyond her own personal life, the Romulan people in recent times had faced great hardship: the war against the Dominion; the assassination of Hiren and the mass murder of the Senate; the death of Shinzon; the division of the Empire, which had led to shortages of food and medicine among the population; the battle against the Borg; the suicide of Empress Donatra; and the demise of Praetor Tal'Aura.

"I've had enough of death," she said aloud. Ventel looked at her, but she could not make out his face within the hood of his robe. She chose to say nothing more.

Past Orventis Arena, Kamemor followed her security detail around the back of the building. A row of hedges, embedded with both a metal fence and a force field, protected the rear of the facility. As her guards fanned out to secure the area, three of their number led the praetor through a narrow gate, and then through a doorway into the arena itself.

Inside, Kamemor found herself in the low lighting of a backstage area. Layers of soaring curtains hung off to one side, and the praetor's gaze climbed upward with them, to the complex maze of cabling, pulleys, and counterweights that crowded the theater's fly loft. She heard a rush of sound, like rain striking the ground, which she immediately identified as applause.

Clustered in a rough semicircle about the door through which she had just entered the arena, Kamemor saw members of the advance team that had helped secure her visit. One of them broke from the shadows and approached her, obviously identifying her by her robe. Though of no particular physical distinction, Ranos Malikan carried himself with an air of imposing authority, befitting the man charged with protecting the leader of the Romulan Star Empire.

"Right this way, Praetor," Malikan said, pointing toward the near corner. Kamemor peered in that direction and saw a short-range lighting panel illuminating a descending staircase. She allowed Malikan to escort her and Ventel down one flight, where they entered a long, narrow corridor bounded by numerous closed doors. Her security director accompanied her and the proconsul to the first door, already guarded by a pair of sentries. Malikan entered a code into a keypad in the wall, and a single panel slid open to reveal a small sitting room.

Kamemor and Ventel stepped inside behind Malikan, who watched to ensure that the door closed and locked behind them. The praetor pulled back the hood of her robe to uncover her head, as did Ventel beside her. Malikan scanned the room quickly, despite the presence of security guards outside the door and a quartet of transport inhibitors, one in each corner. The arena itself obstructed the use of transporters as a matter of course, but Kamemor knew that her security director trusted nothing, always preferring to employ his own equipment in the discharging of his duties.

Cupboards lined one side wall of the room, topped by a counter filled with various light foods and beverages. In the center of the room, a sofa and several easy chairs surrounded a square table, which featured a large, artistically arranged tray of assorted fruits. Opposite the cupboards, two large and half a dozen smaller viewscreens bedecked the other side wall.

"We've set up our own surveillance teams to feed into these monitors," Malikan said, indicating the six smaller screens. "We're also observing from our own secure location." He didn't need to point out the content of the two larger monitors, which clearly showed views of the arena's stage. There, a young woman spoke at a podium, though no sound attended the movement of her lips. "If you wish, the volume can be adjusted," said Malikan, who walked over and indicated controls on the bottom right-hand corners of the monitors. He then made a sweeping gesture that seemed to encompass the entire room. "All of the food and drink here have been delivered from the Hall of State, and are therefore safe for you to ingest." He paused and surveyed the room once more, as though checking everything he saw against an internal inventory. "Is there anything else you require, Praetor?"

"No, Director," Kamemor said. "Only to complete the task I set myself in coming here."

"Very well, Praetor," Malikan said. "When would you like your meeting to commence?"

"As soon as is feasible."

"I will see to it at once," Malikan said. He quickly moved to the door, punched in a sequence on an interior keypad, and exited.

Once the door had closed again, Ventel turned to face Kamemor. "This probably won't seem the appropriate time to ask, but I may not have another opportunity," he said. "Are you certain that you're doing the right thing?"

"Am I certain?" the praetor said, walking over to the counter. She found a pitcher of citrus juice and poured herself a glass of the yellow liquid. She offered it to Ventel by holding it out toward him, but he declined with a shake of his head. Kamemor took a sip, then settled herself on the sofa. "No, I'm not certain," she said. "I suspect that not all of our allies will support the action I propose, and some are likely to object vehemently. But given the precarious political situation, we must do something to restore balance in the region."

The startling news of Andor's secession from the United Federation of Planets would have troubled Kamemor no matter the circumstances, but the role of the Tholians in the destabilizing event redoubled her concerns. Not only had Andor been a significant part of the UFP for more than two centuries, it had been one of its five founding members. Its loss no doubt had sent shockwaves through the Federation, weakening it at a time when it continued to rebuild from the Borg assault.

"The Tholian Assembly may consider your actions as intended to undermine what they have accomplished," Ventel noted.

"Perhaps," Kamemor said, "but they did not deign to inform the Romulan Empire of their own intentions to hobble the Federation until they stood on the brink of doing so. Considering the relative importance of Romulus and Tholia to the Typhon Pact, I am less concerned about the possibility of the Assembly's disapproval of my actions than I am about the repercussions of theirs."

"We've already seen some of the consequences," Ventel said, moving to sit in a chair beside the sofa. "With the Ferengi Alliance and the Cardassian Union joining the Khitomer Accords, tensions continue to ratchet upward. I'm just concerned that what you want to do, rather than calming those political tensions, will end up igniting them into armed conflict."

"And what would you propose?" Kamemor asked. "The Romulan Empire seceding from the Typhon Pact?"

"That is an option," argued Ventel. "Without the Empire, the remaining powers would likely lack the firepower necessary to succeed in an attack on the Federation and its allies, and would thereby preserve the peace."

"If I thought seceding from the Pact would preserve the peace, I'd take it to the Imperial Senate at once," Kamemor said. "But just because a weakened Pact wouldn't attack the Khitomer Accords nations, that doesn't mean it wouldn't attack the Empire."

Ventel nodded. "I'm not sure we could prevail in such a war."

"Even if we could," Kamemor said, "the price of victory would prove steep in blood and treasure." She thought about all the actions and counteractions that had so recently taken place. The Breen—and to her chagrin, the Romulans—stealing the plans for the quantum slipstream drive. The Federation sending two Starfleet operatives into the Breen Confederacy to corrupt those plans and destroy a prototype vessel. The Tzenkethi harrying relocated Federation settlements. The Tholians fomenting Andorian secession. The Ferengi and the Cardassians joining the Federation and the Klingons in the Khitomer Accords. At every stage, reaction followed action, one alliance attempting to gain a tactical advantage over the other.

And why? Kamemor wondered. *To what purpose?* If diminishing the Federation and its allies would have raised the chances of a lasting interstellar peace, she would have supported doing so. But it seemed clear to her that the Tholians, as well as the Tzenkethi and perhaps others, sought to damage the Federation not to guarantee amity, but to permit conquest—or worse, to permit eradication.

Fear, she thought. *It's all about fear.* The Breen and Praetor Tal'Aura feared that Starfleet would utilize its technologically superior slipstream drive to open a first strike on the Typhon Pact nations. The Tholians feared the overall strength of the Federation and its allies. The Tzenkethi feared UFP encroachment on their territories. And the Federation feared the rise of a coalition comprising many of their historical adversaries.

"Fear cripples everything," she told Ventel. "It provokes violence between neighbors, distrust among friends, the sowing of blame against aliens. It allows cynicism and ignorance and brutality to triumph over art and intellect and romance."

Before Ventel could respond, a tone sounded in the room, obviously signaling a request for entry. Kamemor glanced at the wall of monitors, and saw on one screen the closed door that led to the room in which she and Ventel sat. Between the two security guards stood Director Malikan and the man whom the praetor had come to the Orventis Arena to see.

Kamemor stood, and Ventel followed suit. "Please come in," she called.

A moment later, the single panel slid into the wall, exposing Malikan and his charge. "Praetor, may I present Ambassador Spock."

Upon seeing Kamemor, one of Spock's eyebrows rose high on his forehead. Per her instructions, he had not been told with which governmental official he would be meeting.

"Mister Spock," the praetor said, recalling that he preferred not to be addressed with the honorific of his former position. "Please join us."

The leader of the Reunification Movement entered the room alone, while Malikan remained outside in the corridor. The door glided shut, offering Kamemor the privacy she sought. She could have summoned Spock to the Hall of State or to her residence, but once she had made her decision, she'd wanted to meet with the former Federation ambassador as quickly as possible, and in a manner that instantly conveyed her seriousness of purpose, her resolve, and her respect for Spock. She hoped that by going to him, she could accomplish all of that.

Very deliberately, Kamemor raised one hand and offered the traditional Vulcan salute. "Welcome, and thank you for coming," she said.

"It was unclear to me whether or not I had a choice in so doing," Spock said.

Ventel looked to the praetor, an expression of anxiety dressing his face. Kamemor lowered her hand. "You did have a choice," she said, "and you *do* have a choice. If you wish, you may depart right now, with no consequences to yourself or to your cause. But I urge you to stay, to at least listen to what I have come here to discuss with you. I can assure you that it is an important subject, worthy of your attention."

"Indeed," Spock said, and he took a step forward. "I am . . . intrigued."

"Please have a seat, then," Kamemor said. Spock seemed to consider this for a moment, and then he sat in a chair on the other side of the table from her. "You remember Proconsul Anlikar Ventel, I trust."

Spock nodded in Ventel's direction. "Proconsul."

"Mister Spock," Ventel acknowledged.

Kamemor and Ventel took their seats, and after Spock declined the praetor's offer of refreshments, she launched into the reason she had come to see the Vulcan. "Mister Spock, I wanted to speak with you because the Alpha and Beta Quadrants have become nothing less than seething cauldrons of fear and paranoia. If something isn't done to curb the escalating tensions and the continuing attempts to overcome the balance of power, I'm concerned that the situation could boil over and lead to open hostilities."

"You refer, I take it, to the Tholians' role in Andor's secession from the Federation," Spock said.

"Among other things, yes," Kamemor said. "But I contend that *all* sides are culpable to one degree or another. The Federation's development of a superior engine technology has fueled fears among the Typhon Pact nations of a first strike against them."

"And I would submit that since Starfleet has to this point elected not to launch such an attack," Spock said, "the benignity of their motives is clear."

"Their motives notwithstanding," Kamemor said, "the very existence of their advanced starship drive has unsettled the political situation. As has their relocation of several colonies to the Tzenkethi frontier."

Spock seemed to consider this. After a moment, he said, "Praetor, with all due respect, I am in no position to offer an informed defense of the Federation. As you know, I have spent the majority of the past decade and a half here on Romulus. My knowledge of interstellar affairs in general, and of Federation policies in particular, is therefore limited."

"I do not seek justifications for recent Federation actions," Kamemor said.

"Then may I ask what it is that you *do* seek?"

"Your trust," Kamemor told him. "I need you to trust me, and I need to trust you."

"I . . . do not understand," Spock said.

Kamemor peered over at Ventel, looking, she realized, for his support. He nodded once, and she looked back over at Spock. "I need you to deliver a message for me," she said. "For the Romulan Empire, and really, for all the people of the Alpha and Beta Quadrants."

This time, both of Spock's eyebrows danced upward.

Kamemor steeled herself as she set out to alter the path of the Romulan people. "I need you to deliver a message to President Bacco."

II

Naked Frailties

Banquo: And when we have our naked frailties hid,
        That suffer in exposure, let us meet,
        And question this most bloody piece of work,
        To know it further.

                          —William Shakespeare,
                  The Tragedy of MacBeth, Act II, Scene 3

13

The Argelian freighter *Jorvan* heaved to starboard after dropping out of warp. In the ship's cramped command hub, the captain sat at one of the four control stations surrounding the central console. On the small monitor set into his panel, he watched the star field as it whirled about, until it fixed on the white, G2-class star of Laskitor.

"Set course for the third planet," said the captain. Despite the heavy thrum of the impulse engines, he did not raise his voice, nor did he need to do so; his tone left no doubt that he expected the few members of his crew to follow his orders at once. Though relatively new to *Jorvan,* the captain had commanded several vessels throughout his career, which had lasted a considerable length of time. He'd long ago grown comfortable in a leadership role.

Although perhaps not quite as comfortable as I used to be, he thought.

"Laying in a course for Laskitor Three," said the flight controller from her position to the captain's right, her panel perpendicular to his. She tapped at her controls, and a digital overlay representing their flight path appeared on the captain's monitor.

"Ahead one-half impulse," he said, choosing the slower speed consistent with the practice of conserving fuel in older, less-efficient freighters such as *Jorvan*.

"One-half impulse, aye," said the half-human, half-Vulcan flight controller. "Estimated time to orbital insertion, one hour, forty-seven minutes." With *Jorvan* lacking both the sophistication of a starship's warp navigation and the extreme precision of its sensors, the crew had brought the freighter into the system above the plane of the ecliptic. As a result, they would have to make the final leg of their journey to the planet at sublight velocity. Again, their procedures did not deviate from those expected of an older freighter.

"Anything on sensors?" the captain asked.

"Negative," replied the tactical officer, who crewed the station to the captain's left, opposite the flight controller. "But our range *is* limited," she added.

"Of course," the captain said. "It just makes it difficult to sit here and wait for the possibility of an attack." He pushed his seat back from his station and stood up, the heels of his boots tolling against the metal decking. He straightened the dark-brown flight jacket he wore over his heavy work pants and pale-blue cotton shirt. He really had nowhere to go in the confined space of the command hub, other than to circle the four conjoined control panels at its core. He resisted his inclination to do so, figuring that it might set the flight controller and tactical officer on edge.

On the other side of the central console from the captain, the final control panel sat empty. The fourth member of *Jorvan*'s crew maintained watch on the freighter's power and drive systems from the engineering compartment, located in the lower, aft section of the ship's boxy structure. Between the command hub and engineering, four enormous cargo bays composed the bulk of the freighter.

Filled to capacity, the hold carried food, medicine, and equipment bound for the inhabitants of Laskitor III. Displaced from Entelior IV, which had been devastated by the Borg, the quarter of a million surviving colonists had spent months being relocated to the Laskitor system. Two years after the invasion had forced them to find a new home, the colonists still struggled to establish a stable infrastructure that would sustain them independently. Freighters made irregular but much-needed runs to the planet, ferrying all manner of supplies from the Federation.

Had the narrative of the people late of Entelior IV been unique, it would have been a sad but potentially uplifting story, but because some variation of it had occurred on world after world, it formed just one small part of an overarching tragedy. Only recently had the Federation's efforts to transport provisions begun to fulfill the needs of the relocated and recovering populations. In the Bajoran sector, relief efforts—

"Captain," said the tactical officer, a note of expectation in her voice, "sensors are picking up a vessel approaching on an intercept course, bearing—" She hesitated while she worked over her controls. "Strike that, sir. I read two vessels, bearing three-five-three mark six-one."

"Can you identify them?" the captain asked, though only one answer made sense.

"Trying to," said the tactical officer. "These old sensors don't have the refinement that . . . got it. Two vessels, each with a limited profile, shields and weapons energized . . . and a helical structure."

"'Helical,'" the captain repeated. "Tzenkethi harriers."

"Yes, sir."

"Standard shields," said the captain. He placed his hands on the back of his chair but did not sit down. "Bring us about. Lay in our escape course and engage."

As the two officers acknowledged his orders, the captain thought about what lay ahead. Off and on for months, the Tzenkethi Coalition had sent agile, heavily gunned assault ships out beyond their borders, in the direction of Federation space. Distinctively shaped, the aptly classed harriers attacked freighters carrying supplies to colonies newly resettled in the Laskitor, Corat, and Ergol systems. The Tzenkethi refrained from striking the colonists directly, perhaps because the settlements possessed virtually no planetary defenses and no weapon systems—or perhaps because the Coalition wished to stop short of committing an irrevocable act of war. In intercepting freighters, the Tzenkethi claimed encroachment on their sovereign territory. The harriers typically turned the Federation vessels away, occasionally disabling them or destroying their cargo. Two freighters had gone missing during the previous six months, but no solid evidence existed to implicate the Tzenkethi in the disappearances. The Federation had warned the Coalition against interfering in humanitarian efforts, and President Bacco had used particularly strong language in lamenting the two lost vessels, but the Tzenkethi had responded with their usual mix of belligerence and anti-UFP rhetoric.

"They're approaching at high speed," said the tactical officer. "Less than five minutes to intercept."

"How long before we can safely go to warp?" the captain asked.

"Two minutes, ten seconds."

The captain reached forward and touched a control surface on his console. A boatswain's whistle sounded two high-pitched tones, indicating the activation of the freighter's internal communications system. "Bridge to engineering."

"Go ahead, Captain," came the immediate response.

"We'll be going back to warp within five minutes," said the captain. "Are we ready?"

"On your order," said the engineer.

"Very good. Bridge out." He looked once more to the tactical officer. "Open an audio channel, standard Tzenkethi frequencies."

"Aye, sir," said the tactical officer, working her panel once again. "Channel open."

"Tzenkethi vessels," the captain intoned, "this is the Federation freighter *Jorvan*. We are on a humanitarian mission to Laskitor Three. We respectfully request that you stand down and allow us safe passage." The captain waited, but he heard only silence.

"Nothing, sir," the tactical officer said quietly. "But they are receiving us."

"Tzenkethi vessels," the captain said again. "This is the freighter *Jorvan* from the Federation. We ask that you allow us to proceed on our mission of mercy to the inhabitants of Laskitor Three. We are delivering food and medicine, as well as agricultural and other equipment. We would consent to being scanned so that you can assure yourselves that we are introducing no weapons of any kind into the system."

After a few seconds, the tactical officer said, "Still nothing. They remain headed directly for us."

Of the flight controller, the captain asked, "You know their top speeds?"

"Yes, sir," the flight controller replied. "I've programmed our course accordingly, with a slightly slower maximum velocity. If the harriers should gain too quickly on us or fall back too far, I can adjust our speed so that it reads like phase variances in the warp coils."

"Well done," the captain said. "Time to warp?"

"To stay out of their weapons range," said the flight controller, "we'll need to begin our run thirty-nine seconds before they arrive."

"Make it so."

The captain waited, tense but anticipatory. At one minute prior to when they would need to flee the harriers, the flight controller announced the time, and then again at ten-second intervals. At ten, she counted down by ones. The captain listened to the sound of the ship as the warp drive engaged, the heavy vibrations of its operation well in excess of those produced by the impulse engines. The old freighter seemed to shudder beneath his feet.

"The Tzenkethi are in pursuit," said the tactical officer.

The captain felt his hands tighten on the back of his chair, and he forced himself to relax. *None of it's as easy as it once was,* he thought. Age had something to do with that, of course, but more than that—or at least in concert with it—everything had changed. No longer defining himself as the brash cadet, nor even simply as the vastly experienced captain, he had settled into different roles in his life: husband, father. He had long imagined such a change in his personal circumstances, but he had not foreseen the depth and profundity of the changes that had occurred within him. His personal life colored his professional life in a way he had never thought possible.

"The harriers are gaining on us," reported the tactical officer.

"As expected," said the flight controller. "There's no need as yet to alter our velocity."

Minutes passed, and the captain kept counsel with his own thoughts. He trusted his crew to perform their duties without issue, though he sometimes wondered if he still trusted himself. Not only had both his personal and professional lives changed, so too had the whole of life within the Federation. Even as entire world populations fought to recover from the Borg invasion, so too did Starfleet, its primary focus of voyage and discovery almost entirely placed on hold. Recently, rumors had begun to surface about a renewed commitment to exploration, but it remained to be seen whether—

"Captain, the Tzenkethi are closing to within weapons range," said the tactical officer.

"On-screen."

The tactical officer manipulated her controls, and the image on the captain's monitor shifted, revealing the two harriers in flight. Unlike the great, teardrop-shaped battle cruisers of the Tzenkethi Coalition, the hulls of the smaller assault vessels wore not a silver, lusterless coating, but a rainbowlike sheen. Narrowing toward their aft sections, the harriers resembled an artist's modern interpretation of the spiral end of a conch shell.

"We're nearing the debris disk of the Beta Eneras system," said the flight controller before the captain even asked.

"Their weapons are on a buildup to discharge," said the tactical officer. She looked up at the captain. "They're not looking to disable us."

"Shields?" the captain asked.

"They can withstand an initial volley," said the tactical officer, "but probably nothing more."

"Understood," said the captain. "After the first hit, raise the upgraded shields."

"Aye, sir."

He returned his attention to the monitor. On it, he saw bright specks of light growing in brilliance at the aft tips of the Tzenkethi ships. As he watched, the illuminated points began to spin quickly around the curving hulls of the harriers, racing forward until they reached the bows of the ships and fired spiral torrents of energy out into space.

A roar tore through *Jorvan*'s command hub, as though a substantial asteroid had crashed into the freighter. The captain flew from his feet and landed hard on the deck, pain slicing through his hip, his wrist twisting unnaturally as he tried to cushion his fall. Within his own body, over the cacophony surrounding him, he heard the sickening sound of a bone breaking. The lighting panels went dark, throwing the space into an eerie glimmer generated solely by the glow of the instrument panels in the center console.

"Shields down," called out the tactical officer, somehow still at her station. "Raising upgraded shields."

The captain glanced toward the conn and saw the flight controller climbing back to her feet. "We've fallen out of warp," she yelled, even as the din around them settled into a relative calm. The meaty pulse of the warp drive had vanished, and the drone of the impulse engines failed to replace it. "We're drifting."

The freighter shook again as another salvo pounded into *Jorvan,* but without even hearing a report from his tactical officer, the captain could tell that the upgraded shields had protected the ship far better than its regular defensive system. Still, he felt no desire to learn how long the new shields could endure. He reached up and took hold of his chair with one hand, holding his other arm close against his body as he sought to protect his injured wrist. As he pulled himself back up, he said, "Where the hell's the cavalry?"

"They're here," said the tactical officer.

On his monitor, the captain saw the Tzenkethi ships altering their courses, but too late. The impressive figure of a Federation starship swooped into view. The great ellipse of the primary hull, the squat form of the engineering section, and the angular, streamlined warp nacelles distinguished the Starfleet vessel as one of the *Sovereign* class. The captain knew that, concealed among the larger bodies of Beta Eneras's debris disk, the ship and its crew had lain in wait for the opportunity to halt a Tzenkethi attack in progress.

The captain watched as bands of gold energy sliced through space, landing on their marks. It did not take long for the larger, more powerful vessel to compromise the shields and weapons systems on both harriers. Then blue-white curtains bathed the assault ships, the tractor beams tethering them to their captor.

Concerned about his crew, he peered at his officers. "Are you all right?"

From the tactical station, Lieutenant Choudhury nodded. At the conn, Lieutenant Chen said, "Just a few bumps."

The captain stabbed at a control surface to open an internal comlink. "Bridge to engineering," he said. "Mister Taurik, what's your status? Are you all right?"

"Yes, sir," said the engineer. *"I was thrown from my feet during the attack, but I have suffered no injuries."*

"Very good," the captain said. "Report to the bridge."

As the engineer acknowledged the order, the tactical officer said, "Captain, we're being hailed."

"And it's about time," the captain said with a half-smile. "On-screen."

The image of the two harriers hanging in tow winked off, replaced by that of a starship bridge. At its center stood a tall Klingon, clad in the black-and-gray uniform of Starfleet, his red turtleneck indicating his place in the command division. *"Captain Picard,"* he said, *"are you all right?"*

"Yes, we are, Mister Worf," said Picard. "Have you taken the Tzenkethi crews into custody?"

"We have, sir," Worf said. *"After disabling their shields, we transported them directly to the brig. Medical teams are currently examining them for injuries."*

"Well done," Picard said. Knowing that the danger to his crew had passed, he felt a sudden playful urge—a side of himself that fatherhood seemed to trigger. "But what took you so long?"

"So long?" Worf said, visibly confused. But then the captain saw a twinkle in his eye, and his first officer said, *"I was curious to witness the firepower of the latest generation of Tzenkethi harriers."*

"Indeed," Picard said, appreciating how far Worf's sense of humor had advanced over the years. "I trust it was illuminating."

"Yes, sir," Worf said. *"And I trust it was of no inconvenience to you."*

"Nothing more than a broken wrist," Picard said, motioning to the arm he still held steady against his body.

Worf's mouth dropped open, a stark look of concern freezing the rest of his features. *"Captain, I can assure you, we proceeded according to the plan and with the utmost haste."*

"Of course you did," Picard said, forcing a toothless smile onto his face as his wrist began to throb. "This occurred during the first attack. There's nothing you could have done about it." He paused, then added, "And it's nothing Doctor Crusher won't be able to mend."

The mention of Picard's wife appeared to distress the first officer further. *He's right to feel apprehensive,* Picard thought. *But it's not Worf who Beverly's going to take to task about this.*

The turbolift door slid open, and Lieutenant Commander Taurik stepped into the command hub. Refocusing his attention on what needed to happen next, Picard said, "Prepare to release the Tzenkethi ships from the tractor beam and to transport the *Jorvan*'s cargo into the *Enterprise*'s holds. We still have supplies to deliver to Laskitor Three. Then we'll return here to make whatever minimal repairs are needed on the *Jorvan* so that it can travel back to the nearest starbase under its own power."

"Aye, sir," Worf said.

Picard looked to his officers, and then back at the image of his exec on the monitor. "Four to beam aboard," said the captain.

14

When Sisko walked into the cargo bay, a sudden sense of déjà vu bloomed in his mind, claiming his attention like an almost-remembered song lyric or a not-quite-recognized scent. He stopped abruptly at the sight of the hold loaded with shipping containers of various shapes, sizes, and colors, with Brathaw and Pardshay apparently confirming the delivery against a manifest. As Kasidy emerged from *Xhosa* through the circular hatchway of the airlock, the eerie feeling of reliving an already experienced moment seemed complete.

Is this the same cargo bay where we first met? Sisko asked himself. He couldn't recall the designation of the hold he'd visited after Jake had pushed him to make Kasidy's acquaintance. With Deep Space 9's many bays, though, it seemed unlikely to him that—

"What's wrong, Daddy?" Rebecca asked, breaking Sisko's spell.

"What?" He turned and squatted down to face his daughter, her small hand still clasped in his larger one. "Nothing's wrong, honey. I was just looking for Mommy." He allowed himself the fib, wanting to avoid describing a happy, significant time in his relationship with Kasidy, concerned that Rebecca might ask questions. While he and Kasidy had admitted to their daughter that they would continue to spend their marriage largely apart from each other, they had chosen not to tell her precisely why, instead cleaving to the justification that Starfleet needed its experienced officers to help protect the Federation. They did not wish to lie to Rebecca, but neither did they want to frighten her with the actual reasons Sisko had left Bajor. And so, for the present, they settled on a lie of omission. Because of that, they also elected to delay their divorce—Sisko withdrew from the Adarak court his petition for the legal dissolution of their marriage—fearing that word of their official separation would become public and that their daughter would eventually hear about it in school.

"Mommy's right there," Rebecca said with her visible six-and-a-half-year-old sense of exasperation. She dropped her hold on the antigrav sled she towed along behind her, and on which she had insisted that Sisko place her carryall. He had picked it up in his quarters aboard *Robinson,* where he and Rebecca had been staying, but she'd wanted to manage the bag herself. In the hold, she pointed toward Kasidy, who saw them and started in their direction.

Sisko stood back up and turned to greet Kasidy with a hug. She wore a two-toned, formfitting brown coverall, with a blue shirt beneath. The outfit accentuated her attractive curves. "Hello, Kasidy."

"Hello, Ben."

Since he had first returned to Bajor seven months ago to visit Rebecca, he and Kasidy had achieved a rapprochement of sorts. While she remained hurt and angry about his leaving and continuing to stay away, she also understood his reasons for doing so—although she believed him completely wrong. For his part, Sisko recognized and concurred with her reasonable demand that he play an active role in his daughter's life. He also suspected that she thought that seeing her regularly would tug at his heartstrings and perhaps eventually drive him back home for good.

About Sisko's longing for her, Kasidy could not have been more right. But he also could not dismiss the Prophets' admonition to him, or overlook all of the terrible events that had occurred before he'd left Bajor and that underscored the verity of the warning he'd received. Despite Kasidy's pain and his own, as well as the impact on Rebecca, Sisko could not allow himself to falter in his resolve to safeguard his family. He continually reminded himself that what he did, he did for them.

To Rebecca, Kasidy said, "And how's my big girl?"

"Hi, Mommy." She took her hand from Sisko's and held her arms up to her mother. Kasidy bent and picked her up, offering a grunt as she did so. "Oh, my. You're getting too big for this."

Though still below the average size for her age—she weighed just twenty kilos and reached only a hundred fifteen centimeters—Rebecca continued to develop at a healthy pace. Since he'd begun visiting his daughter, Sisko could see her growth. He thought that was probably due to the fact that he only got to see her every couple of months, though they did send each other subspace messages every few days.

"So how did you like Deep Space Nine?" Kasidy asked. Ever since Sisko had given Rebecca the models of *Robinson* and *Xhosa,* she had become fascinated with space travel. She had pleaded with Kasidy to take her aboard her freighter, and after making that first journey, Rebecca asked to visit both *Robinson* and Deep Space 9, the latter of which she had learned about in school. When Sisko's orders brought his starship to the station, there seemed no better opportunity. While Kasidy made a shipping run aboard *Xhosa,* Sisko spent a week on Bajor with Rebecca, and then three days on *Robinson* and DS9. Having completed her job with a final stop at the station to offload shipments in transit, Kasidy would take Rebecca home from there.

"It was great, Mommy," Rebecca said. "Daddy showed me ops and the giant docking arms and the airlocks and I went in a holding cell—"

"Wait," Kasidy said, cutting off Rebecca's excited narrative stream. "You went *where*?" She peered past their daughter at Sisko.

"We were on the Promenade, and Miss Rebecca wanted to go through each and every door," Sisko explained. "The new security chief, Blackmer, was gracious enough to give us a tour of his office. Since there was nobody in any of the holding cells, he very generously offered to lock our daughter up."

"'Generously,' huh?" Kasidy said, with an inflection that indicated she didn't know whether or not she approved. "And how was that?" she asked their daughter.

Rebecca appeared to think for a moment, and then said, "I liked it and I didn't like it." She hesitated, then added, "It was neat to see the force fields, but it was like when I was taken and couldn't go anywhere."

Sisko felt his blood run cold. He saw a look of dread pass over Kasidy's face, which she quickly hid away. Rebecca's abduction had taken place three years earlier. After the ordeal, she met regularly with a counselor for a couple of months, but mercifully, at not even four years of age, she seemed to suffer no ill effects from the experience. She'd said nothing about remembering any of it during her time in the security office, and as far as Sisko knew, she had not spoken about her kidnapping outside of her counseling sessions, nor even made reference to it, since it had taken place.

"Did that make you feel bad, honey?" Kasidy asked.

Rebecca shrugged, a movement that seemed to involve most of her small body. Then her eyes grew wide as she appeared to recall something. "Oh, and I got to go to Earth in a sweet hollow."

Kasidy's brow wrinkled in confusion, but Sisko laughed loudly, his emotions swinging quickly to the other end of the spectrum as his daughter delighted him. "We were talking about where you and I came from," he told Kasidy, "so I decided to show Rebecca. Quark has some Earth programs, so we visited a—" He reached forward and playfully squeezed his daughter about the middle. "—*holosuite*."

"Oh," Kasidy said with a smile, clearly amused by their daughter's malapropism.

"Mister Quark wears clothes that looked like I colored them in my coloring books," observed Rebecca.

"He certainly does," Kasidy said. "And what did you think of Earth?"

Rebecca shrugged again. "It was good," she said. "Kinda like Bajor, but different. I liked it, except the baseball was boring."

"Daddy took you to a baseball game, did he?" Kasidy said. She looked at Sisko. "Ebbets Field?"

"Dodger Stadium, actually," Sisko said. "I was going to show Rebecca one of your brother's games too, but . . . well, she's young. We've still got plenty of time to teach her the game."

"Ugh!" Rebecca said, and she buried her face in Kasidy's shoulder.

Kasidy snickered at their daughter's reaction. Then she asked Sisko, "So when do you leave?"

"Tomorrow at oh-seven-hundred," he said. "The crew is finalizing preparations right now." After an absence of more than six years, Starfleet would finally resume its exploration of the Gamma Quadrant. Since Elias Vaughn and the *Defiant* crew had completed a three-month journey of discovery on the other side of the wormhole, numerous events had conspired to prevent a return there: the emergence of the Eav'oq from subspace on Idran and the relocation of that world's planetary system to the Gamma Quadrant terminus of the Bajoran wormhole; the arrival of the Ascendants, led by the crazed Iliana Ghemor; the *Even Odds* disaster; the calamity on Endalla; and ultimately, Starfleet's decimation by the Borg. But with the Cardassian Union and the Ferengi Alliance joining the Federation and the Klingon Empire in the Khitomer Accords, the influx of starships and crews to protect the four powers, coupled with Starfleet's rebuilding efforts and Cardassia's recovery from the Dominion War, freed up resources for an increase in the number of exploratory missions. When Starfleet Command had proposed six months of exploration in the Gamma Quadrant, Sisko had utilized his experience in the region to lobby for and win *Robinson*'s assignment to the mission.

"Are you still excited about it?" Kasidy asked.

"I am," Sisko said. When the prospect for the mission had first arisen, he'd spoken with Kasidy about it before putting in his request. Since he had begun visiting Rebecca every two months, something he would be unable to do for half a year if he took *Robinson* to the Gamma Quadrant, he wanted to consult with her before pursuing the mission. Since they could easily and honestly explain Sisko's longer absence to Rebecca, and since he would still exchange messages with his daughter every few days—even though it would take longer for each message to reach the communications relay that carried messages through the wormhole—they had agreed that he should go. "After my time on Deep Space Nine, and after everything that's happened since, I'm anxious to do something actively constructive," he said, "rather than just trying to help avert destruction."

She peered at him with an expression of sadness. In it, he could see her love for him, and her sorrow over their separation, but more than anything, he thought he saw pity in her eyes. The look touched him and scared him at the same time, though he could not say exactly why.

"I really hope you find what you need out there, Ben," said Kasidy.

"Thank you," Sisko said, because he could think of nothing else to say—at least nothing safe. "Are you going right back to Bajor?"

"Yes," she said. "I want to get home again early enough so that Rebecca can get a good night's sleep before going back to her regular school." While she had been with Sisko aboard *Robinson* and Deep Space 9, Rebecca had attended the station's school.

"Have a safe trip back," Sisko said. "And you—" He nuzzled his face against the curve of Rebecca's neck. "—be sure to mind your mother and do well in school."

Rebecca looked from Kasidy to Sisko and back again. "I want to stay on Deep Space Nine." She elided the name of the station and ran the words together: *DeeSpayNine*.

"Don't you want to go home, honey?" Kasidy asked gently.

"No."

"But you'll be going on Mommy's ship again," Sisko reminded her.

"Oh," Rebecca said, gazing over at the airlock hatchway. "Right." Kasidy set her down on the deck, and Rebecca grabbed her antigrav sled and raced toward *Xhosa*.

Kasidy looked to Sisko and rolled her eyes. "I'm not sure where she gets all her energy."

"She's definitely got a miniature warp core somewhere inside that little body," Sisko said. "She wore me out. I'm looking forward to the Gamma Quadrant mission just so I can get some rest."

Kasidy smiled at the jest, but then her mien grew serious. She reached up and placed her hand on Sisko's upper arm. "Be careful out there," she said. "Rebecca needs her father."

"And I need her," Sisko said. "I'll be careful."

Kasidy dropped her hand, and the two hugged once more. Then she caught up with their daughter, who stood waiting in the hatchway. Sisko waved. "Bye, Rebecca. I love you."

"I love you too, Daddy," she said, waving back. When Kasidy reached her, she took Rebecca's hand and led her into *Xhosa*.

Sisko stood there motionless, peering after his wife and child. After a moment, movement caught his eye, and he turned to see *Xhosa* crew members Brathaw and Pardshay looking at him from where they worked over the cargo they'd just offloaded from the ship. Suddenly self-conscious, Sisko nodded curtly, then quickly headed out of the bay.

Sisko waited until later that night to leave the confines of *Robinson* again. Three days earlier, after he'd returned with Rebecca from visiting her on Bajor, he'd spent much of their ensuing time together showing her around the ship. His daughter also wanted to see Deep Space 9, though, and he needed to take her to school there as well, so he hadn't been able to stay away from the station completely.

But he'd wanted to stay away—and still did.

As a lift whisked him down from where *Robinson* had moored to the top of one of DS9's docking pylons, he examined his reticence to walk the familiar corridors of the station. He had spent seven years there—seven years that, while filled with challenges and even tragedies, had proven the most satisfying time of his life. His son grew into a man during that period. He met and married Kasidy, became a captain, successfully defended the Federation against the Dominion, and positioned Bajor for its eventual admission into the Federation. He initially resisted becoming a religious icon for the Bajorans, but came to accept and even embrace his position as Emissary.

Sisko did not fear or dread being on Deep Space 9 again. Since leaving the station after the end of the Dominion War, he'd been back a number of times. Nor did he shrink from the possibility of running into old friends and colleagues; indeed, so many of the people he knew best—Kira Nerys, Worf, Miles O'Brien, Odo, Ezri Dax—had long ago departed DS9. Of those who remained, Sisko might not necessarily enjoy catching up with them because he would not wish to discuss his personal life, but the last couple of years had made him adept at deflecting uncomfortable questions directed his way. When *Robinson* had first arrived at the station, he'd reported in person to Captain Ro without experiencing a moment of discomfort.

What is it then? he asked himself as the lift carried him through a crossover bridge toward the central core. He could not deny that during Rebecca's stay with him, he had resisted showing her the station, and when he had shown her, he'd done so in a way that mostly allowed him to see as few of its residents as possible. In reserving a holosuite to show Earth to his daughter—*Robinson*'s holodecks had been powered down during preparations for the ship's upcoming mission—he even communicated with Quark via the comm, rather than in person.

The lift changed direction, and so too did Sisko. *Maybe I am afraid of something,* he told himself. If so, that still left him with his unanswered question: what was it that troubled him about returning to the station?

When the lift slowed to a stop, Sisko stepped out onto the Promenade. Most of DS9's social, entertainment, and services hub lay in the dim lighting and the resultant quietude of the station's simulated night. Farther down from where he stood, though, bright lights shined from the entrance of Quark's and bathed the deck in multiple colors. Sisko also heard the general hum of a crowd, interrupted by the raucousness of a few revelers, doubtless from around the dabo table.

It's nice to know there are some constants in the universe, Sisko thought. He smiled, despite his downbeat mood. The urge to head over to Quark's rose in his mind. He could have a glass of *grosz* and listen to Morn spin one of his endless tales—during his tour of the station with Rebecca, the only person Sisko had run into whom he knew, other than Ro Laren, had been the loquacious Lurian. Afterward, Sisko could even take in an old baseball game in one of the holosuites, perhaps revel in the daring play of the great Jackie Robinson.

First things first, Sisko thought. *You came here for a reason.*

He made his way to the infirmary. Also shrouded in the shadows of the station's virtual night, the outer compartment contained only two medical staffers, one Sisko didn't recognize, and one he did. Both looked up as he stopped just inside the main doorway. Standing at a lighted cache of equipment, a tricorder in hand, a med tech said nothing, obviously waiting for the officer on duty to address their visitor. Seated at a workstation, a woman with long, reddish blond hair and blue-green eyes looked surprised when she saw the captain. Krissten Richter had been assigned to Deep Space 9 perhaps a decade earlier, during Sisko's own tenure on the station. Pushing away from her console and rising to her feet, she said, "Captain."

Sisko moved farther into the room. "Lieutenant Richter," he said, reading the rank insignia on her uniform. She had been promoted a grade since he had last seen her. "How have you been?" he asked.

"I'm well, sir, thank you," Richter said.

"And how is Ensign Etana?" he asked, recalling the identity of Richter's romantic partner.

The question elicited a wide smile from Richter. "Very well, sir," she said. She reached up to her right ear and pointed to the piece of jewelry she wore there. Bajoran in origin, the earring attached to her lobe, and two connected chains draped from there up to the top of her ear. Indicating the second loop by taking it between her thumb and forefinger, she said, "We got married."

"That's wonderful," Sisko said, offering up a genuine smile of his own. "Congratulations."

"Thank you, sir. We're very happy," Richter said, stating the obvious. "How is Captain Yates? And your daughter?"

"Both doing well," Sisko said. Before Richter could inquire further, he quickly added, "I don't have much time, but before I depart aboard the *Robinson* tomorrow morning, I wanted to visit Captain Vaughn."

Richter's smile wilted. "Of course," she said, lowering her voice. "He's in one of the secondary-care rooms. Right now, he—"

"Captain," said a voice Sisko knew well. He turned to see Doctor Bashir crossing the threshold from the infirmary's primary ward. The doctor approached Sisko with a hand extended. Sisko took it. "It's so good to see you, sir. I was hoping you'd stop by while the *Robinson* was here."

"It's good to see you, Doctor," Sisko said. "How are you?"

Bashir seemed to draw himself up. "Actually, I'm excellent," he said. "Maybe never better."

"That's good to hear," Sisko said. "Is there some particular reason?"

Still standing beside Sisko, Richter attempted to cover her smile with one hand. Bashir saw the nurse's expression, and then he motioned deeper into the infirmary. "Shall we go into my office?"

Sisko allowed the doctor to lead him out of the main room. Once in his office, Bashir asked, "Do you remember Sarina Douglas, Captain?"

Sisko thought for a moment. "The woman from the Institute," he said at last. "The one with cognitive-sensory dissonance, who you treated."

"That's right," Bashir said. "That was more than eight years ago. Since then, she's become her own woman and a productive part of society. She's actually in Starfleet now."

"I suppose all of that's a good thing," Sisko said, "but I suspect you didn't bring me in here to talk about this woman's professional record."

"No, sir," Bashir said. "Last year, we reconnected, and she transferred to Deep Space Nine. She's on Chief Blackmer's security team."

"And back in your life as well, I take it?" Sisko asked.

"Yes," Bashir said. "Yes, she is."

"I'm very happy for you, Julian," Sisko said. "I know things haven't always been easy for you here."

"No," Bashir agreed, "but that seems to have changed now. What about you? How are you and—"

"Doctor," Sisko said, "I'm sorry to interrupt, but as I was just telling Lieutenant Richter, I'm afraid that I don't have much time before I need to get back to the *Robinson*. I was hoping that I could see Captain Vaughn before I need to be back aboard."

"Of course," said Bashir, his feelings clearly hurt at being dismissed so quickly by a man—a friend—that he hadn't seen in more than two years. "We've placed him in a secondary-care compartment. I don't know if you're aware, but he was removed from his respirator eight months ago."

A sense of hope flickered across Sisko's mind. "That sounds like good news."

"No," Bashir said. "I'm sorry, but it's not. It simply means that the autonomic functions of Captain Vaughn's brain remain unimpaired. Unfortunately, ever since his injury, there's been no sign of higher brain function."

"How is he even still alive then?" Sisko wanted to know.

"Since the accident, a feeding tube has provided him sustenance," Bashir explained. "Without that and a hydration line, he would die within a matter of days."

"There's no chance for recovery?" Sisko asked.

"I'm afraid not."

"But then why hasn't his body been permitted to die?" Sisko said.

"That's not my decision to make, Captain," Bashir said, clearly implying that Vaughn's daughter had chosen to keep her father—or the husk of what he once had been—from perishing.

Sisko nodded slowly. "I'd still like to see him, if I may," he told the doctor.

"Of course," Bashir said. "Lieutenant Tenmei is in there with him now." When Sisko gave him an inquiring look, he said, "She visits him most mornings and nights."

"Do you think she would mind if I stopped in?"

"Not at all," Bashir said. "Truthfully, another face besides mine in there might do her some good."

Sisko nodded again, and Bashir led him from his office back into the main room. From there, they entered the primary-care facility, which included a surgical table and half a dozen diagnostic beds, all of which stood empty. Bashir gestured to a doorway on the far side of the room. Sisko thanked him, and the doctor withdrew.

Sisko crossed the room and peered inside the smaller compartment. Elias Vaughn lay on a bed beneath a pale-blue sheet, his flesh ashen. His eyes closed but his mouth hanging open, he lacked any sign of the vitality that he had displayed even in the second century of his life. A pair of lines snaked from small devices hanging above him, down onto the bed and below the covers. Outlined beneath the sheet, the shape of his body attested to his condition, his once strong physique diminished by the injury he had borne in the service of his crew and a planetary population in danger. His life had ended heroically—but it clearly had ended.

Sitting in a chair beside her lost father, Prynn Tenmei had one arm outstretched in order to rest her hand on Vaughn's lifeless fingers. A padd perched on her lap appeared filled with text, though she did not read it. Instead, her gaze seemed focused—or unfocused—on the middle distance. Her face appeared drawn, and dark crescents floated under eyes that seemed vacant.

Is it any wonder? Sisko thought. Beginning and ending most days by sitting beside the inert form of her effectively dead father, how had she even retained her sanity? He sympathized with her plight.

For the first time since Sisko's own father had died, he considered that it might have been his good fortune not to make it

to Earth before Joseph Sisko had succumbed to his many infir-
mities. How much more difficult would it have been for him
to watch his father die? And how would Sisko have handled a
situation similar to Tenmei's? Would he have had the strength
to allow the last remaining vestige of his father to pass from
existence? Could he have given permission to remove from his
father's failing body the only things that continued to sustain it?
He wanted to answer the question *Yes,* but in the end, he settled
for the truth: *I don't know.*

Not wanting to startle Tenmei, Sisko rapped lightly on
the doorframe. She looked up at him and blinked, and for a
moment, he didn't think she recognized him. The last time he
had communicated with her had been from Starbase 197, on the
world of Alonis. After the Borg invasion ended, Sisko recorded
and sent a message to Tenmei explaining her father's fate aboard
U.S.S. James T. Kirk.

Recalling that, Sisko feared for a moment that, when she
realized his identity, he would see resentment or even hatred in
her eyes. After all, in addition to delivering to her the news of
her father's devastating injury, he had survived the battle that,
for all intents and purposes, Vaughn had not. *Why shouldn't she
hate me?*

But when recognition flashed across Tenmei's eyes, she
followed it with a smile. Her lips didn't part, and the shallow
expression didn't light up her face, but it nevertheless seemed
genuine. "Captain Sisko," she said. "Please come in."

Sisko did so, glancing down at Tenmei's padd as he neared
her. "Are you reading to your father?" he asked.

Tenmei peered down at the padd as well, almost as though
she had forgotten it. "I was," she said. "I like reading aloud to
him. I know he can't hear me, but it makes me feel . . . not better,
but somehow still connected to him." She let go of her father's
hand, picked up the padd, and touched a control. The text disappeared, replaced by two larger words above a third, presumably
the title and author. "Have you read it?" Tenmei asked.

"*The Iliad,*" Sisko said, "by Homer." He nodded. "Yes, but
not since high school." He thought he recalled that one of the

book's major themes involved the power of destiny, and how one cannot avoid one's fate. He wondered if Tenmei had known that before selecting the epic, or if not, whether she had perceived it in her reading.

"It's interesting," Tenmei said. "I never read it, and I have no idea whether or not Dad did, but it seemed like his type of story."

"I can see that," Sisko said.

"I heard that you were here aboard the *Robinson*," Tenmei said. "I thought about asking to come and see you. . . . I *wanted* to, but . . ." She looked down. "I'm sorry. It just seemed too hard."

It shocked Sisko to hear Tenmei's apology, and he realized that he had underestimated the depth of her despair. The guilt he managed to shunt aside in his daily life for having disregarded the warning of the Prophets suddenly threatened to overwhelm him. The idea that his decision to spend his life with Kasidy had somehow resulted in Vaughn's injury seemed absurd on the surface of it, he knew, but he had lived the reality of it. "Lieutenant," he said, and then started again. "Prynn, you have nothing to be sorry for." He wanted to throw himself down and beg for Tenmei's mercy, plead for her forgiveness, but it would have caused *her* to think *him* insane. "I just wish that there was something I could do for you now to ease your burden."

She peered up at him, and he saw tears in her eyes. "It's not my burden," she told him. "It's just my life."

The sentiment rocked Sisko, echoing as it did his attitude about the recent events of his own life. "Prynn, your father loved you," he said. "Nothing pleased him more than that the two of you reconnected after all those years estranged from each other." He paused, attempting to invite a response.

"I know," she said at last. "I loved him, and I was so happy to have my father back again." She peered over at the body that had once housed Elias Vaughn. "But now . . ."

"But now your father would not want you here," Sisko said, gently but firmly. "It would satisfy him to know how much you loved him, but it would destroy him to see you sacrificing so much of your time, and experiencing so much misery, to sit vigil for him in a hopeless cause." Sisko imagined stepping over to the head of Vaughn's bed and tearing the feeding and hydration tubes from the machines that controlled them. But of course he could not do that. Instead, he simply said, "There comes a time to move on, Prynn."

"I know," Tenmei said, wiping the back of her hand across her eyes. "Really, I do know that. I'm just not there yet."

"I understand," Sisko said. "And I'm not trying to tell you what you should do, or when. I'm just saying that you have options. You can stay here as long as you want to, as long as you *need* to, but you can also have a life—a *full* life—on the other side of that door." He pointed back to the entrance to the compartment. "When you're ready, there will come a time when you can move on."

Prynn regarded Sisko for a long time, her eyes seeming to study his. Finally, she inhaled deeply, as though trying to calm her fraying nerves. "Thank you, Captain," she said.

Sisko waited a moment, then walked around Vaughn's bed to stand beside him. Quietly, he reached his own hand out to rest it atop Vaughn's. His skin felt smooth but fragile, warm but somehow empty. "I felt a special closeness with your father that I've never quite been able to put into words," he said. "And I know he felt it too. He and I connected on a deep level that I don't think either one of us quite understood, but it meant a great deal to both of us."

"He held you in high regard, Captain."

Sisko looked at Prynn, hoping that the gratitude he felt for her statement showed on his face. "Thank you," he said. "Obviously, I had the highest esteem for your father." Sisko leaned in toward Vaughn. He could see the stubble of his beard, which clearly had been shaved off at some point to facilitate keeping his face clean. He saw the slight movement beside Vaughn's Adam's apple that revealed his pulse, keeping time with his heart. He saw the rise and fall of his chest as his body, against all odds and for no real purpose, continued to breathe. At that moment, Sisko knew with absolute certainty that, in the next instant, his friend would open his eyes and return to the world of the living.

But Vaughn didn't.

"Good-bye, Elias," Sisko whispered. He stood back up and headed for the door. When he got there, he turned back toward Tenmei. "If you should ever need anything . . ." He let his sentence dangle unfinished, and Tenmei nodded.

"Thank you," she said.

Sisko headed back through the primary ward and back into the infirmary's outer compartment. According to Lieutenant Richter, Doctor Bashir had retired for the night. Grateful that he could make good a quick escape, Sisko thanked the nurse, congratulating her once more on her nuptials. Then he stepped back out onto the Promenade.

For just a fleeting moment, Sisko thought about escaping into an old baseball game in one of Quark's holosuites, or even to Vic's Las Vegas lounge. But he didn't want to—at least not on Deep Space 9. He had spent so much time on the station, had lived through so much there, but the words he had said to Prynn Tenmei recurred to him: *There comes a time to move on.*

Sisko entered the lift and ordered it to take him back to his ship.

15

Accompanied by the security detachment assigned to protect the chairwoman, Sela boarded a Tal Shiar shuttle bound for orbit above Terix II. There, the shuttle would deliver her to *En'Vahj*, one of the personnel transports used by the intelligence agency. The *Lanora*-class vessel would carry Sela back to Romulus—but not before she completed one additional task, the primary reason she had traveled to Terix II.

Inside the shuttle, the chairwoman looked into the cockpit, confirming for herself the identities of the pilot and navigator, a pair of former military officers. Satisfied, she retreated to the rear of the main cabin, which could accommodate a dozen comfortably. She took a seat along the rear bulkhead, between the side wall and an open hatchway that led to an aft compartment housing a transporter pad, a refresher, and emergency equipment and supplies. Her guards knew enough to sit at the front of the main cabin, affording her whatever privacy they could.

As soon as the shuttle's outer and cockpit hatches closed, the pilot's voice emerged from the comm system. *"Chairwoman Sela,"* said Commander Retind, *"we are prepared to depart as soon as you give the order."* His voice sounded even and professional, and implied a clear awareness that he understood the importance of his passenger.

"I'm ready right now," Sela said, knowing that the comm system would automatically pick up her words and transmit them to the pilot. "Alert me once we've reached orbit."

"Yes, ma'am."

As Sela felt the vibrations of the shuttle's engines powering up, she reached beneath the hem of her gray Tal Shiar uniform tunic and retrieved a small data tablet attached to her belt. She keyed it on, entered a trio of access codes, then brought up a directory of the reports provided to her over the previous day by the intelligence field office on Terix II. She looked forward to returning to Romulus, but after her recent ordeal—first aboard *IRW Stormcrow,* and then with the Federation crew aboard Starfleet's *U.S.S Challenger*—it pleased her simply to be back in the Empire.

When Sela had attended Praetor Kamemor on her state visit to Glintara, the chairwoman had welcomed the opportunity to break from the confines of her office in Ki Baratan, despite the diplomatic nature of the duty. She anticipated trouble beforehand, but underestimated the bond between her predecessor, Rehaek, and the head of the Tal Shiar's Technical Directorate, Jano Vellil. After an act of sabotage set *Stormcrow* on an unstoppable collision course with a pulsar, Director Vellil delivered a simple message to Sela, claiming his part in avenging Rehaek.

Foolish arrogance, the chairwoman thought. After escaping the attempted assassination, she surely would have found him out anyway, but the director's statement of vengeance had allowed her to deal with him quickly and efficiently upon her safe return to the Empire. A disciplinary hearing immediately removed him from the Tal Shiar, and a Senate trial just as swiftly sent him to prison. Only a day after his incarceration, and well before his scheduled execution, Vellil had taken his own life.

I need to be more careful, Sela told herself—a sentiment that she'd continued to repeat after narrowly averting her own death.

She looked up from her data tablet and through a port to her right. The shuttle had lifted off, she saw, and as it rose from the city of Vetruvis, it arced to starboard, bringing into view the magnificent extent of Galixori Canyon. Sela peered out at the vast chasm, at the brilliant greens and blues that climbed its walls, at the raging band of white water that tumbled through it. She recalled vividly when her father had brought her there as a girl, a reward for her academic performance in school. The three-day outing remained an important and powerful memory of her childhood.

Sela pulled her gaze away from the canyon, aware that she must compartmentalize such sentimentality and not permit it to interfere with her professional life. She could tell herself that she should have exercised more caution regarding Vellil, but in actuality, she'd had him under surveillance during the time he'd plotted to kill her. She would need to reevaluate some of her personnel, but she also recognized the simple fact that people such as Vellil often made formidable adversaries.

The director's plan would have succeeded too, if not for the chance presence of the Starfleet vessel near the Neutral Zone. In the end, though, it had been the Romulan crew of *Tomalak's Fist* who had rescued the *Challenger* crew. Sela had considered holding on to the Starfleet officers to interrogate them, and she also had given serious thought to executing them, but had judged the benefits of both actions as limited. Freeing them, she'd concluded, might have fostered some measure of goodwill with the Federation, but of far greater importance, it provided her cover with the praetor.

Returning her thoughts to her current undertaking, Sela read through the directory of reports she'd received on Terix II, then selected one with a touch. Rounded blocks of Romulan text filled the screen alongside a column of photographs. The chairwoman reviewed the list of operatives she'd sent beyond the confines of the Empire, searching for those who had recently communicated their status to their Tal Shiar handlers. She ran agents on Qo'noS and Earth, on Cardassia and Ferenginar, and on a dozen worlds besides those. Her people had gained access to manufacturing plants and government offices, public works and private industry, starbases and starships.

Working with both Commander Marius of the *IRW Dekkona* and the Breen Intelligence Directorate, Sela had helped install an operative, Kazren, at Starfleet's Utopia Planitia Shipyards, from which he had stolen the schematics for the quantum slipstream drive. She had done so, and had seen Kazren safely retrieved, all without the knowledge of Gell Kamemor. Since the chairwoman perceived that the praetor's avowed pursuit of peace would have spelled an end to such endeavors, she chose not to reveal her involvement in them. Indeed, assigned by Kamemor to assist in the efforts to unmask those responsible for planning the Utopia Planitia operation, Sela had pinned the blame four-square on the previous praetor, Tal'Aura, and her Tal Shiar head, Rehaek—both of them since expired.

As she studied the list, the chairwoman noted that the Tal Shiar had received recent word from two of their deep-cover agents within the Federation. The communications did not rise to the level of actual intelligence, amounting to no more than coded bursts of seemingly random noise. The signals did indicate, though, the ongoing success of those missions.

Studying the reports of other operatives—several of them Romulans physically altered to produce Vulcan life signs—Sela felt particularly satisfied with the efforts of the Breen. In light of the shared allegiance to the Typhon Pact of both the Romulan Star Empire and the Breen Confederacy, the chairwoman had reached out to the Breen Intelligence Directorate. Initially, Sela sought to unmask the mysterious aliens, a goal she had at least to some degree accomplished; she knew of three distinct species among them, and suspected more.

To her surprise, though, the Breen demonstrated considerable abilities as spies. No doubt because of their physical variation, they managed to place agents on worlds notoriously difficult for Romulans to infiltrate. In the course of her term as chair of the Tal Shiar, Sela had developed a reliable working relationship with Haut, the director of the BID.

"Chairwoman Sela," came the voice of Retind over the comm system, *"we have achieved orbit. We are setting course for the* En'Vahj.*"*

"Understood," Sela said. She peered again through the port. Splashed with the white of cloud formations, the blue-green world of Terix II hung majestically in space. About it, sunlight glinted off numerous spacecraft, testament to the popularity of the famed tourist destination. The chairwoman saw many Romulan vessels, but also noted quite a few that originated outside the borders of the Empire: the asymmetrical ships of the Gorn Hegemony, the angular ships of the Tholian Assembly, the teardrop-shaped ships of the Tzenkethi Coalition.

Looking back down at her data tablet, Sela closed the document she'd been examining. She then searched for another and opened it, revealing a single line of numbers. She stood up and, passing between her two security guards, made her way to the shuttle's cockpit. Outside its closed hatch, she activated the comm unit set into the adjoining bulkhead. "Commander Retind," she said, "I need to speak with you." She added the classified but seemingly innocuous phrase that indicated to the pilot that she did not speak under duress. After a moment, she heard the locking mechanism of the cockpit hatch release. When it glided open, she stepped inside, and the hatch closed behind her, locking once again.

Retind looked up at her, as did the navigator. The pilot's dark eyes regarded her from beneath black hair dusted white from age. "Commander," Sela said, "we'll be making an unscheduled stop." She looked through the wide front ports at the abundance of ships in the space about Terix II, though she could not distinguish her intermediate destination. She held out her tablet so that Retind could see its display. "Take the shuttle to these coordinates."

"Yes, ma'am." Retind signaled the navigator, who entered the coordinates enumerated on Sela's tablet into his control panel. The shuttle altered its trajectory.

"Inform me when we arrive," Sela ordered. She nodded toward the hatch, and Retind touched a control on his own console. The hatch unlocked and slid open, and Sela passed back into the main cabin.

She did not stop there, though, instead continuing on into the aft compartment, where she secured the hatch. Sela then reconfigured her data tablet as she awaited word from the cockpit. It arrived a short time later.

"Chairwoman Sela," said Retind, *"the shuttle has reached the specified coordinates."*

"Very good," Sela said. "You will wait here until—" She checked the chronometer on her tablet, then provided the pilot with a definite time. "If you have not heard from me by then, inform my security team and proceed to the *En'Vahj*. Once aboard, report this conversation to the lead Tal Shiar officer."

For a moment, Retind did not respond, and Sela conjectured that, as doubts and concerns rose in his mind, he fought the urge to voice them. Experienced in dealing with the Tal Shiar, the commander clearly knew better than to question one of its members—particularly the chairwoman herself. *"Yes, ma'am,"* he finally replied.

Sela operated her data tablet, sending a signal to a second set of spatial coordinates she had brought with her. She received a confirmation at once. Calling up a set of instructions she had programmed into her tablet, she executed it. On her display, she saw verification that the shuttle's shields had temporarily lowered, and an instant later, her vision clouded with the bright motes of a transporter effect.

Sela materialized in a dark place, barely illuminated by the glow of a freestanding console across from her. Behind it stood a pair of armored Breen. They both walked forward, around the control panel, and approached her. Neither appeared to carry weapons.

They don't need to, Sela thought. *Not while we're standing in the middle of a Breen starship.*

"Chairwoman Sela," said one of the two Breen, his words translated into the electronic output of his helmet, and then interpreted by Sela's universal translator. *"I am Haut. It is good to see you again."*

Sela took a step toward the two Breen, leaving the pad onto which she had transported. The pulse of the ship's power hummed through the decking. "Director Haut," she said. She understood that she had no way of confirming his identity, but he had proven himself trustworthy in their previous encounters. If somebody had replaced him, if somebody sought to dupe Sela, it mattered little; Haut had called for their meeting, and so while the chairwoman expected to learn something new, she had no intention of conveying any classified information herself. Turning to the second Breen, she said, "May I ask who your colleague is?"

"This is Trok," Haut said. *"He is an engineer working to restart the development of a quantum slipstream drive for the Typhon Pact."*

Sela regarded Trok. Other than a slight difference in their postures, she could not tell the two uniformed men apart. "I see," she said. "And he has something to report to me?"

"I do," Trok spoke up. *"I have been working on a means not just of constructing a safely functioning slipstream drive, but of creating one easily installable across a wide variety of starship classes. To that end, I have been studying deflector and structural integrity technology—and I think I've found what I need to make this work."*

Sela looked to Haut. "And what is it he needs?" she asked.

Haut turned to Trok. *"Tell her."*

"Let me first say that we have in our possession a Jem'Hadar vessel that crashed within Confederacy territory during the Dominion-Federation War," Trok said. *"We found the ship relatively intact, and we have subsequently repaired its deflector and structural systems in an effort to test them. What we have learned is that we can adapt those Dominion technologies to provide us a sustainable, cross-platform slipstream drive."*

The report surprised and impressed Sela. With the current balance—or *im*balance—of power between the Typhon Pact and the Khitomer Accords, the realization of a quantum slipstream drive for the Pact remained a top priority. After the debacle that ended the Breen's first attempt to develop such a technology, Sela had expected neither such perseverance nor progress from the Confederacy. "That is welcome news," she said. "And so am I to understand that you require a fully functioning Jem'Hadar starship?"

"No," Haut said, to the chairwoman's surprise.

"No," echoed Trok. *"While we have confirmed through exhaustive testing that Jem'Hadar deflectors and structural integrity fields will allow us to produce the quantum slipstream drive, we have so far been unable to replicate those technologies ourselves, and to this point, we have no expectation that we will be able to do so anytime soon."*

"I don't understand," Sela said, though she feared that she actually did. "Are you saying that for every ship in which you install the quantum slipstream drive, you require a separate Jem'Hadar vessel from which to pirate its structural integrity and deflector systems?"

"No," Haut said. *"That would be unworkable in the extreme."*

"I'm glad you see it that way," Sela said, "because short of going to war against the Federation to gain control of the Bajoran wormhole, and then fighting the Dominion, I don't see how we could accomplish that."

"We don't need Jem'Hadar ships from which we can remove their deflector and structural integrity systems," Trok said. *"We need the equipment they employ in the production of those systems so that we can manufacture them ourselves."*

The idea, Sela thought, seemed as absurd as trying to take a fleet of ships from the Jem'Hadar. *But is it?* she asked herself. She recalled Praetor Kamemor's recent proposal to the Typhon Pact, and the likelihood before long of its approval. If Sela could convince the praetor to add another component to her proposal—

Or better still, she thought, *if one of her proconsuls could convince her.*

"I understand what you need—what *we* need," Sela told Haut. "And it just might be possible."

Haut tilted his head slightly to one side, a nonverbal sign that appeared to cross cultural boundaries to indicate surprise. *"Indeed,"* he said. *"As always, I am impressed by your abilities, your confidence, and what I assume must be your ingenuity."*

"And I'm impressed by the progress you've made on the slipstream drive," Sela said. She turned and stepped back onto the transporter pad. "If there's nothing else, Director Haut, I'd like you to return me to my shuttle."

"Of course," Haut said. He retreated to the console, and Trok followed. *"Whenever you are ready, Chairwoman."*

Sela raised her data tablet and touched a control that would again lower her shuttle's shields, which she had programmed to reactivate after she'd beamed over to the Breen vessel. "I am ready now," she told Haut. "But I will contact you again soon."

Haut worked the controls, and once more, the transporter effect took Sela. She materialized back in the aft compartment of the shuttle. After checking to ensure that her command sequence had once more raised the shields, she contacted the cockpit. "Sela to Retind."

"Retind here."

"Commander, make your best possible speed to the *En'Vahj*," Sela ordered.

"Yes, Chairwoman."

Sela unlocked the compartment hatch, went back into the main cabin, and returned to her seat along the aft bulkhead. As she looked through the port at the sight of Terix II receding below, she already set to composing the argument Tomalak would need to make to the praetor. If he could convince Kamemor, then Sela felt confident that Kamemor could convince the other leaders of the Typhon Pact. And the Federation, ever desirous to appear that it sought peace, would doubtless fall in line.

Fools, Sela thought. *Not just the Federation, but* all *of them.* Had she lived, Tal'Aura would not have allowed the Federation's tactical technological advantage to stand. Once she had reunited the divided Empire, she had begun planning to take on the Federation and its Khitomer Accords ally. *And since Kamemor won't do that,* Sela thought with steely resolve, *that duty shifts to the chairwoman of the Tal Shiar.*

And I won't fail Romulus.

At the scheduled time to which all parties had agreed, Federation President Nanietta Bacco walked down an elegant hall toward the Grand Assembly Chamber. By her side walked her chief of staff, Esperanza Piñiero, and behind followed a pair of guards from Bacco's security team. Under normal circumstances, she knew, the head of presidential security would have insisted on additional protectors for her, but the Boslics had been firm in their requirements. When their government offered their world as a neutral site to host a summit between the nations of the Khitomer Accords and those of the Typhon Pact, they stipulated specific conditions in order to minimize any possible threat to the visiting heads of state.

Marching along with her small entourage through the impressive hall, Bacco felt the weight of the moment upon her, the importance of the event manifest in the imposing surroundings. Great fluted columns lined the walkway, and the stone walls and floor had been buffed to a reflective gloss. High overhead, the walls curved outward, capped by a transparent half-cylinder from one end to the other, affording a long view of a stately mountain range. The incorporation of the vista into the architecture emphasized the Boslics' general appreciation for nature.

"Well, if this is a trap," Bacco said to Piñiero, breaking their tense silence, "at least we'll be going in style."

"It's not a trap, Madam President," replied Piñiero. Despite her use of formal address, her tone conveyed her frustration with Bacco for even joking about such a notion.

"It doesn't matter anyway," the president told her. "If we've been duped, if this is all an elaborate ruse designed by the Typhon Pact to assassinate all of us, it's too late now to turn back." Bacco did not think for a moment that the Romulan praetor had requested—had virtually pleaded—for the summit as a means of weakening the Khitomer Accords states, or as the first shot in a massive interstellar war. From a practical standpoint, the Federation maintained technological superiority over the Pact by virtue of Starfleet's quantum slipstream drive. More than that, even in the wake of the loss of Andor, the addition of the Cardassian Union and the Ferengi Alliance to the Accords reinforced both the size and strength of the military force available to defend the UFP and its allies.

On a less strategic note, but perhaps of greater importance, the president believed that Gell Kamemor genuinely wanted peace. After she had succeeded to the praetorship of the freshly reunited Romulan Star Empire sixteen months earlier, Kamemor's background of diplomacy and public service had served as a beacon of hope for Nan Bacco. That hope faded several months later when a Romulan starship employing a new, advanced cloak aided in the theft of the quantum slipstream drive schematics from Utopia Planitia. Since that time, though, and despite Starfleet's own successful covert operation to destroy the Pact's slipstream prototype, the praetor had taken no other provocative action, not even engaging in any bellicose rhetoric.

But such had not been the case with other members of the Typhon Pact. The Tholians had worked to drive a wedge between the Federation and one of its founding members, leading directly to Andor's secession. The Tzenkethi, too, had continued to harass several of the UFP populations relocated after the Borg invasion to planets near Coalition space, to the point where Starfleet had needed to intervene. For the previous two months, the Federation had detained thirty-five members of the Tzenkethi military who had attacked an Argelian freighter carrying humanitarian aid through unclaimed space—and on which Captain Picard had sprung his own trap. Despite repeated efforts to open a dialogue with the Coalition about the release of the soldiers, the autarch and the Tzelnira had refused even to talk to Bacco or her representatives. All of which, to Bacco's way of thinking, generated a real need for a meaningful summit, but also confused her about the aims of the Typhon Pact as a whole.

"It might be too late for us to avoid a trap," Piñiero said, "but at least *I* won't be the target."

"Nonsense," Bacco said at once. "You play an absolutely vital role in our government. I'll make sure the Typhon Pact knows that."

"Thank you, Madam President," Piñiero said. "You're too kind."

As they approached the end of the corridor, a massive block, made of the same polished stone as the floor and walls, glided open. Initially, it appeared to Bacco as though the doorway led to the outside, but when she passed through it, she saw differently. Before her, a wide, shallow staircase—one of several such sets of steps—descended between raked sections of empty seats, down to an open space dominated by a large, semicircular table. Glancing quickly around, she saw that half of the round chamber echoed the interior design of the corridor through which they had just passed: tall, grooved columns rimmed walls of gleaming stone. But the walls and ceiling in the other half of the chamber, beyond the conference table, had been constructed of a transparent material so clear that it seemed as though the neighboring landscape reached directly into the room. Just off to one side and slightly angled with respect to Bacco's point of view, a waterfall plunged perhaps a hundred and fifty meters to a passing river, throwing up a delicate mist and providing a spectacular backdrop.

"Wow," Piñiero said in a whisper.

"Wow is right," Bacco agreed, just as quietly. "Makes me think we need to take a field trip the next time the Federation Council is in session."

Peering down at the conference table, the president saw that several other dignitaries had already arrived. Along the left arc of the table sat the Cardassian and Ferengi leaders, Castellan Rakena Garan and Grand Nagus Rom, while along the right arc sat their Breen and Gorn counterparts, Domo Brex and Imperator Sozzerozs. One of the three members of the Boslic Triumvirate, Letix Kortaj, stood at the center of the table's diameter, her back to those already assembled, and apparently waiting to greet the other delegates as they arrived.

Bacco turned and nodded to her two presidential guards, who responded in kind. As one of the conditions for hosting the summit, the Boslics had demanded that all security officers remain just inside one of the five entrances to the Grand Assembly Chamber. While the Boslics did not confiscate any energy weapons, they made it clear that a dampening field surrounding the entire government complex housing the chamber rendered such arms useless. Looking around again, Bacco saw other security duos at the heads of the other staircases, as well as a number of Boslic personnel. To Piñiero, the president said sotto voce, "Wish me luck."

"I wish us *all* luck," Piñiero murmured.

Bacco started down the stairs, knowing that Piñiero would follow. The president saw that four other individuals sat in the first row of seats, facing the conference table. She assumed, based on their species and the Boslics' allowance of a single advisor per head of state, that they each played the same role for their government that Piñiero did for the Federation.

As Bacco reached the floor of the chamber, Piñiero moved off to the side and took a seat beside the other advisors. Triumvir Kortaj stepped forward and bowed her head, which the president recognized as a Boslic sign of respect. Characteristic of her people, smooth but pronounced ridges angled up from the bridge of Kortaj's nose and above her eyes. Between them, three grooves, joined at their bottom ends like an arrow pointing downward, carved out a distinctive biological feature in the flesh of her forehead. Her eyes flashed an electric red, which precisely matched the color of her long, flowing hair.

"President Bacco, I am Triumvir Letix Kortaj," she said. "On behalf of the Boslic government and its people, I welcome you to our world, to our capital, and to our Grand Assembly Chamber."

"Thank you, Triumvir Kortaj," Bacco said. "On behalf of the government and people of the United Federation of Planets, I thank you for your generosity in agreeing to host this summit."

Kortaj turned and walked toward the center of the straight side of the table, across from the gathered dignitaries, and Bacco followed. "I'm sure that, even if you've never met them in person, you know all of your fellow officials," the triumvir said. "I thought I'd wait until all of you are present before I—"

A loud report rang out from behind and above Bacco. She spun around and looked to the upper part of the chamber, scanning the doors for the source of the sound. At the head of a staircase to the left, she saw the burly form of Martok, chancellor of the Klingon Empire, apparently alone. He wore full Klingon regalia: a long, sweeping robe over dark pants and tunic; high, black boots; and twin silver baldrics that crossed over his chest. "Peace or war?" he bellowed, his deep, booming voice easily filling the large space. "Let's make up our minds and be done talking." He lifted a thick, gnarled cane in one hand and brought it down on the floor, sending a second bang resounding through the chamber.

Kortaj immediately started toward the stairs, but then peered back at Bacco for a moment. "If you would please have a seat," the triumvir said, pointing toward the side of the conference table at which Garan and Rom sat. Bacco moved in that direction, but then stopped to watch as Kortaj addressed the Klingon leader.

"Chancellor Martok," she said, bowing her head toward him, and she repeated the words with which she had greeted Bacco.

Martok tramped down the stairs, swinging his cane out before him and bringing it down noisily on each successive step. When he reached the floor of the chamber and faced Kortaj, he lowered his voice to a respectful tone. "Triumvir Kortaj," he said, "I thank you for the invitation to your world. Your people are honorable and generous." He walked past the Boslic and regarded the Breen and Gorn leaders. "But as for these *petaQ,* I'm not so sure."

A cumbersome silence rose in the chamber. Bacco waited, fighting the urge to explain away the chancellor's behavior. She had spent enough time working with him through the years to recognize Martok's harsh sense of humor, as well as the way he often utilized it to measure his opponents. Though she wanted to speak up and somehow make this plain to Brex and Sozzerozs, she realized that she risked not only offending the chancellor, but also demonstrating that she believed his behavior inappropriate and truly insulting, thus signaling to the Typhon Pact dignitaries that they should feel affronted.

Before anybody could say anything else, a hand came down on the end of Martok's cane. The thick, twisted object resembled a walking stick less than it did a petrified tree branch. The chancellor turned slowly to stare at Kortaj's hand, and then at the triumvir herself.

"Chancellor Martok," she said, "I'm afraid that a condition of my government hosting this summit is that no weapons of any kind are permitted in the Grand Assembly Chamber."

At first, Martok said nothing, and Bacco feared that he might challenge the triumvir's authority. As she considered how she might defuse the situation, though, he said, "A weapon?" He laughed, a short, loud bark. "This is part of the price I have paid for a lifetime of glorious battles. I am merely—" He paused, surely to set up what he would consider another punch line. "—a tired, wounded old man."

Kortaj looked Martok in the eye, her hand still on his cane. "Regardless," she said, "I must impound this." She pulled at the cane, with which, Bacco did not doubt, the chancellor could beat senseless everyone present. For a long moment, Martok held on to his cane, but then finally he loosened his grip. "Thank you, Chancellor," Kortaj said. "Now if you and President Bacco would have a seat alongside your allies."

Only then did Bacco look around at Garan and Rom, Brex and Sozzerozs, to see how they had reacted to Martok's entrance. The grand nagus sat with his mouth hanging open, clearly stunned, while the castellan sat calmly beside him. Bacco could not read the domo in his Breen armor, but he remained in his chair. Of all those present, only the imperator had risen to his feet. The president noted Sozzerozs's posture, the tension in his impressive Gorn musculature, and she wondered how close Martok's brashness had come to instigating an interstellar incident even before the summit had begun.

As Bacco and Martok took their places at the conference table, she noticed the chancellor unburdened by even the slightest hint of a limp. Then the president spied another head of state: Praetor Gell Kamemor stood at the top of the central set of stairs, gazing with an air of quiet dignity toward the chamber floor. Two Romulan guards had already stepped aside and taken up positions along the wall behind her. Proconsul Tomalak accompanied her. Bacco wondered how long she had been standing there, and whether she had witnessed any of Martok's outburst.

A Boslic guard quickly came down a different set of steps

and collected Martok's cane from Kortaj, which he quickly carried out of the room. Once he had, the Romulan praetor strode down to the chamber floor, the proconsul trailing behind her. At the base of the stairs, Tomalak moved to the first row of seats with the other advisors, while Kortaj again offered her official greeting, this time to the praetor. Once Kamemor had made her way over to Brex and Sozzerozs, the triumvir moved to the middle of the table, and looking across it, spoke to all of the visitors to her world.

"The Triumvirate of Cort," she said, giving the official title of the three-person executive panel that ruled the Boslics' government, as well as the name of their planet, "our Congress, and our people are honored to host this historic summit. We feel particularly privileged to assist in such vital efforts to bring peace and stability to both the Alpha and Beta Quadrants."

A century ago, Bacco knew, the Romulans had occupied Cort for ten years. Although the Boslics eventually repelled the invaders, they lived under the continued fear that they would again have to face the Empire or some other aggressor. The cultural memories and collective fears of the Boslic people made their resistance to a military alliance—with the Federation or any other nation—all the more impressive. They unwaveringly maintained their independence and neutrality even in the face of the major strategic value of their world's location in space.

As Kortaj went on, Bacco wondered why the triumvir had begun to welcome the delegates as a group when clearly three had yet to arrive: the Kinshaya pontifex maxima, one of the Tholian high magistrates, and the Tzenkethi autarch. The president looked to her allies, who also seemed confused by the seemingly premature start of the summit. Bacco waited for Kortaj to pause so that she might ask about the missing dignitaries, but then the triumvir addressed the matter.

"As I'm sure you have noticed," she said, peering directly at the heads of state representing the nations of the Khitomer Accords, "several leaders from the Typhon Pact have not arrived. I will ask Praetor Kamemor to speak to this." Kortaj sat down, and Kamemor stood up.

"Before I say anything else, I would like to thank everyone here today for their willing participation in this summit," she said. "It is my firm belief that initiating a dialogue among our worlds is not just a reasonable way to ensure the safety of all our peoples, but the *only* way."

Bacco listened to the praetor's words, agreed with them, and believed that Kamemor meant what she said. Ever since the Ferengi Alliance and the Cardassian Union had allied with the Federation and the Klingons, the praetor had sought a dialogue with the president and the other Khitomer Accords leaders. Through former Federation ambassador Spock, Kamemor sent word to Bacco that she wished to defuse the seemingly continual escalation of tensions in the Alpha and Beta Quadrants. The two heads of state exchanged a number of messages in the ensuing months, until the praetor proposed a summit of all the Khitomer Accords and Typhon Pact leaders, advocating that they come together to find a method of cementing a lasting peace. It required some time for all the involved parties to agree to the meeting, and even longer to find a mutually acceptable place and time for the unprecedented conference.

"I regret that because of certain events," Kamemor continued, "several of my fellow leaders within the Typhon Pact have chosen not to participate at this time."

"And how are we to 'ensure the safety of all our peoples,'" Castellan Garan said, "if not all parties agree to do so?" Bacco saw the set of the Cardassian's jaw, and knew that the absence of the three Typhon Pact leaders both troubled and angered her—as it did Bacco herself.

Chancellor Martok rose, his chair pushing back noisily on the stone floor, his body language suggesting to the president that he intended to leave at once. "It is unfortunate," he said, "that you did not elect to inform us of this development *before* we made the long journeys from our homeworlds."

"Please, please," Kamemor said, holding the palms of her hands up to the Khitomer Accords representatives. "While the Kinshaya, the Tholians, and the Tzenkethi have decided not to attend this summit, they have consented to abide by whatever agreements we can negotiate here."

"You have their proxies, then?" asked Grand Nagus Rom.

"In essence, I do," Kamemor said.

Bacco peered up at Martok, who had neither left the table nor sat back down. Then she posed a question of her own. "May I ask to what events you refer when you offer them as the reasons for the other Typhon Pact leaders opting to stay away from this summit?"

"Of course," Kamemor said. "With respect to the Holy Order of the Kinshaya, while the pontifex maxima initially agreed to take part, the Episcopate pressured her not to involve herself in such a categorically secular, and therefore 'unholy,' assembly."

Martok grumbled, apparently at just the mention of the Kinshaya. The Klingons had clashed with them repeatedly for many decades, and the Order evidently remained a problem for the Empire. Although the Federation had encountered the Kinshaya infrequently and knew little about them, Bacco understood the extreme religiosity of their culture, lending credence to the praetor's explanation.

Kamemor ignored Martok's exclamation. "The Tholian Assembly informed me that they believed their presence at the summit would prove counterproductive," she said. "They attributed this to their developing relationship with the people of Andor, and the Tholians' inadvertent role in the Andorians' secession from the Federation."

Bacco choked back a pointed response of her own at the praetor's use of the word *inadvertent*. The Tholians had acted surreptitiously in involving themselves in the search for a solution to the reproductive crisis facing the Andorian people. They also clearly calculated the timing of their revelation that they had provided critical data to Andorian scientists that the Federation had not, which then led directly to Andor's secession.

"And the Tzenkethi refuse to speak with the Federation as long as it holds their citizens captive," Kamemor finished. She sat down again, leaving Martok the only one at the table still standing.

Bacco joined him. With the Klingon chancellor apparently still on the cusp of leaving, and the summit already stumbling along even before it had really begun, she felt that she needed to say something—to *do* something. Looking to Martok, she said, "Chancellor, if I may?" Martok appeared to measure her for a second, then took his seat, granting her the floor. Bacco peered across the length of the table. "Praetor Kamemor," she said, deciding in that moment to take an action that she had mulled for a while, but that her advisors had petitioned against taking. "In the spirit of goodwill, and in an effort to foster positive relationships among all the worlds of the Khitomer Accords and the Typhon Pact, I will release the members of the Tzenkethi military currently in Federation custody. I take this action unilaterally, and without condition." She turned to the first row of seats in the gallery. "Esperanza, would you please see to it at once?"

Although the president's instruction probably surprised her chief of staff, Bacco also knew that Piñiero would do as she'd been asked. "Yes, Madam President," she said. She immediately rose and headed back up the nearest stairs toward one of the chamber's exits.

Bacco peered back over at the three Typhon Pact leaders. "I do this despite recorded evidence that the Tzenkethi harrier crews wantonly attacked a freighter bringing medicine, food, and infrastructural equipment to a displaced population in need," she said. "But I am releasing the prisoners without reservation because I recognize that one of us must take a first step toward peace if we are ever to reach that destination. I feel that Praetor Kamemor has opened the door for all of us, and I have just stepped through that door. I welcome all of you—" Bacco looked around to include Martok, Garan, and Rom. "—to join me."

The president sat down again. For several seconds, nobody spoke. Finally, the Gorn imperator broke the quiet with a series of hisses, which Bacco's universal translator interpreted into Federation Standard. "Most impressive, Madam President," Sozzerozs said. "I cannot speak for the Tzenkethi, but for myself and for my people, I thank you." Bacco acknowledged the imperator with a nod.

"Now then," said Triumvir Kortaj, "let us commence as we had planned, with opening statements from each of you." She looked to Bacco's end of the table. "Castellan Garan, would you please start?"

The Cardassian rose and gazed around at both her allies and adversaries. As she started to speak, Bacco realized that the group assembled had already accomplished something. Despite all that had been said already, as well as the unwillingness of the Kinshaya, Tholians, and Tzenkethi to contribute directly to the gathering, Kamemor and Bacco and the others had somehow found their way past those obstacles.

To the president's great satisfaction, the summit had truly begun.

Gell Kamemor walked through the Boslic government complex to the Grand Assembly Chamber, where she made her way down the central stairs and back to the conference table. Most of the heads of state had already returned from their break, she saw, among them Domo Brex and Grand Nagus Rom, who huddled together and spoke animatedly with each other. Each held up his own data tablet for the other to see, occasionally pointing at one of the displays.

As the praetor sat down, she realized that she felt both exhausted and invigorated. Through nearly four full days of talks that had included conversations, questions, debates, and arguments, she counted the summit as an unqualified success. At times, words had grown heated and tempers had risen, but not one of the dignitaries had abandoned the proceedings, nor even threatened to do so—not even the ever-combustible Klingon chancellor.

During the course of the gathering, several trade agreements had been reached, but more than anything, issues long the province of military brinkmanship—or worse, of actual military action—had become subjects for discussion. The parties made little progress on matters such as the martial advantage that quantum slipstream drive provided the Federation. Imperator Sozzerozs raised a concern about the UFP and the Klingon Empire increasing the *im*balance of power by allying with the Cardassians and the Ferengi, while President Bacco objected to the Tholians' part in doing the reverse by helping drive the Andorians to secede.

Despite the lack of resolution in such areas, though, Kamemor welcomed the new dialogues, believing them an essential prologue to a durable peace. She also appreciated the unselfish action taken by President Bacco in releasing the Tzenkethi raiders, without making any demands of the Coalition in return. Although Kamemor had not heard from the autarch during the summit, she had contacted Chairwoman Sela, who in turn checked with one of the Tal Shiar operatives stationed within the Federation; the agent confirmed the release of the Tzenkethi harrier crews from UFP custody.

The idea of Tal Shiar personnel posted secretly on other worlds concerned Kamemor. She appreciated the efficacy, even the necessity, of placing undercover observers among the adversaries of the Empire, but she also understood the potential for diplomatic disaster, which could readily lead to military engagement. Because of the Tal Shiar's long record of abuses, as well as Sela's own personal history of antipathy toward the Federation, Kamemor had kept a watchful eye on the chairwoman. Thus far, Sela had demonstrated no propensity for plotting against the UFP, or for supporting anti-UFP sentiment. The chairwoman had even unmasked her own predecessor, as well as the previous praetor, as the perpetrators of the deadly theft of the slipstream drive plans from Utopia Planitia. More recently, Sela had rescued and then released the crew of a lost Starfleet vessel.

Castellan Garan, the only dignitary not yet back at the table in the Grand Assembly Chamber, appeared at the top of one of the sets of stairs. As she paced down toward the chamber floor, Kamemor saw Grand Nagus Rom pull a small handheld device from within his tailored, olive-colored jacket. Amazed, the praetor watched as Brex accepted a stylus from Rom and affixed his signature to the device. When the castellan resumed her place at the conference table, Rom announced that he and Brex had agreed in principle to a redrawing of the borders between the Ferengi Alliance and the Breen Confederacy, potentially settling a conflict of considerable duration.

Everyone present met the news with muted but seemingly authentic enthusiasm. With the summit nearing its natural conclusion, Kamemor judged the moment right for her to introduce the two proposals that she had brought with her. After considering input from Proconsuls Ventel and Tomalak, and conferring with the Imperial Senate, the praetor had decided on two ideas that she believed would promote familiarity and trust generally between the Typhon Pact worlds and those of the Khitomer Accords, and specifically between the Romulan Star Empire and the United Federation of Planets. If the two alliances wanted to establish amity and make it endure, there could be no better start than between the largest, most powerful nations among them.

"In the same spirit of cooperation that Domo Brex and Grand Nagus Rom have just demonstrated," she said, "I would like to suggest not an adjustment of borders, but an opening of them." Kamemor saw that she had everybody's attention, including that of Brex and Sozzerozs, with whom she had not previously shared her intentions. "Because trade can entwine interests and encourage closer relations, I would like to advocate that the nations of the Khitomer Accords and the Typhon Pact allow each other's civilian vessels to traverse one of their major trade routes."

Skeptical expressions greeted Kamemor, including one on the face of the Cardassian castellan. "While I can see how, under the best circumstances, such a loosening of borders could spur improved relations," Garan said, "I can also see it leading to even more confrontations."

"Are you espousing a practice that would see Kinshaya ships in Klingon space?" President Bacco asked. "Tzenkethi ships in Federation space? Federation ships in Tholian space?"

"Actually, I am," Kamemor said. "Not all at once, and not everywhere. But I submit that we cannot effectively put aside our differences, that we cannot become allies—even *friends*—without exposing our cultures to each other. I am not saying that we should throw open every border, that all states should send ships to every sector of the Alpha and Beta Quadrants. We can limit our exposure to each other by selecting individual areas of space in which to trade."

"Ferenginar welcomes all vessels of commerce," declared the Grand Nagus.

"That would be a beginning," Kamemor said, "though I would at the outset choose a region of space with greater diversity, such as the Rigel Corridor."

"The Rigel Corridor does host a wide diversity of cultures," said Bacco, "but it is also the heaviest traveled trade and passenger route within the Federation. I'm not sure that the sudden influx of Tholian and Tzenkethi vessels at this time would be readily and peacefully accepted."

Kamemor nodded her head in understanding. Proconsul Tomalak, who had first recommended using civilian ships along the trade routes, had also predicted the Federation president's reaction to doing so in the UFP's most populous areas. He had therefore offered another suggestion. "Perhaps a less crowded trade route then," Kamemor said. "An area such as the Bajoran Sector."

Castellan Garan looked at President Bacco. "Most of the traffic around Bajor and even Cardassia these days comes and goes through the wormhole," said Garan. "You could allow Typhon Pact freighters and trading ships into the sector and into the Gamma Quadrant."

Bacco seemed to consider the possibility. "There could be no military vessels," she finally said. "And the civilian ships could not be armed other than for basic protection."

"I imagined that they would have to consent to random inspections as well," Kamemor said.

"And what about you, Praetor?" Martok asked. "What region of Romulan space would you open to Klingon traders?"

"Not Romulan space," said Rom. "Typhon Pact space."

"What do you mean, 'Typhon Pact space'?" asked Brex.

"The Typhon Expanse," Rom said. "As far as I know, it's a

region of space only lightly explored by the Klingons, the Romulans, and the Federation, primarily because of several conflicts that have taken place there. But trade routes there could be opened back up to each of those worlds."

"'Opened *back* up'?" Sozzerozs asked.

"Until the Typhon Pact decided to build a starbase there and militarize the region," Rom explained, "the Ferengi Alliance had established numerous shipping lanes through it."

The praetor turned to Brex and Sozzerozs. Kamemor had intended to offer the Devoras Division, an area within Romulan space near both the United Federation of Planets and the Klingon Empire, but the Typhon Expanse made more sense, considering its familiarity to the Ferengi. She saw no objection from either the domo or the imperator. "The Typhon Expanse would be acceptable," she said.

"We would need to work out the details, of course," Garan said. "As President Bacco already indicated, there would have to be limits on vessels' armaments, prescribed procedures, inspections, a timeframe."

"We would have to establish a method and schedule for reviewing the status of the program," Martok added.

"And a mutually acceptable means of mediating any disputes that might arise," said Brex.

Suddenly, several voices spoke at once across the table as separate conversations started. To her great satisfaction, Kamemor perceived widespread interest in her idea. She allowed the multiple dialogues to continue for several moments, but she wanted to capitalize on the others' eager acceptance of her suggestion. She stood from her chair and waited as voices trailed off and faces turned toward her.

Into the hush that followed, she said, "I have a second proposal. While we seek to demystify our people for one another, while we seek to acquaint them so that they might better understand one another, we cannot do so only among the civilian population. The Romulan Imperial Fleet, the Klingon Defense Force, Starfleet, the Breen Militia, and all the other military forces contain sizable numbers of our citizens. And since they have been at the forefront of our armed conflicts, they most especially need to learn to accept the people whom they have so often called *enemy*."

"You can't be saying that you want to allow the starships of the Typhon Pact states to travel within Khitomer Accords territory," said Martok, an expression of incredulity on his face.

"No," Kamemor said. "I have no desire to invite tension and conflict. I'm suggesting something smaller, something that would not jeopardize the inhabitants of either political alliance." The praetor saw expectant looks around the table as the dignitaries waited for her to explain herself, but then awareness seemed to come to the Federation president.

"Exploration," Bacco said simply.

"Yes," said Kamemor. "A joint mission of exploration, well beyond the borders of the Typhon Pact and the Khitomer Accords."

Once again, the people around the table looked to each other, as if they might find answers in one another's eyes. Finally, Martok spoke. He said words that Kamemor wanted to hear, offering a sentiment that she hoped the others shared.

"It could work."

June 2383

16

The fusion core pulsed with power. Though noticeably cold, the entire space hummed with energy, as if charged, like the air before a planetside electrical storm. In the center of the vertical conduit—one of six that attached above to the midcore power-transfer hub of Deep Space 9—an immense, brilliant column of harnessed force flowed upward, carrying the output of one of the four fully functioning reactors to the rest of the space station.

Security Chief Jefferson Blackmer paced around the metallic mesh walkway that circled the coruscating pillar of energy, headed for the ladder that would take him down to the reactor itself. He looked everywhere about him, not allowing his gaze to dart, but trying to take in every surface. In the bulkheads along the round walkway, as with the bulkheads enclosing all twenty-five levels above the reactor, few control panels or access plates interrupted the many rows of sensors that kept a meticulous watch on the flood of magnetically contained power. The security officer thought—and hoped—that he would be able to distinguish anything out of place.

Blackmer rarely visited the lower core, although circumstances had brought him down there just two days before. He still felt relatively new to DS9, having transferred from the *Perseverance* less than a year earlier. He had replaced Lieutenant Commander Evik Nath, a middle-aged Bajoran whose death from natural causes clearly shocked and saddened the crew and residents of the station. Perhaps because Evik had been so well liked and so highly regarded—Blackmer still heard the man's name fondly mentioned around DS9—the reception of the new security chief had trended toward the cool side. In particular, while Captain Ro treated him professionally, she also plainly resisted establishing the sort of easy familiarity she demonstrated with Colonel Cenn and Lieutenant Tenmei and other crew members. After ten months' active duty on the station, Blackmer had essentially given up attempting to gain the friendship of his commanding officer, settling instead for her respect and a utilitarian working relationship.

When he'd finished inspecting the grid on which he stood, Blackmer swung onto the ladder and climbed down to the reactor chamber. As he understood it, Deep Space 9's original lower core had been jettisoned and destroyed some years earlier, then replaced with the core of an abandoned Cardassian station. The half-dozen energized-plasma generators had been manufactured more than three decades earlier. Over the course of the seven or so years since the second core had been installed, Starfleet engineers maintained and upgraded the reactors, but only four of the complex mechanisms continued in regular use. The other two reactors remained off line, though the engineering staff sporadically coaxed them into service to ensure that they could serve as functional backups during repair cycles or in the case of an emergency. Since DS9 did not operate as an ore-processing facility—one of the major uses for which the Cardassians had originally constructed the station—the four reactors provided more than sufficient power.

Blackmer moved slowly about the huge compartment at the base of the lower core. The generators towered above him as he visually scanned the area. His flesh prickled, a sensation like a colony of insects swarming over his body. He wanted to leave, but since he hadn't finished what he'd gone there to do, he didn't think that he should.

The security chief didn't know for precisely what he searched, but he understood how to categorize it: something left behind. *A tool, a tricorder, a phaser . . . something.* He acted out of concern and even fear, because he'd learned long ago to trust his instincts. In his position, he could rely on little else.

As Blackmer studied one of the massive reactors, he wondered about the methods employed to secure the lower core. Deflector shields and a specially designed hull protected the station against unauthorized transport from beyond its confines, but had measures been taken to ensure that nobody could beam in to the reactor compartment from within DS9? He didn't

know with certainty—though he recognized that he should—
but he also doubted it, as such a scheme would compromise the
safety of Starfleet personnel. The engineering team did not continuously crew the lower core during the normal operation of the
generators, but emergency transport protocols would still need
to be available in the event of a mishap.

*Except that the power flow probably inhibits beaming in or out
anyway,* the security chief realized. Again, he didn't know, but
he should.

A plate on the nearest reactor identified it as reactor three.
Around its circumference, numbers and symbols paraded across
a host of display screens. Blackmer studied them for a moment,
not really searching for anything out of the ordinary, as he likely
wouldn't have discerned an abnormality even if he saw one. He
also knew that any problems with the reactors, or any alterations
to their performance, would trigger warnings in the operations
center.

Taking a few steps back, Blackmer peered beneath the
inward curve of the generator's base. He moved slowly around
it until he returned to where he'd started. Finding nothing that
caught his attention, he moved on.

In the same way, Blackmer examined each of the reactors,
including four and six, despite their nonoperational status.
Doing so, he circumnavigated the compartment. Choosing caution over expedience, the security chief then made a second circuit, examining not the generators, but the workstations that
lined the bulkheads. Sometimes, when he spotted access panels,
he pulled them off and peered inside. He felt like a blind man
searching for color.

Once he returned to reactor three a second time, Blackmer
stopped. His eyelids had grown heavy, notwithstanding the
great vibratory drone that enveloped him. He doubted himself, wondering just how observant he'd been on his last circuit
around the compartment. More than that, he had yet to scale the
power-transfer conduits for four of the reactors so that he could
subject those spaces to his scrutiny.

With fatigue fast washing over him, he moved to the nearest

companel. He raised a hand and jabbed at it, bringing it to life. "Computer, what time is it?"

"The time is zero-one-twenty-seven hours," said the familiar, feminine voice of the station's primary processor.

Great, Blackmer thought. *Not just after midnight, but* well *after.* He'd spent more than two and a half hours roaming through the lower core. He'd intended only to make a cursory pass through the reactor deck, had even planned on a quick stop by Quark's afterward. Obviously, he'd gotten caught up in a search that had quickly become painstaking, and he'd lost track of the hour.

No time to visit Quark's now, he thought. He'd hoped to visit the bar before turning in because he would have little opportunity to do so after tonight, at least in the near term. With preparations continuing in earnest for the arrival of the Typhon Pact vessels later in the week, Blackmer would need to rise early and work long hours in the coming days.

Maybe just a quick stroll on the Promenade, he thought, *if only to catch a fleeting glimpse of Treir's smile.* Then, alone in the lower core, Blackmer shook his head and chuckled at himself. He grasped the scope of his foolishness, given what he'd come to Deep Space 9 to accomplish. Additionally, he had to admit that Treir had shown no interest in his advances. Or rather, she responded to his flirtations in the same way that she did with everyone else who wooed her, men and women alike: with a flip of the red hair she'd grown long, with a smile, a laugh, a stroke of one hand along the curve of her hip. Whatever game anybody played with her, she played it right back, and she always appeared to emerge victorious—usually netting nothing more than an increased tip, as best the security chief could tell, but she had a gift for rebuffing admirers without turning them into disgruntled customers. But even though Treir seemed to enjoy taking on the role of coquette, Blackmer saw past that, perceiving a strong personality and fierce intellect behind her dancing eyes and radiant green skin. When he spoke with her, she often—

Blackmer didn't know if he heard some foreign sound amid the constant rumble of the lower core, or if maybe he saw the flicker of a reflection on the companel screen. Regardless, he all at once knew that somebody else had entered the reactor compartment and stood behind him. He knew it even before he turned and saw a phaser leveled in his direction.

Ro Laren woke with a start. Pushing herself up in bed, she heard a voice, but it sounded unintelligible, as though muffled or far away. Fully asleep just a moment before, her foggy mind could not make sense of the words. As she worked to rouse herself, she waited, expecting that the message would be repeated. It was.

After the light tones that signaled the opening of a communications channel, a voice said, *"Ops to Captain Ro."*

She recognized the speaker as Lieutenant Aleco Vel, the officer on duty in ops during the delta shift. "Ro here," she said. Her voice sounded gravelly, and she quietly cleared her throat. "Go ahead."

"Captain, this is Lieutenant Aleco," he said. *"We've got an unscheduled entry into the reactor core."*

Unscheduled, Ro thought. *Not unauthorized.* Which likely meant that one of the engineering crew had decided to conduct maintenance after hours. "Is there a problem?" she asked. "I've stressed to the crew that, whenever possible, they should take the initiative, rather than just being reactive. That's especially the case, considering who we'll be seeing by the end of the week."

"Captain," said Aleco slowly, as though reluctant to divulge something that he knew he must. *"It's Chief Blackmer."*

Blackmer! Ro threw aside the bedclothes and bounded from atop her mattress. She'd slept in her underwear, and so she reached at once for the uniform she'd worn the previous day, which lay draped across the back of a comfortable chair in the corner. "Did he just enter the reactor core now?"

"No, we only found out about it now," Aleco said. *"But it appears that he's been there for at least an hour, maybe longer. The reactor compartment was empty, and we think he overrode the security seal. We wouldn't have even known except that Lieutenant Merimark was running diagnostics on the reactors and happened to notice a slight increase in the power usage to cool the compart-*

ment. That only happens when there are personnel there, and since there was nothing on the schedule, the lieutenant mentioned it. The computer confirmed the chief's identity. We thought you'd want to know."

Because you're aware that I don't completely trust our new chief of security, Ro thought. Although she'd never said anything of the kind to her crew, she also knew that sometimes she projected her apprehensions about Blackmer.

After stepping into her uniform pants, she pulled her red, command-division undershirt over her head. "Have two armed security officers meet me outside the main entrance to the lower core," she said. "Make sure nobody contacts Mister Blackmer before we get there." She declined to refer to him as *lieutenant commander* or *chief,* rejecting the esteem inherent in the use of his Starfleet rank or DS9 position.

"Yes, Captain," Aleco said.

"Ro out." She grabbed the gray-shouldered overshirt of her uniform and raced from her bedroom, across the living area of her quarters, and out into the corridor. Only when she'd entered a lift and specified her destination did she finish donning her official captain's attire.

As the cab accelerated through the habitat ring on its way to the lower core, Ro worried about the newest addition to her senior staff, and about what he might be doing in the reactor compartment. Ever since he'd first arrived at Deep Space 9, she'd felt uncertain about him. She understood that, at least initially, her misgivings probably resulted from the sudden and not entirely explicable death of Evik Nath. But even as the crew dealt with the upsetting loss of their colleague and friend, Ro continued to feel unsettled about Blackmer. She couldn't isolate the source of her concern, and so she allowed for the possibility that Evik's abrupt death persisted in coloring her estimation of his replacement.

Ro had said nothing about her unease to anyone—least of all to Blackmer himself. Instead, she waited to get to know him better, and for her qualms about him to pass. When that didn't happen, she set about researching his service record. He'd had a middle-of-the-pack ranking at Starfleet Academy, choosing early on in his training to pursue the path of command, but before too long getting shunted over to security. Upon his graduation, Starfleet assigned him to Starbase 189, where he served for five years before being sent to Helaspont Station along the Tzenkethi border for another five-year stretch. During those periods, Blackmer received generally positive performance reviews, and he made steady, if unspectacular, progress up through the security ranks. He also received an occasional demerit along the way, mostly attributed by his senior officers to his being in the wrong place at the wrong time, but that—if Ro understood the subtext of some of the reports—seemed to point to something else going on, though she could not tell what.

Well, it seems like he's in the wrong place at the wrong time right now, she thought. The lift eased to a stop, then began to descend.

After Blackmer's postings on Starbase 189 and Helaspont Station, Starfleet detailed him to a series of starships—*Trieste, Nova, Sarek, Bellerophon, Perseverance*—on each of which he generally stayed for a year or two. Aboard *Perseverance,* he achieved the rank of lieutenant commander and the position of security chief, but soon after, when the same responsibility opened up on Deep Space 9, he immediately requested a transfer to the station.

Why? Ro wanted to know. Why would Blackmer finally reach one of the highest levels of his profession in one place, then almost at once leave there for another assignment? *Maybe there's an understandable reason, a perfectly* innocent *explanation,* she told herself. But that still wouldn't explain why his presence on DS9 vexed her.

"Helaspont Station," Ro said aloud in the empty cab. She kept going back to Blackmer's lengthy duty along the edge of Tzenkethi space. Two ideas occurred to her. Both seemed absurd, but particularly the first: the notion of a Starfleet officer allying—or even sympathizing—with a difficult, belligerent adversary of the Federation enough for him to take direct action against the UFP. She found it only marginally more believable that somebody in Starfleet could develop such a hatred of a Federation enemy that he would take independent action against that enemy. With the first wave of civilian vessels due to arrive at the station in just a few days, though, Ro could not afford to ignore her intuition.

The lift glided to a halt, and a pair of doors parted to reveal security officers Cardok and Hava, both of whom had served directly under Ro when she'd been the station's chief of security. They stood in a small antechamber outside the lower core, a large blast door closed behind them. Both carried phasers in their raised hands, and Cardok consulted a tricorder.

Ro exited the lift. "He's still in there?" she asked.

"Yes, sir," Cardok said. "We've verified that he overrode the security seal at twenty-five-forty-six hours." His tone sounded tentative.

"Do you have an issue, Lieutenant?" Ro asked sharply. She peered over at Hava, who also seemed to carry an air of reluctance about him, and then back at Cardok.

"No, Captain," said the Benzite officer. "But this—" He waved his tricorder toward the blast door. "—is Chief Blackmer. What's he done?"

Ro's grip on the certainty with which she had rushed from her cabin down to the lower core loosened. "Maybe nothing more than forgetting to properly schedule a security check down here," she said. Then, softening her stance even more, she added, "*Probably* nothing more than that. But we're going to have Romulans and Gorn and Breen on this station in just a few days, and possibly even Tzenkethi and Tholians, so we can't take any chances when even the slightest deviation from procedure occurs. Understood?"

"Yes, sir," Cardok said, with no hesitancy.

Ro looked to the other guard. "Lieutenant Hava?"

"Understood, sir." Hava held out his other hand and offered the captain a phaser of her own.

Ro took the weapon, confirmed its stun setting, and switched off its safety. Then she turned and moved over to where a smaller hatch stood closed within the larger blast door. "Is it locked?"

Cardok studied his tricorder. "Yes, sir, but the security panel doesn't appear to have been reprogrammed. Any one of us should be able to override the seal."

Ro nodded. "Is he armed?" she asked.

"Chief Blackmer has a standard-issue phaser," the lieutenant said, without having to consult his tricorder. Then he did peer at the device's display, motioned to the hatch, and made a circling motion with his arm until he indicated a point back behind the turbolift.

Ro knew that the shaft for the lift led down through the center of the station's core, and that the reactor compartment spread out around it. "Let's go, then," she said. She reached up to the keypad set into the smaller hatch and tapped in her individual security code. A tone signaled acceptance. She inserted her fingers into the sunken latch and slowly pulled open the hatch.

A current of nondescript noise immediately pushed its way out of the lower core. Ro hoped it covered the noise of their entrance, as well as their footsteps on the deck. As Cardok moved to take the lead, she stopped him with a touch to his upper arm. He stepped back as ordered, allowing the captain to enter first.

Inside, a pair of reactors stood directly ahead, to either side of the blast door. Bright, shimmering light emanated from them at several points, and the displays ranged around their midsections seemed almost alive as constant streams of glyphs marched across them. Looking back at the two security officers, Ro pointed to Hava, then directly down at the deck, indicating that he should stand guard at the door. Hava nodded once. Ro then gestured to Cardok that he should circle around the lower core to the left, while she would go right. He nodded as well.

As Cardok started in one direction, the captain started in the other. As she moved past the first reactor she came to, she saw Blackmer at once. He stood before a companel in the outer bulkhead, his back to her. She padded over to him, but before she could say anything, she saw him stiffen, as though he had heard her approaching. As he began to turn, she lifted her phaser and aimed, prepared for him to spring at her.

He didn't.

"Captain Ro," he said.

"Chief," she said, forcing herself to use his title. "What are you doing here?"

"I think probably the same thing as you," he said.

"I don't think you are," Ro said, "since I'm looking for *you*."

The captain saw Blackmer's eyes glance past her. She did not follow his gaze, but after a few seconds, Lieutenant Cardok arrived at her side. Like her, he kept his phaser at the ready.

"Why are you looking for *me*?" Blackmer asked.

"I'll ask you once more," Ro said, her attitude stern, "what are you doing at this time of night in the lower core?"

Blackmer peered over at Cardok again, and then back at Ro. "Captain," he said, "I think you and I need to speak privately."

Ro studied Blackmer's face, tried to measure the serious expression he wore. She could not judge his motives, and she did not trust her own. "You're right," she said to him. "We do need to talk." She reached up and tapped her combadge. "Ro to security."

"Security," came the immediate response. *"This is Si Naran."*

"Lieutenant," Ro said, "are any holding cells occupied at this time?"

"No, sir," Si Naran said.

"Good," Ro said. "Prepare cell number one to receive a prisoner. Notify ops when you're ready."

"Yes, sir. Right away."

Ro activated her combadge a second time to contact the operations center.

"Ops. Aleco here."

"Lieutenant," Ro said. "Site-to-site transport. I want you to beam Mister Blackmer from the lower core into holding cell number one once Lieutenant Si Naran notifies you that he's ready."

"Yes, sir."

"Ro out." For the first time, she looked away from Blackmer, who appeared to accept his impending incarceration with composure. She peered up and around the reactor compartment, at the vast space so important to the continuing operation of

Deep Space 9—so important, and so vulnerable. Looking back at Blackmer, she said, "What have you done here?"

"Done?" he said. "Nothing but conduct a security sweep."

Ro nodded. "We'll see."

Blackmer opened his mouth to respond, but then the whine of the transporter rose in the compartment, the distinctive sound audible even through the blur of reactor noise. The security chief disappeared in eddies of shimmering light. Ro waited for the beaming process to complete, then turned to Cardok.

"I want all available security officers and engineers down here right now," she ordered. "I want a complete sweep of the entire lower core, up through the power-transfer conduits."

"What are we looking for, Captain?"

"I don't know," Ro said, a sinking feeling in her gut. She gazed around again at the huge space in which energized-plasma reactors generated all of Deep Space 9's power, and at the complex equipment needed to accomplish that. Locating, or even identifying, an act of sophisticated sabotage could take a long time—perhaps *too* long. "I don't know what we're looking for," she told Cardok, "but I intend to find out."

Ro turned on her heel, headed for the security office on the Promenade—and holding cell number one.

After dismissing Jang Si Naran, Ro stood alone in the central holding area, peering into the first of the three cells that surrounded the large room. Jefferson Blackmer faced her from his three-walled space, on the other side of the force field that kept him confined. "All right, Chief," she said, working to keep her voice level. She knew that antagonizing the lieutenant commander would not net her any answers. "Now we can have the private conversation you wanted."

"Thank you, Captain," Blackmer said.

The polite reply momentarily disarmed Ro, considering that she had just trained a phaser on a member of her own crew and then taken him into custody, based only on vague suspicions. "I'd like to ask you again," she said, "what were you doing in the lower core in the middle of the night?"

"I was conducting a security sweep."

"By yourself?" Ro asked, unable to completely mask the doubt she felt, which crept into her voice.

"Yes, by myself," Blackmer said. "I didn't have much choice, since I'm not sure who on this station I can trust."

"What?" Ro said. *Is he trying to place blame on us?* she thought, thinking of her crew. She knew that she hadn't been the only one aboard who'd had a difficult time accepting the death of Evik Nath and then the arrival of his replacement. But her emotions had given way to a genuine, though not fully formed, suspicion of Blackmer—and he probably knew that. *So is he blaming me?* she asked herself. *And for what?*

But Ro expressed none of those questions. Based on her training and experience as DS9's chief of security for two years, she cautioned herself not to permit her own preconceptions and expectations to color what Blackmer revealed to her. She needed to allow him to explain his thoughts and actions, after which she could reach her own conclusions.

"Why can't you trust people on Deep Space Nine?" she asked.

"Because I had a member of the crew come to me a few days ago," Blackmer said. "They told me that they harbored suspicions about *another* member of the crew based on a conversation they overheard."

Ro wanted to ask the identities of the mysterious crew members, simply so that she could corroborate Blackmer's claim. She refrained from doing so, though, since she felt committed to letting the security chief tell his story. "Go on," she said.

"I looked into what I was told," said the security chief. "But I uncovered conflicting information. I couldn't be sure if the initial report from the first crew member was truthful, or if they'd come forward as a means of covering their own transgression. Regardless, it seemed to me that one or more of the crew might be lying to me, so I thought it wisest not to confide in anybody. That's why I continued investigating on my own."

"But investigating what?" Ro asked.

Blackmer raised his arms and then brought his hands together, a gesture that exposed his own frustrations. "Honestly,

Captain, I'm not sure," he said. "But my greatest fear is that somebody intends to sabotage Deep Space Nine."

The revelation didn't surprise Ro—after all, she had suspected Blackmer of attempting to perpetrate such an act—but it did distress her. "Why didn't you come to me with this?" Ro asked, but the answer seemed immediately obvious. "Or am I one of the people you suspect?"

Blackmer sighed heavily. He turned in the small cell and stepped over to its built-in bunk, where he sat down heavily. He wore his fatigue and frustration like a great weight. "I don't suspect you, Captain," he said. "But it's challenging for me to trust you when you clearly don't trust me."

Ro felt an urge to reject the charge, but circumstances made such a denial irrational. Following Blackmer's lead, she moved to sit on the low, backless bench in the center of the room. "At this point," she said, "I think you need to trust somebody, whether it's me or maybe somebody farther up the chain of command at Starfleet."

"Believe me, Captain, I know."

"Then, since you don't suspect me," she said, "why don't you give me the details of your investigation."

Blackmer shook his head. "Because I'm not interested in making unfounded accusations."

"How do you know they're unfounded?"

"I don't," Blackmer said. "Which is why I've been trying to find out."

"Sometimes," Ro tried to prompt him, "there are good reasons to make accusations. Full investigations can follow, and the truth can be uncovered."

"And sometimes accusations are *groundless*," Blackmer shot back, his voice rising. He rose to his feet and paced forward to the front of the cell, just shy of the force field, which issued a short, low hum at his approach. "I'm sorry about the death of your friend," he said. "I'm sorry about Evik Nath. But taking over his position is not a crime."

"No," Ro agreed quietly, suddenly feeling a sense of shame. "What have I done in my time here to warrant your distrust?" Blackmer said, almost pleading for an answer. "What actions have I taken to make you so wary of me?"

Ro said the only thing that occurred to her. "Why did you transfer here?"

"What?" he asked, apparently confused by the question.

Ro stood up and crossed the room until she stood facing Blackmer from only centimeters away, the force field frizzing between them. "Why did you transfer to DS-Nine?" she repeated. "You'd only just been promoted to security chief aboard the *Perseverance,* but when the position opened up here, you immediately requested a transfer. Why?"

Unexpectedly, Blackmer smiled. "That's it?" he asked. "That's why you don't trust me? That's why you haven't accepted me into your crew?"

"Let's just say that it's a question that's been bothering me."

Blackmer threw up his hands, one of which made contact with the force field. It flashed and crackled in response, sending him backward a step, but it appeared to faze him for only a moment. "I don't want to tell you, Captain," he said heatedly. "If you'd asked me over a cup of raktajino sometime, or even if you'd sat me down as a new member of your crew and demanded it of me, I'd have been happy to tell you. But instead, you allowed this unanswered question and maybe some others to create this . . . this . . . amorphous mistrust."

Is that what I did? Ro thought. She wanted to mention her wayward concerns involving the Tzenkethi, but how could she put into words something that she had yet to fully work out for herself? And even if she could, would that invalidate what Blackmer had just said?

Ro looked away. What had she done? How could her instincts have been so wrong?

Nath, she thought. Had she let the loss of yet another close friend influence her so much as to distrust his professional replacement without just cause? The idea seemed unlikely to her; she had lost so many people throughout her life—in the refugee camps, on Garon II, in the Maquis—how could one more make such a difference?

But then she realized. *They* all *made a difference.*

Into the silence that followed, Blackmer said, "I like space stations."

At first, the words struck Ro as a non sequitur. She looked back up at him, and he went on.

"I spent the first decade of my Starfleet career on two space stations, and the next seven years on five different starships," he said. "On a space station, you stay in one place, in one star system. You're usually on or near a habitable world, so you don't have to experience nature exclusively in artificial environments like holodecks. It feels more stable, with fewer dangers." Blackmer shrugged. "I just like space stations better than I do starships."

Ro smiled. "That's it?"

"It's not complicated."

"No, I guess it isn't," Ro agreed. Making a calculation, she walked over to the control panel set into the bulkhead beside the cell. She keyed in her security code, then lowered the force field, which deactivated with a flash and a buzz. "For whatever it's worth to you, I'm sorry." Blackmer's explanations—about his presence in the reactor core, about his lack of trust in the crew and in the captain herself, about his transfer to DS9—all rang true to Ro, but they did not fully convince her of his trustworthiness. She recognized the risk in freeing him, but that risk threatened only Ro, not the station or its crew. The captain had left Cardok and Hava as sentries outside the holding area, with orders to take Blackmer back into custody if he exited alone.

Instead of standing aside to allow the security chief to leave the cell, Ro walked past him and sat down inside. When he turned to gaze down at her, she said, "You need to tell me specifically what drove you down to the lower core tonight."

Blackmer appeared to give the matter some thought, then sat down beside Ro. "Three days ago," he said, "Lieutenant Douglas reported to me that she'd overheard a heated exchange."

After embarking on a mission for Starfleet Intelligence with Doctor Bashir, Sarina Douglas had transferred to Deep Space 9 and joined the security staff. She and Bashir shared quarters in the habitat ring, and Ro knew that Quark had taken hundreds of wagers throughout the station on both the date they would announce their intention to marry, and the date of the wedding itself. Ro had already missed out on the former, but still hoped to recoup her losses by winning the latter.

"Douglas was on duty at the airlock where the *Vren-thai* was docked," Blackmer continued. "While she was there, she claimed that Ensign th'Shant arrived to say good-bye to Ensign zh'Vesk." Of the thirty-nine Andorian Starfleet officers on DS9 at the time of their world's secession from the Federation, seventeen had immediately resigned their commissions. In the intervening eight months, another eleven had followed suit, including two who departed the station three days earlier: Ensign zh'Vesk and an enlisted crew member, ch'Rellen. "Douglas claimed that in a whispered conversation, both th'Shant and zh'Vesk became agitated, and she heard one of them make reference to avenging themselves on the Federation."

"That sounds like angry hyperbole," Ro said.

"Maybe," Blackmer said. "But Lieutenant Douglas considered the words menacing enough to report the incident to me. She interpreted it as a threat to Deep Space Nine, and she believed that it was Ensign th'Shant who made that threat."

An engineer on the station for more than two years, Rahendervakell th'Shant had reacted to Andor's secession much the way many Andorians in Starfleet had: with a mixture of confusion, depression, and anger. Many became conflicted about whether to remain in the service or return to their homeworld. Not only had some stayed and some gone, but some had left and then come back, while others had at first stayed and then gone later.

"Did you speak with th'Shant?" Ro asked.

"I did," Blackmer said. "He denied that either he or zh'Vesk ever said such a thing. Another security officer there at the time, Jacob Smith, also said that he didn't hear anything resembling that conversation."

"Do you feel that either Douglas or th'Shant was lying to you?" Ro asked.

"I don't know," Blackmer said. "It could be just a misunderstanding: misheard words or a misinterpretation. But it seemed too serious a situation to ignore, so I've been monitoring Douglas's and th'Shant's movements on the station. Yesterday, both of them ended up in the lower core, Douglas as part of a security exercise, and th'Shant on an engineering maintenance team."

"Which is why you ended up there tonight," Ro deduced.

"Yes," Blackmer said. "Particularly with civilian ships from the Typhon Pact set to arrive here in a few days, I just felt that I had to."

"You're concerned that Douglas or th'Shant sympathizes with the Typhon Pact and is looking to help them take action against the Federation?"

"Or that they could pass vital information to the Pact," Blackmer said. "Or that they could commit violence *against* citizens of the Pact in a way that implicates the Federation." The security chief stood up and strode forward, out of the holding cell, before turning back to face Ro. "I know it was foolhardy for me to visit the lower core; anybody who would commit an act of sabotage on the station wouldn't leave it visible for the naked eye. I didn't even intend to stay there for long, but then I found myself searching the entire compartment, even up into the power-transfer conduits."

"You were doing your job," Ro said gently. She waited, not rising, providing Blackmer the opportunity to quickly raise the force field and imprison her in the holding cell. While she found the security chief's recounting of events believable, she didn't assume that they were true. Blackmer could have visited the lower core because he feared that he or a confederate had left behind a tricorder or a tool or something else when *they* had sabotaged the station.

"It's obviously not a job for one person," Blackmer said, making no move toward the control panel.

"No," Ro said, finally getting up. "But now we can launch a full-scale investigation."

"That might just drive any potential saboteurs to exercise more caution," Blackmer said.

"Yes, but it will also make their task more difficult to accomplish," Ro said. "The crew will be alert to anything out of the ordinary, and it will give us more resources to determine if there even is a threat to the station from among the crew."

"You're right, of course," Blackmer said.

Ro moved forward and out of the holding cell, and together she and Blackmer started toward the exit. "I'll convene a meeting of the senior staff," she said. "After that, we can talk to the security team. We're already on high alert for the arrival of the Typhon Pact ships, so we'll just have to tighten our procedures to include restrictions for our own crew."

As the captain and the security chief walked out of the holding area, Ro understood the seriousness of the situation. A threat might have been made against the station and lies might have been told. Worst of all, after her encounter with Blackmer, she came away suspecting not just one of her crew in plotting to sabotage Deep Space 9, but three.

17

Tenmei walked out of the infirmary and stopped in the middle of the Promenade. Somebody jostled past her, but she paid them no attention. She stared down at the deck, pressure mounting behind her eyes. She felt like crying—she *wanted* to cry, wanted a release—but she had wept so often since her father's torpid body had been brought to Deep Space 9's infirmary that she wondered if any tears remained.

What am I doing? Tenmei asked herself as the people on the Promenade maneuvered around her. For so long, she'd sat by her father's bedside, missing him and irrationally hoping that the terrible injuries his body had suffered would eventually heal. Reading aloud beside his dormant form, she pretended to connect with him, told herself that in some fashion he could hear her, but really she connected only with her memories of him. She recalled the merry, carefree times of her childhood, and then much later, at DS9, all the joys she'd shared with her father after their reconciliation. She remembered so vividly the world of the

Prentara in the Gamma Quadrant, where she at last began to really know herself, and to grow, and to understand her father and all the reasons for their ruptured relationship. When her mother had died—

No! Standing outside the infirmary, where her father's fractured body still lay swaddled in a veneer of life, she could not allow herself to think about her mother too. That Tenmei had effectively become an orphan pained her in a way that seemed almost impossible to endure.

Maybe that's why I can't let go, she thought.

It had taken eighteen months from the time of her father's injuries at Alonis, but Tenmei had eventually summoned the courage to have Doctor Bashir remove him from the respirator that breathed for him. But his body hadn't died then, and nearly a full year later, it continued to survive. Tenmei still hadn't been able to bring herself to order the elimination of her father's feeding and hydration tubes, the last steps in allowing him to slip into his final rest.

Do it, she told herself. *Give the order and let him go.*

But how could she? He was her *father.* He was all she had left.

Tenmei raised her head, wanting more than anything to stop thinking, to stop *feeling.* She looked left and right down the Promenade, saw the late-night activity as people bustled about, mostly to and from Quark's. Without consciously deciding to do so, she started toward the bar.

Inside, the place brimmed with activity. Voices competed with the clink of glassware and the chirp of the dabo wheel. A cornucopia of colors splashed across the scene from the bottles on the shelves, the attire of the customers, and the three-story red, orange, and yellow lighted mural that dominated the main room. At the bar itself, she spotted Morn, a small group massed around him, no doubt listening to one of his interminable stories.

Tenmei made her way into Quark's and peered toward its far periphery, where shadows muted the vibrancy of the place. She looked for an empty table, but didn't see one. She almost abandoned her impulse to visit the bar, but then she saw Cenn Desca,

Jeannette Chao, and John Candlewood sitting together at a table for four. Not giving herself a chance to change her mind, she headed toward them.

When she arrived at the table, her friends did not see her as they talked spiritedly with each other. But then Candlewood, the station's lead science officer, glanced up and noticed her standing there mutely. "Prynn," he said loudly, though his raised voice barely competed with the din of the bar. "Come join us."

"Yes, come have a drink," said Chao. Turning to Cenn, the chief engineer made a shooing motion with her hands. "Move, move." Cenn shifted over to the one empty chair at the table, right beside the bulkhead. Then Chao moved over as well, freeing up the seat in front of Tenmei.

She sat down. Across from her, Cenn leaned forward, presumably so that she could hear him. "How are you, Prynn?" he asked. "It's good to see you on the Promenade."

And not heading into or out of the infirmary, Tenmei thought, completing what she thought must have been the first officer's full sentiment. Forcing a smile, she said, "I'm fine. It's good to be out."

Chao started to say something, but then a voice at Tenmei's shoulder asked, "And what can I get for you?" She looked up to see Quark, who carried a tray filled with empty glasses in a wide array of sizes, shapes, and colors. He quickly reached in over the table and collected two more empty glasses, one from in front of Cenn and one from Chao. When he tried to grab Candlewood's, though, the lieutenant commander pulled it back, a finger or so of liquid still swilling around inside it.

"Not done yet," Candlewood protested.

"When you've only got that much *kiriliona* left," Quark insisted, "you've lost all the infused vapor." He lunged for Candlewood's glass, this time seizing it and placing it on his tray with the others. "So then, another round?" After nods from Cenn, Chao, and Candlewood, the barkeep turned to Tenmei. "And for you, Lieutenant?"

"Double vodka on the rocks," she said. "The real thing," she added, not wanting synthehol and its easily dismissed intoxicating effects.

"I love a discerning palate," Quark said. "Like father, like daughter." Then he dashed away as quickly as he'd come, headed back toward the bar. He left behind an uncomfortable lull.

Tenmei quickly peered at each of her friends to include them, then said, "I didn't mean to interrupt your conversation."

"You didn't," Candlewood said. Silver strands had begun to weave their way through the dark-brown ringlets on his head, Tenmei saw, and she wondered when that had happened. "We were just talking about our visitors," Candlewood said. "What do you think?" He nodded past her, indicating the main room of Quark's, through which she had just passed.

Tenmei turned in her chair and gazed around. At first, she saw nothing more than an unusual preponderance of Vulcans in the bar. But then, over in an alcove, she spotted large, golden orbs peering out from the green, leathery scales of a saurian face. The Gorn's presence on a Federation space station seemed so incongruous that, despite knowing that civilian Typhon Pact vessels had begun arriving at Deep Space 9 earlier that day, Tenmei did not immediately make the connection. But then she looked back around the room and realized: *Not Vulcans. Romulans.*

Tenmei had earlier spent her duty shift aboard *Defiant,* helping to keep the ship at full readiness should trouble arise. She also knew that *U.S.S. Canterbury,* a *Galaxy*-class starship, orbited Bajor, its temporary presence in the system designed to discreetly discourage any deviation from the procedures that the Federation had negotiated for Pact vessels traveling to and from the wormhole through UFP space. In addition to being prohibited from encroaching on Dominion space—a quiet peace had held sway for seven and a half years, since the Dominion had withdrawn from the Alpha Quadrant and closed its borders—the civilian craft could carry only minimal armaments and defenses, and no cloaking devices. Further, their cargo could include no martial wares.

Looking back through the crowd at the Gorn, Tenmei saw another seated at the same table, and beside them, a fully armored Breen. At once, a rash of memories crowded in on her, bringing her back to her days of piloting *Sentinel* during the war. She remembered well the crew's encounters with the Breen, hard-fought battles that not all her shipmates had survived.

There were tears then too, she thought, realizing just how much of her life had been spent in mourning.

"It feels strange to have them around," Chao said, "but then I guess it probably once felt strange to have Klingons around." She turned to Cenn. "The way it once did for Bajorans to have humans around."

"Depending on the particular human," Cenn offered with a smirk, "it still feels strange."

At that moment, Quark swooped back to the table, the tray he carried balanced atop one hand packed not with empty drinks, but full ones. He placed a small, stemmed glass in front of Chao, its tall bowl filled with a dark-green liquid. "A syntheholic Finagle's Folly for the chief," he proclaimed, as though bestowing an award. Before Candlewood, he set down a tall, straight glass from which a curl of light gas emanated, dissipating just above the rim. "A *kiriliona* for the scientist." When Quark gave Cenn a tall glass of a pink beverage, he pronounced it a "Trixian bubble juice," then set down Tenmei's tumbler of vodka and ice, saying, "And the good stuff for the lieutenant."

"Thank you, Quark," Cenn said.

"Happy to be of service," said the Ferengi with a wave of his empty hand, though he'd already started away from the table, obviously rushing to deliver the next set of drinks.

Tenmei looked down at her glass and then past it, past the edge of the table to her lap, to where she saw herself twisting her hands together. None of her friends said anything for a moment. She wanted to fill the conversational void, or if not fill it, then at least pour something of herself into it, but she felt wholly incapable. Suddenly, she felt the urge to bolt, to run from the bar and isolate herself in her quarters.

"How's your father, Prynn?" Candlewood asked. "Has there been any change, any improvement?"

Tenmei raised her head in time to see Chao throw Candlewood a withering glare. "That's all right," Chao told her, reaching forward and giving her shoulder a squeeze. "You don't need to talk about it."

"I *like* talking about my father," Tenmei said sharply. She plucked her drink from the table, the movement dislodging Chao's grasp on her shoulder. Tenmei brought the tumbler quickly to her mouth and upended it. The cold alcohol paradoxically warmed her gullet as she drank it down in three quick gulps.

"Prynn," Chao said, looking visibly rebuked, "I didn't mean—"

"He's a good man," Tenmei said. She put her tumbler back on the table, careful not to give in to her emotions and slam it down. "And it seems like everybody wants to forget about him."

"Nobody wants to forget Elias Vaughn," said Cenn. "And nobody *has* forgotten him. He was an excellent commanding officer and a fine man."

"He *is* a fine man," Tenmei said, firing her words across the table at Cenn. "He's not *dead.*"

"Oh, Prynn," Chao said softly, impossible to hear over the clamor of other voices, though Prynn saw the words forming on the chief's lips. Chao reached forward again, this time placing her hand on Tenmei's uniformed forearm.

Tenmei jerked her arm away. Chao's jaw fell open in a look of surprise. Tenmei's thoughts began to swirl. "Don't tell me," she said, sure that her friends meant to declare her father dead.

"Prynn," Cenn said from across the table. "You need to calm yourself."

"Don't tell me what I need!" she yelled back at him. Around her, she could hear voices quieting. Anxious about people turning their attention to her, she stood up, but too quickly, and her chair toppled over backward, landing on the deck with a loud clang. She straightened her uniform, then addressed Cenn in a calmer tone. "Don't tell me what I need, *sir.*"

She turned as she heard Chao and Candlewood call after her. Tenmei pushed past other customers in the bar. She intended to leave, to go to her quarters. *Or maybe to go read to my father,* she thought. But as she stumbled past the crowd at the dabo wheel, she saw the two Gorn and the Breen peering across the room at her.

"Murderers," she said, more to herself than to them. She lifted her arm to point and offer up her appraisal of them in a louder voice, but then she felt an arm around her shoulder and a hand on her right biceps. Tenmei felt her body spun halfway around, but her mind seemed to continue swirling. A jumble of images crossed her field of vision, and then she saw the entrance to the bar. She started to walk that way, but then realized that somebody was leading her in that direction.

Outside, on the main walkway of the Promenade, Tenmei reached up and pushed at the hand gripping her biceps. "No," she said, and twisted away from the arm around her shoulders. She backed down the Promenade, and saw that it had been Jeannette Chao who had conducted her out of Quark's.

"Prynn," Chao said gently, "it's all right."

Tenmei heard herself yelp, a short, quick sound she'd intended as a laugh, but that even to her own ears contained no trace of humor. "Nothing's all right," she said. "Nothing." She continued to back down the Promenade, and Chao followed after her. Tenmei saw people coming around her on either side, obviously making way for her as she walked backward. Many stopped and watched her retreat.

"Maybe things aren't all right," Chao said. "But they will be."

"*How?*" Tenmei yelled. Then, in a high-pitched but small voice, she said, "My father . . ." She closed her eyes and let go of whatever small amount of control she still had over her own body. Her knees buckled, and the artificial gravity of DS9 began to pull her down to the deck. But then she felt Chao take hold of her once more, this time wrapping her arms around her and holding her up.

"I've got you, Prynn," Chao whispered to her. "I've got you."

Tenmei buried her face in her friend's shoulder and began to cry. Great sobs racked her body. She couldn't stop.

She didn't know for how long she stood there with Chao, but it seemed like a long time. Her weeping slowed eventually, and then stopped. It had given her the release she'd needed, but she also understood that it solved nothing.

When Tenmei finally pulled away, Chao took her by the arm

and led her to the nearest door. The two panels that blocked the octagonal opening parted, and Chao guided her inside to a chair. Once seated, Tenmei looked around to see Chief Blackmer at his desk in the security office. As she wiped at the drying trails of tears on her face, he looked back at her, and she saw his expression of surprise transform into one of sympathy.

"May we borrow your office for just a few minutes, Chief?" Chao asked.

"Of course," Blackmer said, rising out of his seat immediately. "I was just going to check on my deputies over in Quark's anyway."

"It threatened to get bumpy a couple of minutes ago," Chao said, "but otherwise it's been quiet."

"That's good to hear," Blackmer said. He walked toward the door, but turned back just as it opened before him. "Take as much time as you need," he said, and then he left.

Chao took the second chair in front of the security chief's desk and faced Tenmei. "Can I help?" she asked.

Tenmei didn't know what to say. Finally, she simply said, "No. There's nothing anybody can do."

Chao sighed, a sound not of frustration, but of compassion. She leaned forward, resting her elbows on her knees. "Prynn, I don't want to pry, but I'm your friend, and I hate seeing you like this," she said. "Have you talked with Counselor Matthias?"

"Yeah," Tenmei said. "Just not in a while."

"Well, maybe you should think about seeing her again," Chao suggested. "Or at least talking with somebody."

"Yeah, I'm sure you're right," she said. Chao did not respond to the clearly noncommittal answer.

They sat that way for a time, no words passing between them. Tenmei felt grateful for both the silence and the company, which at least approximated a moment of peace. But she knew it couldn't last, and it didn't.

"Prynn, I've known you for more than a decade," Chao said, "since you graduated from the Academy. I'm not telling you anything you don't know when I say that you've always carried a bit of darkness around inside of you. When you eventually told me about the loss of your mother, and about your estrangement from your father, I understood. But even before you reunited with your father, you somehow managed your pain." She paused, as though trying to conjure the right words. "You didn't *manage* your pain. You let your happiness—your genuine love of life— be the dominant force within you."

Tenmei listened, and recognized the truth of what her friend said.

Chao smiled. "Do you remember when Captain Hoku taught us to surf on the holodeck?" she said, referring to their days as shipmates aboard *Mjolnir*. "Well, when she taught *you*. I could never get the hang of it."

Unexpectedly, Tenmei felt herself smiling too. She remembered well Kalena Hoku's lessons. "*He'e nalu,* the captain called it," Tenmei said, remembering the words from Hoku's native Hawaiian tongue. "Wave sliding."

"That's what she called it for you," Chao said. "For me, it was *hā'ule nalu*: wave falling."

Tenmei laughed, picturing all the times poor Jeannette had tried to hop up on her board, only to lose her balance almost immediately. "It's amazing you made it through Starfleet Academy's fitness courses," she joked.

"Hey, the Academy doesn't require the ability to walk on water," Chao said with mock indignation. "But if you want to grab some environmental suits and match up our EVA skills . . ."

"No, no," Tenmei said. "I believe you."

Chao looked at her, still smiling, but then Tenmei saw something in her eyes, some quality that seemed to pair hope with mercy. "You see," she said. "It's not that difficult." She reached up and touched a finger to the side of Tenmei's lips. "This," she said, obviously referring to her smile, "is who you are."

Tenmei looked down. She saw her hands twisting together again in her lap, and she willed herself to stop. "That's who I was," she said.

"No," Chao said firmly. "That's who you *are*. You're just a little lost." She paused again, and as the silence drew out, Tenmei looked back up. "I don't want to tell you what to do, Prynn.

And I don't want to ask you what you think your father would want you to do, because that doesn't seem fair or right, but also because it doesn't matter. I'm sorry, but your father's not here right now, and he's never going to be." Chao reached forward and took Tenmei's hands in her own. "But you *are* here. As your friend, I don't want you to waste the time you have."

"I—" Tenmei started, but she didn't know what to say.

"I miss you," Chao said. "Everybody on board misses you."

"I know," Tenmei said, her voice a mere whisper. She squeezed her friend's hands. "Thank you." She knew Chao was right. Tenmei didn't know how that made her feel, or how it *should* make her feel, but she thought that maybe the time had finally come for her to do something.

Because she missed herself too.

18

Tomalak pushed open the tall doors to the praetor's audience chamber. He expected no trouble, no resistance whatsoever, to the announcement that he would deliver to her, though he had prepared for such a possibility anyway. He had not survived for so long in the Imperial Fleet, and then within the corridors of power, without planning for contingencies.

The proconsul entered the chamber, wincing at the bright illumination that threw the normally beautiful embellishments into harsh contrast. Before him, sprawled across the center of the space, stood a conference table, its prosaic, functional design yet another feature introduced by Gell Kamemor that detracted from the room's splendor. As the doors closed behind him, he glanced across the chamber to where a throne rose on a high platform, allowing the praetor to look regally down on whomever she granted an audience.

It surprised Tomalak not at all that the throne sat empty. He had served as one of this praetor's advisors for nearly five hundred days, and so he had become accustomed to her willful gestures, meant to humble not just her office, but the entire government. She fancied herself a populist, he knew, a notion that struck him as absurd in an empire where virtually nobody believed him- or herself to be an ordinary citizen—where most found the very idea of an "average Romulan" odious.

Tomalak peered to his right, to where a smaller table sat along the circumference of the room, and where he expected to see the praetor. She sat there, a ceramic tea set laid out before her. When Tomalak made eye contact, she put her cup down and addressed him.

"Proconsul," she said. "Please join me." Tomalak walked over to the praetor, who gestured to a chair at the table. "You are as prompt as ever. Would you care for some tea? This is a Vulcan blend called *relen*."

"Thank you, no," Tomalak said as he sat down. He kept his expression neutral, despite his disapproval of the leader of the Romulan Star Empire indulging not just in an offworld beverage, but in one of *Federation* origin. *If only that were her greatest offense against her own people,* he thought.

From the very beginnings of her reign, Kamemor had promoted multiculturalism in a subversive, insidious manner. Though her predecessor, Tal'Aura, had tied the Empire to the Typhon Pact, she had done so with the idea that Romulus would lead that alliance as its most powerful member. Kamemor, though, collaborated with the Pact allies as equals, working to persuade them of her positions rather than demanding that they follow her leads. Worse, she had convinced enough of the Typhon powers—namely, the Breen Confederacy and the Gorn Hegemony—to seek a rapprochement with the Khitomer Accords worlds.

Fortunately, Sela and I were able to move quickly enough to turn that to our advantage, Tomalak thought. His visit to the praetor would allow him to promote that advantage. Soon— and, he hoped, soon *enough*—the Federation would no longer enjoy the military advantage provided by its exclusive possession of quantum slipstream drive.

"My scheduler did not specify the nature of the meeting you requested," Kamemor said. "With the opening of the Typhon Expanse to Khitomer Accords vessels, and of the Bajoran wormhole to the Typhon Pact, I naturally assume it has something to do with those initiatives."

"No, Praetor," Tomalak said. "I am here, really, on a matter of a personal nature."

"Oh," Kamemor said, clearly surprised. "I hope that all is well with your clan."

"It is, thank you," Tomalak said. "I come not to request assistance, but to ask if I may take my leave of the government."

Kamemor raised an eyebrow. "You wish to resign as proconsul?"

"As one of two proconsuls," Tomalak noted.

"I see." The praetor rose from her chair and paced away from the table and toward her throne. She wore a tailored, deep-green shirtwaist that flattered her. Tomalak noticed that she wore soft-soled shoes, as they padded along the polished stone floor with almost no sound. Several steps away, Kamemor turned to face him. "May I ask the reason for your decision?"

That the praetor would, even as a formality, request information from him, rather than require it, appalled him. Tomalak hid his disgust, just as he had each day he'd functioned as proconsul to Kamemor. "When Tal'Aura took over the praetorship," he said, reciting the words he had rehearsed, "I agreed at her behest to leave the Imperial Fleet. I did so because my praetor called upon me to serve at her side, in the cause of leading the Romulan people. I did so for more than seven hundred days, until the time of Tal'Aura's death."

"And you served ably," Kamemor said. She walked back to the table, where she rested her hands on the back of her chair. "At a particularly low point for the Empire, and in a time when we needed strong leadership, you successfully argued to the Hundred that they must reconstitute the Imperial Senate. For that alone, Proconsul, the people of Romulus and beyond owe you a debt."

"You are generous to say so, Praetor," Tomalak said. "As you know, when you accepted the responsibility of succeeding Tal'Aura, I offered you my resignation. I did so because it was expected of me, and for good reason: so that you could form the government around you that would best allow you to lead the Empire. I must say—" Tomalak bowed his head to Kamemor, intending her to take it as a sign of both gratitude and deference. "—I was humbled when you asked me to stay on as proconsul, and to stand beside Proconsul Ventel as we both offered counsel and assistance."

"As you have come to know, I value opposing viewpoints," Kamemor said. "Yours was an important one, although you and I concurred far more often than I surmised we would at the start. But when we did not, you brought me to a greater understanding of many issues. And on occasion, you even changed my mind."

"Again, I am humbled by your kind words," Tomalak said. "I have come to feel, however, that there is a redundancy in having both Proconsul Ventel and myself in the same position. Although he and I certainly do not agree on all matters, I would argue that we are both capable of supplying you with the many opposing sides of an issue." Tomalak paused, and behaved as though he struggled to decide whether or not to say what would come next. "In truth, I welcome the redundancy, because I feel it allows me to resign my position as proconsul in good conscience."

"What will you do?" Kamemor asked.

"I will petition you to return me to my previous life," Tomalak said.

"The Imperial Fleet."

"Yes. Until called upon by Praetor Tal'Aura," he said, "I spent essentially all of my adult life in the Fleet. I would welcome a return to its ranks."

Kamemor nodded. "Of course," she said. "Do you have your statement of separation as proconsul?"

"I do." Tomalak stood up, reached to his hip, and retrieved a small data tablet from where it hung. He examined its display, then touched a control surface. "I have transmitted it to your files."

"Very well," Kamemor said. "I will speak to Fleet Admiral Devix at once." She stepped forward and looked directly into Tomalak's eyes. "I genuinely thank you for your service to this government, and to me."

"I was honored to have the privilege," Tomalak said. He offered a stiff bow, then turned and headed for the main doors.

Outside the audience chamber, Tomalak walked for what he hoped would be the last time through the Hall of State. He had accomplished many things there—important, necessary things—but he had never belonged. He did not shun power, but he sought it in a different form, in a different forum.

It pleased him that his conversation with Kamemor had gone precisely as he'd planned. He knew that the praetor believed all that he had told her. Of course, it helped that not everything he'd said had been a lie: he truly did look forward with great anticipation to rejoining the Romulan Imperial Fleet.

When he did, though, he would do so as an agent of the Tal Shiar.

The Breen privateer *Ren Fejin* swept along the arc of the established shipping lanes. Light-years behind the vessel floated the Idran system, a convenient marker for the Gamma Quadrant terminus of the Bajoran wormhole, but the worlds of which had been designated by the Khitomer Accords powers as off-limits to Typhon Pact ships. Ahead lay civilizations as yet unvisited by the Breen and their allies, though familiar to the Federation and theirs: Parada, Argrathi, Stakoron, Rakhari, Wadi, and others. And unknown to *any* denizens of the Alpha and Beta Quadrants, still many more planets and societies awaited beyond those.

Trok sat off to the side on the cluttered bridge of the small vessel, attempting to calm his nerves. Across from him, the Romulan specialist Joralis Kinn also appeared ill at ease. Unlike the smooth, hushed operation of the great Breen Militia starships, *Ren Fejin* ran almost as though it might blow apart at any instant. Vibrations from the faster-than-light drive sent tremors coursing through the deck plates and set equipment to rattling, and deep, continuous undertones saturated the ship's interior. Already, Trok had adjusted several settings in his environmental suit—gravitational compensators, visual stabilizers, auditory inputs—but he still felt uncomfortable.

How can they stand it? he wondered of the three Breen who crewed various consoles on the bridge, and of the three down in engineering. *And how can the others possibly rest?* Six other crew members supposedly slept belowdecks so that they could later take their shifts to run the ship.

They're probably all Amoniri, Trok thought, although he knew he shouldn't. The standardized exteriors of all Breen uniforms ensured the equal treatment of every individual within the Confederacy, eliminating biases based on their species or other physical attributes. The wholly democratic culture inhibited prejudice, forcing judgments based solely on actions and performance. Still, certain species excelled in particular roles within Breen society, and along with the Paclu, the Amoniri dominated both military and civilian starship operations. Trok knew that Amoniri uniforms contained internal refrigeration units to prevent their mostly liquid bodies from evaporating, so it occurred to him that their fluidic nature might allow them to better tolerate the rough travel aboard *Ren Fejin*.

And being a Vironat doesn't help me in this situation, he thought. While the many extremely responsive and exactingly accurate sensory organs along his two sets of cleft limbs provided a natural benefit in his vocation as an engineer, they also disadvantaged him with a sensitivity to vigorous motion. Once more, Trok modified the gravity fields within his environmental suit, and to his relief, the second alteration in the settings steadied his vestibular system. He took several moments to allow the relative tranquillity to soothe his distress.

Freed from the misery of motion sickness, Trok turned his attention to the holographic display projected in a sphere above the navigational console in the center of the bridge. At the heart of the hologram, a large, not-to-scale representation of *Ren Fejin* held steady: two mismatched curves of hull two decks through at their tallest points, and linked off-center by a one-deck connecting dorsal. The bridge, Trok knew, sat in a superstructure atop the connector.

A splay of bright, blue light emanated from the endpoint of the Bajoran wormhole near the edge of the navigational projection and reached across the middle of the display. Beld, the master of the vessel, had explained the blue zone as the region of space that the Accords powers deemed permissible for Pact ships to travel after emerging into the Gamma Quadrant. The specified area expanded as it moved away from the Idran system, ultimately ending and allowing Pact vessels unlimited movement far from the gateway back to the Alpha Quadrant. As he studied the display, Trok realized that nowhere in it did he see the serpentine mass of interstellar gas and dust that formed the Omarion Nebula. He asked Master Beld about it.

Beld approached the hologram near the representation of the entrance to the Bajoran wormhole, then lifted a gloved hand to indicate an area away from it, in a direction opposite that of the blue light. *"It is here,"* Beld said, his words delivered in the electronic scratch emitted by his helmet.

"There?" Trok asked. *"But the Omarion Nebula is located within Dominion space. We're traveling* away *from our objective."*

"We are traveling along the path best suited to successfully achieving our objective," said Joralis Kinn, stepping over to stand beside Beld. The usual green cast of the Romulan's skin seemed deeper, almost bilious. "We will wait to reach the far end of the prescribed shipping lanes—" He pointed to the wide mouth of the blue cone in the navigational projection. "—and then circle back around to the Dominion." He drew his finger through the air, around the spherical display, until he reached the relative point where Beld had placed the Omarion Nebula.

"Do you know how much time that will add to our journey?" Trok objected. *"If we wish to ensure the safety of the Breen Confederacy and the Romulan Star Empire and the rest of the Typhon Pact, we need to develop the slipstream drive now, not in five hundred or a thousand days from now."*

"Yes, we seek to develop the advanced drive in the shortest possible time," Kinn agreed. "But we must also be mindful of not allowing the Federation to impede our efforts to facilitate that development." He pointed toward the blue light in the display, then looked to Beld. "Show him," Kinn said.

Beld reached to the console below the projection and worked

some controls. As Trok watched, a series of red dots blinked on in the display. They all bordered the blue swath identifying the Federation-mandated shipping lanes.

"These," Kinn said, "represent Starfleet sensor buoys seeded along the mandated routes of Typhon Pact vessels after entering the Gamma Quadrant. I do not know if this has been explicitly stated, but it is reasonable to assume that if Federation sensors detect a ship deviating from this region—" He spread his hands along the blue expanse. "—then Starfleet will send a starship to investigate, and probably attempt to apprehend the offending vessel and crew."

"If they can find us," Trok said.

"Irrelevant," Kinn said. "Even if this ship cannot be located— and perhaps *especially* if this ship cannot be located—the Federation and their Khitomer allies would accurately claim a violation of their agreement with the Typhon Pact. In such a case, they would probably abrogate the arrangement. They would also fortify their defenses at the wormhole, and they would not allow this ship to travel back to the Alpha Quadrant and then on to Breen space."

"We do have contingency plans to fight our way through the wormhole, but only if absolutely necessary," Beld said.

"Those plans rely on normal operations on and around Deep Space Nine," Kinn said. "If the Federation expects a battle, they will be far better equipped for it, which would necessarily diminish our chances of success."

Trok studied the navigational display, hoping to find a means of invalidating what Kinn had said. *"If we destroy one of the buoys,"* he finally suggested, *"make it look like a system failure . . ."* He did not bother to finish his statement, knowing that he had made his point, but also recognizing its simple flaw.

"Even if we could disable one of the buoys and mask our complicity," Kinn said, "we would disappear entirely from the coverage of the numerous remaining sensor platforms, which would alert Starfleet of our actions. Additionally, the coverages of the Federation's sensors overlap, making the disruption of a single buoy inadequate to the task of eluding their efforts to track Pact vessels."

Trok uttered an expletive, which his helmet translated into an electronic squawk.

"It is no matter, Engineer Trok," Kinn said. "It will take us longer than we wished to reach the Dominion, but we will reach it."

Trok nodded. The Romulan made the task ahead of them sound effortless, but the engineer suspected it would not be that easy. *Which is probably why I'm so anxious to get started,* he realized. The sooner they reached the Dominion and acquired what they needed—without, Trok hoped, the intervention of either the Founders or the Jem'Hadar—the sooner they could be on their way back to the Confederacy.

And the sooner I can nullify the Federation's technological advantage over the Typhon Pact, he thought. *And if I can bring the slipstream drive to the entire Breen fleet and to the starships of the other Pact powers, utter defeat will be at hand for the Khitomer Accords powers.*

August 2383

19

Ro Laren stood on the upper walkway of the Promenade, peering out into space through an oval window that reached twice her height. In the distance, a brilliant point of light flared in the darkness, and then a circular mass of churning blue eddies swirled into existence, as though out of nothing. Ro had never counted herself among the Bajoran faithful, and yet a few seconds later, as she watched the wormhole collapse into itself in a flurry of motion, and then disappear completely in a single bright flash of white light, she thought that she could understand at least some measure of their reverence. Whatever the physics of the artificial wormhole—which, as far as Ro knew, Federation scientists had begun to comprehend, but had yet to replicate— the illuminated dervish *seemed* special, *felt* like some extraordinary marvel of the universe.

If you're going to believe somebody a god, she thought, *there are certainly far less compelling reasons than their ability to create something like that.*

For long moments, Ro continued to stare out at the patch of space where she had seen the wormhole. Behind her, she heard sounds of movement from down below, on the first level of the Promenade, as some of the station's shopkeepers no doubt readied for the day ahead. She wondered if Quark might be among them, but she knew that he rarely opened his place himself; even Treir typically slept in after her late nights there, usually leaving Broik to unlock the bar and prepare for business.

Maybe I'll go pay Quark a visit in his quarters, Ro thought. She felt unsettled, and so she wanted some company. But she knew that Quark would still be in bed, and like anybody else, he needed his sleep. *Besides, I already know what he'd tell me.*

As Ro went on looking straight ahead, out past Deep Space 9's habitat and docking rings, out at empty space, she felt the gray cloud of fatigue dulling her thoughts. She had slept poorly through the night, waking often, and always with her mind focused on a particular impending arrival at the station. She tried to tell herself that the continuing travel of Typhon Pact vessels to and from DS9 troubled her, but in the two months since the program had begun, there had been no incidents beyond an occasional, usually drunken skirmish in Quark's. And her suspicions about her chief of security, and his own alleged suspicions of two other crew members, had proven unwarranted. Investigations, including interviews and deep-background checks, exonerated them all. Most important—and most telling—the station had suffered no acts of sabotage.

I know what's bothering me, Ro thought. *I'm just not sure exactly why.* That morning, she had chosen to stop by the Promenade on her way to ops, not so that she could watch the wormhole cycle into and out of reality, but to get a glimpse of a part of the station not visible from her office.

Finally ready to do so, Ro lifted her gaze. Having arrived within the hour, docked at an upper pylon, one of Starfleet's best known vessels hung above DS9: *U.S.S. Enterprise.* Although Ro had not served aboard the *Sovereign*-class vessel, designated NCC-1701-E, she had spent more than a year of her Starfleet career as a flight controller on its predecessor, the *Galaxy*-class NCC-1701-D. To Ro's eye, the newer *Enterprise* appeared sleeker than its antecedent, with a less rounded and more elongated primary hull, streamlined warp nacelles, and an overall shallower profile.

But neither the older nor the newer ship carried any meaning for Ro. Their captain did.

Jean-Luc Picard had been a significant force in Ro's life. After standing court-martial for her role in the disastrous events on Garon II, she'd spent more than three years in the stockade. Upon her eventual release, Picard supported the resumption of her Starfleet career, a decision not especially popular with Starfleet Command. Later, he recommended Ro for enrollment in Starfleet's demanding Advanced Tactical Training program. She welcomed the challenge and met it head-on, but it unexpectedly sent her life spinning in another direction, ultimately leading to her betrayal of the *Enterprise* captain.

Ro had wholeheartedly believed in the worthiness of the cause for which she had committed her act of treachery. The self-styled Maquis had been displaced from their homes when the Federation had ceded a number of planets to the Cardassian Union. Having grown up on a world occupied by the brutal Cardassians, Ro not only sympathized with the Maquis, but *empathized* with them. Although she would sooner have chosen to remain loyal to Captain Picard, she could not allow herself to be party to the arrest of people simply fighting to protect themselves and their homes.

Nearly six years passed before Ro saw Picard again. By that time, the Maquis had been utterly defeated by Dominion forces, and she had joined the Bajoran Militia, which had posted her at DS9 as its chief of security. When *Enterprise* visited the station, Captain Picard appeared in her office, where he faced her not with anger or acrimony—though he would have been justified in doing so—but with acceptance and a seemingly genuine interest in her career and her life.

Later, when Bajor became a member of the Federation, Ro had confronted the choice of attempting to rejoin Starfleet— over the objections of more than one admiral—or opting for the path of least resistance and moving on from DS9. She gravitated toward the latter alternative, until Captain Picard somehow overcame the voices in Starfleet Command opposing Ro. He also offered her his support in a simple but powerful way: he had a Starfleet uniform delivered to her office on the station, along with a handwritten note encouraging her to remain on DS9.

In some ways, Jean-Luc Picard had become like a *vintern* to Ro—an older, experienced figure who provided personal guidance, an exemplar of behavior and principle. Although they had communicated on only those two occasions in the past dozen or so years, she still felt connected to him. Her father had been tortured to death when she'd been just seven years old, causing her great anguish and leaving a void in her life that had led her more than once down the wrong path, and few others—not family members, not vedeks, not Starfleet admirals—had been able to point her in the right direction. Picard's interest and belief in her had been like a beacon in the night, guiding her forward to better places.

Then why am I so nervous? Ro asked herself. She knew that Captain Picard intimidated her, but she still thought that she should be excited and happy to see him, especially after such a long time.

I will *be happy to see him, of course,* she thought. But her emotions seemed more complicated than that. Though he had behaved as though he had forgiven her disloyalty to him, she could not help wondering if he truly had. Regardless, how could Ro ever repay the captain for all that he'd done for her, for all that he'd allowed her to accomplish?

You're being ridiculous, she told herself. In her life, she had leaped into battle, outnumbered and outgunned, against the formidable Jem'Hadar, and yet she felt anxious about seeing a man she respected and admired, and who seemed to hold her in high regard. It made no sense.

Ro pulled herself away from the window and headed for the nearest turbolift. She resolved to go to her office and see if the *Enterprise* crew had yet filed an itinerary for the few days they would spend at the station. Then she would contact Captain Picard and ask if she could, at his convenience, board the ship to see him.

As Ro headed for the lift, she glanced over the railing toward the main entrance of Quark's. She saw the doors thrown wide and the counter that opened directly onto the Promenade ready for business. She saw three people inside—Broik, Frool, and M'Pella—but not her . . . what? Friend? Companion? Paramour?

Ro smiled. *He's just my Quark,* she thought, content not to define their relationship. Whatever they had together, it had worked for them for some time. There seemed little reason to risk spoiling it by assigning it a label.

She entered the turbolift and stated her destination. When the cab arrived at ops, still several minutes before the start of the alpha shift, it pleased Ro to see that most of her command crew had already taken their posts to begin the day: her first officer and the Bajoran liaison, Cenn, sat at his general-services console,

Chief Chao at the main engineering station, Candlewood at sciences, and the station's newest transfer, Slaine, at tactical. It still felt peculiar to see a Cardassian working alongside Bajorans, but since the addition of Cardassia and Ferenginar to the Khitomer Accords almost a year earlier, a limited integration of personnel had taken place across the various military services.

Zivan Slaine held the grade of *dalin* in the Cardassian Guard, which roughly equated to the rank of lieutenant commander in Starfleet. In the few months that she'd been stationed on DS9, Dalin Slaine had performed well in her position, particularly given the high volume of Typhon Pact vessels traveling within the Bajoran Sector and through the wormhole. Though understandably reserved when she'd first come aboard, Slaine had lately displayed a willingness to mix with the crew in off-duty hours.

As Ro descended to the lower, central level of ops, she saw Cenn look up from his console, then quickly cross to intercept her at the base of the steps. "Good morning, Captain," he said quickly. Before Ro could even respond, he nodded his head in the direction of her office and said, "You've got a visitor."

Ro looked up, but even before she saw the rigidly postured figure, she guessed that Captain Picard had come to her office before she'd been able to visit him aboard *Enterprise*. He stood before her desk, with his back to the rest of ops, his head turned toward the left. In profile, he appeared strong and regal.

"Thank you, Desca," Ro said to her first officer. "Anything else to report?"

"Nothing that can't wait," Cenn said. "We had routine activity through the gamma and delta shifts, with a few ship arrivals and departures." He pointed up toward her office and Captain Picard. "Most notably, the *Enterprise*."

"All right," Ro said. "I'll check back with you after my meeting." She walked past Cenn and started up the stairs that led to her office. To her annoyance—and really, to her confusion as well—she felt her heart race inside her chest. *What is it about this man?* she thought, but she had no answers for herself.

The doors to Ro's office parted with an audible click. At the sound, Picard turned in her direction. He looked much the same as the last time she'd seen him, seven years earlier, though the small line of gray hair that had ringed his head back then had vanished, leaving him completely bald. He appeared fit, though perhaps the flesh of his face had sagged a bit, and the lines around his mouth and eyes had deepened.

"Captain Ro," he said, and he surprised her by smiling— an actual face-brightening, tooth-filled smile. Picard had supported her and provided a strong influence in her adult life, but his reputation of being a man reserved by nature, even austere, had been well earned.

Ro felt the sudden inclination to step forward and embrace her former commanding officer. Thinking that the gesture would likely embarrass both of them, she resisted. "Captain Picard," she said, pleased that she managed to keep her voice level and mask her nervousness. "It's good to see you."

Picard raised an arm and motioned across the room. "I was just admiring your artwork," he said, walking over to the side of the office where a painting hung on the outer bulkhead. Bordered by a simple, gilt frame, it depicted a starscape with a green-and-white planet hanging in the lower right-hand corner. Visible through the cloud cover, recognizable coastlines identified the world as Bajor. Four moons orbited above it, while a shard of Endalla, its largest natural satellite, showed over the horizon. "If I'm not mistaken," Picard said, "the stars are accurately represented. I think I can make out a number of the better-known Bajoran constellations." He traced his fingers just above the canvas as he enunciated the historic stellar configurations: "The Runners . . . the Dawn . . . the Falls . . . the Tears . . . the Temple." He glanced back over at Ro. "I think that may be all of them I know."

"And right in each case," Ro said, moving over to join him in front of the painting. "It's called *Bajor at Peace*." Ro indicated a triangular star formation on the left side of the work. "This is the Flames," she said, "and that—" She pointed to one of the lower stars. "—is Sol."

Picard nodded at the mention of his home star. "Is the artist Bajoran?"

"Yes," Ro said. "A woman named Acto Viri."

Picard seemed to consider the name. "I don't believe I'm familiar with her work."

"I'm not either," Ro said. She appreciated art for art's sake, but she knew little about the subject. For that reason, she rarely spoke about it, though she felt comfortable discussing *Bajor at Peace* with Picard.

Abruptly, Ro realized that her heart had stopped galloping, and that the captain had made it so. Apparently either anticipating or recognizing her disquiet, Picard had adroitly driven their conversation in a manner clearly designed to put her at ease. She felt grateful for his perceptiveness and consideration. "Captain Kira acquired the painting when she was in command of the station. When she left Deep Space Nine to enter the seminary, she gave it to me."

"Very generous." Then, changing the subject, Picard said, "So: *Captain* Ro."

"I know," she said. "It's been more than a year since my promotion, and I still can't believe it myself."

"I didn't say I couldn't believe it," Picard said. "Actually, your success doesn't surprise me at all."

"Now *you're* being very generous," Ro told him. "But you probably had more to do with my making captain than I did."

"Nonsense," Picard said, in a way that implied he would brook no argument. "Your abilities, your performance, and your leadership brought you to where you are now. Not me."

Ro nodded, fully aware that without the captain's efforts on her behalf, she never would have been permitted to resume her career in Starfleet when Bajor had entered the Federation. Rather than contradict Picard, though, she instead asked if he would care for something to eat or drink. He asked for hot tea, which she ordered from the replicator, along with a glass of *pooncheenee* for herself. She handed the cup of tea to Picard, took the glass of reddish orange fruit juice for herself, and led him to the sitting area on the other side of her office. They sat together on the cushioned bench there.

"So how has the transition to captain been for you?" Picard asked.

"Honestly, things didn't really change much for me," Ro said. "I'd already been commanding Deep Space Nine for three and a half years at the time."

"So no alteration in your mind-set?" Picard asked. "No compulsion to recheck your work three times instead of two, to spend twice as much time second-guessing your decisions, that sort of thing?"

"Well," Ro said with a shrug, recalling that her advancement to the rank of captain had initially undermined the confidence she felt in her own abilities. "Is that common?"

"I don't know if it's common," Picard said. "But it seems to me that it's not *un*common."

"Did you go through it?" Ro wanted to know.

"That and more," Picard said, and for the second time, the edges of his mouth curled upward.

For a strange moment, Ro actually wondered if a Founder had infiltrated DS9 or *Enterprise* and masqueraded as Jean-Luc Picard. She could in no other way immediately account for the apparent change to his disposition. He seemed . . . lighter.

Returning to their conversation, Ro asked, "Do you think you'll go through that again when Starfleet Command finally makes you an admiral?"

"Oh, I've made it quite clear that I have no intention of flying a desk for the rest of my Starfleet career," Picard said. "However long or short that might be."

"Somehow I don't see you walking away from the *Enterprise* anytime soon." Even as Ro uttered the words, she understood that she didn't necessarily believe them. As much as she'd always thought that Captain Picard belonged on the bridge of a starship, she sensed that, somehow, that might no longer hold true, despite his protestation to the contrary.

"My circumstances have changed," Picard said, as though echoing Ro's thoughts. "I got married."

Ro felt her mouth open wide in surprise, and she made a conscious effort to close it. "Did this just happen?" she asked.

"Almost three years ago now."

Ro's jaw dropped open again. "Three *years*?" she said. "How have I not heard about this? This is a Starfleet space station. Ships dock here all the time. And I'm in touch with Command. You'd think somebody would have mentioned it."

"You don't strike me as one for idle gossip," Picard noted.

"No, but . . ." As her voice trailed off, Ro realized her impoliteness. "Congratulations," she said. "I'm so happy for you."

"Thank you," Picard said. "I married Beverly Crusher."

Ro nodded. "There always did seem to be a spark between the two of you."

"Well, after many years and several false starts, we finally managed to fan that spark into a flame," he said. "When it came down to it, it really didn't take much at all, other than each of us being ready to share our lives in that way." He paused enough to offer Ro another smile. "We have a son."

Ro's mouth didn't drop open again. Instead, she threw her head back and laughed, a merry sound that accurately captured the joy she felt.

"That's a new reaction," Picard said.

"I'm sorry, Captain," Ro said. "I think it's wonderful that you have a son, but I was just remembering back when I served aboard the *Enterprise,* when we were returning to the ship from Marlonia." Along with Keiko O'Brien and Guinan, Ro and Picard had traveled aboard a shuttlecraft. When they'd become caught in an energy anomaly, the shuttle had broken up in space, and the *Enterprise* crew had needed to transport them to safety—only to find that the bodies of the four had been transmuted into their preadolescent selves, although their adult minds had remained intact.

Picard offered a knowing chuckle of his own. "I trust René won't be quite as precocious as I was when that happened." Even in the body of a twelve-year-old, the captain had helped thwart the takeover of *Enterprise* by a band of renegade Ferengi.

"He's a Picard," Ro said, "so you never know."

"I suppose not," said Picard. "But we still have time before he reaches that age. He'll be two next week."

"Do you have a picture?" Ro asked.

"I'm afraid that I don't," Picard said. "But he is on board the *Enterprise,* and I hoped you might like to meet him."

"Of course," Ro said, trying to imagine the captain himself at such a young age.

"The *Enterprise* won't be heading to the Gamma Quadrant until our Romulan counterparts arrive," Picard said. "That's why I've come to your office: to invite you to join Beverly and me for dinner in our quarters this evening."

Ro felt honored by the invitation—and at the same time, unworthy of it. *It's just dinner,* she thought, but then something else occurred to her. To Picard, though, she simply said, "I'd like that very much."

"Good. Let's say nineteen hundred hours then," Picard said. He stood up and faced Ro, who also got to her feet. "It is so very good to see you, Laren. I'm delighted that you are doing so well."

"Thank you," she said. "It's very good to see you, sir."

"Jean-Luc."

She considered his request that she use his given name a privilege. "Thank you, Jean-Luc."

He turned and exited the office. Ro felt a twinge of disgrace as she watched him leave. It still troubled her that she had once betrayed Picard's trust in her, despite the fact that it had happened so long ago.

Ro turned and collected his cup and her glass from the sitting area. As she carried them to the replicator to be recycled, she faced her realization. It seemed completely clear that Captain Picard had forgiven her for her past failures, but she also saw that, even after all the time that had passed, she had yet to forgive herself.

"Maybe it's time," she said in her empty office. And she knew that it was.

Captain Jean-Luc Picard waited in DS9's wardroom, seated at the head of the long conference table that filled most of the elongated, narrow space. Even with the capacity to accommodate more than a dozen people at the table, and perhaps as many at either end of the room, and even with the five large, eye-shaped ports that lined the outer bulkhead, the place felt cold and confining. *And not just the wardroom,* Picard thought.

The entire station seemed like an agglomeration of shadows, collected together in a hard, uninviting framework. The setting reminded him of a starship in battle, with emergency lighting and instrument panels barely able to keep the darkness at bay. *In other words,* Picard thought, *not a friendly place.*

At the captain's right hand sat *Enterprise*'s chief engineer, Geordi La Forge. The two meetings that afternoon called for one of Picard's senior staff to accompany him. With so many Typhon Pact vessels ranging through the sector—he could see four freighters, three Breen and one Gorn, through the wardroom's ports—it made sense to leave his exec and his security chief aboard ship, in the event that an incident arose requiring the *Enterprise* crew to take immediate action.

"Do we know who the Federation Council is sending along with us?" La Forge asked.

"We did," Picard said, not without some frustration. "Tel Ammanis Lent had been appointed, but she's subsequently been withdrawn."

"She's the Alonis ambassador?"

"Yes," Picard said. "And she's had more experience in dealing with the Romulans over the past decade than any other Federation diplomat. Her assignment to this mission made eminent sense." When *Enterprise* and the Romulan Imperial Fleet starship *Eletrix* embarked on a joint exploratory mission to the Gamma Quadrant two days hence, each would carry a liaison to aid in the lines of communication between the two crews.

"Then why was she withdrawn?" asked the engineer.

"That's a good question, Mister La Forge, one for which I do not have an adequate answer," Picard said. "When I received word directly from President Bacco's office yesterday about the change, they did not offer an explanation."

"It sounds like somebody somewhere is playing politics," observed La Forge.

"It does appear as though that might be the case," Picard said. "Although, considering the importance of this venture to the stability of the—"

Before the captain could complete his thought, the farther of the wardroom's two doors parted and glided open. He expected the station's first officer to escort the Federation liaison to the meeting, but instead, Captain Ro entered. A moment later, he understood why as a familiar, lanky figure stepped inside behind her. He wore traditional black vestments, his arms hidden within their folds. Picard stood up from the table, as did La Forge beside him.

"Captain Picard," Ro announced formally, "I would like to present Ambassador Spock."

"Of course," Picard said quietly. He raised his hand and offered the customary Vulcan gesture of greeting, palm out, paired fingers forming a *V*, thumb straight out to the side. "Welcome, Ambassador."

"Thank you, Captain," Spock said, extracting his arm from within his robe and returning Picard's manual salutation. He then turned to Ro and thanked her as well.

Ro bowed her head in acknowledgment. Then, to Picard, she said, "The Romulan ship *Eletrix* has just docked at the station."

"When their party is ready, Captain," Picard said, "would you please have them escorted down here?"

"I will," Ro said, and then she left the wardroom.

Once the doors had closed behind her, Spock approached the conference table and the two officers. "I trust you remember my chief engineer," said Picard, "Commander La Forge."

Spock turned his head slightly to one side, the small movement clearly signaling curiosity, and reminding Picard of his lost friend, Data. "*Commander* La Forge?" said the ambassador. "When we last saw each other, you had been promoted to the rank of captain of engineering."

Beside Picard, La Forge shifted from one foot to the other. "I was," he told Spock. "But when the command of the *Musgrave* opened up, Starfleet wanted to transfer me there as its new captain. I considered the opportunity, but . . ." He shrugged and glanced at Picard. "I'm pretty confident in my engineering abilities," he said, "but I think my command skills could still use a little seasoning."

"He's now the *Enterprise*'s second officer," Picard noted.

"Starfleet didn't think the chain of command worked with two captains in it," La Forge explained, "so I accepted a rank reassignment to commander."

"Nevertheless," Spock said, "I am certain that our mutual colleague would have been pleased and impressed with the path of your career."

Picard nodded in agreement. "I believe that Scotty considered Mister La Forge a kindred soul."

"He said as much to me," Spock said, before bowing his head and casting his gaze downward. "With Captain Scott's death, Starfleet lost one of its finest engineers."

"He saved two crews," La Forge said solemnly. "One aboard the *Challenger* and one aboard a Romulan ship."

Spock looked back up. "As I've mentioned to you, that is of no surprise to me," he said. "Dying in the service of saving others has become something of a staple among the senior officers—and former senior officers—of the *Enterprise*."

As the captain of the current generation of that ship, Picard glanced at La Forge, and then back at the ambassador. "I hope that you're not offering a prediction for the mission we're about to begin."

"A prediction?" Spock said. "No." Then he raised an eyebrow and added, "But there are always possibilities."

Picard did not visibly react to the remark, but he thought that the dryness of the Vulcan's sense of humor could bring drought to Pacifica. He indicated that Spock should take the seat across from La Forge. Once all three men had sat down at the conference table, Picard said, "So you are taking the role of the *Enterprise*'s liaison to the crew of the *Eletrix*."

"I am," Spock said. "President Bacco personally requested that I take the position. As I understand it, she made the decision to do so jointly with Admiral Akaar. While the Federation Council's first choice for the position, Ambassador Lent, possesses a wealth of diplomatic experience with the Romulans, I do as well. In addition to my own years of service as a Federation ambassador, I have also resided on Romulus almost continuously for the past fifteen years. Furthermore, I believe that President Bacco and Admiral Akaar viewed my decades of active duty aboard Starfleet vessels as an advantage. There is also the matter of my familiarity with Praetor Kamemor."

"Familiarity?" Picard asked.

"Since she became the leader of the Romulan Empire," Spock explained, "she and I have had several meetings. Most recently, she asked that I carry an olive branch from the Typhon Pact. Specifically, I delivered her invitation to President Bacco for the diplomatic summit that was ultimately hosted by the Boslics."

"I see," said Picard. "And obviously your presence here demonstrates your commitment to the cause of entente. Clearly, you view it as even more important than your work on Vulcan-Romulan reunification."

"I do actively support the current state of governmental amity in the Alpha and Beta Quadrants," Spock said. "But my decision to depart Romulus, while hastened by the praetor's call for me to act as an envoy to the president, did not begin there. I had already determined to leave the Empire and return to the Federation."

"I must say, that surprises me," said Picard. "I thought that over the last couple of years, since first Tal'Aura and then Gell Kamemor permitted the open public discussion of reunification, the Movement had grown considerably."

"It has," Spock said. "But my place as its leader, and as the face of the Movement, has outlived its usefulness. Romulan voices—in many cases, younger voices—have replaced mine in the ongoing debate. While I will freely provide counsel to the owners of those voices if asked, I am content to step aside and allow them to carry the cause into the future."

"Does that mean that you've left Romulus for good?" La Forge asked.

"I do not know if I will ever reside within the Empire again," Spock said. "I am sure that I will maintain a relationship with the Romulan people, and with Praetor Kamemor, but I now believe that I can be of most use back in the Federation."

"A claim well supported by your participation in our upcoming mission," Picard said. "Do you have a plan for how you will conduct the communications between the Federation and Romulan crews?"

"Nothing specific," Spock said. "I intend to discuss the nature and details of our interface with my Romulan counterpart before establishing any definite procedures. It seems to me, though, that our roles should be more administrative than participatory."

"Meaning that you intend to allow the crews to communicate among themselves?" Picard asked.

"That will be my recommendation," Spock said. "There should be limitations in place in order to avoid confusion. I would restrict such communications to a small number of senior officers in both crews."

"Will that include the chief engineers?" La Forge asked. "Because in my experience, while too many voices can muddy the waters, technical solutions often require a high level of coordination among the experts."

"I have to agree with Commander La Forge," Picard said.

"I think we need to manage such interactions," Spock said, "but I concur. I envision connecting the heads of departments from both crews, such as the chief engineers, the lead scientists, the communications directors, and the chief medical officers."

They spoke for several more minutes about the joint mission, including the historic nature of the Federation and Romulan Empire exploring the universe together. The plan called for the two ships, *Enterprise* and *Eletrix,* to travel independently but in relative proximity to each other, with their crews charting star systems and interstellar phenomena. If either vessel encountered a habitable world or something else worthy of extended study, both crews would then work together.

As Picard started to discuss the intended flight path through the Gamma Quadrant, the nearer doors opened, and Captain Ro once again entered the wardroom. Two Romulans, a man and a woman, both in Imperial Fleet uniforms, followed her into the room. Picard recognized the rank insignia of the woman as that of a commander, the Romulan equivalent of a Starfleet captain. Tall, with striking green eyes and loose brunette hair, she carried herself with confidence and dignity.

Picard stood—as did La Forge and Spock—and waited for Captain Ro to make formal introductions. Before she did, though, a third Romulan crossed the threshold behind the others, a man whom Picard recognized from numerous encounters across many years. After the doors closed, Ro said, "Captain Picard, I would like to present Commander Orventa T'Jul of the Romulan vessel *Eletrix*; her second-in-command, Subcommander Venalur Atreev; and the Romulan liaison, Tomalak."

All at once, the optimism with which Picard anticipated the joint mission faded, replaced by a feeling of dread, and a concern about the true aims of the praetor.

20

Vedek Kira Nerys walked through the murky lighting of the habitat ring on Deep Space 9, inundated by memories. It had been some time since last she'd visited the station, but her many experiences there remained vibrant in her mind. That had always been her way. She certainly could not recall every moment of her youth, but she could still visualize so much, from her time as a girl in the Singha refugee camp to her days as a teen in the Resistance. For fully a quarter of a century— for the *first* twenty-five years of her life—she lived within the cruel reality of the Cardassian Occupation. Because she knew nothing else, that harsh existence had long defined her, during its thousands of interminable days, and in the days that followed.

In the aftermath of the liberation, Kira had clung to her anger and to her hatred—both emotions well justified. She initially came to Deep Space 9—the erstwhile Terok Nor—as the Bajoran liaison to the Federation contingent there, who took over the operation of the station at the request of the barely functioning provisional government. At the outset, Kira viewed the UFP as merely another usurper, perhaps not as ruthless as the Cardassians, but to her way of thinking, just as invasive. Over time, though, the situation changed, or her understanding of it did, and eventually she also changed.

Kira recalled Aamin Marritza, the Cardassian file clerk who'd served at the notorious Gallitep forced-labor camp on Bajor. Years later, aboard DS9, he impersonated the brutal commandant of the camp, allowing himself to be captured as a war criminal, in the hope that he—and by extension, all of Cardassia—would stand trial. Horrified by the merciless treatment of the Bajorans at Gallitep but powerless to stop it, Marritza suffered terrible guilt for what he considered his cowardice. He wanted not only to atone for his personal inaction, but to lay bare the sins of his people in occupying Bajor.

Marritza had been a tortured man, and perhaps he'd even been right to condemn himself for not risking his own life to save those interned at Gallitep. But Kira vividly remembered coming to recognize and appreciate the quality of Marritza's character, to realize that despite the occupation of Bajor by the Cardassian Union for decades, she could not rationalize painting all Cardassians with the same brush. Whatever small amount of wisdom she might have gained in the course of her life, she traced its beginnings to her interactions with Marritza.

Well, and to my time with the Emissary, she thought.

Seemingly surrounded by her past, Kira turned a corner into another shadowy corridor, at last approaching her destination. It amazed her to think that she had spent nine years on Deep Space 9. For such a long time—for all her life to that point—she truly believed that she would never stop battling the Cardassians, even after they left Bajor. But when she met Marritza, when she came to understand him, she finally foresaw a time when she would lay down her sword. After that revelation, she came to feel that she would never leave DS9, which became a home for her in a manner that no other place ever really had.

But then Benjamin had ascended into the Celestial Temple, and even when he'd returned, he'd never gone back to the station, other than to visit. And even though Kira rose to the highest position on DS9, even though her term as its commander fully satisfied her, it also brought new challenges. By sending

Taran'atar, a Jem'Hadar soldier, to reside on the station, Odo boldly attempted to change so many things: the nature of the Alpha Quadrant's relationship with the Dominion, the Founders' view of their interactions with "solids," the very character and self-identity of the Jem'Hadar. Other complications arose, including the parasite invasion and the death of First Minister Shakaar. The Eav'oq reappeared after millennia, the Ascendants rose, and Iliana Ghemor wove a thread of madness from Cardassia to Bajor, from Idran to Deep Space 9. Kira remembered well Taran'atar's betrayal—though he had not committed it of his own volition—and she surely would never forget his final, fevered act, which had transformed everything.

All of which had led Kira to pursue true peace and understanding for her own life. None of her experiences—struggling just to survive in the refugee camp, shedding the blood of Bajor's occupiers, wrestling with her place in a free society, and even commanding Deep Space 9—nothing she ever did in her life made her think that her path would lead her to religious service. At Singha, a friend of her parents, Istani Reyla, introduced Kira as a child to the teachings of the Prophets. From that time forward, she always believed, always found strength in her faith, but it never occurred to her to even consider becoming a novice.

Until the day that it finally did occur to me, Kira thought with a smile. As the old adage went, "The path the Prophets lay out for you may not be straight."

That was almost six years ago, Kira thought with a sense of wonder. Sometimes, it felt as though her life hurtled by at warp velocity. As she got older, the speed with which time passed only seemed to increase.

Upon deciding to join the Bajoran religious order, Kira had resigned her commission from Starfleet and had gladly turned over command of the station to Elias Vaughn. She took up her official religious studies at the Vanadwan Monastery in Releketh Province, in some ways far more scared than when she stormed Dominion Headquarters on Cardassia Prime during the war. But she committed to her newfound calling, and her personal journey took her to places within herself that she never knew existed. She felt tranquil and happy, and to her surprise, she also felt of greater service to her people than she ever had before that, even as a freedom fighter or as the commanding officer of Deep Space 9.

Finally arriving at the quarters to which she'd been heading, Kira reached up and touched the control panel set into the bulkhead. A moment later, the door slid open. Kira stepped inside, over the raised threshold.

Although the furniture in the sitting area had been rearranged since the last time she'd been there, the cabin looked much as she recollected it. On one bulkhead, a large, abstract clock, composed of metal sheets and rods—more a work of art than a timepiece—ticked away the seconds of the twenty-six-hour Bajoran day. On that same bulkhead, on the other side of the room's replicator, three prints hung in silver-gray frames, all of them presenting an image of a Starfleet vessel: *Mjolnir, Sentinel,* and *Defiant.* A mobile hanging from the overhead in one corner depicted Bajor and its five moons. Various other pieces of art, most of them kinetic in nature, adorned the rest of the space. Kira also saw a number of framed pictures on tables and shelves, some of them showing the faces of people she knew, including Kalena Hoku—the captain of *Mjolnir*—and Elias Vaughn.

Dressed in her uniform, Lieutenant Prynn Tenmei stood in front of the sofa, a padd depending from one hand. "Vedek Kira," she said. "Thank you so much for coming."

"It's good to see you, Prynn," Kira said, taking another step forward, allowing the door to glide shut behind her. "And we've known each other too long for formalities. It's Nerys." She glanced down at the simple, earth-toned pantsuit she wore, not particularly immodest, but flattering. "This isn't exactly a vedek's robe."

Light shined from Tenmei's eyes as though reflecting tears. Then the lieutenant moved, extracting herself from the sitting area and reaching her arms out to Kira. The two embraced.

"Thank you for coming, Nerys," Tenmei said.

Kira waited until her friend pulled away, and then she said,

"I'm only sorry I couldn't come sooner. I was at a retreat, teaching young acolytes."

Tenmei laughed, though Kira saw no humor in her expression. "Believe me, there's no hurry."

"Well, good," Kira said. "I'm glad to be here." When she'd received Tenmei's message asking if she intended to visit Deep Space 9 anytime soon, Kira had replied with the dates of her earliest availability. She did not know why Tenmei wished to see her, but she could guess.

After Tenmei offered refreshments, and then retrieved two steaming mugs of raktajino from the replicator—Kira's extra hot, with two measures of *kava*—the two women moved into the sitting area. Kira sat on the sofa, and Tenmei took a comfortable chair opposite her across a low, oval table. They both sipped at their mugs before Kira said, "How are you, Prynn?"

"I'm all right," Tenmei said with a flat smile. Kira imagined that she wore that expression often these days in a futile attempt to disguise her emotions.

"That doesn't sound very convincing," Kira told her lightly. Then, soberly, she said, "I know how difficult it's been for you to deal with your father's condition."

"Yes, it's difficult," Tenmei said. Kira felt grateful that at least she could admit that. "When I'm on the station and not away on the *Defiant,* I spend time with my dad every day, usually before and after my duty shift."

Kira counted back in her head and calculated that Vaughn's injuries had occurred two and a half years earlier. She thought that spending so much time with a patient who suffered from a traumatic brain injury—with, essentially, a lifeless body—must have been terribly debilitating for Tenmei. "Has your father shown *any* improvement?"

"No," Tenmei said. "And Doctor Bashir says that there's really no hope."

"I'm sorry, Prynn."

"Thank you," Tenmei said, and she swiped a hand across her eyes. "It's been a year since we removed my dad from his respirator. The only things keeping his body alive are a feeding tube and a hydration line." She picked up her mug, raised it almost to her lips, then set it down again without drinking from it.

More than anything, Kira thought, Tenmei looked like somebody acting on automatic pilot. She seemed sad and alone and lost. Kira hoped that, for whatever reason Tenmei had wanted to see her, she could help.

"I called you *vedek* before because that's the capacity in which I need to speak with you," Tenmei said. "I mean, you're my friend—I wouldn't have contacted you otherwise—but . . . it's just—"

"Prynn, it's okay," Kira told her. "I want to be here for you. What is it you need?"

"I . . . I'm not really sure," Tenmei said. "But I recently decided to have my dad's feeding and hydration tubes removed. For so long, I've been holding so tightly to the idea that, someday, he'll just wake up and be himself again. But that's a lie. A lie I chose to believe because I love my dad so much. And because, even when we were estranged, there was always that possibility that we would reconnect. I don't think I knew it back then, but I wanted that possibility—I *needed* it. I guess I still do." She looked to the side, and Kira could see her fighting back tears once more. When she spoke again, she did so in a whisper. "But I know that my dad's not coming back this time."

"I'm sorry," Kira said again. She wanted to say more, but she knew from bitter experience that words could provide only so much salve. At that point, just her presence in the room with Tenmei probably meant more than anything she could possibly say.

The lieutenant inhaled deeply and slowly, her nostrils flaring, and she appeared to gather herself. "My dad wasn't religious," she said. "He didn't hew to any particular creed, he didn't believe in a deity. But he thought about life a lot, thought about his place in the universe, and how he could best fulfill himself while also making a positive contribution. In that way, I consider him a spiritual man."

"Your father and I grew pretty close during our time together here on the station," Kira said. "He talked enough about his ambitions to be an explorer that I could tell that he'd been dreaming of such a life for a long time—probably since he was a boy. But I also know that he spent the majority of his career in Starfleet as an intelligence officer. I never got the sense that he disliked his work as an operative until maybe the end, but I could tell that missions like *Defiant*'s three-month exploration of the Gamma Quadrant satisfied him much more."

"He *loved* taking the ship and crew on that mission," Tenmei said, her face genuinely brightening for the first time since Kira had seen her. "A lot happened, and we all faced our share of dangers, but I don't think I'd ever seen him happier up to that point. He *reveled* in those eleven direct first contacts."

"Don't forget the exchange of friendship messages with sixteen other civilizations," Kira said.

Tenmei continued to smile, which altered the contours of her face considerably. Without the wide, joyful expression, she could look so serious, even in the best of times. "You were right about my dad, Nerys," she said. "About his wanting to explore the galaxy back when he was just a boy. When I was young, he talked a lot about it. His mother taught him about the stars in his own youth, and I always got the feeling that's where his passion for space travel came from.

"But his other work—his intelligence work—got in the way," Tenmei went on. "I guess, when you don't foster your dreams for a while, you lose sight of them. But do you know what brought him back to wanting to explore?"

"His Orb experience?" Kira asked, knowing the answer.

Tenmei's eyes widened. "He told you about it," she said. "I'm glad that he did, but I'm surprised. He didn't seem to want to talk about it much. I think maybe because he couldn't explain it . . . maybe because he doubted the reality of the experience."

"No, I don't think he doubted," Kira said softly. "I don't want to contradict you about your own father, Prynn—"

"No, go ahead," Tenmei said, a note of excitement seeping into her voice. "If you know something about him, I'd love to hear it."

For just an instant, Kira worried about betraying Vaughn's confidence. But Tenmei was right: he was never coming back.

And Kira thought that if she could somehow ask Vaughn's permission to share that particular piece of information about him with his daughter, he would gladly allow it.

"Actually, your father had two Orb experiences, and I don't think he doubted either one of them," Kira said. "When he found the Orb of Memory on a Cardassian freighter lost in the Badlands, just before he first came to Deep Space Nine . . . I dreamed about him finding it."

"What?" Tenmei asked. "I don't understand. What do you mean?"

"I essentially saw your father aboard the freighter," Kira said. "I saw him find the Orb of Memory. And yet we'd never met, and he was out in space, and I was here on the station."

"And you told him about your dream?"

"I did," Kira said. "I confirmed some of the details of his time aboard the freighter before he revealed them to me."

Tenmei seemed to consider Kira's story, and then, in something approaching an awed tone, said, "Wow."

"I know," Kira said. "Orb experiences can be like that."

"It's no wonder you two became close friends."

Kira nodded. "I certainly think that connection helped set us on that course."

Again, Tenmei grew quiet as she appeared to think about what Kira had told her. Then she said, "You mentioned that my dad had a second Orb experience. Was it like the first?"

"I don't think so," Kira said. "We only talked about it once, though I asked him about it more often than that. I don't think he liked to talk about it because . . . because it involved you and your mother."

"Oh," Tenmei said, evidently surprised, though she didn't seem upset. "Would you tell me about it?"

"I can't tell you much, because your father didn't tell me much," Kira said. "But when he experienced the Orb of Unity, he confronted the guilt he felt for the loss of your mother. And for what he did to you."

Tenmei nodded. Kira had thought that her friend deserved to hear the truth, and that it might someday help her, but she'd also thought that what she had to say would likely distress Prynn. But that didn't seem to be the case.

Unexpectedly, Tenmei chuckled. "You know, it's funny," she said. "When people learned about the troubles I had with my dad, and about my childhood and about what happened to my mother, they almost always drew the wrong conclusions. It didn't matter what I told them; they heard a few facts, ignored a few others, perhaps didn't understand the complexity of it all. Maybe I just didn't explain it properly."

Tenmei laughed again, louder. "Of course, until a few years ago—until my dad and I were on the *Defiant*'s mission to the Gamma Quadrant—I didn't entirely understand it myself. My dad didn't either, not really. But what happened out there . . . we figured it out together."

The smile on Tenmei's face faded. "And then when we found my mother . . . when we found what she had become . . . and my dad had to . . . had to . . ." She stumbled over the words, and tears began to run down her face. Kira rose, intending to go to her, but Tenmei held up her hands. "I'm all right," she insisted. "I know what the Borg did to her, why she had to die again . . . because that wasn't her, and never would be."

Kira thought about what had happened to the Borg Collective, and wondered if Tenmei ever thought about the possibility that, had her mother survived long enough as one of their number, she might ultimately have gained her freedom. If she did, or had, she gave no indication. Still crying, she continued to speak.

"People always thought my dad was a bad father when I was a child," Tenmei said. "They thought that he was always absent, off on one mission or another, leaving my mother and me at home. Except that sometimes my dad stayed and my mother left. And sometimes we were all together. When we weren't, we all looked forward to when we would be. I mean, I missed them when they weren't there, but . . . I had a happy childhood. I was loved, and nurtured, and supported.

"Later, when my dad sent my mother off on her mission . . . on the mission she never returned from . . . people always thought I blamed him for that," Tenmei said. "And probably I did to some degree. But I knew that he loved my mother, that he wouldn't have willingly sent her on her mission if he knew that she wouldn't come back.

"What mattered," Tenmei said, "was that my dad blamed himself. And because I was grieving, he allowed that to validate his guilt. He pulled away from me, punishing himself, telling himself that he didn't deserve my love, that I *should* hate him.

"But I didn't. Not then." Tenmei shrugged. "But when I needed him most, when I needed him to help me work through the pain of my mother's loss, he abandoned me emotionally. He didn't intend to. He thought he was giving me what I wanted: distance from him, because he thought I *already* hated him.

"And so, eventually, I did."

Kira didn't know what to say. Vaughn's relationship with his daughter, when it had been bad, had been a subject he did not discuss. Neither had Tenmei. And when father and daughter had grown close again, neither ever seemed moved to talk about what had so long divided them.

"I feel privileged that you're telling me this," Kira said. "I didn't know. I didn't understand, at least not in the way you just explained it."

Tenmei wiped the tears from her face. "I've never really told anybody all of it," she said. "Not in that way. I mean, I talked about the different aspects of what happened, but . . . I don't know. I just let people think what they wanted to think, what they felt comfortable thinking."

"Well, I'm not sure exactly what your father experienced when he encountered the Orb of Unity," Kira said, "although the one time he talked with me about it, I got the impression that he had somehow relived the tragedy of the loss of your mother, and of his relationship with you.

"What I do know," Kira concluded, "is that when your father emerged from his second Orb encounter, Benjamin Sisko was with him."

"I remember that," Tenmei said. "I guess I didn't understand that was an Orb encounter. I just knew that my dad went to talk to Opaka Sulan on Bajor, and that while he was there, Captain Sisko reappeared."

Kira thought for a moment about the course of her conversation with Tenmei. "Can I ask you, Prynn, why you brought up your father's Orb experience?"

"Because I know that it had a profound influence on him," Tenmei said. "And because when I made the decision to have his feeding tube removed, I informed Doctor Bashir. We went together to my dad's bedside, but simply taking him off his last remaining life support didn't seem right. I mean, I still believe it's the right choice, but it seemed wrong to do so without some sort of ceremony or . . . I don't know, something . . . to mark his passing, and to honor his life.

"I thought about taking him back to Berengaria Seven, where his mother raised him, but he never liked to go back there. He lost his mother when he was young. So, I don't know, I just thought that, since he found something of real value to him in the Bajoran religion . . ." She left her question unasked, but Kira answered it anyway.

"I can do something for him, Prynn," she said. "*We* can do something. There are several Bajoran funerary rituals. Many of them have ancient origins and have fallen into disuse. Many of them, such as the Bajoran death chant, are long and complex."

"I don't think that's what I'm looking for, Nerys," Tenmei said. "I'm talking about something basic, but heartfelt. Maybe even something lyrical, because I really think my father had the heart of a poet." She shook her head. "When I think of him breathing his last breath on an old Cardassian mining station, so angular and cold . . . it just seems like he deserves more."

"I understand," Kira said. "Maybe . . . you know, there are hospices on Bajor. We have one at the Vanadwan Monastery. Normally, when patients are brought there, they're conscious and aware, and the caregivers help them spend their final days in relative peace, surrounded by loved ones. But the experience is important not just for the patient, but for whom they leave behind."

"That sounds nice," Tenmei said. "Can we do that for my dad, even though . . ."

"Yes, of course," Kira said. "I can arrange for him to be taken to Bajor in the next day or two, I'm sure. When you're ready, you can bring whoever you need to so that they can say good-bye with you."

"I would like you there, Nerys, of course," Tenmei said. "My dad always thought so highly of you, and he thought he owed you a debt for allowing him a place on Deep Space Nine."

"He owed *me* a debt?" Kira said. "As I recall, the first time he came aboard, he stopped a rogue Jem'Hadar soldier from blowing up the station."

"He told the story differently."

"Of course he did," Kira said. "I'm touched that you want me there, Prynn, and I want to be there. I'll just need to find a replacement for me on a trip—"

"A trip?" Tenmei asked.

"I was supposed to be on my way tomorrow to Cardassia Prime for a gathering of vedeks together with adherents of the Oralian Way," Kira explained.

"I don't want you to give that up," Tenmei said.

"I'm happy to do it," Kira told her.

"I know," Tenmei said. "But it's been two and a half years since my dad sustained his injuries. We don't have to rush."

Kira wondered if Tenmei actually welcomed the delay, given the finality of what would happen. "I may be gone a few weeks."

"That's fine," Tenmei said. "In the meantime, we can have my dad moved to Bajor, and I can invite who I need to invite, maybe prepare some words to read."

"I think that would be lovely."

Tenmei stood up and moved around the low table to sit beside Kira on the sofa. "Thank you, Nerys," she said. "This means so much to me." She reached out and hugged Kira.

"You're welcome." Then, trying to lighten the mood, she asked if Tenmei wanted to have dinner together, perhaps on the Promenade, at T'Pril's or the Replimat—or even at Quark's, if she preferred.

"I'd love to have dinner with you," Tenmei said. "I want to find out about everything going on in *your* life. But I don't think I'm quite up to going out to the Promenade."

"That's fine," Kira said. "We can eat here."

"Terrific."

As Tenmei got up and headed for the replicator, Kira wondered when the lieutenant had last been to the Promenade, other than to visit her father in the infirmary. Kira had felt grief often in her life—far *too* often—but she couldn't quite imagine the scope of Prynn's pain, horribly prolonged by Vaughn's condition. She only hoped that, when she returned from Cardassia Prime and helped Tenmei to finally lay her father to rest, Prynn could find her way back to a normal and happy life.

21

Trok observed from his customary place on the side of the bridge as the holographic projection hovering above *Ren Fejin*'s navigational console changed. Where for scores of days the spherical display had depicted vast volumes of space and the astronomical objects that populated them, and then the more focused but still sizable extent of an entire star system, it had at last shifted to present only a single world. The surface of the planet showed large landmasses separated by dark, almost colorless oceans, all topped by intermittent cloud cover.

With the ship no longer at warp, its interior had finally stilled. Though during the journey Trok had continually made finer and finer adjustments to the internal settings of his environmental suit, and in that way had combated the noise and vibration surrounding him, those measures could not compare to the genuine calm that had settled within *Ren Fejin*. And yet the newfound quiet within the ship did not quell his anxiety.

"We have achieved high orbit above Overne Three," Dree announced, in a voice digitally standardized by the vocoder of his snouted Breen helmet. He reported from the other side of the bridge, where he stood at the pilot's station.

"Can passive scans identify planetary defenses?" Master Beld wanted to know.

"Yes," replied another Breen, Zelk, from where he consulted a sensor readout. *"They appear considerable."*

"Show me," Beld ordered.

Zelk worked his controls, modifying the hologram once more. The image of the planet contracted to half its size, while representations of the objects in orbit expanded about it, making them plainly visible. Trok readily recognized the distinctive forms of Jem'Hadar starships. *I spent enough time on Goventu Five watching the excavation team dig up one of their vessels,* Trok thought. *I certainly should know what they look like.*

Except that the ships Trok saw in the navigational projection glowed with power. They did not sit dark and lost beneath masses of frozen soil, but brimmed with energy and the capacity to destroy. And above Overne III, there were *many* of them.

"Reading what's visible in orbit, and extrapolating to the far side of the planet," said Zelk, *"I estimate that there are thirty-six Jem'Hadar vessels."*

Inside his environmental suit, a chill shook Trok. It reminded him again of his time in the frigid climes of Goventu V. But even as Trok shivered, he felt beads of sweat tracing down the side of his head.

"There are also six weapons platforms," Zelk added. He touched a control, and four of the six platforms joined the Jem'Hadar ships in the display. They each featured a cubic base from which emerged an articulated arm that ended in a concave dish—doubtless an energy emitter. *"I also read several dozen construction scaffolds, though most appear empty and uncrewed."* He operated his console again, bringing into view a number of large, skeletal frames, all but one of them empty; the exception contained a half-assembled Jem'Hadar starship.

"What about on the surface?" Beld asked.

Zelk again manipulated the controls on the console before him. *"It's difficult to know with certainty because of the cloud cover, and because of the large number of industrial facilities there,"* he said, *"but I'd say there are at least six land-based defensive emplacements."*

From their alliance with the Dominion during its war with the Federation, the Breen knew of several worlds on which the Gamma Quadrant power manufactured starships, including

Overne III. But even though the crew of *Ren Fejin* had traveled so long to reach the planet, Trok suddenly wanted to be back in the Breen Confederacy. For all of his research and all of his careful planning, and despite the threat posed by the Federation, he wanted to be home, not tens of thousands of light-years away, in the hostile space of the Dominion. Yes, the Founders and the Breen had once joined forces, but Trok did not doubt that, should the Jem'Hadar detect *Ren Fejin* so deep within their territory—particularly at one of their primary starship-manufacturing locales—they would immediately destroy the Breen vessel. *Or capture it,* he thought, *and then interrogate us.* Trok did not know which fate he feared more.

"Is there any indication that they know we're here?" Beld asked.

"If the Jem'Hadar knew we were here," said Dree, *"we* wouldn't *be here."*

Trok agreed with that sentiment, but he still had difficulty trusting the Romulans. The Federation hadn't permitted any of the civilian Typhon Pact vessels passing through the wormhole and into the Gamma Quadrant to carry cloaking devices, and so *Ren Fejin* hadn't. But it did keep scattered throughout its various cargo holds the components necessary to construct such a device. The Romulan specialist who had joined the crew, Joralis Kinn, had spent the time in the Gamma Quadrant assembling the equipment. If he'd done his job correctly, and if the latest version of the Romulan stealth technology functioned as well as the Empire claimed, then the crew of *Ren Fejin* would accomplish their objective; if not, they would likely never see home again.

The ship's master stepped over to the side of the bridge, raised a gloved hand up to a panel on the bulkhead, and pressed a button. *"Beld to engineering,"* he said. *"Kinn, what's your status?"*

"The cloak is performing within expected tolerances," replied the Romulan, his voice sounding tinny as it emerged from the comm unit. His words failed to rouse much confidence in Trok. Apparently Beld felt the same.

"'Within expected tolerances'?" the ship's master repeated. *"It's not working at its optimal level?"*

"*Master Beld, your vessel is not a Romulan starship,*" Kinn explained. "*We had little time to test the use of a cloak on a ship of Ren Fejin's size and configuration. Variances are unavoidable.*"

"*I don't care about avoiding variances,*" Beld said. "*I care about avoiding the Jem'Hadar.*"

"*The cloak is functioning,*" Kinn maintained. "*We are already at Overne Three, and we clearly haven't been detected. I don't expect that to change.*"

"*You don't 'expect' that to change,*" Beld said, and even though his helmet transformed his voice into an electronic blur, his words conveyed frustration. "*That hardly sounds like a guarantee of success.*"

"*That's because it isn't a guarantee,*" said Kinn. "*But if the ship sustains consistent power, we should remain undetectable to the Jem'Hadar.*"

Beld did not respond for a moment, instead looking around at both of his subordinates in turn, and then at Trok as well. Finally, he turned back to the comm unit. "*Very well, Kinn,*" he said. "*Let me know the instant you even anticipate a problem with the cloak.*"

"*Understood,*" Kinn said.

Beld reached up and punched at the comm control with the side of his gloved fist. Then he turned and moved to face the navigational hologram at the center of the bridge. He regarded the swarm of Jem'Hadar starships more or less evenly spaced about the planet, before asking, "*Are you reading their manufacturing plants?*"

"*Yes,*" Zelk said. "*All but the warp-engine construction plants appear to be on the surface. Most shipyard operations are centralized on the largest continent, but there are facilities scattered all over the planet.*"

Trok stepped away from the bulkhead and interjected. "*Can you tell where deflector systems and structural integrity generators are produced?*"

"*No,*" Zelk said. "*Not without engaging active sensor scans.*"

Beld pointed to the hologram, where the outsized representations of Jem'Hadar starships, weapons platforms, and engineering scaffolds ensphered Overne III. *"Show me the location with the highest concentration of large industrial facilities."*

Zelk complied with the order, and once again, the holographic image shifted. The Jem'Hadar ships and other objects in orbit vanished, and the planet grew in a dizzying rush of movement, until only a segment of its surface showed. Across a flat plain spread a compound comprising dozens of buildings, many of them interconnected. A distance scale along the display's equator indicated the great magnitude of the complex. *"These facilities are located in the center of the largest continent,"* Zelk said.

Beld turned toward Trok. *"Could any of these be what we're searching for?"*

Trok moved closer to the hologram and studied the buildings. *"A few of them appear to be large enough to allow for the full-scale testing those systems would require,"* he said. *"But I can't tell just by looking at them from the outside."*

"No, of course not," Beld said. *"But we need to know where to begin."* Peering over to the pilot, he said, *"Take us down, Dree. Bring us in over these buildings."* He waved over the complex display in the hologram.

Dree acknowledged the order, and Trok heard and felt the operation of the thrusters as they altered the ship's trajectory. The holographic projection changed once more, reverting to a view of the planet from high orbit, with the Jem'Hadar ships and weapons platforms circling above it. As the ship began its descent toward the atmosphere of Overne III, Trok could only hope that the Romulan technology installed on *Ren Fejin* would allow them to reach the surface, do what they'd come there to do, and escape back to the Alpha Quadrant.

But he had his doubts.

Trok watched the industrial complex grow in the holographic display, and he imagined *Ren Fejin* hovering above it, plain for all the Jem'Hadar crews in orbit to see. He tried to concentrate on the features of the buildings so that he could estimate the possibility of their containing the equipment used to manufacture either structural integrity field generators or deflector systems. But a portion of his mind remained on edge, his body tensed as though expecting a Jem'Hadar torpedo to come hurtling through the bridge, sending the ship and everybody aboard it to their destruction.

"Do you notice anything?" Master Beld asked in his short, electronically encoded bluster.

"I'm looking," Trok said. *"It's not as though the buildings have windows in them or signs identifying their purpose."*

"No, I'm not asking about what you think might be inside," Beld said. *"I'm asking if you notice anything unusual about what's outside the buildings."*

Trok walked around the spherical display, peering at the complex from different angles, searching for whatever Beld wanted him to see. *"I'm afraid I don't know what you mean,"* he said at last. *"I don't see anything."*

"Precisely," Beld said, somewhat mysteriously. *"There's nothing to see, no activity. The place seems abandoned."*

Trok looked closer, actually leaning in toward the display. He saw no movement whatsoever. While he surmised that the Founders, and therefore the Jem'Hadar, would insist on the Overne maintaining strict security procedures in the construction and testing of starships and weapons, he still would have expected to espy some indication of the workforce at the plant, and of work being performed.

"Remember the assembly scaffolds in orbit," said Zelk from his place at the sensor panel. *"There were dozens of them, but only one contained an actual starship under construction."*

"That's right," said Trok, recalling the large, empty frames floating above the planet. He turned away from the navigational hologram and toward Beld. *"Could this place be abandoned?"*

"If it's abandoned," Dree asked from the piloting console, *"then why would there be so many Jem'Hadar ships in orbit?"*

Beld looked at Trok, the horizontal light of the shipmaster's helmet like a fluorescent green eye. *"If the place had been abandoned permanently, wouldn't the Founders want it destroyed or dismantled?"* Beld finally asked. *"Since it all appears intact, doesn't that suggest* temporary *disuse?"*

"*But why would the Dominion stop the manufacture of starships and weapons?*" said Zelk.

"*These aren't their only such facilities,*" noted Beld.

"*All right,*" Zelk said. "*But even if the other complexes are still functioning, the question remains essentially the same: why would the Dominion reduce the manufacture of starships?*"

Trok thought about that, and could find only one answer. "*The Dominion closed its borders after the war with the Federation,*" he said. "*If there are no aggressors challenging them, then perhaps they have no need at the moment for large-scale starship production.*"

"*Perhaps,*" Beld allowed. "*Zelk, I want you to scan inside one of the buildings below. Narrow beam, low intensity. Try not to set off any alarms.*"

Zelk's gloved fingers marched dutifully across his sensor board. Again, Trok waited anxiously, anticipating a sudden Jem'Hadar attack. None came.

"*The entire complex is sheathed in a material that's scrambling my scans,*" Zelk said. "*But I'm reading a continuous thermal envelope, which you'd expect from external solar radiation. I'm not seeing any signatures to indicate functioning industrial production. But I can't tell with certainty from the outside.*"

Trok understood that if *Ren Fejin*'s sensors couldn't penetrate the buildings, then neither could transporters. But he suspected that Beld didn't intend to beam any of the crew into the complex anyway. A moment later, Beld confirmed that when he moved to the bulkhead, activated the comm system, and contacted the Romulan specialist down in engineering.

"*We need to look inside these buildings,*" the shipmaster told Joralis Kinn via the ship's comm system.

"*The phasing cloak is fully operational,*" replied Kinn. "*Proceed with care, and I'll monitor from down here. I'm tied into the ship's sensors and navigational display, so there should be no problems.*"

"*Acknowledged.*" Beld closed the comm channel, then stepped back over to the holographic display. Of Trok, he asked, "*Any suggestions as to which building we look at first?*"

Trok examined the three-dimensional images before him.

He knew that, at least for Breen engineers, integrated shipwide systems such as those they sought required testing at full scale. That suggested that any structures that housed the construction of those systems would be large enough to essentially accommodate an entire Jem'Hadar vessel. Trok checked the scale superimposed on the display, then pointed out two buildings that seemed sizable enough for their purposes.

"Dree, take us in," Beld ordered. *"Nice and slow."*

"Yes, Master Beld," Dree said.

Trok watched the navigational hologram with interest and trepidation. He understood the concept behind the Romulans' phasing cloak, and Trok supposed he trusted their claims of its successful operation, but the idea of taking the ship *through* a solid object unnerved him. Then again, just being in Dominion space disturbed him, let alone being beneath the watchful eye of a Jem'Hadar squadron.

One of the two buildings Trok had pointed out grew larger in the display as the ship descended toward it. When *Ren Fejin* seemed almost on top of its flat roof, the image suddenly blurred. Trok imagined the ship passing through the solid mass, the monitor recording an actual cross section of the matter it penetrated.

Suddenly, the navigational hologram changed dramatically, transforming from a smudge of motion to darkness.

"Full stop," Beld said.

"Full stop," said Dree.

"Adjust for low-spectrum infrared," Beld ordered.

"Adjusting," Zelk said.

The image shifted, and a large, open space came into view. Trok said the first thing he noticed. *"There's nobody here."*

"No," Beld agreed. *"It does appear that the Dominion has abandoned these facilities, at least for now. Whatever their reason, it will make our task easier to accomplish. Trok, do you see what we need here?"*

Trok peered at the holographic display, taking the measure of what he saw. In the center of the space, two massive convex shapes lay on the floor, likely baffle plates of some kind, or possibly hull sections. A pair of channels in the floor cut below them. All around, considerable amounts of other materials sat in heaps, and huge banks of apparatus lined the walls. *"I need to examine the supplies and the equipment,"* Trok said. *"This will take some time."*

"If you require it, Trok," Beld said, *"you can study all of this in person. Since the exteriors of the buildings are closed to scans from without, then the Jem'Hadar ships in orbit will not be able to read life-forms within. While we're inside the building, we can set you down."*

This time, Beld's information did not trouble Trok, but rather excited him. They hadn't anticipated empty facilities on Overne III. Rather, he'd expected to have to make his determination of the Dominion starship-manufacturing equipment visually and via narrow, passive scans. What Beld proposed would allow him a much better chance of locating and confirming what they needed.

"Let me out," Trok said.

22

Picard sat in the command chair, atop the rear, highest tier of the *Enterprise* bridge. He peered forward, past Lieutenant Faur at the conn and Glinn Dygan at ops, toward the main viewscreen. There, a great rock of a planet hung in space, mostly colored a grimy brown, but with ebon gashes smeared across its surface. "Science officer, report," Picard said.

"I'm having a difficult time categorizing the planet, sir," said Lieutenant Dina Elfiki. She sat along the starboard bulkhead, at the center console configured to host the primary science station. "It doesn't fit neatly into the standard classification schema."

The statement didn't surprise Picard. The dirty globe about which *Enterprise* orbited didn't *look* standard. It seemed somehow alive to Picard, yet it displayed none of the hues normally associated with life-sustaining worlds: blues and greens and whites. "What are its characteristics?" he asked.

"It resembles typical terrestrial planets in many ways," Elfiki said, her words lightly clipped by her Egyptian accent.

"Distance from its star, one-point-zero-seven astronomical units. Diameter, thirteen thousand seven hundred kilometers. Gravity, nine-point-eight-one meters per second squared. I'm reading an iron core . . . but with a mantle of titanium carbide and silicon carbide, and a crust of—" Elfiki paused, and Picard glanced over to see her peering over her shoulder at the main viewer.

"It's a carbon planet," said Spock. He sat immediately to Picard's left, in the chair customarily reserved for Hegol Den, the ship's senior counselor. Lieutenant Hegol had graciously offered up his usual seat for the ambassador, while he took one of the ancillary stations along the port side of the bridge.

"I'd say so," Elfiki agreed. She turned back to her console. "The crust is composed of two allotropes of carbon, primarily graphite, but at its deepest reach, diamond."

"Diamond?" Picard said.

"Yes," Elfiki said. "There's a crystalline shell approximately seventy kilometers beneath the surface, all around the planet."

"Can that be a natural formation?" Picard wanted to know.

"Yes, absolutely, sir," said Elfiki. "Planets are ultimately formed from the condensing and coalescing of materials in the protoplanetary disk orbiting a star. As a general occurrence, there is twice as much oxygen as carbon around young stars, which leads to the development of worlds composed primarily of silicon-oxygen compounds. But if there is as much carbon as oxygen surrounding a burgeoning star, then a planet such as the one below can form."

"Does it have an atmosphere?" asked the ship's executive officer, Worf, from where he sat to Picard's right.

"It does, but nothing breathable by our standards," said Elfiki. "Mostly methane, with a percentage of carbon monoxide."

"What about the black streaks?" Picard asked.

Elfiki tapped at the controls of her station. "There's virtually no hydrosphere on the planet, Captain, but the black veins are rivers of a sort, filled with condensed hydrocarbons. They're essentially flows of oil." She continued to operate her console, presumably reading through a wealth of sensor readings. "I'm also detecting volcanic activity."

"I'm assuming there are no life-forms down there," Picard said.

"No, sir," confirmed Elfiki. "I see no indications of life."

Turning to Spock, Picard said, "What do you think, Ambassador? This world does not sound particularly hospitable."

"No," the Vulcan said. "But it *is* intriguing."

"I agree, sir," said Elfiki. "Closer examination could definitely add to our knowledge of planetary science."

"The Romulans are right, then," Picard said. Together with the Romulan vessel *Eletrix, Enterprise* had set out a week previously from Deep Space 9. The two vessels had traveled through the Bajoran wormhole to the Gamma Quadrant, and then set a course into unexplored space. Their planned flight path intentionally took them in a direction away from Dominion space, avoided regions already navigated by other Federation ships, and kept out of the Typhon Pact travel lanes.

The crews of *Enterprise* and *Eletrix* had begun their joint mission by separately locating and mapping star systems along their route, then sharing the data collected. Both parties had agreed that, should one crew discover something especially noteworthy, something that called for extended scrutiny, they would call in the other crew so that they could study the find cooperatively. That had happened for the first time earlier that day, when Commander T'Jul contacted Captain Picard and informed him about the unusual planet below, the lone terrestrial world orbiting a seemingly ordinary main-sequence star.

"Yes, the Romulans are right," Elfiki said.

"Do you recommend an away team, Lieutenant?" Worf asked.

"Yes, sir," said Elfiki. "With the amount of metallic compounds down there, and the need for the use of environmental suits in any direct exploration, I'd suggest taking a shuttle down rather than employing the transporter."

"Understood," Picard said. "Lieutenant Choudhury, open a channel to the *Eletrix*."

At the freestanding console behind and to the right of Worf, *Enterprise*'s chief of security acknowledged the order and worked her controls. After just a moment, she said, "I have raised the *Eletrix*, sir."

"On-screen," Picard said. On the main viewer, the brown-and-black orb of the carbon planet winked off, replaced by a view of the Romulan vessel's bridge. It appeared larger than *Enterprise*'s own, with wider spaces between its detached consoles and built-in stations, and all of it tinted lightly but distinctly green. The ship's commanding officer stood at its center, and so Picard rose to his feet as well before addressing her. "Commander T'Jul," he said. "As I'm sure you're aware, the *Enterprise* has arrived at the planet about which you informed us."

Though still in its early stages, the joint mission had so far unfolded successfully, and exactly as planned. Picard knew that his crew had provided their Romulan counterparts with complete sets of data on each astronomical object they had charted and scanned, and the data they'd received in return appeared to contain no holes. Coordination between the two crews had proceeded smoothly, overseen by Spock and Tomalak, without a single issue arising. As best Picard could tell, and substantiated by Spock, the former proconsul had acted with no trace of his former bellicosity. *Or perhaps Tomalak's time in government has taught him to better camouflage his intentions.*

"*Captain Picard,*" T'Jul said. "*Yes, we registered the* Enterprise*'s approach. Has your scientific team had an opportunity to take any readings of the planet?*"

"They have," Picard said. "They concur with your scientists that it is worth extending our time here and studying it further."

"*Excellent,*" T'Jul said. "*Shall we discuss requirements for a combined landing party?*"

"I leave such matters in the capable hands of my first officer," Picard said. "I would suggest a meeting between Commander Worf; my senior science officer, Lieutenant Dina Elfiki; Ambassador Spock, of course; and their counterparts from your crew."

"*I oversee landing assignments myself, Captain,*" T'Jul said. She spoke as though simply delivering a fact, with no hint of superiority or accusation—a rarity among the numerous high-level Imperial Fleet officers with whom Picard had dealt in his career.

*"But I will bring my chief science officer, Sublieutenant Selus, as
well as our liaison, to such a meeting. May I invite your contingent
over to the* Eletrix *for that purpose?"*

"That would be perfectly acceptable, Commander," Picard
said—although for a moment, the idea of Worf interacting with
Romulans aboard their own ship almost brought him up short.
But the *Enterprise* captain had been privileged through the years
to watch his exec grow—not just as a Starfleet officer, but as a
man. Whatever prejudices Worf had once possessed—born out
of hard experience—he had come to understand and discard.
Picard did not doubt that he would work with the commanding
officer and crew of *Eletrix* with the utmost professionalism. "As
soon as our group has assembled in the transporter room, Commander Worf will contact you."

"Very good, Captain," T'Jul said, her tone one of conclusion.
An instant later, the Romulan commander's image vanished,
and the screen reverted to a view of the carbon planet.

Picard turned to his first officer. "Number One," he said,
"make it so."

The hatch of the Romulan shuttlecraft *Vexia* folded outward
with a low hum that translated through the deck plating and
up into Worf's environmental suit. He peered out from the
open hatchway as the moving section of hull angled down to
become a ramp, which led to the rugged, filthy-looking surface
of the carbon planet. *Enterprise*'s sensors had detected no signs
of life—not even microscopic life—on the strange world, and
scans by the combined away team aboard *Vexia* had verified
those findings. Still, Worf liked to trust his own senses when
possible, and he also recognized that the lack of life-forms on the
planet did not necessarily mean a lack of danger.

The *Vexia* pilot, a young Romulan woman named Torlanta,
had set the shuttle down at the edge of a vast plain. In the near
distance, Worf spied a range of tall, jagged peaks, mountains
that looked as though they had been thrust violently up through
the ground. Off to the right, even closer, an enormous volcano
rose from the terrain and dominated the landscape. One side of

its crater had collapsed away from the structure, perhaps blown apart during an eruption. Visible gases spewed forth from several points within the crater, as well as from fumaroles that dotted the surrounding topography.

Worf looked down at himself, at the fitted white shell that enclosed his body and kept him safe from the toxic atmosphere. He reached to a control on the lower sleeve of his environmental suit and activated the audio pickups in his helmet. Behind him, he heard the rustle of other away team members as they prepared to disembark. From outside, only the sound of an empty wind reached him.

Utilizing the communicator built into his helmet, Worf confirmed the readiness of the officers he led. In total, ten members made up the away team, five from *Enterprise* and an equal number from *Eletrix*. Worf had been assigned command of the mission, backed up by Lieutenant Torlanta, who had also been given the task of ferrying the crew to and from the planet's surface. After the meeting aboard the Romulan vessel to plan the expedition, each crew had sent along its senior science officer, a planetary scientist, and a geologist, while *Enterprise* had also contributed a chemist, and *Eletrix* an aerologist.

Worf marched down the ramp and stepped cautiously onto the ground. The boots of his environmental suit displaced dark, granulated matter. Beneath the sandy dirt, the land felt solid, but it also seemed to give slightly, dense but perceptibly soft.

Pacing away from the ramp, Worf turned back toward the shuttle. The auxiliary craft, of the same olive green as its parent ship, measured approximately twice the linear dimensions of *Enterprise*'s largest shuttles. As with so many Romulan craft, *Vexia* resembled a bird, though not one of the raptor-like avians after which the Empire modeled its starships. Rather, its general shape evoked the shape of a songbird, with its short wings and blunt, conical beak. Through the wide, narrow port at the front of the shuttle, Worf could see the figure of Lieutenant Torlanta, still seated at her pilot's console.

The *Enterprise* first officer watched as the eight scientists descended to the planet's surface, all of them carrying various types of handheld equipment. The Starfleet officers wore white environmental suits, while their Imperial counterparts wore deep-blue. *At least when the fighting breaks out, I will know who to shoot,* Worf thought, amusing himself.

During the planning of the away mission, the issue had arisen of whether or not to arm the participants. Perhaps not surprisingly, none of the scientists from either ship had voiced the need to carry a weapon, while both Commander T'Jul and Worf had argued that nobody should visit an unexplored world without some means of defending themselves. Mission liaisons Spock and Tomalak had ultimately sided with the latter point of view, and so each member of the away team had been supplied with either a Starfleet phaser or a Romulan disruptor. There had been some talk of providing everybody with the same type of weapon to ensure all an equal footing, but doing so would have implied the suspicion of possible trouble between the two crews. Considering that the Khitomer Accords and Typhon Pact leaders—particularly President Bacco and Praetor Kamemor—had pushed for the joint mission specifically to promote better relations among all the Alpha and Beta Quadrant powers, it seemed more in keeping with that philosophy to simply outfit each member of the away team with their own standard gear.

After all of the scientists had alighted, Worf faced them and activated the comm system inside his helmet, knowing that it would carry his voice to the same system in everybody else's environmental suit. "You have three hours to perform your preliminary field work," Worf reminded them. "I will contact each of you every half-hour to ensure that you are safe. Report any potential dangers immediately." Worf asked the members of the away team to acknowledge their orders, and they all did so in a prescribed sequence. He released them to their duties, then contacted Lieutenant Torlanta to have her seal the shuttle.

After seeing *Vexia*'s hatch close, Worf watched the away team spread out across the land, though he noted that the pairs of planetary scientists and geologists stayed together. Everybody appeared to move deliberately, encumbered by their environmental suits, by a slightly stronger gravitational field, and by the debris strewn about their surroundings. Rocks and boulders littered the uneven geography that stretched away in one direction toward the mountain range, and in another toward the massive volcano.

Depending on the away team's reports and recommendations, Worf knew, *Enterprise* and *Eletrix* might remain in orbit of the carbon planet for an additional two or even three days. While the basic execution of the joint mission would probably help establish a better relationship between the Federation and the Romulan Empire—and by extension, between the Khitomer Accords and the Typhon Pact—the people involved believed that the actual shared accomplishment of real goals would prove even more beneficial. Captain Picard, among others, thought that charting a region of unexplored space, mounting exploratory operations, and performing meaningful science would go a long way toward uniting the two crews and toward laying a substantial foundation for future interactions among their peoples.

As Worf paced about outside *Vexia,* he thought about where he stood on the matter. In general, he had never held Romulans in high regard, not because he believed them intrinsically inferior in some way, but because in his experience, their culture fostered duplicity and treachery, their citizens routinely engaging in behavior he considered dishonorable. Romulans had killed his parents in the sneak attack on the Klingon colony at Khitomer, Romulans had schemed to foment a Klingon civil war, Romulans stood as avowed enemies of both the Klingon Empire and the United Federation of Planets.

Except that *Klingons* had conspired with Romulans both to assault Khitomer and to provoke the civil war. And when the human madman Shinzon and his Reman forces had plotted to destroy Earth, it had been *Romulan* Commander Donatra and her crew aboard *Valdore* who had fought with honor to help the *Enterprise* crew avert disaster. Even with the prevailing mores of the Romulan Empire, Worf had learned that he could not reasonably generalize a Romulan character—just as he could not necessarily esteem a member of Klingon society merely because the person was a Klingon.

In his contact with Commander T'Jul, Worf had found her intelligent, efficient, and professional. She had treated Spock, Lieutenant Elfiki, and himself with dignity and respect. While he would not say that he trusted her, he did not *dis*trust her.

As Worf stood watch outside *Vexia,* immediately available should any of the scientists need his assistance, he considered returning inside the shuttle so that he could interact directly, on a one-to-one basis, with Lieutenant Torlanta. During preparations for the joint mission, Captain Picard had emphasized the importance of the opportunity it would afford the *Enterprise* crew to get to know their Romulan counterparts, not just on a professional level, but also on a personal one. The captain believed that such relations would only serve to buttress the ongoing efforts to bring true peace. Worf understood and agreed with the captain's view, but at that moment, he felt a responsibility to remain on alert as eight men and women in his charge roamed about a pristine, unfamiliar world—a world with a lethal atmosphere and an unknown number of other perils.

Peering up at the nose—*the beak,* Worf thought—of *Vexia,* he once more spotted the vessel's pilot through the forward port. Though not an accustomed action for him, Worf raised one arm and moved it quickly from left to right, offering Lieutenant Torlanta a quick wave. For a few seconds, she did nothing, and Worf wondered if she had even seen him, but then she raised her own hand and returned the gesture.

Satisfied, Worf turned his back to the Romulan shuttle and gazed out across the carbon planet, to the expanse along which the members of the away team had spread. He quickly counted the number of environmental suits he could see, and to his consternation, tallied only seven. Reaching to the controls on his sleeve, he activated a sensor display that, projected on the inside of his faceplate, showed the relative positions of all eight scientists. As he looked out across the land, though, he still saw only seven. Anxiously, he hurried toward the area where sensors indicated one of the scientists *should* be, but whom Worf couldn't locate.

As he reached for the tricorder tucked into a receptacle at

his hip, his right boot kicked through a pile of rocks. He almost fell forward, but managed to keep his balance. As he steadied himself, a flash of light suddenly flared up ahead. He stopped and searched for its cause, and saw a ray of sunlight glinting off something on the soil, about thirty meters away. Alarm gripped Worf as he spotted a helmet at ground level, but then he saw it moving, and he realized that one of the Romulan scientists had descended into a gully, thus becoming difficult to see. *Enterprise*'s chief geologist, Catherine Rawlins, worked nearby, and Worf guessed that the channel in the earth allowed them to study different rock strata.

Worf replaced his tricorder in its place at his hip, and started back toward the shuttle. Ahead of him, he noticed something else flickering on the ground. He reached the spot where his boot had struck and scattered some stones, and he bent down to see chunks of translucent rocks brightly reflecting the daylight—not just reflecting the light, but refracting it, acting as prisms and throwing rainbows across the surrounding dirt. Worf retrieved his tricorder again and scanned the stones, identifying them as diamonds. He recorded his readings so that he could later pass them on to the scientists.

Back at the shuttle, Worf resumed his position. On the half hour, he checked in with each member of the away team, including Lieutenant Torlanta aboard *Vexia*. They all responded, with no issues to report. The same cycle occurred at the next three intervals, but then, with just thirty minutes before the end of the expedition, he received a different response from one of the scientists.

"Worf to Tornot." A Bolian, Tornot served aboard *Enterprise* as a chemist. "Status report."

"Tornot here," the man said. *"Commander, I think there's something here you should see."*

Worf grew instantly concerned by the deviation from procedure. "Are you all right?" he asked. He gazed out across the land, but according to the sensor display on his faceplate, a rock formation stood between the shuttle and the chemist's location five hundred meters away.

"Yes, sir, I'm fine," Tornot said. *"But I'd really like you to take a look at something I've found."*

"What is the nature of it?" Worf wanted to know.

"I'd really prefer you see it and make your own judgment," Tornot said.

"Very well," Worf said. "I will be there in five minutes. Worf out."

He quickly checked in with the remaining scientists, and then contacted Lieutenant Torlanta. He informed her that one of the away team had requested his help, and that he would be leaving the vicinity of the shuttle for a few minutes. Then he started toward the chemist.

Alert to the possibility of danger despite what Tornot had said, Worf utilized his tricorder as he approached the scientist's position. A scan confirmed Tornot's life signs as strong and vital, as well as the fact that he waited alone. Nevertheless, before rounding the rock formation, Worf exchanged his tricorder for a phaser.

Tornot came into view, standing away from the rocks on a flat patch of ground. His scientific instruments sat off to the side, a few meters away. He held nothing in his hands, nor did there seem to be anything near him other than his equipment. He waved.

Worf holstered his weapon and approached. "Worf to Tornot," he said, reopening a comm channel with the chemist. "What is it you wish me to see?"

In reply, Tornot squatted down and pointed to a spot of disturbed soil. *"Here, sir,"* he said. *"Do you see the hollow?"*

Worf lowered himself onto his haunches beside Tornot. He saw a depression, rectangular in shape, though some of the dirt along its edges had fallen into it, spoiling any precise lines it might have had. About twenty-five or thirty centimeters deep, it measured more than a meter on its longer dimension, and about two-thirds that length along its shorter. "I see it," Worf said, "but I do not understand its significance. What is it? What caused it?"

The chemist stood back up, as did Worf. *"I'd like you to make that assessment, sir,"* Tornot said, *"but I haven't finished showing you everything."* He paced away on a straight line, and Worf followed. After almost half a minute, Tornot stopped and squatted down again. He did not have to point out the second hollow before Worf saw it.

Crouching, Worf saw that the hollow appeared similar to the first. He glanced up through the faceplate of his helmet at Tornot, whose pale-blue features had drawn into a look of concern. *"We're about twenty-five meters from where we started,"* the Bolian said. *"There are two more similar hollows to either side, about fifteen meters apart."* He reached down to the ground, poked four holes into the dirt, then connected the opposite pairs. It resulted in a longer and shorter line meeting at right angles, forming a shape like a lowercase *t*.

Worf rose and looked back across the flat land, visualizing the four hollows. *Not hollows,* he thought. *Indentations.* "A ship landed here," he said.

"That was what I thought," Tornot said. *"I would have just listed the finding in my report, but . . ."* He did not complete his sentence, perhaps not wanting to voice his concern. Worf did it for him.

"But these marks at least roughly correspond to the landing gear of the *Vexia*," Worf said.

"Not just roughly, sir."

Worf nodded, understanding Tornot's concern, and sharing it himself. If the *Eletrix* crew had sent down a shuttle to the carbon planet prior to notifying the *Enterprise* crew about the strange world, then why hadn't Commander T'Jul revealed that? Keeping such a piece of information hidden amounted to a violation of the terms of the joint mission, which called for full disclosure on all operations. From such an action, Worf inferred a lack of trust: either the *Enterprise* crew could not count on the Romulans, or possibly the Romulans had acted as they had because they did not rely on their Starfleet counterparts. Whichever the case, such a failure of the mission, and so quickly, would mean a blow to efforts to craft a durable peace.

But the possibility that the Romulans had already breached

the mission agreement brought Worf a more immediate concern. A lie, even one of omission, suggested Commander T'Jul might possess a different agenda than Captain Picard. Worf needed to know the repercussions of that with respect to the safety of the away team in particular, and of the *Enterprise* crew in general.

Of Tornot, Worf asked, "If the crew of the *Eletrix* brought down the *Vexia* or another shuttle to the planet's surface before the *Enterprise* arrived, what did they hope to accomplish? Have you detected anything else in the area that might offer a clue?"

"No, sir," Tornot said.

"No residual energy readings? No footprints?"

"No, sir," Tornot said. *"Nothing."*

Worf looked around, attempting to puzzle out what had taken place there, and why. "If Commander T'Jul did send down a shuttle from the *Eletrix* before the *Enterprise* arrived here, and if she wished to conceal that fact, then why would the *Vexia* set down so close to the first landing site?" Worf asked, and then offered a possible solution. "Typhon Pact vessels have been entering the Gamma Quadrant for a couple of months now. Perhaps a Romulan ship with a footprint similar to that of the *Vexia* landed here."

"But those are civilian vessels," Tornot observed.

"Yes, but military designs can migrate to nonmilitary usage," Worf said. "And military vessels can be converted to civilian use."

The questions and possibilities vexed Worf. He checked his chronometer and saw that seventeen minutes remained in the expedition. In that time, he needed to decide what course of action to take. If he falsely accused the Romulans of deceit, it could ruin the mission. If he withheld the discovery of the evidence of a landing on the planet, even until he could inform Captain Picard about the situation, and if the Romulans learned of the *Enterprise* away team's holding back that information, that could undermine the mission as well, as it would constitute a contravention of the terms of the joint mission.

It occurred to Worf that perhaps the Romulans had intentionally engineered such a dilemma in order to test the fidelity of the *Enterprise* crew to the mission and to the conditions of the agreement on how to conduct it. The Romulans' covert intelligence service, the Tal Shiar, had a history of conducting far more complex, even convoluted, plots to accomplish their aims. Worf knew of no Tal Shiar agents aboard *Eletrix,* but that did not mean that Chairwoman Sela had not sent along one or more of her operatives.

Worf looked over at Tornot. "We have little time left before we return to the ship," he told the chemist. "You should gather your equipment and head back to the shuttle."

"Yes, sir," Tornot said.

Worf waited as the scientist collected his gear, and then the two started back toward *Vexia*. It would only take a few minutes to reach the shuttle, and shortly after that, once the rest of the away team had boarded, the time would come for all of the data gathered on the carbon planet to be pooled for examination by the crews of both *Enterprise* and *Eletrix*. Worf had until then to decide how to proceed.

23

Ben Sisko stood at the top of the tower and took in the view of the magnificent city for the final time. Laid out in a series of concentric circles, with the tower at its hub, the great metropolis looked almost like a diorama, like a scale model presented on a holodeck. A stunning, low-lying mass of subtly colored glass and steel, it ebbed and flowed like some cubist vision of a translucent, aquamarine ocean, its vast waters frozen in place. Cutting through the city radially and in rings, wide pedestrian thoroughfares allowed citizens to walk freely and easily, and when seen from a height, added to the overall impression of designed beauty. Numerous parks also dotted the urban landscape, as did public displays of artwork.

In some ways, Sisko thought, *the Vahni Vahltupali are themselves works of art.* Though reminiscent of humanoids in shape and size, the builders of the city differed in many ways. They had a long, narrow torso; a large, bulbous head; two legs; and two tentacles that functioned more or less as arms. They stood tall and slim, with a highly articulated skeleton that endowed them with extreme flexibility. They had no senses or organs that allowed them to hear or speak, but possessed a single, complex eye that circled their entire head. They communicated via conscious alterations to the colors, patterns, and textures of their flesh.

Although only a handful of the city's buildings reached higher than one or two stories, the place nevertheless *seemed* tall. Sisko had anticipated such an effect, having heard Elias Vaughn speak about the *Defiant* crew's contact with the Vahni Vahltupali. Seven years prior, Vaughn had taken the ship on Starfleet's first extended exploration of the Gamma Quadrant after the end of the Dominion War. At that time, other than the towers at the hearts of cities, no structure anywhere on the Vahni world reached higher than two stories, since they had for more than two centuries experienced massive, planetwide temblors—not geologic in nature, but caused by a powerful pulse of energy intermittently surging through their solar system. During *Defiant*'s visit there, such a pulse had caused horrible devastation, including shattering the planet's lone moon. Vaughn and his crew had tracked down the source of the pulse and put a permanent end to it, for which they occupied a revered place in the history of the Vahni.

It troubled Sisko to think about Elias Vaughn. Not only did he mourn the loss of a man to whom he'd felt particularly close—despite the fact that they hadn't spent all that much time together—but he had *expected* something different for him. After all, it had been Vaughn who had helped usher Sisko out of the Celestial Temple so that he could be back on Bajor for the birth of his daughter. That alone—Vaughn acting as an instrument of the Prophets—had led Sisko to believe that his friend could and should serve as the Emissary in the so-called mirror universe, at least on a temporary basis. When that hadn't happened, Sisko had thought some other important fate awaited Vaughn—more than the role he'd played with the Eav'oq and the Ascendants, more than what he'd done on Endalla.

And more even than sacrificing his own life to save both the Alonis and the crew of the James T. Kirk, Sisko thought. He envisioned Vaughn still lying in bed in the DS9 infirmary, his body alive only in a technical sense, his mind long since dead. It hurt Sisko to think of Vaughn in that way, and it pleased him that the Vahni remembered him only in his vitality, that they held him in such high regard.

Moments earlier, at the entrance to the rooftop of the five-story tower, Sisko's guide had read him the contents of a plaque commemorating the previous tower that had stood there, on which Vaughn and a Vahni named Ventu had been standing when the last pulse had struck. When that occurred, the loss of the planet's single natural satellite caused several physical effects on the planet itself. Without its moon, the world's rotation speeded up, consequently shortening the length of its day by several seconds. The magnitude of the tides also decreased. But the greatest impact of the annihilation of the Vahni moon had been psychological. The plaque on the rooftop told of the collective dread and fear that had gripped their society, but also how Vaughn had survived the destruction of the previous tower— though Ventu had not—and how he and his crew had then gone on to forever end the terrible threat of the pulse.

The Federation had maintained relations with the Vahni Vahltupali in the years since first contact with them, though it had not done so initially. Because of the Vahni's status as a pre-warp culture, UFP policy, much like Starfleet's Prime Directive, precluded even basic communication with its people. Vaughn and his crew, bound by regulations, had not initiated contact with them. But despite lacking the capability to travel faster than light, the Vahni possessed a technologically advanced society. By the time the *Defiant* crew had come to explore the Gamma Quadrant, the Vahni had already toured their own solar system, had discovered subspace, and had begun major scientific and engineering efforts to develop both warp drive and transporter technology. Also, they had already been visited by two other spacefaring civilizations, and therefore understood that they were not alone in the universe. And so it had been the

Vahni who had established contact with the crew of *Defiant*, rather than the other way around.

But the president of the Federation at that time, Min Zife, had successfully lobbied the Council not to resume ties with the Vahni once *Defiant* had returned to the Alpha Quadrant. That embargo lasted three years, until Zife's successor, Nan Bacco, convinced the Federation Council to reverse its earlier prohibition. With the help of Vaughn, Bacco argued that the maturity of the Vahni people, their prior contact with other warp-capable species, and their significant technological achievements made such a prohibition not only unnecessary, but ludicrous.

In the seven years since *Defiant*'s first visit there, the Vahni had yet to achieve faster-than-light travel. Nor had they solicited the Federation's assistance to do so, thus relieving the Federation Council and Starfleet Command of having to make difficult choices. But the Vahni had recently cracked the secret of the transporter. It had yet to gain widespread use in their society, though, with many of their population continuing to use the efficient mass-transit systems entrenched beneath their cities.

"Your world is stunning," Sisko said, turning to face his guide, "outshined only by your people." An intricate optical net worn atop the chest of Sisko's uniform shirt flashed a series of shapes and colors across it, translating his words into the visual language of the Vahni.

Sisko's guide, a male Vahni whose name approximated as Brestol, served on a government council charged with establishing and maintaining offworld relations, and he'd led a large group in hosting the *Robinson* crew. In response to Sisko's comment, he shifted in place, and his flesh, normally bright blue, wavered in a complex sequence of hues, shapes, and textures, mostly long, striated ripples in the orange and yellow range. The processor set into the top corner of Sisko's optical net read the communication and rendered it into Federation Standard via his universal translator. *"Our world is richer for having you and your crew as our guests,"* Brestol said.

Robinson had departed Deep Space 9 more than five months before, forging a new path for Starfleet through the Gamma

Quadrant. The journey had been productive, with the crew making several first contacts and more than a few discoveries along the way, despite also facing numerous dangers. On the final leg of *Robinson*'s voyage, Sisko had taken the ship to the world of the Vahni Vahltupali, on a visit planned before the mission had begun, combining diplomacy with shore leave.

The crew had spent six days there, and everyone raved about the hospitality of the Vahni. Sisko had certainly enjoyed his time on the planet. With Relkdahz and several others from the ship's engineering team, Sisko had explored the Vahni's Museum of Innovation, which traced their ambitious technological development; although they still lacked warp drive, some of their achievements surpassed those of civilizations that traveled the galaxy. In particular, their ability to reuse and recycle a huge percentage of their natural resources had enabled them to live in near-perfect harmony with their environment.

Sisko had also seen a great deal of their artwork, both in public rights of way and in staged exhibitions. The Vahni, upon hearing his account of baseball, had also shared with him their sport of *gestalus-ru,* which required more than three dozen players on a team, featured round-robin play within a single game, and had such complicated, many-conditioned rules that Sisko found it impenetrable. Still, he'd liked watching the sheer athleticism of the Vahni, and he'd acquired both the recording of a competition and a rule book so that he could study it at his leisure.

And yet, as much fun as he'd had on his shore leave, and even as satisfying as his diplomatic exchanges with the Vahni had been, Sisko looked forward to being on *Robinson* when it departed their world later that day. He expected a message from his daughter in just a few hours, and nothing during *Robinson*'s mission satisfied him more. In the months that he'd been away and unable to visit Rebecca, they had both assiduously recorded and sent messages to each other every three days—though there had been a few exceptions, when Sisko had been unable to do so because he'd been away from the ship for an extended period. In such cases, though, he attempted to make up for the missing message by sending the next few with shorter intervals between them. Of course, as *Defiant* traveled farther and farther from the wormhole, and from the communications relay to DS9 and Bajor, it took longer and longer for Rebecca's messages to reach him, and for his to reach her. But they always arrived eventually, and Sisko valued those times when a comm packet arrived from Deep Space 9 containing another interaction with his daughter, however distant, however removed. And Rebecca, despite being not even seven years old, understood the principles of time, distance, and velocity that impacted the deliveries of their communications with each other.

More than receiving a message from his daughter, though, Sisko looked forward to leaving the world of the Vahni because *Robinson* would then begin the final stage of its expedition. On their way back to the Bajoran wormhole, and beyond it, to the Alpha Quadrant, the crew would spend a couple of weeks retracing *Defiant*'s initial course of seven years earlier, painstakingly recording detailed sensor scans for comparative analysis with previous readings. In only a matter of days—*In less than a month,* Sisko thought excitedly—he would see Rebecca in person, would hug her, speak with her, *rejoice* in her.

I can't wait, he thought.

To Brestol, Sisko said, "On behalf of my entire crew, thank you for your many kindnesses in hosting us on your world." Colors and shapes flew across the captain's chest.

"Your people are always welcome here," Brestol said, his flesh a kaleidoscope. *"The Vahni Vahltupali look forward to the day when we can visit some of your many worlds."*

Sisko knew that the Federation Council had discussed proffering an invitation to the Vahni, to allow some of their citizens to travel to the UFP aboard a Starfleet vessel. Ethical concerns arose again about having such a relationship with a pre-warp society, but more practical fears included the unknown health impact on the Vahni of introducing them into a new ecosystem. Without their own portable environment and a considerable support system, which ships of their own would provide, some councillors thought bringing the Vahni to any Federation world too great a risk. Still, the prospect surfaced in communications with the Vahni, but while they appreciated the opportunity, they also objected to leaving their own solar system before developing the ability to do so themselves.

"I look forward to seeing you in the Federation one day too," Sisko said. He reached above the optical net on his uniform and tapped at his combadge. "Sisko to *Robinson*."

"Robinson *here*," came the reply. "*This is Rogeiro.*"

"Commander, have all our crew members returned to the ship?" Sisko asked.

"*They have, Captain,*" Rogeiro said. "*We'll be ready to break orbit within the hour.*"

"Very good, Commander," Sisko said. He looked at Brestol, to the single eye that wrapped around his head. Sisko nodded, and the Vahni returned the gesture. Then, into his combadge, the captain said, "One to beam up."

Sisko heard the warble that signaled the opening of an internal comm channel aboard *Robinson*. He looked up from the sofa in the living area in his quarters. In his hands, he held a padd on which he worked to finalize his report of the diplomatic meetings he'd held with the Vahni Vahltupali.

"*Bridge to Captain Sisko,*" said Ed Radickey, one of the ship's communications officers.

"This is Sisko," said the captain. "Go ahead, Ensign."

"*Captain, we've just received our regular comm packet from Deep Space Nine.*"

"Any messages from Starfleet Command?" Sisko asked, hoping for a negative reply.

"*No, sir,*" said Radickey, obliging the captain.

"Any other messages from Starfleet?"

"*Just acknowledgment of the receipt of the last comm packet we sent,*" Radickey said. "*You do have a personal message from Bajor.*" It sounded as though the young officer spoke through a smile.

"Thank you, Ensign. Pipe it down here," the captain said. "Sisko out."

The comm channel chirped its closure. Sisko set down his

padd on the low table before the sofa, then stood and made his way over to the companel. He activated it and sat down, feeling a smile spread across his face, as though Radickey's had been contagious. The thrum of the warp engines, more felt than heard, coursed through *Robinson*. To Sisko's right, through the tall ports that lined the outer bulkhead, the stars streaked past, their elongated forms like motion lines in animation, signaling speed. The crew had left the world of the Vahni Vahltupali behind, and ahead lay the Idran system, the Gamma Quadrant entrance to the Bajoran wormhole, and Deep Space 9—and beyond those, Bajor and Rebecca.

"Computer," Sisko said, "retrieve incoming personal messages for Captain Benjamin Sisko."

"One incoming personal message," said the computer in its familiar female voice. *"Source: Rebecca Sisko, Kendra Province, Bajor."*

"Play message."

The display blinked, and a view appeared of the room he and Kasidy had set up as an office, or a place for overnight guests, in their home. Rebecca stood with her back to the companel, gazing through the window that looked out from the rear of the house. Sisko could see large flakes falling outside, the ground already covered in white with what appeared to be a significant accumulation of snow.

"Honey," Sisko heard Kasidy say from somewhere offscreen. *"We're recording."* Kasidy appeared from the right, moving over to take Rebecca by the hand and lead her to the companel. It looked to Sisko as though his daughter had grown in the nearly half a year since he'd been in the Gamma Quadrant, perhaps three centimeters or more. But then, despite seeing her in messages every few days, she almost always seemed taller and older to him, a bittersweet feeling that left him worried that Rebecca's childhood would slip away too quickly.

"Hi, Daddy," she said as she climbed onto the chair before the companel. She wore a pretty purple dress.

"Hi, Ben," Kasidy said, leaning in beside Rebecca. She didn't usually talk or even appear in their daughter's messages to Sisko,

but obviously she'd been caught when Rebecca had abandoned the companel for a look out the rear window at the snow. *"I guess you could say we're a little distracted today."*

"It's snowing!" Rebecca announced, peering back over her shoulder, as though she wanted to ensure that the wintry scene hadn't suddenly vanished. *"Mommy said we can go out later and play."*

"That's right, honey, I did say that," Kasidy agreed. *"But what else did I say?"*

Rebecca gazed up at her mother. *"Um . . . that . . . um . . . I don't know."*

Kasidy shook her head. *"You don't know because you don't remember,"* she asked, *"or because you weren't paying attention?"*

"Um," Rebecca said, hesitating. *"I don't 'member."*

"You don't remember," Kasidy said, emphasizing the missing syllable.

"I don't remember," Rebecca repeated, precisely mimicking her mother.

Alone in his cabin, Sisko couldn't help but laugh. Rebecca, he suddenly saw, had begun to resemble Kasidy more than she did her father. And when she'd imitated her mother, she'd looked *just* like her.

"What I said was that we could go out and play after *you recorded a message to your father,"* Kasidy told Rebecca, *"and after you finished your homework."*

"Oh, yeah," Rebecca said. Instead of looking at the companel, though, she peeked back over her shoulder at the window and the snow beyond it.

"Rebecca Jae Sisko," Kasidy said, her tone stern. She walked over to the window, reached up, and swept the burgundy drapes closed.

"Ma-a-a," Rebecca complained.

"Do not whine to me, young lady," Kasidy said. *"And do not be rude. We're recording a message to your father, so you should be paying attention to that."* She pointed toward the companel.

"I'm sorry," Rebecca said, sounding duly chastised. She shifted around on her chair so that she fully faced the companel.

"Why don't you tell Daddy about school?" Kasidy suggested. Rebecca had recently begun attending first grade.

"Oh. Yeah," Rebecca said. *"It's good."*

"How do you feel about your teacher?" Kasidy prompted her.

"I like Ms. Wyse. She's nice," Rebecca said, and then giggled at the rhyme she'd made. *"We're doing letters and sounds and counting, but I already know a lot of that, so it's pretty easy."*

"Then you shouldn't have any trouble doing your homework, should you?" Kasidy said.

"No," Rebecca said. *"But then we can go outside, right?"*

Kasidy smiled at their daughter, then peered at the companel. *"She's certainly got* some*body's stubbornness."* It pleased Sisko to hear her sound less angry than amused. Looking back at Rebecca, she said, *"Yes, honey. You finish your homework and then we'll go out and build a snowman."*

*"A snow-*captain*!"* Rebecca said, and Kasidy laughed.

"That's right," Kasidy said. *"Have you told your father what you've decided to be when you grow up?"*

Rebecca beamed. *"A captain,"* she said. *"Just like you and Mommy."*

"Ever since you brought her those spaceship models," Kasidy explained, *"and then when I took her aboard* Xhosa—*"*

"We're going on your ship again soon, right, Mommy?" Rebecca asked.

"We'll see, honey," Kasidy said. *"But only little girls who do all their homework get to go on trips like that."*

"Okay," Rebecca said. Then she leaned in toward the companel. *"I have to go do my homework. I love you, Daddy."* She brought her face right up to the screen and gave it a quick peck, as though kissing her father through all the light-years that separated them. Then she leaped down from the chair and scampered out of sight.

Kasidy watched her go, then turned back to the companel. *"Sorry about that, Ben,"* she said. *"Rebecca's got a few days off from school coming up, right when Wayne's got to be on Alpha Centauri for his sister's wedding."* With *Xhosa*'s first mate away from the ship, Kasidy would obviously want to make any shipping runs herself. *"Since Jasmine's not available to watch Rebecca all that time, and with Jake and Rena not yet back from their trip to New Zealand, I made the mistake of musing out loud that maybe I should just take Rebecca with me. Now it's all she can talk about."*

Kasidy had other friends with whom Rebecca could stay, but Sisko knew that Kasidy would never thrust such a burden onto anybody other than family or Jasmine Tey. After Rebecca had been abducted, asking somebody else to take responsibility for her safety, even for a short time, seemed unfair. Although after three and a half years, the emotional wounds left by the kidnapping had scabbed over and perhaps even healed, caution had become a way of life for Kasidy.

"I'm still not sure I want to take Rebecca on a full freight run," Kasidy continued, *"but I'm not scheduled to head near the Badlands or into any sensitive areas. I've got some wares coming back to Deep Space Nine too, and I know she's wanted to visit the station again, so maybe I will bring her along."*

For a moment, Kasidy paused, and a strange expression crossed her face. Sisko couldn't quite read it, but she looked— *What? Uncomfortable? Surprised? Melancholy?* He couldn't tell, but he thought that maybe unexpectedly finding herself talking alone with her estranged husband affected her in some way.

"Anyway," she went on, clearly pushing past the awkward moment, *"I'm sorry about Rebecca. She loves recording her messages to you, and she loves receiving your messages even more. By the way, speaking of your messages, we spent all day yesterday reading about the Vahni Vahltupali. She was fascinated by the way they communicate. Actually, so was I.*

"Other than that, and the snow today, Rebecca has been fixated on coming with me on a shipping run aboard Xhosa,*"* Kasidy said. *"But I'll try to sit her down and record another message tomorrow. She does miss you, Ben."*

Kasidy paused, and Sisko felt a jolt that seemed to mix anticipation and fear within him. He wanted Kasidy to say that she missed him too, and he also dreaded that she would. But he knew that he still missed her—still *loved* her—though he could do nothing about those emotions.

"Come home safe, Ben," Kasidy said. Then she reached forward and ended the recording.

Sisko leaned back in his chair, a bit disappointed that Rebecca's message hadn't been longer, and that she really hadn't said much. "But she wants to be a spaceship captain," he said aloud, once more feeling a smile bloom on his face. When he'd brought Rebecca the models of *Robinson* and *Xhosa,* it hadn't been with the intention of interesting his daughter in spaceflight, so much as wanting her to understand what he and Kasidy did. But Sisko couldn't deny an element of satisfaction in Rebecca's attraction to space travel. He'd never imagined her entering Starfleet Academy, but the thought suddenly filled him with delight.

Sisko leaned forward and touched a control on the companel. "Computer," he said, "record a message to Rebecca Sisko, Kendra Province, Bajor."

24

Trok stood alone in the enormous building, the darkness thick and heavy around him, the accompanying silence broken only by the scrape of his environmental suit's boots along the concrete floor. He had extinguished the ghostly green glow emanating from the horizontal glass band on his helmet so that he could maintain whatever cover the building's interior night afforded, but he needed no light source to expose the secrets around him. His suit's wide, narrow eyepiece, though no longer illuminated, reached into the shorter wavelengths to discern the extensive arrangement of equipment lining the high walls and scattered across the floor.

A slew of numbers and words marched across the internal display within Trok's helmet, measurements and descriptions fed there by the scanner he held in one hand. He read through the data, then did so a second time. He wanted to make certain that he comprehended what the sensors told him, and that he didn't mistakenly interpret the information merely so that he would see what he *wished* to see. How many facilities had he searched through on the surface of Overne III? How much time—*How many days now?*—had he hunted for the gear that would allow him to manufacture high-performance structural integrity field and deflector generators, and that would in turn provide him the ability to install quantum slipstream drive on existing Breen and other Typhon Pact starships?

And each day that I search, each moment, I expect a polaron beam to come slicing through the roof of whatever building I'm in and reveal my presence there, Trok thought. *Or I anticipate a troop of Jem'Hadar soldiers suddenly materializing around me.*

He tried to tell himself that his fears came from his vocation as an engineer. Trok knew the basic principles of the Romulans' cloaking technology, and given the preponderance of the evidence that it had worked in practice for a very long time, he accepted its usefulness. But their phasing cloak had been a relatively recent advance, and though he'd witnessed it operating, allowing the crew of *Ren Fejin* to deliver him into one Overne industrial plant after another, he nevertheless felt skeptical that the Breen privateer remained undetected by all the Jem'Hadar on the many starships circling the planet, and invisible to internal security systems. And so he waited day by day, moment by moment, for some member of the Dominion—an Overne, a Vorta, a Jem'Hadar, even a Founder—to abruptly appear and take him into custody—or to abruptly appear and do something far worse.

Trok also realized that his status as an engineer—even one directing as important a project as the development of the slipstream drive—implied another fact: he was *not* a soldier. While he'd agreed to travel to the Gamma Quadrant to look for the apparatus he required for his work—*As though I'd had a choice in the matter*—he hadn't foreseen the magnitude of the peril he would face. He absolutely wanted to succeed as an engineer and as the leader of the slipstream effort—for himself, for the Confederacy, and for the Pact—but he wanted even more to go on living.

It still chilled Trok to consider how fortunate he'd been to be away from the Alrakis system when the Federation operatives had destroyed Thot Keer's slipstream prototype, along with the

shipyard that housed it. So many Breen engineers and techni-
cians had perished in the assault, and if not for Keer assigning
him the usually unenviable task of briefing Domo Brex, Trok
would have died as well. That he had survived Alrakis when so
many of his colleagues had not, only made him more wary of
placing himself in danger.

But as Trok for a third time read through the details collected by his scanner, he thought that he might finally have
arrived on the verge of escaping the Gamma Quadrant with his
life. It had taken some time, but he'd located what he'd come
to the Dominion seeking. The crew of *Ren Fejin* needed only to
take possession of it all and haul it back to Breen territory. Then
he could at last leave the sleuthing behind him and return to
actual engineering work.

"*Trok* to Ren Fejin," he said, opening up a communications
conduit to the ship.

"*This is Beld*," came the shipmaster's immediate reply. "*What
is it, Trok? Are you finished already? Do you need to move on to the
next building?*" Beld's words seemed to register his own annoyance that the mission had continued for so long without success.

"*No*," Trok said. "*I mean, yes, I'm finished, but not because I
have to keep searching. I found the equipment.*"

A noticeable silence followed, and Trok wondered if he'd lost
contact with the ship. But then Beld asked him to repeat his
message. He did.

"*All right*," Beld said. "*Stand by.*"

Trok waited. He could do little else. He comforted himself
with the knowledge that he would soon board *Ren Fejin* again,
and before long, head for home.

A noise suddenly rose within the building, a hum reminiscent of the whine of a transporter. It sounded thin in the huge
space, insufficient to fill the area from wall to wall and floor
to rooftop. Trok recognized the noise, but with the thought of
Jem'Hadar soldiers still fresh in his consciousness, he took a step
backward. Then, at one end of the building, in a sizable open
area likely given over during production to large-scale starship
systems testing, bright pinpoints penetrated the darkness, reduc-

ing it to a mere gloom. Then the form of *Ren Fejin* began to take shape, the hull becoming substantial beneath the vessel's running lights.

At the back of the dorsal that connected the two main structures of the ship, a hatch rotated inward. A Breen—no doubt Beld—emerged from within and swung onto a line of hand- and footholds punched into the hull of *Ren Fejin*. As he began to descend, Trok headed over to the base of the built-in ladder. The metallic ring of Beld's boots against the hull contrasted with the scuff of Trok's footsteps on the concrete.

When Beld reached the floor, he said simply, *"Show me."*

Trok handed him the scanner. The shipmaster worked the controls of the device, obviously routing its readings to the display within his own helmet. Then he passed it back to Trok, who adjusted it to highlight the great machines that they would have to beam onto the ship and haul back to the Alpha Quadrant.

"All of these?" Beld asked.

"Four sets of equipment, yes," Trok said. *"One set that produces a ship's deflector generator and the associated infrastructure, another for structural integrity, and the other two to perform full-scale testing on each."*

"These machines are massive," Beld said.

"They have to be," Trok told him. *"They produce those systems as holistic components for a starship. That's their strength. Vulnerability is minimized because there's no in-system integration required, and thus no possibility of connectivity weaknesses."*

"Can the machines themselves be disassembled?" Beld asked.

"I'm sure that they can be," Trok said, *"but you see how complex they are. It would require a thorough research project to figure out how to do so."*

Beld did not respond right away, and silence once more descended within the building. Trok felt pressure to fill the gap in the conversation, and to ameliorate the problem he inferred from Beld's questions and comments. *"If necessary, we can leave the testing equipment behind. It might take some time, but we should be able to create a means ourselves of analyzing systems performance."*

Beld still hesitated. At length, he reached for Trok's scanner again, which the engineer once more handed to him. Beld held up the device in the direction of the ship, worked at its controls, then returned it. Trok took the scanner and routed the feed of the shipmaster's readings to the display in his own helmet. He saw a representation of *Ren Fejin,* along with a series of dimensions and volumes. *"What am I looking at?"* he asked.

"The size of our cargo holds," Beld said. *"Even if we leave the testing equipment behind, and even if we dismantle the production equipment, it's still too much. It's possible we might be able to fit one of the production machines on the ship, but not both."*

Trok's satisfaction at having found what he needed for the slipstream project melted away like ice on a summer afternoon. *"We have to bring* all *the manufacturing gear,"* Trok said. *"That's the entire reason for us being here. It's not as though we can take one set of equipment, then come back later for the other one."*

"No," Beld said. *"But that's why we have a contingency plan."*

Trok had heard of no such plan. *But then,* he reminded himself, *I'm just an engineer.* *"What's the plan?"* he asked.

In response, the shipmaster turned and started climbing back up the hull to the open hatch. Trok quickly switched off his scanner and tucked it into a compartment in his environmental suit. Then he followed Beld back into the ship.

Moments later, Trok stood on the bridge of the cloaked *Ren Fejin* as it soared upward through the atmosphere of Overne III.

"Encode the message," Beld ordered.

Trok, as he had so often during the long journey within the Gamma Quadrant, stayed off to the side and out of the way in the small confines of *Ren Fejin*'s bridge. The Romulan specialist waited beside him. Trok watched and listened to the shipmaster, who stood next to the navigational display. The holographic images of the starship-manufacturing installations on the surface of Overne III had given way, first to the squadron of Jem'Hadar vessels orbiting high above the planet, and then to open space. The ship remained within the Overne system, but outside the plane of the ecliptic.

"*Append all data, including the readings of all the equipment Trok requires and its location, so that they can pinpoint it easily,*" Beld continued. "*We don't need to remain in Dominion territory any longer than absolutely necessary, and certainly not just to tell them what to look for and where to look.*"

Trok concurred completely with Beld's last sentiment. Although the engineer would have preferred to have chaperoned the equipment back to the Confederacy aboard *Ren Fejin,* it also satisfied him to know that it would at least follow him home, and that he no longer had to prowl through the industrial plants of Overne III. Liberated from his task as a thief, he turned his mind to what lay ahead: a slipstream fleet for the Breen Confederacy and the Typhon Pact.

"*Your message has been encrypted,*" said Zelk.

"*Kinn?*" Beld said, turning toward the Romulan. "*Will you affix your verification?*"

Kinn had studied the readings Trok had taken of the equipment, and he'd voiced his agreement with Beld that they should implement their contingency plan at once. At the shipmaster's request, he crossed the bridge, jockeying around the navigational hologram, until he stood beside Zelk. The Breen officer touched a control, then nodded to the Romulan. "This is Engineering Specialist Joralis Kinn," he said. "I request assistance. Authorization code: *eleth risu t'ren evek norvad.*" Kinn nodded back at Zelk, who then worked at his console once more.

"*Your message has been sent, Master,*" said Zelk.

"*Very good,*" Beld said. "*Dree, plot the shortest possible course to take us out of Dominion space. From there, head us back to the Idran system. As soon as we receive a reply, I want to make the best possible speed to the wormhole.*"

"*Plotting your course,*" Dree said, operating his navigational console.

"*We're not leaving yet?*" Trok asked, surprised.

Beld peered over at him. "*We don't know the location of the vessel we just tried to contact,*" he said. "*We can't even be sure that it's in the Gamma Quadrant at all. We only have an idea of approximately where it's supposed to be, and when. And so, no, we're not leaving yet—not until we receive the coded signal indicating that the other ship is on its way."*

"But what if we don't receive such a response?" Trok asked, displeased with the apparent uncertainty in Beld's contingency plan.

"Then we resort to the tertiary plan," Beld said.

"Which is what?"

"Which is none of your concern unless we get to that point," Beld said, clearly having no patience for Trok's questions. *"Your concern right now is to figure out how you're going to adapt the equipment we're working so hard to acquire for you into Breen starships with slipstream drive."*

"Into *Typhon Pact* starships," Kinn said quietly.

"Of course," Beld said. *"Forgive me for misspeaking."*

Kinn bowed his head in obvious acceptance of Beld's apology. "If you have no further need for me at the moment, then, I'd like to repair to my quarters." When the shipmaster did not object, Kinn strode to the bridge's only door, waited for a moment as the single panel glided slowly open, then exited into the corridor.

Trok thought to go to his own tiny cabin, but he didn't want to feel that he'd been chased from the bridge. Instead, he withdrew his scanner from its place in his environmental suit and reviewed the data he'd collected on the Overne machinery. He would do as Beld had suggested, and begin determining how best to use—

Ren Fejin jolted as a roar filled the bridge. Trok flew from his feet, his scanner hurtling out of his hand as he landed hard on the deck. The back of his helmet struck a bulkhead with a loud crack. He felt dazed, but he reached up to the nearest console, found a place to grip, and started to pull himself up. But then the ship shook fiercely again, and he crashed back down to the decking.

"They're polaron bursts," he heard one of the Breen officers call out in a rush of electronic static. *"Shields are down sixty-four percent. I don't think we're cloaked anymo—"*

A sound like thunder blasted through the ship, and the

bridge shuddered and then canted, the inertial dampers failing
for a moment. Trok rolled across the deck and into something
solid. Even with the protection of his environmental suit, he felt
battered. He tried to focus and look around the bridge. He spotted a scanner, presumably his own, smashed to pieces. He saw
one Breen officer down, but another still on his feet.

"*Shields down eighty-one percent,*" somebody called out,
though Trok could not tell who.

"*Evasive maneuvers,*" said somebody else, probably Beld. "*See
if you can cloak us again.*"

Trok thought he heard the tap of gloved fingers on a control
panel, but then another weapons strike landed. He listened to see
if he could hear the ship's hull coming apart. *What would that
sound like?* he wondered idly.

As Trok waited to die, he spared another thought for all of
his colleagues who had lost their lives in the Alrakis system.
Somehow, it still pleased him that he had survived when they
had not.

Then he lost consciousness, expecting never to wake up
again.

25

"Captain, we're receiving a message from the *Eletrix*,"
reported Lieutenant Choudhury from the tactical console. In the command chair, Picard heard the urgency in the
security chief's voice even before she continued. "It's a distress
signal."

Picard responded calmly, out of long experience. After
decades as a Starfleet captain, he delivered his next words almost
automatically. "Put it on-screen."

The tactical station emitted several reactive chirps beneath
Choudhury's touch. "Sir," she said, a sense of uncertainty entering her tone, "the message is audio only."

"Let's hear it, then, Lieutenant," Picard said.

"Aye, sir."

Picard glanced over to see Choudhury operating her controls. She worked deftly, but the captain could see the tension in her face. An instant later, the recognizable voice of the Romulan commander spilled onto the bridge.

"Eletrix *to* Enterprise. *This is T'Jul.*" The message crackled with static. "*We've suffered an accident, possibly an . . .*" The signal dropped out for a few seconds, and when it returned, some of what the commander said had clearly been lost. "*. . . tage. We are facing . . . tainment, and may . . . ject the singul . . .*"

In his mind, Picard filled in T'Jul's missing words and syllables: *An act of sabotage. A loss of containment. May have to eject the singularity.* The captain knew that an artificial, microscopic black hole drove the engines of every Imperial Fleet starship, and that a complex system of containment held the quantum singularity safely in check, keeping it from consuming the vessel it powered.

"*. . . may need to evac . . . quest immediate assist . . .*"

The message quieted again. Picard visualized a loss of data on a display of text, leaving letters missing and holes in words. He waited for the message to resume, but it didn't.

After a few more seconds, Choudhury said, "That's all there is, Captain. I'll attempt to clean it up, see if I can capture some of the missing content."

"Very good, Lieutenant." A mix of thoughts and emotions vied for supremacy within Picard. He first felt concern for the crew of *Eletrix,* and an earnest desire to help them. But he also thought of the joint mission and what its failure would mean to the Federation, to the Khitomer Accords, and beyond. And after what Commander Worf had discovered on the carbon planet, Picard could not ignore the seed of distrust that had been planted within him.

"Do you have a fix on the location of the *Eletrix*?" asked Worf, seated at Picard's right hand.

Choudhury continued to work her console. "Spatial coordinates were appended to the message, but they're incomplete because of the signal loss," she said. "I'm tracking back along their transmission path now."

With Choudhury occupied, Picard called on the ship's senior

science officer to answer his next question. "Lieutenant Elfiki, is there anything of note on long-range sensors?"

From her position along the starboard arc of the bridge, Elfiki said, "No, sir, nothing out of the ordinary."

That judgment provided Picard with at least a measure of relief. The aftereffects of an explosion resulting from the loss of containment about the singularity driving *Eletrix* would be readily detectable via subspace readings. Even the loosing of the microscopic black hole from within its cage, short of causing an explosion, would have registered on long-range scans.

"Captain," Choudhury said, "the message from the *Eletrix* originated in or near a star system approximately half a light-year distant."

"Lieutenant, transfer the coordinates to the conn," Picard said. "Lieutenant Faur, set a direct course."

At the conn, Joanna Faur's hands raced across her panel. "Calculating the course now, Captain," she said. "Estimated travel time would be one-point-two hours at maximum warp."

Picard looked to Worf, who nodded his agreement. "Make it so, Lieutenant," Picard said. The stars on the main viewscreen shifted as the conn officer brought the ship about and headed it toward its new destination. The warp drive seized control of *Enterprise* and pushed it faster than light through the void of space. "Lieutenant Choudhury, send a message to the *Eletrix,* just in case they can still receive. Let them know that we're on our way."

"Aye, sir."

The captain rose from the command chair and straightened his uniform. "Mister Worf, I'd like you to join me in my ready room." Then, gazing to the main systems display at the aft section of the bridge, he addressed the ship's second officer. "Mister La Forge, you have the bridge."

As the chief engineer acknowledged the order, Picard crossed to the forward doors on the starboard side of the bridge. Worf followed. Inside his ready room, the captain moved behind his desk, while his first officer took a chair opposite.

"Commander," Picard said, "what is your analysis of the situation?"

"It is difficult to judge with certainty," Worf said, his careful words matched by his manner. "It may be that the Romulan vessel has indeed endured an accident of some kind, or an act of sabotage, as Commander T'Jul's message indicated."

Picard noted how his first officer did not rush to accuse the Romulan commander or her crew of deception. Not for the first time, Picard marveled at how much Worf had grown in his Starfleet career. Impulsive and outspoken as a junior officer, he had learned to measure not only his words, but the thoughts behind them. Worf had served as Picard's exec for nearly four years, and the captain could not have been more satisfied with his performance.

"I'm afraid that the question I have to ask," Picard said, "is whether or not you *believe* that the message we received is truly a distress signal."

Worf looked away and shook his head, clearly not answering the question, but showing his obvious doubt. Peering back at the captain, he said, "I am unsure about the validity of T'Jul's message, mostly because of what took place at the carbon planet."

After one of *Enterprise*'s scientists had discovered physical evidence that a small vessel—possibly one of *Eletrix*'s shuttle-craft—had landed on the carbon planet, Worf had been conflicted about what action to take. He did not wish to jeopardize the mission—and with it, the prospect of peace—either by withholding information from the Romulans or by accusing the Romulans of withholding information themselves. At the same time, he had explained to Picard, the safety of the *Enterprise* crew remained his top priority.

Ultimately, Worf had simply handed over to the crew of *Eletrix* all of the data that the *Enterprise* away team had collected while on the carbon planet, doing so without comment. Later, when the Romulan crew reviewed it and notified their commanding officer of the indications of a prior landing, T'Jul contacted Captain Picard to discuss the matter. She recognized what the evidence must have looked like to him, but she claimed that her crew had not set down on the carbon planet until it had done so with the *Enterprise* crew. Offering up a possible explanation, T'Jul suggested, just as Worf had, that perhaps another vessel had landed there, possibly one of the Romulan civilian craft that had entered the Gamma Quadrant during the previous couple of months.

Picard had accepted her denial, in part because T'Jul had seemed sincere and convincing, but also because he'd *wanted* her explanation to be true. The *Enterprise* crew already exercised caution in working with their counterparts aboard *Eletrix,* so he saw no reason to modify existing procedures. In the days that followed, Picard let the incident go.

But then, even before receiving the distress call, something else had happened. "There is also the matter of the encrypted transmission," Picard reminded Worf. The *Enterprise* crew had been unable to decode a brief message they had detected.

"But I feel that neither that nor the situation on the carbon planet, even considered together, are compelling enough evidence that the Romulan distress signal is not real," Worf said.

"Agreed," Picard said. "I think it is important for the success of this mission that we treat Commander T'Jul's message as genuine." He paused, unwilling to ignore his concerns. "But I think that we must also prepare for the alternative possibility." The captain breathed in deeply, then expelled a heavy sigh. "Of what possible benefit could it be for the Romulans to dupe us into thinking that they are in danger?"

"It could be an attempt to lure us into a trap," Worf proposed.

"It could be," Picard said, "but even if it is, the question remains: to what end? The Romulans need not have participated in this mission, but allegedly did so in the spirit of cooperation and establishing a friendship. If they have other aims in mind—if they wish to sow ill will, trigger a war, or something in between—then why the intricate subterfuge? The recent attempts at entente notwithstanding, suspicion and antipathy are rife among the nations of the Khitomer Accords and the Typhon Pact. The Romulans didn't have to tempt a Federation starship crew into the Gamma Quadrant in order to stir up trouble; politically and militarily, it takes a great deal of effort these days to *prevent* trouble."

"All of that is true," Worf said. "But perhaps Commander T'Jul is acting on her own, rather than according to the instructions of the praetor."

Picard shook his head slowly. "That could be," he said. He stood up, and as he considered the idea, he paced toward the near corner of his ready room, to where a reproduction of an ancient Taguan amphora sat on a pedestal. He peered at the tapering neck and curved handles of the clay piece, then turned once more to face his first officer. "Even if T'Jul is operating based upon her own interests, I still don't see what she hopes to accomplish. The capture of the *Enterprise* crew? Appropriation of the ship itself?"

"The execution of our crew?" Worf posited.

"But how would any of that benefit the Typhon Pact, or the Romulan Star Empire, or even just T'Jul herself?"

"There is always the motive of revenge," Worf said. "And Tomalak is aboard the *Eletrix*."

"Yes, he is," Picard said, recalling his misgivings about the former starship commander taking part in the mission. The *Enterprise* captain had certainly encountered Tomalak often enough through the years, and had frustrated enough of the Romulan's plans, to make an enemy out of him. "Revenge *can* be a motive," he said, "but it is so mindless. We may not consider Tomalak a genius, but neither is he an empty vessel. I can't see him seeking retribution in this situation without there being some other objective."

"I see your point," Worf said. "It is also true that counterfeiting a distress call hardly guarantees that the *Eletrix* will be able to defeat the *Enterprise* in any sort of confrontation."

Picard agreed, but his imagination conjured up another scenario. "Perhaps the many civilian Typhon Pact ships that have traveled here through the wormhole in the past couple of months managed to secrete away weapons, or perhaps they acquired them here in the Gamma Quadrant. Perhaps when we arrive to assist the crew of the *Eletrix,* we will find an armada waiting for us."

"While that is at least conceivable," Worf said, "it still does not answer your fundamental question about this situation: why?

The capture or even the destruction of the *Enterprise* will have no impact on the current balance of power, and it can only cause the deterioration of the political situation. Even if the Romulans could somehow convince every nation in the Alpha and Beta Quadrants that the *Enterprise* crew were the aggressors in such a confrontation, that would not sway any of the major powers to switch their affiliations."

Picard paced away from the corner and into the center of his ready room, out past Worf. When he reached the end of the room, he looked back at his first officer. "Maybe this doesn't have anything to do with us," he said. "Maybe it doesn't have anything to do with the Federation, or even the Typhon Pact."

"The Romulans?" Worf said, clearly trying to follow Picard's train of thought. "Praetor Kamemor has been in power for twenty months, and in that time she has shown herself to be a far more moderate leader than any of her recent predecessors."

"Precisely," Picard said. "But there must still be anti-Federation hard-liners on Romulus, and likely in Ki Baratan."

"If so," Worf said, "then it is likely that they are the praetor's political enemies. Perhaps they would seek to use the failure of our joint mission to undermine her labors in the cause of peace—and to undermine Gell Kamemor herself."

"*That,* Number One, sounds less like the approach of a Romulan starship commander," Picard said, "and more like that of a Romulan agent."

"It does." Worf nodded, his eyes widening in realization. "And we know the identity of the current chairwoman of the Tal Shiar."

"Not exactly one of our admirers," Picard said. "We know from experience that Sela would have no problem attempting to use this ship and its crew to her own ends, which she would no doubt proclaim the best interests of the Romulan Empire. That she could simultaneously avenge herself on us would no doubt make the prospect sweeter still for her."

"It might be of value for us, then, to learn more about Praetor Kamemor," Worf suggested, "and if possible, about Sela's leadership of the Tal Shiar."

"Agreed," Picard said. "Fortunately, we happen to have a valuable resource on board." The captain strode back across his ready room and sat down behind his desk again. "Picard to Ambassador Spock," he said.

26

Captain Ro sat at the desk in her office, a padd in her hand, long past the end of alpha shift. She had managed to ease up on her excessive, subconscious efforts to justify her promotion, thanks in large part to Counselor Matthias, who had helped her understand the nature and cause of her anxiety. It had also been of no small consequence that Captain Picard had revealed his own such struggles to her. Just knowing that a man of his stature had experienced his own crisis of confidence, and that he'd overcome it to achieve such great success, had allowed Ro to finally move past her insecurity—for good, she hoped. Since Picard's visit, she certainly felt stronger and more capable than ever.

None of which gives me any extra time to complete all my duties, she lamented. Since the civilian Typhon Pact vessels had begun arriving at Deep Space 9, the amount of work for Ro and her crew had grown considerably. The increased traffic through the station meant scheduling arrivals and departures almost around the clock, as well as conducting many more ship inspections. The number of reports Ro needed to read and approve—for the Bajoran Ministry of Commerce and for the Federation Interstellar Affairs Department, not to mention for Starfleet—had begun to take up more and more of her time. She gladly would have delegated some of her responsibilities if any of her staff weren't already overworked.

"I just have to press my requests for more personnel," she said aloud. In the past two months, Starfleet had assigned seven new officers to the station—including one from the Cardassian Guard and two from the Ferengi Treasury Guard—but she had asked for thirty. "This is why they promote you, Laren," she told herself. "So you can't quit."

For all of that, though, DS9 had been running relatively

smoothly. The number of vessels and their crews from the Typhon Pact induced her to intensify security throughout the station, and Chief Blackmer and his team had met the challenge. And despite having to deal with higher volumes of ships, goods, and visitors, Ro and her crew had somehow kept up.

Still at her desk, she tried once more to focus on the report on her padd, but when her gaze passed over the same sentence three times without her actually reading it, she gave up. She dropped her hand down more forcefully than she'd intended, and the padd skittered across her desk and off the other side. "I wish I could make all the reports go away that easily," she said. Ro got up and went to retrieve the padd. Just as she placed it on her desk and prepared to leave for the day—*Maybe get some dinner at the new Argelian place*—the comm system chimed.

"Ops to Captain Ro," said a female voice.

Rather than reply, Ro took the three steps to her door and entered ops. "What is it, Zivan?" she asked of the station's tactical officer.

Dalin Slaine glanced up from her console, as did the rest of the crew. "Captain," she said, sounding a bit surprised. "I wanted to inform you that we've just received the latest communications packet from the *Robinson.*" Although the Cardassian officer had made friends during her time on the station, she tended toward formality while on duty.

"Anything requiring my immediate attention?" Ro asked, moving over to Slaine's station.

"Negative, Captain," Slaine said. "The ship just left the world of the—" She had to peer back at her console to read the name. "—the Vahni Vahltupali. There's a full diplomatic report for Starfleet Command and the Department of the Exterior, and a précis for you."

"Thank you, Zivan," Ro said. "I'll take a look at it in the morning." She leaned in to Slaine's console and glanced at its chronometer. "Shouldn't you be off duty?"

The dalin looked down, and Ro thought she seemed embarrassed. "Everybody on alpha shift should be off duty now, Captain," she said. "Since you weren't, I thought I should stay as well."

"Zivan, just because I work late doesn't mean that you have to," Ro told her. "I appreciate your dedication, but if I need your support, believe me, I'll let you know. In the meantime, I prefer my officers to be well rested."

"Yes, Captain."

"Anyway, I was just about to leave ops myself," Ro said. "I was considering trying the new Argelian restaurant."

"I've eaten there," Slaine said with a trace of excitement. "They have an incredibly eclectic menu—even a Cardassian dish—and the food is excellent."

"You've convinced me," Ro said. "Would you care to join me?"

"Thank you, Captain, but I already have plans this evening." She tapped at a control on her panel, securing her station.

"Some other time then," Ro said. She started around the outer, raised section of ops, headed for the turbolift. Slaine walked beside her.

A cab arrived in ops a moment later, carrying one rider: Prynn Tenmei. She did not appear completely hale and hearty, but Ro thought she looked better than she had in quite some time. The captain knew that Tenmei had recently moved her father from DS9's infirmary to a hospice on Bajor, and she guessed that had everything to do with the improvement in her appearance.

"Captain," Tenmei said. "Are you leaving?"

"Are you here to see me?" Ro asked.

"I was, but if you're done for the day . . ." She left her sentence unfinished.

"A captain's work is never done," Ro said, making sure to punctuate her words with a smile. "Let's head into my office." As she started back in that direction, Slaine took a step that way as well.

"Captain, if you'd like me to stay too—"

"No, definitely not, Zivan," Ro said. "Please, enjoy what's left of your evening."

"Thank you, Captain." Slaine stepped into the cab of the turbolift and specified a destination in the habitat ring—a destination nowhere near Slaine's own quarters. It pleased Ro to think that somebody so new to the station—and a Cardassian—had already made friends—and perhaps more than friends.

Ro walked back to her office with Tenmei beside her. When the doors had closed behind them, she offered the lieutenant something to drink, but Tenmei declined. Ro motioned to the sitting area to one side, and the two women sat down on the padded, built-in bench there. "I have to say, Prynn, you look well."

"Thank you, Captain," Tenmei said. "I feel better, so I'm glad the outside matches the inside." She smiled hesitantly, but after the continuous emotional pain she'd endured for more than two years, she might as well have been turning cartwheels, so dramatic was the difference in her.

"So what did you want to speak with me about?" Ro asked.

"You know that I took my father out of the infirmary," Tenmei said. She twined her hands together in her lap, clearly uncomfortable despite her more positive demeanor.

"Yes, of course," Ro said. "You moved him to Releketh, I believe."

"Yes, to the hospice at the Vanadwan Monastery," Tenmei said. "Vedek Kira arranged it for me."

Ro nodded, but Tenmei didn't continue. Ro didn't know what to say, so she said nothing. She waited as Tenmei stared down at her tangled fingers.

Finally, Tenmei said, "I'm going to take my father off the feeding and hydration tubes." She looked up at Ro with eyes mercifully dry, but still seemingly filled with doubt. Ro could only nod again. "When he . . . when he dies . . . I want it to be somewhere nice." She paused, and then added, "Not . . ." She lifted her hands from her lap and gestured to their surroundings, which Ro took to mean the entirety of the former mining facility, built by an occupying army and originally staffed with slave labor.

"Of course," Ro said. "I understand."

"I'm also hoping that the people who meant the most to him will come and say good-bye." Tenmei awkwardly reached forward and took Ro's hands in her own. "I know I don't have any right to ask anybody to do this, but I really hope you'll consider coming. My father thought a great deal of you. He talked about you a lot, and I think he saw something of himself in you."

Ro could not help but smile. "I take that as a high compliment," she said.

"Don't feel too admired," Tenmei said, the side of her mouth rising up to form half a smile. "I think, particularly when he and I were estranged, he saw a part of me in you too. You were like another daughter to him—and, for a while anyway, like his *only* daughter."

Ro had thought before that Vaughn had seen her sometimes as a surrogate daughter. But hearing it from Tenmei, she unexpectedly felt her own eyes moisten. "We worked so closely together, especially after he took command of the station and offered me the position of first officer. But it was so much more than that. He was a . . . a calming, steadying influence on me." A multitude of memories rose in Ro's mind. Unable to focus on any one of them, she simply laughed, happy to see the vital form of Elias Vaughn in her recollection. "I loved that old man," she said.

"He loved you too."

Ro squeezed Tenmei's hands, and then pulled her own away so that she could wipe away the tears in her eyes before they spilled down her face. "Of course, I'll be there. Do you know when this will be?"

"Not exactly," Tenmei said. "Within a couple of weeks, I think. I want to wait for Vedek Kira to return from Cardassia, and I'm also hoping that I can persuade Captain Sisko to be there as well. I've recorded a message to him to go out with the next comm packet we send to the *Robinson*."

"I'm sure Captain Sisko will be there if it's at all possible," Ro said.

"I think so too." Tenmei exhaled loudly, almost as though she'd been holding her breath. She slapped her hands down on her thighs and stood up. "Thank you, Captain. I won't take up any more of your evening." She headed for the doors, but Ro called after her.

"Prynn," she said, but then hesitated. Ro had often tried to bolster Tenmei's flagging spirits by inviting her to Quark's, to play a game of springball, to watch a film—to do almost anything—but as far as Ro knew, it had been a long time since Tenmei had done anything personal with anybody. Still, she felt compelled to ask. "I was going to try the new Argelian restaurant. If you wouldn't mind, I'd love some company."

Tenmei looked at her blankly for several seconds, and Ro thought that the lieutenant might not have even heard her. But then, in a small voice, she said, "Okay."

"Okay," Ro said, delighted. She stood up and joined her friend, and together they left her office.

27

How long has it been? Trok wondered. *Has it even been a day? Two days? Ten?*

He knew that the answer didn't matter, because a worse question awaited asking: *How many days* will it be?

He shifted where he lay on the hard deck of his cabin aboard *Ren Fejin.* The Jem'Hadar had removed the few pieces of furniture—a bed, a chair—that had once cluttered the small, basic space. Trok didn't believe that they had done so in order to cause him discomfort, but so that he would have no materials available to help him mount an escape attempt.

Which is probably why they also took my environmental suit, Trok thought. He peered down the narrow length of his body, covered only by the thin layer of fabric he wore. He shivered, as though just thinking about his missing environmental suit reminded him that he should feel cold.

But not cold enough, he thought. Without his environmental suit, Trok found the ship's internal temperature unpleasant, but not unbearable. But for the Amoniri among the crew, the interior of *Ren Fejin* did not reach anywhere near as cold as they required in order to survive. Trok did not actually know the species of any of the crew members, but the Amoniri and the Paclu dominated not just the Breen Militia, but also civilian spaceflight within the Confederacy. *Maybe their cabins are refrigerated,* he thought—

and hoped. If not, and if the Jem'Hadar had removed the environmental suits of any Amoniri, then those Breen had died. Trok had never witnessed the evaporation death of an Amoniri, but he had heard how much pain they felt as their mostly liquid bodies turned to vapor, how they suffered a slow loss of physical function, and how they ultimately descended into madness before finally dying.

Trok pushed himself up on the deck and leaned against the bulkhead. His muscles aching, he tested his limbs, first stretching and tensing both branches of his cleft legs, then doing the same with his similarly cleft arms. He did not look healthy. His gray flesh looked desiccated and inflexible, the stipples of the sensory organs on his arms unresponsive. In places, his skin had turned bright pink, the result of injuries sustained at the hands of the Jem'Hadar.

Well, mostly not the hands *of the Jem'Hadar,* Trok corrected himself. *Mostly their polaron beams.* The bulk of the physical damage to his body had occurred during the initial attack on *Ren Fejin.* He'd lost consciousness while being thrown about the bridge as the ship absorbed volley after volley of polaron blasts.

After that, Trok had awoken—briefly—in the clutches of two Jem'Hadar. Later, he came to when he felt his environmental suit being ripped from his body. The Dominion soldiers had not handled him gently, but neither had they beaten him. But that didn't mean that they wouldn't.

Trok trembled again, not from the cold, but out of fear. He wanted to feel hope because the Jem'Hadar had so far left him alive, but he didn't. At that moment, Trok saw no way for him to survive the situation and return home safely.

It frankly surprised him that he'd woken up at all after the ship had come under attack. He wondered if the Jem'Hadar had tracked the movement of *Ren Fejin* while supposedly rendered invisible by the phase cloak, or if they had detected Trok's presence in the industrial plants. Because of the timing of events, he suspected that it had been the subspace message that Beld transmitted that had given up the ship to the Jem'Hadar.

I guess a contingency plan isn't much help if it brings a squadron of soldiers bred for war down upon you, Trok thought bitterly. At the same time, it caused him to wonder about the "tertiary plan" Beld had claimed. *Was he serious about that?* Trok wondered. *Was there really a third plan, and if so, was there somebody on board still alive who could—*

The single panel of the cabin's door slid open. Expecting a squad of Jem'Hadar soldiers, Trok looked over—and froze. From the other side of the threshold, a creature from his nightmares stared back at him with a dozen shining, jet-black eyes. With a pale, segmented body and long fangs flowing with neurotoxins, the *rinculus* lived along the desert sands of Grevven II, a hellish world within the Breen Confederacy. Though low to the ground, the beast could rear up on its two pairs of hind limbs, bringing it to a greater height than most Breen. Its venom did not kill its prey, but immobilized it, so that the rinculus could then puncture its flesh and devour its internal organs.

Trok didn't know what to do. Inside his Breen armor, he could have survived an attack by a rinculus; defenseless and virtually naked, he would live only long enough to feel the brutal predator chewing through his viscera. If Trok could have ended his own life at that moment, he would have, just to evade the terrible pain he knew he would soon suffer.

In the doorway, the rear legs of the rinculus tensed, as though the creature prepared to pounce. Trok felt his bladder let go, the warmth of his urine spreading beneath his body. He looked to the side, for anything—a weapon, a hiding place, *anything*—though he knew the empty cabin offered him only a place to die.

As Trok turned his head, he saw movement from the doorway. He screamed, wrapping his two-pronged arms about his head and rolling into the corner. He pulled his legs up to his body and cowered, waiting for the end, and hoping that death would come quickly.

Nothing happened.

Trok did not move, other than breathing in large, desperate gasps. He knew he hadn't imagined the rinculus, and that if he looked, it would still be there. And if he looked, then it would attack, incapacitate, and consume him.

Something hot fell on the back of Trok's neck, and still he didn't move. *Maybe I should move,* he thought. He envisioned the razor-sharp fangs on either side of his neck, pushing back against their edges, allowing them to slice easily through his flesh and deliver a merciful death.

Instead, Trok felt himself hauled upward. His feet left the deck, and yet he continued upward, higher even than the rinculus could have risen on its hind legs. His cranium hit the overhead, and then he hurtled downward, still held by his nape. When his legs struck the deck, the grip on his neck released. Terrified and dazed, he crumpled.

"Get up, you filthy monoform."

A rinculus could not speak. Faint from the impact of his head on the ceiling, Trok looked up from where he lay on the deck in a heap. He did not see the rinculus. Instead, a man stood there, peering down at him from deep-set eyes and a strangely expressionless face. He looked humanoid, but even in his stunned state, Trok knew better.

"I said, 'Get up,'" the Founder repeated.

Trok attempted to position his feet beneath him and rise, but he felt drained. The blow to his head, his fear, the Jem'Hadar attack, and everything else that had taken place to bring him to that point—all of it had worn him down, had depleted the core of his being as thoroughly as if a rinculus had feasted upon his entrails. He dropped back to the deck. He did not even look back up at the Founder.

A whorl of motion encircled Trok, bands of glowing matter curling around him. A peculiar sound reached him, like that of deep-water currents. And then the Founder faced him from an arm's length away, a humanoid head at the end of a serpentine column of coruscant gold.

"You are the only one left," said the Founder. "Well, you and the Romulan. The others . . . the Jem'Hadar say they dissolved into mist." As he said the final word, the surface of the Founder's body rippled and changed, shifting from a solid form to an indefinite fog.

The abilities of the Founder fascinated Trok. He watched the cloud as it hung in the air, his gaze following its changing contours. As he did so, he caught sight of the open door, and for one brief moment, he considered attempting to race through it. But he immediately saw the folly of such an action. The Founder could pursue him in a hundred, a thousand, perhaps an infinite number of ways, and even if somehow Trok eluded the shape-shifter, surely the Jem'Hadar still occupied and controlled *Ren Fejin*.

Directly in front of Trok, he saw a section of the cloud roil, until it formed an approximation of a mouth. "Why are you here, I wonder," the Founder said. "Certainly you could not have been intending to make war on the Dominion in such an insignificant vessel."

The fog swirled around as though caught in a vortex, until it spun itself out into the Founder's humanoid form once more. "Perhaps you meant to destroy the starship-construction facilities on Overne Three." The Founder glanced around, then said, "Although even that is too ambitious for this ship and crew. Did you mean to steal something from here? Or did you simply wish to test the Romulans' new cloaking device against Jem'Hadar defenses?"

"Founder," Trok said, but before he could say more, the shape-shifter interrupted him.

"I am *not* a Founder," he bellowed. "I am Laas. The Founders are superstitious cowards."

The assertion startled Trok. He recalled learning that the Founders, though sometimes encountered as individuals, considered themselves a single, communal being, spending much of their time bound physically together—and presumably intellectually and emotionally together as well—in a shared existence called the Great Link. There had been the case of the Changeling who'd fought with the Federation in the war, but Trok had never heard of a shape-shifter opposing his own people *within* the Dominion.

"Laas," he said, "what do you want from me?" Somewhere deep within Trok, the desire to survive still burned. He thought to bargain for his life, though he knew that he had little to offer the shape-shifter.

"Want?" Laas said. "From you?" He laughed, a flat, strange sound that contained more contempt than humor. "You have nothing I want—other than perhaps to provide me some diversion. It is an awesome responsibility to lead the Dominion, but it is also a chore. I tire of the monoforms who I'm told I'm meant to protect." Laas crouched, bringing his eyes down to the level of Trok's own. "But I have no mandate and certainly no interest in protecting you, or the Romulan, or those to whom you sent your signal."

Trok felt his eyes widen as he realized that he'd been correct, that Beld's transmission had alerted the Jem'Hadar to their presence in the Overne system. He also wondered if the message would bring help—and if so, if that help would arrive in time to rescue him. "Laas," he said, trying to give himself as much time as he possibly could. "What . . . what can I do to save my life?"

Laas stared at Trok, as though measuring him in some way. Then he rose and stepped backward. "There's nothing at all you can do," he said, "except start running." Once more, Laas's flesh rippled and changed, transforming him. The mass of quivering bio-matter dived toward the deck, spread, and then captured another form.

Even before Trok saw Laas solidify completely as a rinculus, he found the strength to leap to his feet and bolt from the cabin.

28

Picard watched the main viewscreen closely, but he saw only stars spread across space like glistering jewels in the night. Leaning in toward Worf, who sat beside him on the *Enterprise* bridge, he said quietly, "I cannot refrain from thinking about Romulan cloaking technology." He paused, then added, "The *Eletrix* could be anywhere out there."

"That would presuppose that Commander T'Jul's distress signal was not genuine," the first officer noted, his gaze also riveted to the main viewer. "If the Romulans required aid, they would not seek to conceal themselves from us."

"No," Picard said. "But perhaps it is not the *Enterprise* from which they are hiding."

Worf's head snapped toward the captain, as though Picard had offered a possibility the first officer had not considered. He quickly stood up and mounted the single step to his right, to where Lieutenant Choudhury crewed the tactical console. "Is there anything at all on sensors?" Worf asked, peering down at the panel.

"Negative," replied Choudhury.

"How many planets are there in the nearby solar system?" Picard asked.

"Six," Choudhury said. "Two rocky worlds, and four gas giants."

"Are either of the terrestrial planets class-M?"

"No, Captain," Choudhury said. "The second planet is class-L, though, with an oxygen-argon atmosphere and some plant life."

"Number One?" Picard said, soliciting his first officer's opinion.

"It *is* possible that if the *Eletrix* was in danger of foundering," he said, "its crew could have sought refuge there."

Picard agreed with Worf's assessment. "Lieutenant Faur," he said, "take us to the second planet. Best speed."

"Aye, sir," said Faur.

As the conn officer adjusted the course of *Enterprise* and sent it racing through the void, Picard turned to his left, to where Spock sat in the counselor's chair. "Any thoughts, Ambassador?"

"Only that I find the apparent disappearance of the Romulan vessel disturbing," Spock said. "If its crew was truly in distress, then our inability to locate the ship does not bode well for their continued survival. If not, then the cause of peace for which we act similarly seems unlikely to survive."

"But you are convinced that Praetor Kamemor's motives in helping to establish this joint mission, as well as the civilian program in the Gamma Quadrant and the Typhon Expanse, are authentic?" Picard asked.

"I am," Spock said. "As we discussed, Gell Kamemor does not seem to be in the mold of typical Romulan leaders—at least not those of recent vintage. Her patriotism does not extend to the need to diminish other species and worlds, but only to maintaining the safety and security of the Romulan Star Empire. She believes that the establishment of endeavors that promote mutual trust with nations formerly viewed as enemies supports that aim."

"If only we could be as sure of the goals of Commander T'Jul and former proconsul Tomalak," Picard said.

"It is difficult to judge without additional information," Spock said. "But it is also difficult to envision how transmitting a false distress call to the *Enterprise* in the present circumstances would aid those in opposition to the praetor."

Before Picard could respond, Worf spoke up from where he still stood beside Choudhury at the tactical station. "Captain, we are seeing residual energy readings in the vicinity of the second planet."

"Energy readings? Can you characterize it further?" Picard asked.

"Scanning," Choudhury said. "I'm reading a considerable amount of antiprotons in the area. It could be the residue of weapons fire."

"But not the residue of *Romulan* weapons," Picard noted.

"No, sir," agreed Choudhury.

"Perhaps if the *Eletrix* was ambushed," Worf suggested, "they might not have had the opportunity to defend themselves."

"Captain, I'm now reading bursts of high-energy radiation near the second planet in the system," Choudhury reported.

"Are there any indications of ships in the area?" Picard asked.

"Negative," Choudhury said. "But it could mean that the *Eletrix* ejected its microsingularity somewhere nearby."

"Without primary power," Worf said, "the Romulans would not be able to maintain a cloaking field." The first officer stepped away from the tactical station and returned to his chair.

"Which means that if they're in the vicinity," Picard said, "we should be able to locate them."

"Approaching the second planet, Captain," said Lieutenant Faur.

Picard saw a green-and-white globe grow in the center of the main viewer as Lieutenant Elfiki spoke up from her science station. "Reading an oxygen-argon atmosphere," she said. "Traces of carbon dioxide, considerable water vapor, but little surface water. Vegetation, but no animal life."

"Captain," Choudhury said, "the high-energy radiation appears to be emanating from near the larger of the planet's two moons. Definitely reading like a microsingularity ejected from a Romulan starship."

"Take us there, Lieutenant Faur," Picard ordered.

"Aye, Captain."

On the viewscreen, the planet drifted downward and to the left, sliding out of view as *Enterprise* circled around it. Beyond, a small, gray orb rose up from the horizon. Half in the shadow of its host world, it looked pale and lifeless.

"Standard class-D planetoid," said Elfiki. "Diameter, approximately seventeen hundred kilometers. Mass, nine-point-one-three times ten to the twenty-first kilograms. Surface gravity, zero-point—"

"Captain," Choudhury interrupted, "sensors are showing considerable antiproton residue on the surface of the moon." She continued to operate her controls. "I'm reading a field of refined metals on the surface."

"An installation of some sort?" Picard asked.

"I . . . I don't think so, Captain," Choudhury said. As she tapped commands into her panel, she added, "I should be able to get a visual."

Picard watched as the main viewer blinked, the image of the moon increasing considerably, with just a fraction of its surface filling the screen. A dark smudge showed in the center of the picture. "Magnify," Picard said, but his people knew their jobs, and already a small, red rectangle flashed around the area of interest. A moment later, the dark area expanded, revealing its identity.

Somebody—Elfiki, Picard thought—gasped, which effectively captured how Picard felt. He stood up and stepped forward, as though a closer look might change the reality of what he saw. On the ashen surface of the moon, the basic outline of a Romulan *Valdore*-class warbird stood out like a sinister scar. Its hull had been obliterated, as though the vessel had plunged keel-first onto the moon, disintegrating on impact.

"Life signs?" Picard said, almost whispering on the quiet bridge. The answer to his query seemed painfully clear.

Controls cheeped beneath Choudhury's touch. "None, sir," she said. "I am reading biological matter, nothing immediately identifiable, but consistent with the remains of a crew after a high-velocity crash."

"Are there any signs of escape pods in the area?" Worf asked.

"No, sir," Choudhury said, "but I'll keep scanning."

Sorrow filled Picard at the loss of a starship with all hands. But he also understood in that moment that the wider repercussions of that loss had yet to be felt. *What will happen when the* Enterprise *returns to Federation space and reports the unexplained loss of the* Eletrix, *and the deaths of the thousand Romulans who served on board?*

Picard knew what he needed to do next, and that he should do it in the privacy of his ready room. At such an emotional time, though, he would not leave his crew. Instead, with Choudhury occupied searching for possible survivors, Picard called on the operations officer.

"Glinn Dygan," he said. "Record a message to Starfleet Command, highest priority and highest level of encryption." As he stood in the center of the bridge and searched for the words to say, he wondered not only what actions Starfleet, the Federation Council, and President Bacco would take, but what the *Enterprise* crew would find when it returned home.

29

Sisko arrived for his shift on the bridge with a spring in his step. Though it would take longer to reach the Gamma Quadrant terminus of the wormhole because of the detailed scans of the region that Starfleet had ordered, *Robinson* flew just days away from the Idran system. Before long, his crew's six-month mission would end, and he would finally get to spend time with his daughter, rather than just seeing her in subspace messages.

Not that I don't love those messages, Sisko thought as he padded down the portside ramp to the main level of the bridge. He looked forward with great anticipation to every transmission he received from Rebecca, who had not missed sending one every third day. A couple of them had been shorter than he would have preferred, such as when Rebecca had been sick or when she'd been preoccupied with the new snowfall or her possible upcoming trip with her mother aboard *Xhosa,* but he gave Kasidy a great deal of credit for helping to keep father and daughter connected.

Commander Rogeiro already sat in the first officer's chair as Sisko took the center seat. "Good morning, Anxo," Sisko said.

"Good morning, Captain," said the exec. "I hope you slept well."

Sisko smiled. "Like a baby," he said. "Must be the smell of *nerak* blossoms in the air." The fragrant, pink flowers bloomed all over the surface of Bajor.

"Isn't it winter in Kendra Province?" Rogeiro said teasingly.

"Ah, but it's summertime in Tozhat and Hedrikspool and Releketh," Sisko said.

"But won't you be visiting your daughter in Kendra when we get back?"

"That's why they invented transporters," Sisko said. "Although Rebecca loves the winter, so we may just wind up playing in the snow for my leave."

"Making snow-*captains*?" Rogeiro said. Sisko had told him about his daughter's youthful ambitions.

"Exactly," Sisko said. "And speaking of that, did I get a message overnight?" Part of his good mood stemmed from knowing that another transmission would await him when he arrived on the bridge that morning. He had expected it to arrive the day before, but the regularly scheduled communications packet from Deep Space 9 hadn't arrived.

"Actually, sir, we may have a problem," Rogeiro said, adopting a more serious manner. "We didn't receive the regular comm packet again last night."

"Two nights in a row?" Sisko said. "Problems with the Gamma Quadrant communications relay?"

"It's probably just that," Rogeiro said. "We just sent a test message. We're close enough that if the station receives it, we should get a reply in just a few hours."

Sisko nodded. "With a ship on a mission in the Gamma Quadrant, standard procedure if the communications relay goes down is to send the *Defiant* through the wormhole so that it can transmit a status to that ship."

"I know," said Rogeiro. "So we should have received something. But maybe the *Defiant* is tied up somewhere."

"In which case they would send a runabout into the Gamma Quadrant," Sisko said.

"Maybe the Deep Space Nine crew are working on the comm relay, or maybe they don't even know it's down yet," Rogeiro suggested. "Just because we're not receiving messages from the station doesn't mean that they're not receiving ours."

"True," Sisko said. "You're probably right. It's probably nothing."

But a knot of concern started to form in Sisko's gut.

30

Denison Morad hastened along the alley, trying to hurry to his destination without appearing either frightened or vulnerable. As he passed through the shadows between the old brick buildings, he pulled his coat tightly closed about him, an action he intended to signal to anyone who saw him that his alacrity stemmed from a desire to escape the elements—a ploy that benefited from its accuracy. A cold rain fell on Relvanek, the wind off the Loren Sea picking up as night descended on the coastal town.

Up ahead, the wet cobblestones led to an intersection. Morad emerged from the alley onto a wider avenue, the dark, recessed waters of one of the town's many canals dividing the road in two from right to left. He peered around, searching for anything that would positively identify the thoroughfare for him. He saw no signs, no characters, no symbols of any kind. Even the clapboard façades of the buildings that fronted on the avenue went unmarked. In Relvanek, he knew—and really anywhere on Dessica II—if you didn't know the place to which you headed, you shouldn't even be on the planet.

Morad leaned into the rain and tramped to the edge of the canal, to where a short, wooden bridge arched over it. He squinted and put a hand above his eyes, shielding them from the rain. He saw several boats tied up in the narrow waterway, their shells clattering against the stone sides of the canal walls. Seeing the swift current and smelling a damp, fetid stench, he wondered just how many dead or dying bodies had been dumped there through the centuries and had drifted out to sea.

Judging his location by the width of the canal, Morad realized that his destination stood on the near side of the waterway. He started away from the bridge and to his left down the avenue. It displeased him to see at least half a dozen other figures moving among the pools of light thrown by a run of unevenly spaced and inconsistently functioning lampposts.

Morad wanted to get out of the miserable weather, but more than that, he wished to flee the notoriously dangerous, crimeridden settlements that spread across the surface of Dessica II. He expected everybody he passed to lunge at him, to attempt to rob him. He carried only a small amount of the locally accepted currency with him, but nothing else beyond the shabby, secondhand clothes he wore. He most assuredly did not bear any identification on his person. What Morad had brought with him of value from the Cardassian Union, he kept in his head. But he harbored no fantasies that possessing no appreciably valuable material objects would keep him safe.

Morad continued to clutch his coat closed as he made his way down the avenue. Rainwater poured down his face. He counted the doorways he passed even as he kept as far as possible from the others desperate enough to be out in the rain, at night, in Relvanek. When he reached the ninth door, he continued on, allowing a Vulcan—*More likely a Romulan than a Vulcan,* Morad thought—to stagger off past him and into the darkness, bellowing drunkenly. Then Morad circled back around, pushed open the door, and dashed through it.

Inside, a haze of blue-hued smoke struck him immediately, its burnt scent assaulting his nose and lungs. A crowd of people thronged the medium-sized room, the heat of their bodies and the discordant lash of their many conversations cramming the space full. Almost as dark within the saloon as it had been outside, the atmosphere did nothing to alleviate the sense of danger that Morad had felt on the streets. Booths constructed of bare wood lined two walls, while a rudimentary, half-stocked bar filled a third. Only two of the lighting panels in the ceiling, both above the bar, provided more than the dimmest illumination; most of the panels over the booths remained completely unpowered, while a few others could do little more than turn the room's milling occupants into silhouettes.

Fighting the urge to turn and rush back outside, Morad instead pulled his coat open in the heat, slicked his hair back with one hand, and wiped his face as dry as he could with the other. Then he flung himself forward, into the mass of people. The place reeked not just of smoke, but of odors he did not recognize, which nevertheless possessed the sickly tang of bodily secretions. He choked back the urge to gag. Struggling forward, he pushed past members of one species after another. He saw the rugged green flesh of a Gorn, the deeply lined face of an Yridian, the pointed ears of one or another of the Vulcanoid races. He spotted a Bolian, a Tzenkethi, a Nausicaan. He worked hard to avoid making eye contact with anybody.

Finally finding an empty spot at the bar, Morad reached into an outer pocket of his coat. Pulling out five of the small objects there, he slapped them down onto the surface in front of him, his hand covering them. He waited until the bartender walked over and stood before him.

"Yeah?" the Corvallen said. His face looked like a piece of pottery that had fractured and then been glued back together.

"*Kali-fal,*" ordered Morad, speaking loudly in order to be heard above the many voices around him.

The Corvallen angled his head to one side and regarded him

with unconcealed suspicion. "Kali-fal?" he said. "That's not a usual drink for a Cardassian."

"I'm not a usual Cardassian," Morad said. He delivered the words as a reflex, simply wanting to meet the bartender's distrust with a show of strength and confidence, but in the next instant, Morad realized the veracity of what he'd said. Indeed, if more Cardassians believed as he did, if they supported the true order of things, he wouldn't have needed to travel to Dessica II. He had gone there specifically because most of his people had lost their way, while he had not. "I am *not* a usual Cardassian," he said again, emphasizing the point to himself.

"I guess not," the Corvallen said. "And here I didn't think any of you spoon heads could appreciate Romulan spirits."

Morad leaned into the bar as though rising to the taunt, fully aware that some weapon somewhere in the building must be trained on him at that moment. "Are you a food critic?" he said, lifting his hand from the objects he had pulled out of his pocket. "Or are you a bartender?"

The Corvallen held Morad's gaze for what seemed too long a time, but then he glanced down. When he looked back up, his hand moved forward, snatching away the slips of gold-pressed latinum. "Right now," he said, "I'll be a bartender." He stepped back from the bar and turned toward the rows of bottles that only partially filled the shelves there. As he reached to pull down an almost empty, transparent container of pale-blue liquid, the bartender also deposited the slips of latinum into a slot in the wall.

After upending the bottle into a low glass, the Corvallen returned to plunk the few sips of kali-fal down in front of Morad. In other establishments, in other places, Morad would have complained that he hadn't received equitable value for his currency. In Relvanek, though, he understood that he hadn't just purchased a drink; he had procured time in the saloon, as well as a measure of anonymity.

As the Corvallen moved back down to the other end of the bar, Morad picked up his drink, leaned on one elbow, and turned to face the rest of the room. He did not know the identity of the individual he would meet that night, but the person would know him. Morad appeared to be the only Cardassian in the saloon, and the clothes he wore and the drink he had ordered would further identify him. He also assumed that the operative would have memorized his face.

Morad raised the glass of kali-fal to his mouth, but even with only a small amount of the drink, its piquant aroma penetrated deep into his sinuses. He snapped his head around involuntarily, then turned to the bar and set the glass back down. When he looked around again at the room, an Andorian had appeared directly behind him.

"You're a long way from home," the blue-skinned alien said. He had a thick, barrel chest and well-muscled arms. He wore a tan vest over a bright red shirt, and he spoke in thickly accented but understandable Cardassian. The pair of antennae that emerged from his coiffure of white hair moved about noticeably, but seemed focused more on the rest of the room than on Morad.

"I like to travel," Morad replied, a planned response to the words that had been spoken to him.

The Andorian immediately turned and started away. Morad grabbed his drink, then pushed off from the bar and followed after him. He struggled to keep up with the Andorian, whose muscular physique cut through the crowd like a disruptor blast through ice. People closed ranks behind him, though, and Morad bounced past one after another, feeling like a spaceship traversing a dense asteroid field.

At last, the Andorian reached the far corner of the room, where a pair of Kressari sat across from each other in one of the ramshackle booths. Morad arrived in time to see the two men quickly extracting themselves from their benches and beating a hasty retreat across the saloon, obviously persuaded that their best interests lay in surrendering their seats to the Andorian. Morad's contact swung himself into the booth, and Morad sat down opposite him, placing his drink on the table.

The Andorian wasted no time. From a vest pocket, he removed a small, cylindrical object, which Morad recognized as an audio-dampening field generator. The Andorian set the silver device down on the table and triggered it with a touch, a gold ring about its center indicating its activation. Then he removed an isolinear optical rod from another pocket and pushed it across the rough surface of the tabletop.

"The rod is encrypted utilizing our third protocol," the Andorian said. "On it, you'll find an account number from the Bank of Luria. The account contains the funds you requested, as well as access to a storage compartment stocked with the equipment you need."

Morad reached down to the table and scooped up the rod, which he then tucked into an inner pocket in his coat. "This will be of tremendous help," he told the Andorian. "It will facilitate all of our operations."

"See that it does," the Andorian said. "And what do you have to report on our current undertaking?"

Despite the presence on the table of the anti-eavesdropping device, Morad glanced around the saloon to ensure that nobody present paid him and the Andorian any undue attention. "We don't anticipate having to use them in the near term," Morad said, "but the explosives are in place."

"It doesn't matter when or even if we use them," the Andorian said. "As long as the bombs are there, they give us an advantage over the Federation."

Morad nodded his agreement. It had taken a long time for his faction to graduate to the bold actions necessary for success, and it had been a struggle to re-form after the war, especially given the direction that the civilian Cardassian government had taken. With their newfound allies, though, and a continued resolve to do what they had to do, the group had begun to make considerable advances for their cause.

"Is there anything else?" the Andorian wanted to know.

"No," Morad said.

The beefy Andorian immediately grabbed up his device from the table, thumbed it off, and replaced it in his vest pocket. He hauled himself up and out of the booth, but as he started away, Morad reached out and took hold of his forearm. The Andorian looked down at him, then leaned in closer as Morad opened his mouth to say something.

"Please pass along the thanks of the movement, as well as my personal gratitude," Morad said, whispering in the Andorian's ear. "We're very appreciative to Chairwoman Sela."

31

From his command chair, Captain Picard looked at the image on the main viewscreen. Although he had seen it many times by that point, a sense of horror and great sadness filled him. He knew that it had an impact on his crew as well. Silence, interrupted only by the sounds of controls being operated, had come to fill the bridge like a rising tide. Counselor Hegol also reported a significant increase in the call for sessions with his staff since the discovery of the tragedy.

It had been a dozen years since Picard's own starship—the predecessor to the one he presently commanded—had crashed on the surface of Veridian III. He hadn't been aboard the ship at the time of the accident, but he'd witnessed its aftermath. The engineering hull had been destroyed by a breach of the warp core, sending the detached saucer section hurtling into the atmosphere of the planet it orbited. Because there had been some small amount of time to react to the disaster as it had unfolded, *Enterprise*'s casualties had been remarkably light, but Picard recalled well seeing such a large portion of his starship downed. Without the drive and secondary hull, the rest of the ship looked alarmingly incomplete, but sitting on the surface of a planet, it also looked *wrong*.

The remains of *Eletrix* looked worse than that.

Whatever had attacked or afflicted the Romulan vessel and its crew had done so with devastating effect. The ship appeared to have hurtled at tremendous velocity into the planet, virtually disintegrating on impact. Not like the corpse of an individual who has fallen to his death from a great height, Picard thought, but like the remnant ashes of somebody who has strapped a jetpack to his back and flown himself *into* the ground.

The moon on which *Eletrix* had crashed possessed no atmosphere, complicating the direct study of the wreckage by requiring away teams to don environmental suits. Worf had spent the last couple of days leading medical personnel, engineers, and scientists down to the surface in an attempt to make sense of what had taken place. Picard wanted to be able to provide a full report, for review not only by Starfleet Command and the Federation Council, but by the Romulan Imperial Fleet and the Romulan Senate.

Initially, a search for survivors had been the top priority, but the severity of the crash had quickly dashed even the most hopeful thoughts. The *Enterprise* crew did not locate a single body, and very few body parts. That could have been cause for suspicion, but if the hull of a Romulan warbird had been reduced to dust, what chance had there been for mere flesh? Sensors did indicate a massive amount of genetic material, though—enough to account for the loss of a crew numbering more than a thousand.

The image on the bridge's main screen showed a view of *Eletrix*'s ruins from above, from one of *Enterprise*'s shuttles. The huge, dark mass of vaporized metal looked almost like something out of an inkblot test. *What do you see here?* Picard thought, and a phrase rose in his mind: *The shroud of* Eletrix.

"Captain," somebody said, snapping Picard back from his thoughts. He had to replay the word in his head to determine who had spoken.

"Yes, Lieutenant," he said, peering over to Jasminder Choudhury at the tactical station.

"It's seventeen hundred ten hours, sir," she said.

For a few seconds, the significance of Choudhury's statement eluded Picard, so focused had he been on the fate of *Eletrix* and its crew. Then he recalled that the *Enterprise* crew should have received their regular comm packet from Starfleet by seventeen hundred hours—if not new orders even sooner than that, given the circumstances. Immediately after discovering the crash of *Eletrix,* Picard had sent a coded message to Starfleet Command, informing them of what had taken place. The transmission had

been marked priority one, and so should have been acknowledged upon routing through Deep Space 9. The *Enterprise* had
received no such acknowledgment. Of even greater concern, no
response had arrived from Starfleet—not in a single message,
not in the regular comm packet the day before, and as he'd just
been informed by Choudhury, not in the regular comm packet
that day.

"And sensors show no local interference?" Picard asked. He
stood up and walked over to face Choudhury from across the
tactical station.

"I see nothing on local or long-range scans," Choudhury
said. "I've also run multiple diagnostics on our communications
equipment, and I've found nothing wrong."

Picard nodded, deeply concerned by the lack of contact with
Starfleet. The *Enterprise* crew hadn't traveled for that long or
across that great a distance since entering the Gamma Quadrant. Along the way, they hadn't encountered any phenomena
that might have forecast future communications problems. "But
something is definitely wrong," he said.

"I think so, sir, yes," Choudhury said. "It's a feeling, maybe
colored by what's happened, but yes, I think something's wrong."

At the main engineering station at the rear of the bridge,
Commander La Forge turned in his chair to face Picard. "I'm in
agreement, Captain," he said.

"And is this a feeling for you too, Mister La Forge?" Picard
asked.

The chief engineer rose and stepped forward. "It is, sir," he
replied. "I've been thinking about this since it happened, and the
circumstances just seem suspect to me." He paused, then added,
"It's a feeling, but I'd say that it's a *well-founded* feeling."

"Well-founded how?" Picard asked.

La Forge shook his head. "I've had plenty of dealings with
the Romulans over the years," he said. "I know we all have,
but . . . I don't know. Their distress call . . . it just sounded . . .
too desperate for a Romulan."

"Surely if the *Eletrix* crew were in genuine and immediate danger," Picard said, "their captain would be anxious to call for help."

"Yes, of course," La Forge agreed. "But add to that the fact that the wreckage of the *Eletrix* is so catastrophic that there are virtually no intact pieces of the ship left, and almost no remains of the crew recognizable as such."

"You're suggesting that Commander T'Jul and her crew have perpetrated a ruse," Picard said.

La Forge walked around the tactical console and descended the steps to the bridge's lowest tier. Facing Picard directly, he said, "Think about it, Captain. Since the supposed incident, we've had no contact with Starfleet. We have no confirmation that they've received any of our messages, and we've received none of their regularly scheduled communiqués. If the Romulans have faked all of this—" He pointed toward the forward section of the bridge, in the direction of the main viewscreen. "—then it could well be the crew of the *Eletrix* who are interfering with our transmissions."

Picard understood the inclination of his chief engineer, or any member of the *Enterprise* crew—or anybody within Starfleet, for that matter—to distrust the Romulans. In agreeing to participate in the joint exploration of the Gamma Quadrant, the captain himself had needed to fight against his own such feelings, to distance himself from the recollections of his many combative experiences with members of the Imperial Fleet—including, specifically, Tomalak. Picard had wanted to believe that the new praetor truly sought peaceful coexistence, and even cooperation, but in his rush to work toward those goals himself, had he been too forgiving?

Picard turned toward the main viewer and regarded the grim scene on the moon about which *Enterprise* orbited. "Lieutenant Choudhury," he said, "how is our study of the *Eletrix* debris going?"

"We're not learning much," Choudhury said, "but we have collected a considerable set of readings. It may take some time, but eventually we should be able to figure out what happened."

"Are you satisfied with the amount and quality of the information we've gathered here?" Picard wanted to know.

"Sir?" she said, apparently sensing that something in particular motivated the captain's question.

"If we depart within the next few hours," Picard elucidated, "would that significantly affect our analysis of the crash?"

"Not significantly, no," Choudhury said.

"Thank you," Picard said. He looked at La Forge, then returned to the command chair. "Open a channel to the *Chawla*."

"Channel open, Captain," Choudhury said almost at once.

"Picard to *Shuttlecraft Chawla*."

"*This is* Chawla. *Worf here,*" came the reply of the ship's first officer.

"Number One, I want you to recall each of your away teams to the *Enterprise*," Picard said. "How long will that take?"

"*I should be able to have all crew and equipment back aboard within ninety minutes, Captain,*" Worf said.

"Very good, Commander," Picard said. "Make it so."

"*Yes, sir.*"

"Picard out." Looking to the conn, he said, "Lieutenant Faur, set course for the Bajoran wormhole. Be prepared to go to warp nine as soon as all of the away teams are back on board."

"Aye, Captain," said Faur.

Picard paused, then said what he thought his entire bridge crew wanted to hear—and what he wanted to hear himself. "We're going home."

La Forge moved to the first officer's chair beside Picard and sat down. "Captain," he said, "before we depart, I think there's something else we might try."

"Yes, Mister La Forge?" he asked.

"There's another Starfleet vessel in the Gamma Quadrant," La Forge said. "If I'm not mistaken, its crew should be nearing the completion of their mission, meaning that they should be even closer to the wormhole than we are. If we try to contact them, perhaps our success or failure to do so can tell us whether or not our communications are being blocked, by the Romulans or anybody else."

Picard nodded. "Well considered, Geordi," he said. La Forge continued to impress in his transition to a senior command position aboard *Enterprise*.

Picard stood from his chair and looked again to his tactical officer. "Lieutenant Choudhury," he said, "record a message to Captain Benjamin Sisko aboard the *Robinson*."

32

"**C**aptain Sisko," said Lieutenant Commander Uteln from the tactical station, "we're receiving a transmission. It's coded priority one, marked captain's eyes only."

Sisko looked up from the command chair on the *Robinson* bridge. "From Deep Space Nine?" he asked. He felt relieved to finally be in contact with the station again, though the urgency of the message concerned him.

The Deltan officer worked the controls on his panel. "No, sir," he reported. "The message originated from within the Gamma Quadrant, but from a different direction than that of the wormhole. It's from the *Enterprise*."

"The *Enterprise*?" Sisko said. He knew from Starfleet Command that Captain Picard's crew had recently embarked on a historic joint exploratory mission with the Romulans, but he'd had no reason to anticipate any communication with them.

"Why are they contacting us?" asked Commander Rogeiro, echoing Sisko's own thoughts. The first officer sat to the captain's right.

"That's a good question," Sisko said, rising from the command chair. Looking toward the tactical station, he asked, "Is it a distress signal?"

"Negative, sir," Uteln said.

Sisko peered down at Rogeiro. "Maybe they've lost contact with Starfleet as well," the captain suggested.

"Maybe," Rogeiro said. "And at least we know with certainty now that our comm system's working."

Sisko nodded, then looked back up at the tactical officer. "Mister Uteln, route the message to my ready room." To Rogeiro, he said, "Commander, you have the bridge."

The captain crossed past the ops console and entered his ready room. Inside, he walked directly to his desk, reached for the computer interface atop it, and turned the screen to face him.

On it, he saw the skewed chevron of the Starfleet emblem, above the words Incoming Transmission. He tapped a control, and the image of Jean-Luc Picard appeared. He looked older than when Sisko had last seen him, though perhaps the serious expression on the captain's face contributed to that impression.

No, it's not that, Sisko thought. *Picard* always *looks serious.*

"*Captain Sisko, this is Captain Picard of the* Enterprise," he said. "*As I'm sure Starfleet Command has detailed for you, my crew have undertaken a mission of exploration into the Gamma Quadrant with the crew of the Romulan vessel Eletrix.*" Picard paused and took a deep breath. "*Captain, we have had an . . . incident.*"

Sisko immediately wondered about the nature of the "incident," as well as why the *Enterprise* captain clearly chose not to discuss it. It occurred to him that perhaps Picard did not want to risk the message being intercepted and thereby revealed to others.

"*The crew of the* Enterprise *are fine, and we are in no danger,*" Picard continued. "*But over the course of the last two or three days, we have lost touch with Deep Space Nine.*"

At the mention of the station, Sisko grew immediately concerned. He could not help but think of Kasidy's intention to bring Rebecca with her on a freight run aboard *Xhosa*, which would end at DS9. Nor did his mind ever stray too far from the warning the Prophets had issued all those years ago.

"*It is unclear whether our transmissions are being jammed somewhere along the way, or whether there might simply be an equipment failure aboard the station or on the Gamma Quadrant communications relay,*" Picard went on. "*If you are receiving this message, then it seems more than likely that the latter is the case, especially if the* Robinson *crew are experiencing the same sort of difficulties.*"

Of course, thought Sisko, *there could be other reasons why the crew of Deep Space Nine haven't responded to messages from either the* Enterprise *or the* Robinson. He visualized the station under attack, something he had experienced numerous times while he'd commanded DS9. And while Starfleet had posted *Canterbury* to aid *Defiant* in defending the station, the wormhole, and

Bajor, it could also be the case that, despite their present locations in the Gamma Quadrant, *Robinson* and *Enterprise* were the next nearest vessels.

"Captain Sisko," Picard concluded, *"if you receive this message, please reply at once and let us know the status of the* Robinson *crew's communications with Deep Space Nine. I await your reply."* The image of the *Enterprise* captain vanished, replaced by the Starfleet emblem.

Sisko walked around his desk and sat down behind it. He considered the situation. Both his crew and Captain Picard's had received no transmissions from DS9 for more than two days. Add to that the presence in the Gamma Quadrant not only of scores of civilian Typhon Pact vessels, but also a Romulan warbird. And though Sisko had no idea what sort of "incident" the *Enterprise* crew had experienced, he suspected that it could not be considered something positive.

With his concerns growing, he reached forward and turned the computer interface on his desk toward him. He touched a control and said, "Computer, record a message to Captain Jean-Luc Picard of the *U.S.S. Enterprise*. Encode it priority one and captain's eyes only."

"Recording," announced the computer, the word itself appearing on the screen.

"Captain Picard," Sisko said, "I have received your message aboard the *Robinson*. Like your ship, mine has also lost contact with Starfleet and Deep Space Nine. We have received none of our regularly scheduled comm packets in the last two days, nor any other transmissions other than the one you sent. And like you, I am concerned about the sudden subspace silence." Again, Sisko saw in his mind's eye some of the vessels that had mounted attacks on DS9 while he'd commanded the station: Cardassian ships, Klingon ships, Breen, Jem'Hadar—

"Computer, pause recording." Two quick tones verified the order. "Sisko to bridge."

"Rogeiro here, Captain," replied the first officer. *"Go ahead."*

"Commander, lay in a direct course for the wormhole," he said. On the last leg of the *Robinson* crew's journey through the

Gamma Quadrant, they would be doing nothing but recharting a region of space already mapped by Starfleet. *And that,* Sisko decided, *can wait.* "Take us to warp nine."

"Aye, sir," Rogeiro said.

"Sisko out."

He would complete his message to Captain Picard, but first he waited. Seconds passed, perhaps half a minute, then another. At last, he felt the change in the vibrations flowing through the ship. His momentum shifted almost imperceptibly as the inertial dampers worked to adjust to *Robinson's* course change, and then the thrum of the warp engines surged in intensity as the ship leaped to dramatically higher velocities. It would take mere days, and not weeks, to reach the Bajoran wormhole, and beyond it, the Alpha Quadrant and Deep Space 9.

Sisko could only hope that would be soon enough.

33

*R*en Fejin floated uncontrolled above the planetary system's orbital plateau, dying, but not dead.

At least, seemingly *not dead,* thought Commander Orventa T'Jul. *But perhaps reanimated.*

Perched on the edge of her command chair on the bridge of *Eletrix,* T'Jul observed the Breen cargo vessel as it tumbled slowly across the primary viewscreen. From his position at the sensor panel, Sublieutenant Vorsat had reported many of *Ren Fejin's* systems down: engines and thrusters, shields, communications, transporter, and as T'Jul herself could see, the cloak. Emergency power functioned, and the entire ship's complement—thirteen Breen and one Romulan—registered as alive, although life support operated at minimal levels. As various aspects of the asymmetrical freighter twisted into the light of the Overne sun, the reason for the vessel's failures became evident: irregular black patches spread across its hull.

"It's taken fire," said Tomalak, noting the obvious. He stood beside T'Jul's command chair, to her right. Opposite him, to her left, the lone Breen aboard waited without comment.

Paying Tomalak no heed, T'Jul looked over at Sublieutenant Vorsat, who stood at the sensor station on the port side of the bridge. "What can you determine about the weapons that caused the damage?" asked the commander. With the Breen ship inside Dominion space, T'Jul knew the answer, but before she acted, she wanted to be absolutely certain of her facts. Something about the state of *Ren Fejin* troubled her, and she needed to figure out what that meant.

"Energy readings on the hull indicate an assault employing polaron beams," Vorsat said.

"The Jem'Hadar," said Tomalak, once again mentioning something readily apparent as though drawing an unexpected conclusion.

During Tomalak's time aboard *Eletrix*, T'Jul had grown to despise him. Aware of his long record of service to the Empire, and specifically of his decades in the Imperial Fleet, she nevertheless characterized his mind as dull. In the short span of the joint mission with the *Enterprise* crew, Tomalak had carried out the role of liaison adequately, but really, almost anybody on board with a modicum of organizational skills could have performed the task. He added nothing of value to the process of interfacing with the Starfleet officers, and he certainly fell far short of providing the knowledge, intelligence, and calming influence she had witnessed in Ambassador Spock.

T'Jul had spent all of her adult life in the Imperial Fleet, not all of it easy. As a young officer, she faced all the same obstacles everybody did at that age and in that position, but her unusual appearance—her considerable height, her lighter hair, her green eyes—also contributed other challenges. Through her rise to warbird command, though, she saw most of the opposition to her, most of the suspicions, disappear in the bright light of her performance, like shadows banished by a noonday sun. She did not receive universal acceptance—nobody did—but she did gain the respect of many of her superiors along the way.

As T'Jul had climbed up through the ranks, some of the resistance to her had come from a single source—though she could hardly claim uniqueness on that front. The Tal Shiar tasked many people, both inside and outside the Fleet. Their representatives often traveled aboard starships as visible components of some particular mission, but they also sometimes slinked onto a vessel, promoting some mysterious agenda of the secretive intelligence agency. Tal Shiar agents could be chillingly calculating and stunningly adept at maneuvering matériel into places, and personnel into actions, for the purpose of achieving specific aims, but they could just as often be petty tyrants whose heavy-fisted meddling in ship operations betrayed their affiliation and rattled the crew. Although Tomalak had been assigned to *Eletrix* under the guise of liaison to the Federation officers, he had arrived with the imprimatur of Admiral Vellon, a known minion of the Tal Shiar. Upon his boarding, Tomalak also revealed to T'Jul a potential mission profile wildly different from the official version. All of that, together with her observations of Tomalak's blunt behavior—particularly after receipt of the coded message from *Ren Fejin*—convinced T'Jul that he acted on behalf of the Tal Shiar. And for that alone, he earned her contempt.

"Yes, the Jem'Hadar," T'Jul said, agreeing with Tomalak while resisting the desire to comment on the mediocrity of his analytical abilities. "But if the *Ren Fejin* battled Dominion forces, then where are those forces?"

"Clearly the Breen vanquished their foes," Tomalak said.

"*That* vessel?" said T'Jul, gesturing toward the viewscreen, unable to conceal her incredulity at Tomalak's suggestion. "The *Ren Fejin* is quite obviously designed for a different purpose than warfare." Irked by Tomalak's useless contributions to their scrutiny of the situation, but also wanting to avoid pushing him too far, the commander turned to another source for validation of her assessment. "What do you think, Kazren?"

The Breen turned to her. The horizontal green light of his helmet, which hinted at the location of his eyes beneath, and the muzzle that evoked the impression of a protruding nose and jaws, masked a being of a different form than the environmental suit implied. Back when she had served aboard *Dekkona* as executive officer, T'Jul had helped retrieve Kazren from Starfleet's

Utopia Planitia station—and she had seen him *without* his environmental suit. He looked like nothing she had expected, and not much like his Breen armor suggested, and that recollection helped fuel her suspicions about the present set of circumstances.

"The possibility of the Ren Fejin *crew succeeding in their endeavors,"* Kazren said in his digitally modified speech, *"was completely predicated upon the stealth they gained from employing the phasing cloak recently installed on their ship."*

"And the advantage of that stealth has obviously vanished," T'Jul said. "So even if the *Ren Fejin* somehow managed to defeat the Jem'Hadar forces that attacked it, where are their reinforcements? The message sent by Master Beld stated that the Dominion defended the shipyard at Overne Three with three dozen ships."

"Commander," Sublieutenant Vorsat said from the sensor panel, "midrange sensors do confirm more than thirty Jem'Hadar warships orbiting the planet."

"Perhaps the Jem'Hadar were willing to send only one or two vessels against a single intruder in the system," Tomalak suggested, "and the remainder are committed to protecting the shipyard at close range."

T'Jul opted not to address the several flaws in Tomalak's argument. Instead, she rose to her feet and reached to her left. Guiding the Breen by the elbow of his environmental suit, she led him off to the port side of the bridge, away from the rest of her crew and the liaison. While she knew what Kazren—and presumably all Breen—looked like beneath the cover of his armor, she doubted that anybody else on the bridge did. The Breen seemed to hide their physical nature zealously, even to the point of misdirection. Indeed, most people seemed to think that the Breen required very cold temperatures in order to survive, something that T'Jul, by virtue of her experience with Kazren, knew to be patently untrue.

Recognizing the cultural choice of the Breen to conceal themselves—to hide their very forms—T'Jul had pulled Kazren away in order to respect that choice. She didn't know if he would under any circumstances answer the question she wanted to ask, but she thought it more likely if she did so in private. "Kazren," she said, leaning in close to his helmet, her voice low, "is there a way that you can use sensors to determine the identity of those who are wearing Breen armor?"

Kazren did not answer immediately, but he regarded her— or at least he gave the impression of doing so, inclining the front of his helmet in her direction. Finally, he said, *"I understand why you are asking this."* Unexpectedly, he reduced his electronically encoded voice in volume. *"I can do what you ask, but I request privacy when I do so, and no recording of my methods."*

"You have my word," T'Jul said, and she meant it. Kazren peered across the bridge at Tomalak, as though deciding whether or not to trust him. Again speaking in a voice meant only for the Breen, T'Jul said, "I will keep Tomalak away."

Kazren nodded, and T'Jul immediately looked over to the sensor panel. "Sublieutenant Vorsat, attend me," she said. T'Jul walked back over to her command chair, where Vorsat met her. As Kazren headed for the sensor panel, T'Jul addressed the sublieutenant. "Have you been monitoring the communications block?"

"Yes, Commander, as you ordered," said Vorsat. "All functions continue to perform at optimal levels."

Once *Eletrix* had received the *Ren Fejin* crew's encrypted request to implement Tomalak's mission, T'Jul had given her crew the new orders. Utilizing materials and equipment left on various worlds in the Gamma Quadrant by Typhon Pact civilian craft, the crew of *Eletrix* staged the crash of their own vessel, with the loss of all hands. After transmitting a ragged distress call to *Enterprise,* they then headed, under cloak and at high warp, for the Dominion. Along the way, they deposited a satellite on the edge of the Idran system. Hidden by its own cloak, the satellite blocked all transmissions to and from the nearby Federation comm station, which facilitated trans-wormhole communications with Deep Space 9, and beyond it, with the rest of the Federation.

With the communications block in place, T'Jul could be sure that the *Enterprise* crew would not notify Starfleet and the UFP president about the apparent loss of *Eletrix*, which might have triggered a state of high alert on DS9. Likewise, depending on what ultimately transpired at Overne III, the Dominion could not warn the Federation. According to Tomalak, the Romulan Empire's operative aboard Deep Space 9—*Doubtless a member of the Tal Shiar*, T'Jul thought—indicated that, as long as Typhon Pact ships traveled within the Gamma Quadrant, calls to high alert on DS9 would lead to Starfleet personnel screening for cloaked vessels traveling through the Bajoran wormhole. Tomalak's superiors wanted to avoid detection of *Eletrix* as it returned through the wormhole in order to avert an interstellar incident, while T'Jul wanted to avoid putting the lives of her crew at risk.

"Very good, Sublieutenant," said T'Jul, acknowledging Vorsat's report on the communications block. "Is there any means of determining whether the Jem'Hadar penetrated the phase cloak?"

"No, Commander, not based on the data we have available to us," Vorsat said. "But since we appear to have gone undetected, that is reason to believe that either the phasing cloak aboard the *Ren Fejin* failed, or that its crew did something that alerted the Jem'Hadar to their presence."

T'Jul agreed with the sublieutenant's assessment. Since the *Ren Fejin* crew had mentioned nothing of an assault on their ship, it followed that the attack had taken place after they'd sent their message. T'Jul further surmised that the transmission itself may have betrayed *Ren Fejin*'s presence and location to the Jem'Hadar.

The commander saw Kazren finish working at the sensor panel. As he walked toward her, she dismissed Vorsat back to his duty. When Kazren reached the command chair, he addressed T'Jul.

"There are thirteen active Breen environmental suits on the Ren Fejin, *as well as one set of Romulan life signs,"* he said, confirming Vorsat's earlier findings. *"Of the thirteen environmental suits, only four are worn by actual Breen."*

T'Jul nodded, her suspicions vindicated. "And the other nine sets of Breen armor are in use by Jem'Hadar," she said.

The crew of *Ren Fejin* had not avoided the destruction of their vessel because they had somehow beaten back an attack by the Jem'Hadar; the Dominion forces intended to use the Breen ship to lure the recipient of the *Ren Fejin* crew's message: *Eletrix*.

"Not nine Jem'Hadar," said Kazren. "Eight. The final suit is being worn by a Changeling."

"A Founder?" said T'Jul, startled. The news unsettled her as well. She took a step back and sat down in her command chair. The Jem'Hadar surely would not protect a Founder with only eight soldiers, which meant that they likely kept *Ren Fejin* under surveillance, with a much greater force at the ready. For a moment, T'Jul thought that would complicate any attempt to help the crew of the Breen vessel—or what remained of them— to complete their mission. But then she realized how she could turn the presence of the Founder to her advantage.

She stood up and quickly headed for the turbolift. "Tomalak, Kazren, come with me," she said.

Trok leaned against a panel in the corner of the *Ren Fejin* bridge, cowering. Despite having his environmental suit returned to him, he felt miserable. He had no idea how long it had been since Master Beld had transmitted the message that had revealed the Breen privateer to the Jem'Hadar, or even how long it had been since the Changeling—*Not a Founder,* he reminded himself in a panic—had arrived to join the boarding party. He didn't know how many of the Breen crew had survived the Jem'Hadar attack and commandeering of the ship; Laas had told Trok that only he remained, but Trok had seen at least one Paclu donning his gear. He'd also seen a Jem'Hadar soldier fitting himself into a Breen environmental suit.

Joralis Kinn stood on the other side of the bridge from Trok. The Romulan appeared physically fit, with no bruises on his flesh or other visible injuries, but his eyes looked vacant. Trok wondered briefly what Laas had done to Kinn, but the thought only served to unnerve Trok even more.

Gazing around the bridge from within the familiar confines of his helmet, Trok observed the other five Breen present. *Or whoever wore the five sets of Breen armor,* he thought. He could not tell with certainty, but based upon their postures, Trok thought that five Jem'Hadar soldiers stood on the bridge.

All of them had waited there for at least half a day, and that time followed other similar days. From time to time, Trok would be escorted to his cabin, where he could eat and sleep and clean himself, but mostly he waited on the bridge or in engineering. For what, he did not know, but he suspected that the Changeling and the Jem'Hadar employed *Ren Fejin*—as well as Breen environmental suits—as bait for the Romulan starship Master Beld had attempted to contact. With what little he knew of that feature of the operation, Trok could not even conjecture when—or even *if*—help would arrive.

Trok could imagine, though, the sort of reception that the Romulan crew would receive from the disguised Jem'Hadar. *Once the—*

Something shifted in Trok's field of vision. For an instant, he thought he might have imagined it, but then one of the other "Breen" turned his helmet sharply, as though he had seen something unexpected just off to the side. Suddenly, the bridge began to glitter and throb, quickly softening into nebulous patches of bluish green. Everything in the room retained its shape, but lost its color and texture, replaced by the pulsing blue-green smudges.

For the first time in he didn't know how long, Trok felt hope.

For day after day down on Overne III, Joralis Kinn had utilized the phasing cloak mounted in *Ren Fejin* to allow at least a part of the ship to travel essentially *through* the roofs and walls of the industrial plants. If the entire hull fit within a building, Trok could just open a hatch and climb out of the uncloaked vessel. If not all of the ship fit, then Trok would mount the phase-transition stage and be uncloaked himself, returning to an unphased state inside the building he wanted to examine.

So Trok recognized the effect of entering and exiting a phase-cloaked ship.

A moment later, the fluid scraps of blue-green focused themselves into shapes once more, but different shapes than those of the *Ren Fejin* bridge. He saw rods and mesh surfaces, and beyond them, the forms of humanoids. When the colors paled, Trok saw a number of uniformed Romulans, and one Breen—a *true* Breen, he hoped.

Trok had just enough time to see the weapons leveled in his direction before several bright-green streaks flashed across the room. One struck him directly in the chest. He felt pain, but, after all that he'd recently been through, no sense of surprise.

He was unconscious before he collapsed to the deck.

T'Jul watched as two of her security officers led the shape-shifter into a conference room aboard *Eletrix*. They stopped at one end of the large table that sat in the center of the space. Another half-dozen of T'Jul's crew ringed the room, all of them with weapons drawn. The commander herself stood at the other end of the table, with Tomalak and Joralis Kinn to her right, and Kazren and Trok to her left.

T'Jul raised her arms and made a quick parting motion with her hands. The two security officers each released their hold on the shape-shifter and stepped away from him. "I am Commander Orventa T'Jul of the Romulan Imperial Fleet," she said. "You are aboard the vessel *Eletrix*."

The Changeling said nothing. He possessed an oddly smooth face, though three wavy lines creased his high forehead. He didn't wear clothing in the traditional sense, but he had formed the appearance of boots, pants, and a long-sleeved shirt about him.

"Your name is Laas, I'm told," T'Jul continued. Once everybody aboard *Ren Fejin* had been phase-shifted to *Eletrix*, they had all been rendered unconscious with a disruptor blast—all but the shape-shifter, who had proven impervious to the stun setting. Instead, T'Jul's security staff had dealt with him in a different manner.

Still receiving no response from the Changeling, T'Jul went on. "All of the Jem'Hadar aboard the Breen vessel are alive and have not been harmed," she said. "They have been divested of their Breen armor, and we are currently holding them in detention cells. We are prepared, though, to set them—and you—free."

The proclamation still elicited no reply from the shape-shifter, who stood there with the eyes he had crafted out of his morphogenic matrix, and he stared down at the deck. T'Jul moved away from the head of the table and walked along its length, toward the prisoner she genuinely hoped to release soon. When she reached the Changeling—careful to remain beyond the length of his arms—she waited for him to look up at her. When he didn't, she decided to go on.

"I'm sorry about the use of our device," she said, pointing to a bulky cylinder standing on a larger octagonal base in the center of the table. It emitted a low hum, and chaser lights circled its upper rim. The Cardassians had initially created the quantum stasis field, and the Romulans had perfected it—at least to the extent that it could be perfected. The device prevented a shape-shifter from changing form, but it functioned only over modest distances. Tomalak had brought several of them onto the ship, knowing that *Eletrix* might need to divert to the Dominion. Before bringing the shape-shifter aboard, he had deployed them throughout the ship, ensuring that the Changeling would be unable to use his abilities while in their custody. "I wanted to be able to speak with you, but if you retained your capacity to change your shape at will, I wasn't sure you'd freely listen to me."

The shape-shifter still said nothing, still peered downward.

Fighting back her frustration, T'Jul charged ahead. "Neither my crew nor that of the Breen vessel have come here to commit violence against your people or any part of your empire."

At last, the Changeling lifted his head. From deep-set eyes, he glared coldly at her. "You come in peace, is that it?" he said, his voice dripping with odium. "I believe that's what monoforms say just before they attempt to commit genocide."

"We are here because the Federation and its allies are threatening *our* people," T'Jul said. She motioned back toward Kazren and Trok. "The Romulans, the Breen, and others."

"All you monoforms like to do is talk and fight," Laas said. "I suppose it is your effort to compensate for living your individual lives in such solitude."

"We do not wish to fight," T'Jul maintained. "We have come

here in the hope of acquiring technology from the Dominion that will put us on an even footing with the Federation. In that way, we will be able to *avoid* war."

"I don't care," Laas said. "Fight. Fight until you are all dead. Leave the galaxy to those who deserve to live in it . . . to those who can appreciate and experience its many marvels."

"We don't want to fight," T'Jul persisted. "As I said, we came here to acquire technology from the Dominion—not weapons, but defensive equipment."

"And so you were going to steal it from us," Laas said.

It occurred to T'Jul to lie, to assert that the Breen had intended to bargain for the technology, but since *Ren Fejin* had entered Dominion space and approached Overne III under cloak, and then enlisted the aid of a cloaked Romulan warbird, such a claim would lack credibility. Instead, she chose to adhere to a version of the truth. "Yes, we were going to steal your equipment for manufacturing deflector and structural integrity shield generators. We did not think you would give them to us."

"And that is your idea of peace?" Laas said. "To steal what is not yours just because you supposedly need it."

"We do need it," T'Jul said. "The lives of our people depend on our ability to match the Federation's technological level of advancement. If we cannot, then we will eventually be overrun and enslaved, or possibly exterminated completely."

"I don't care," Laas said again. "The fewer monoforms, the better."

T'Jul waited a beat without saying anything, fighting the frustration rising within her. Cloaked or not, she did not like having *Eletrix* in the middle of Dominion space. She wanted to leave, to take her ship back through the Bajoran wormhole and back to the Empire as soon as possible. But she also believed in the cause that Tomalak had brought aboard with him, and which she had served previously: matching the might of the Federation. If at all possible, she would not depart the Dominion without obtaining the equipment that her people needed to achieve a balance of power and thereby preclude war.

"From aboard the Breen vessel, we contacted the Jem'Hadar

stationed about Overne Three, as well as several of the Vorta there," she said. "They know that we have you, and that's the only thing that has prevented them from sweeping the system—from sweeping *all* of your territory—in an attempt to locate our cloaked ship. For now, they will allow us to return the Breen vessel's engineers to their ship so that they can repair it and exit Dominion space. They have yet to consent to providing us with the technology we need, though. I was hoping that you might convince them."

"Why would I help you?" Laas asked, his anger unrelenting. "You've taken me prisoner, restricted the essence of who I am, and now you threaten me unless I do your bidding."

"I am not threatening you," T'Jul said. She considered making a gesture of good faith by deactivating the quantum stasis field, but based on Laas's obvious hostility toward "monoforms," she doubted that she could trust him to honor any bargain they struck if she returned his ability to shape-shift. "I'm asking for your cooperation. Allow us to take the sets of machinery we need from the surface of Overne Three, and we will allow you to go free. We will leave the Dominion and return to our own space through the Bajoran wormhole."

"And if I don't?"

T'Jul tried to gauge the answer that would provide the best chance of convincing—or coercing—Laas to agree to the deal she'd proposed. It seemed clear that a light touch would not work with him, nor did she think that the threat of death would either. "If you do not provide us with what *we* need, then I am sorry to say that we will not provide you with what *you* need."

"What does that mean?" Laas demanded.

"It means that we need the equipment we described," T'Jul said, no longer working to keep her tone calm. "You need your freedom. If we don't get what we need, then neither will you. We will bring you through the wormhole and to the Romulan Star Empire, where you will spend the rest of your days confined to a cell and unable to shape-shift."

Laas looked at T'Jul with such hatred that she thought he might launch himself across the corner of the table to get his unchanging but potentially lethal hands around her throat. She felt her own anger rising. She understood all the reasons why the Dominion in general and Laas in particular should be upset about two cloaked alien ships entering their territory to perpetrate a theft—but she didn't care enough to see the situation from their perspective. She had a job to do, and not one for personal gain, but one intended to help her people and their allies protect themselves against the great threat of the Federation, the Klingons, and the others. She would do what needed to be done.

Peering at one of the security guards who had ushered Laas into the conference room, she said, "Lock him up."

34

Colonel Cenn Desca mounted the stairs to the captain's office—though even after the years he'd spent on Deep Space 9, he found it difficult not to think of it as the *prefect*'s office. So much time had passed since the end of the Occupation, and yet the Cardassian presence on Bajor and the terrible legacy they'd left—the physical scars disfiguring the planet, the destroyed art and architecture that could never be recovered, the families that would never be whole again—all of it still haunted Cenn.

In his seven years aboard the station, he'd become accustomed to working and living on DS9—an aspect of himself that he despised. He wanted to cling to his hatred of the Cardassians, and to everything they had ever touched, and for a long time, he had. But time and life moved on, and whether or not he resisted their influences, they carried him along into the future. Counselor Matthias had helped him understand so much about himself, about why he felt and thought the things he did, and that had been the key to letting go of most of his negative emotions.

Most, but not all.

Memories remained of the Occupation, and Cenn refused to cheapen the importance of all that had happened, of all that had been lost, by willfully forgetting. He wanted to remember. He *needed* to remember. But he paid the price for doing so.

Each day on what had once been dubbed Terok Nor—and what from the outside looked almost exactly as it had when Bajorans had first been brought there as slave labor to process the raw ore ripped from their world—each day on DS9 brought Cenn self-loathing. He had yet to discuss it in his counseling sessions, or with any of the numerous friends he'd made on board, but he recognized the unhealthy and destructive impulses within him. Only recently had he realized how comfortable he'd grown on the station, and only then had he begun to castigate himself for the life he'd made in a place with such an evil past.

But I serve the interests of Bajor, Cenn told himself. When his homeworld had joined the Federation, he had chosen not to join Starfleet, but to remain in the Militia. Although he had rarely left the planet prior to his nomination as DS9's Bajoran liaison officer, he'd accepted the position as a means of continuing to promote the welfare of his people. He'd had reservations when Captain Ro had offered him the role of exec, but he'd seen the value in holding such a position of authority even as he remained liaison officer. Vedek Kira had taken on both capacities for seven years, during which time she had done much to safeguard the people of Bajor.

Cenn reached the top of the stairs and the doors to Captain Ro's office. *Not the doors to the* prefect's *office, Desca,* he told himself, and he knew that he would have to speak with Counselor Matthias about the ugly thoughts in his head. He touched the chime control set into the bulkhead, and he heard Ro invite him inside. He stepped forward, and the doors separated.

Ro sat at her desk, her computer interface active, and an accumulation of padds spread out before her. "Desca," she said when she looked up. "I hope you're here with a phaser to put me out of my misery. Between the reports that the Federation, Starfleet, and Bajor require, I'm amazed that I can get any other work done around here."

Cenn stepped up to Ro's desk. Throwing a look of shame onto his face, he held up his right hand, in which he carried a padd. "I'm sorry, Captain," he said. "The scheduled arrivals and departures for the day."

"You mean that's not already here?" Ro said, waving her hands over her cluttered desk.

"Maybe we could just close up the place for a week or so and all head into the holosuites," Cenn suggested.

Ro chuckled. "That actually doesn't sound like a bad idea," she said. "Do you think Starfleet and Bajor would mind?"

"Not if you can figure out a way to stop the traffic to and from the Gamma Quadrant," Cenn said.

"*That*," Ro said, "sounds like an even better idea."

Though the captain had offered her comments in a joking manner, Cenn knew that they contained kernels of truth. "The increase in the number of ships coming to the station *has* been hard," he said. "But I think we've handled it pretty well, and nobody more so than you."

"Thanks, Desca," Ro said. "We do have a pretty good crew here." She held out her hand toward him, and he gave her the padd he'd brought. "Anything else?"

Although he wanted to avoid adding another burden to the already considerable list of the captain's responsibilities, Cenn had little choice. "Unfortunately, we seem to have a problem with the communications relay in the Gamma Quadrant," he said.

"We're still not receiving transmissions?" Ro said.

"No," Cenn told her. "We've received no regular comm packets, and no other word, from either the *Robinson* or the *Enterprise* over the last couple of days."

"I thought we ran a test yesterday," Ro said.

"We did," Cenn confirmed. "We ran remote diagnostics and performed a number of tests that verified all the relay's functions. But still, we don't seem to be picking up anything from the two Starfleet ships out there. It may be nothing; both crews might be engaged in operations that preclude assembling and transmitting their regular comm packets, or perhaps they've both encountered some astronomical phenomena that are interfering with their transmissions."

"Both of them?" Ro asked. "At the same time? They're not traveling anywhere near each other."

"It does seem strange," Cenn agreed. "That's why I've brought it to you."

"Get Chief Chao and Lieutenant Tenmei, and have them take the *Rio Grande* through the wormhole," Ro said. "Have the chief bring whoever she needs to perform direct testing on the relay. Let's find out what the problem is and how we can fix it."

"Right away, Captain," Cenn said. He headed for the doors, but as they parted, Ro called after him. He stopped and turned back around, the doors shutting behind him with a click.

"Is it possible that somebody's intentionally interfering with the operations of the comm relay?" Ro asked.

Cenn shrugged. "I'm not sure what that would accomplish," he said. "The Dominion's been as quiet as ever."

"And we know that the Dominion's been quiet from our sensor buoys in the Gamma Quadrant," Ro said. "But if there's a problem with the relay, then we wouldn't be receiving any alarms."

Cenn nodded. "That's true," he said. "And no alarms have reached us since we noted the missing comm packets from the *Robinson* and the *Enterprise*. But we haven't received any alarms for quite a while, even when we were receiving regular transmissions from those ships."

Ro inhaled deeply, then let out her breath in a noisy exhalation. "Let's not take any chances," she said. "Increase our alert status. As long as we might be deaf and blind in the Gamma Quadrant, we should be prepared."

"Yes, Captain," Cenn said. "I'll see to it."

Deep Space 9's first officer headed through the doors to the captain's office, back into ops. As he descended the steps, he understood that his shift had just gotten considerably more complicated.

35

Chief Engineer Jeannette Chao finished entering commands into the control station, then stepped back and waited for the results. Beside her stood Ensign th'Shant, a member of her engineering team. "What do you think, Vakell?" she asked.

The ensign peered at the display screen, his antennae shifting forward slightly in a subtle way that Chao had come to read as intense concentration. "It is difficult to know," said th'Shant, his words pronounced very carefully in his heavily accented Andorian voice. "But I do not anticipate finding the problem."

Chao and th'Shant had traveled from Deep Space 9 and through the wormhole aboard *Rio Grande,* with Tenmei at the helm. When they reached the communications relay, they pressurized and warmed its interior, and charged the gravity grid. With life support established, they transported inside and began running diagnostics on the equipment. They spent the afternoon executing every test they could, as well as reviewing the performance logs, all with no result. As best they could tell, the relay functioned perfectly.

As if reacting to her thoughts, the final diagnostic finished running, chirping its notification and posting the results to the display before them. Chao read through all of the text, but she needn't have. Every indicator glowed green.

"This does not make sense," th'Shant said. "We have tested the relay in every way possible. We've even run a diagnostic of the diagnostic system itself. Everything reads operational, and yet we know that there's a problem."

"Maybe it's not a problem with the relay, though," Chao said. "They diagnosed the issue when we didn't receive the regular comm packets from Starfleet's vessels in the Gamma Quadrant. Maybe those ships just didn't transmit their packets."

"That's certainly a possibility," th'Shant agreed. "But it's not one we can easily test if we're not in direct contact with the ships."

Chao reached up to the control station and closed down its diagnostic-operations interface as she wrestled with their dilemma. "Maybe there is another test we can try," she said. "Maybe we can stand in for those ships, at least in local space."

"That might tell us more," th'Shant said, his antennae shifting upward a touch.

Chao shut down the workstation, then tapped at her combadge, contacting Lieutenant Tenmei aboard *Rio Grande.* A moment later, the two engineers materialized aboard the runabout's transporter pad. They moved forward into the vessel's main cabin, where Tenmei sat at the helm console. Through the front ports, Chao saw the communications relay floating in space.

The chief engineer sat down beside Tenmei and operated the comm controls. "Opening a channel to the station via the relay," she said, narrating her actions as th'Shant watched over her shoulder. "*Rio Grande* to Deep Space Nine," she said. "Come in, Deep Space Nine. This is Chief Chao."

"Rio Grande, *this is Deep Space Nine,*" said the voice of Colonel Cenn. "*You fixed the relay, Chief. Good work.*"

"Actually, we've done nothing but execute a series of diagnostics," Chao said, "all of which tell us that the relay is in perfect working order."

"*That sounds contrary to what circumstances are telling us, Chief,*" Cenn said.

"I know, Colonel," Chao said. "That's why I want to try something else. I'm going to use this channel to transmit periodically back to the Alpha Quadrant. Please respond as quickly as you can each time I contact the station."

"*Understood,*" Cenn said. "*I'll be here.*"

"Thank you, sir," said the chief engineer. "Chao out." She looked over at Tenmei. "Lieutenant, take us to the edge of the Idran system, to the last planet."

"Yes, sir," Tenmei said. Her hands danced across her controls, and the runabout hummed around them, its impulse engines engaging. Chao knew that Tenmei would pilot the runabout up out of the deepest part of the Idran star's gravitational well, then employ the warp drive to carry them to the outer planetary rim of the system.

Before *Rio Grande* went to warp, Chao contacted DS9 again. Colonel Cenn responded at once. When they finally reached the last planet, they repeated the exercise, succeeding once again.

Frustrated, Chao decided to make one more attempt. "Lieutenant," she said, addressing Tenmei, "take us two hundred light-hours away at maximum warp."

"On what vector, Chief?" Tenmei asked.

"Take us along the path that the civilian Typhon Pact ships have to follow," Chao said.

Nearly an hour later, Tenmei reported that they had reached the specified distance from the Gamma Quadrant terminus of the wormhole. Chao once again opened a channel to the station. "*Rio Grande* to Deep Space Nine," she said, feeling as though she'd repeated the phrase a hundred times that day already. "This is Chief Chao."

The engineer waited, knowing that the greater distance to the comm relay and DS9 would create a lag in the transmission signal. Seconds passed, and then a minute. Tenmei and th'Shant exchanged anxious expressions with her. They waited a second full minute, and then a third.

They received no response.

Chao looked at th'Shant, who said, "I guess there is no problem with the relay."

"No," Chao said, "but there *is* a problem somewhere out here, and we've just gotten closer to finding it."

36

Trok stood at one end of the largest of *Eletrix*'s cargo holds, which easily could have held *Ren Fejin* within its confines several times over. He waited as the ship's executive officer, Subcommander Venalur Atreev, spoke into a communications panel set into the bulkhead. Trok also waited for the possibility of his imminent death—a feeling to which he had lately grown far too accustomed.

"We are ready in both of the larger bays, and in both of the smaller ones," Atreev said, adding the authorization for three other holds on the ship.

Trok believed that the true success or failure of his journey into the Gamma Quadrant would occur within the next few moments. Achieving his goal would see him headed out of the Dominion, toward the wormhole and, beyond it, to the Breen Confederacy. Disappointment would see the atoms of his body scattered throughout open space tens of thousands of light-years from home.

Several sections forward of where Trok stood, he knew, eight Jem'Hadar soldiers sat in detention cells, perhaps anticipating their own fates. In a separate section, guarded by a contingent of more than a dozen security officers, the Changeling continued his refusal to barter with Commander T'Jul. Fortunately, the commander had neither accepted the intransigence of Laas nor the unwillingness of the Jem'Hadar and the Vorta to act without the sanction of their god. T'Jul allowed some time to pass as an opportunity for the shape-shifter to reconsider his position, but she did not wait *too* long.

At some point, T'Jul ordered *Eletrix* uncloaked, after which she contacted the Jem'Hadar and Vorta directly. She issued an ultimatum: allow the *Eletrix* crew to send down transport enhancers so that they could beam up to their ship the equipment they needed from the surface of Overne III, or she would kill Laas. She also warned that if a single Jem'Hadar vessel—or any vessel at all—approached *Eletrix,* she would likewise put an end to the Changeling's life. If they agreed to T'Jul's terms, then once her crew had received the equipment, *Ren Fejin* and *Eletrix* would start immediately out of Dominion space. When they had traversed most of the distance to the wormhole, with scans showing no pursuit by the Jem'Hadar, T'Jul would then release Laas and the captured Jem'Hadar, leaving them on a particular world in that region.

T'Jul had given the Jem'Hadar and the Vorta only moments to decide. Trok did not know what T'Jul actually would have done if she hadn't gotten the response she'd sought. Fortunately, the Jem'Hadar and the Vorta had chosen—at least as far as Trok thought—wisely.

"The cargo transporters have been networked to provide for the sizable mass," said a voice via the communications panel.

"Proceed," Atreev ordered.

"Commencing transport."

In front of Trok, a high-pitched buzz filled the massive, empty space. Vertical streaks of bright white light formed at its center and reached nearly to the overhead far above the deck, then spread apart horizontally. Between them, illuminated green veins formed, reaching in all directions to form shapes. A final white line manifested high above, then descended, filling in as it did so the full existence of the transporter's target.

That quickly, the great mass of equipment Trok had located in an industrial plant had been beamed from the surface of Overne III to the *Eletrix*'s cargo bay. In the brighter light of the ship, it looked smaller, but it still filled the cargo hold from bulkhead to bulkhead, and perhaps two-thirds of the way up to the overhead. Trok gazed at it almost in disbelief. He had traveled a long, winding path over such a long period to realize his goal.

A hand fell on his shoulder. "Go," Subcommander Atreev told him. "Make your scans and verify that this is the equipment you need. We may not have much time."

Trok nodded, then raised a scanner that the *Eletrix* crew had retrieved for him from *Ren Fejin*. He worked its controls, taking detailed sensor readings. It required some time, and when he'd finished, Atreev accompanied him to the other cargo holds, where Trok performed new sets of scans on the equipment that had been transported to those sites.

When Trok had finished, Atreev led him to the bridge of *Eletrix*, where the Breen engineer reported his findings. "We have everything we need," he told Commander T'Jul, who rose from her chair and stood amid the bustle of her command. "With this equipment, the slipstream drive will be ours."

"Excellent," T'Jul said, hearing precisely what she wanted to hear from the Breen engineer. Standing in the middle of the *Eletrix* bridge, she turned toward the communications console off to port. "Lieutenant Tillek," she said, "open a channel to the *Ren Fejin*."

Tillek tapped at his controls. "Channel open."

"*Eletrix* to *Ren Fejin*," she said. "This is Commander T'Jul."

"*This is Tomalak*," came the immediate reply.

Under normal circumstances, T'Jul would have enlisted her executive officer to oversee the repair efforts aboard the Breen cargo ship. While she trusted in the abilities of Subcommander

Atreev far more than in those of Tomalak, the management of the Breen engineers in the mending of their own vessel had not required much skill. It did, however, allow T'Jul to exile Tomalak from her presence, if only for a short while.

"We are prepared to depart," T'Jul said. "What is the status of the *Ren Fejin*?" *Eletrix* required the smaller vessel for cover. If the Romulan warbird traveled through the wormhole, uncloaked and without *Enterprise* accompanying it, T'Jul knew that her ship would be stopped at Deep Space 9. If *Eletrix* navigated the wormhole while cloaked, but by itself, the ship would be unmasked by the suspicious Starfleet crew on the space station when the Alpha Quadrant terminus opened for no visible reason.

"Warp power has been fully restored, and life support brought up to acceptable levels for the journey," Tomalak reported. *"The transporter and the shields are unusable, but that should be of little concern at this point. The cloaking device is in the process of being dismantled. We're ready to leave at any time."*

"Do you have Lieutenant Torlanta's flight plan?" T'Jul asked.

"We do," said Tomalak. *"It's already laid in and ready to execute."*

T'Jul nodded. "That's good work," she said, trying not to sound grudging. "We'll signal you at our departure. T'Jul out." The channel closed with an audible tone.

Looking once more to Tillek, the commander said, "Lieutenant, inform the Jem'Hadar and the Vorta that we have what we need, and that we will be departing at once. Tell them that we will honor our agreement with them as long as they continue to honor it as well. No Dominion ships may follow us until we reach the designated point, where we will leave the Changeling and the Jem'Hadar we captured."

"Yes, Commander," Tillek said, and he started to work his panel. After a short time, he said, "Message transmitted and acknowledged."

At last, T'Jul thought.

"Lieutenant Torlanta, signal the *Ren Fejin* that we are leaving," T'Jul said. She turned, walked to her command chair, and sat down. "Take us home."

37

Kasidy Yates reached up and brushed her hair away from her eyes, then pushed the antigrav sled forward. The cargo floated out of *Xhosa* and down the ramp into one of Deep Space 9's cargo holds. She ran the crate to the right, until she deposited it with the first few that she and her crew had already offloaded.

I hate bio-matter, she thought. *At least the unstable kind.* Normally, she and her crew could have beamed their cargo directly into the hold, but the volatile material required a transporter system with an adjustable phase-transition inhibitor, something her antiquated freighter lacked. That meant that she and her crew would spend the afternoon hauling crates, which would delay her return to Bajor. *I'm definitely going to have to talk with the Petarians again,* she thought. She needed to make them understand how much extra time—

"Kasidy," said a woman's voice.

Kasidy stopped and turned. Just inside the doors to the hold stood Kira Nerys. She wore the traditional raiments of a vedek—a loose-fitting, earth-toned robe with wide sleeves—and a broad smile.

"Nerys," she said. Kasidy moved the antigrav sled off to the side, then walked over and embraced her friend. "It's so good to see you. What are you doing here?"

"I'm on my way back to Bajor from Cardassia," Nerys said. "A group of vedeks had a conference of sorts with members of the Oralian Way."

"Oh, I see," Kasidy said. "Sounds pretty dry."

"Some of it was, but some of it was actually quite interesting," said Nerys. "The diversity of thought on Cardassia these days is really something to see."

Kasidy shook her head. "It's hard to believe, isn't it?" she said, recalling the long, complicated history of Bajor and Cardassia.

"It just shows what you can accomplish when you have faith," Kira said. "So I heard from Captain Ro that you were aboard, and since my transport doesn't leave until this evening, I thought that maybe we could have lunch. It's been a while since we've gotten to visit."

"I'd love to, but we've got a freighter full of cargo to unload," Kasidy said. "I'd also like to finish by the time Rebecca gets out of school."

"Rebecca's here on the station?" Nerys asked.

"She *insisted* that I bring her with me on my run," Kasidy said, then shrugged at her own ridiculous suggestion that her daughter drove such decisions. Rebecca had pleaded to come along, but far more than her pleas had gone into Kasidy's choice to bring her. "It wasn't that long a trip, and I think it's good life experience," she told Nerys. She heard movement behind her, and she glanced back over her shoulder to see Pardshay lifting a crate from an antigrav sled and onto the stack of delivered goods. At that moment, *Xhosa*'s chief engineer, Luis García Márquez, emerged through the hatchway. He saw Kasidy and paced over.

"Vedek Kira," said Luis. "How good to see you again." He extended both his hands, and Nerys took them in greeting.

"It's good to see you too, Mister García Márquez," Nerys said.

"Pardon the interruption, Captain," Luis said, "but I just wanted to let you know that we've finished the systems checks on the engines. Everything's in solid shape. The new deuterium-flow regulator really helps."

"That's great," Kasidy said, pleased at the performance of the new component. She'd acquired it on the secondary-parts market through Quark, and though he'd never actually misled her, she did worry about some of the characters with whom he did business. "Thanks for letting me know."

"Mister García Márquez," Nerys said, "I was just trying to coerce your captain into having lunch with me, but she's claiming too much work."

"Nonsense," Luis said without a moment's hesitation. "Since I'm done inspecting the engines, I can help out with the unloading while you two go eat."

"Luis, you've already been working too much," Kasidy said. To Nerys, she explained, "Since Wayne's attending his sister's wedding on Alpha Centauri, Luis has been pulling double duty as my chief engineer *and* first mate."

"And as your first mate, I say go have lunch with your friend," Luis insisted. "You've been working pretty hard yourself."

Kasidy felt herself relenting. She really did want to visit with Nerys. "You're sure, Luis?" she said. "It's been a heavy run, and you're due for some time off."

"It's no problem at all," he said. "I learned a long time ago that if the captain's not happy, then nobody's happy."

Kasidy smiled. "See?" she said to Nerys, feigning an aside. "I should promote this man to first mate permanently."

As Luis headed for Kasidy's antigrav sled, she and Nerys made their way to the doors of the cargo hold. "Do you want to go to Quark's?" Kasidy asked. "Or the Replimat?"

"Actually," Nerys said, "I hear there's a new Argelian restaurant that people are raving about."

The doors opened before them, and the two women stepped through, on their way to the Promenade.

38

Security Chief Jefferson Blackmer gazed in mute shock at the open access panel before him. For months, he and his staff had been scouring the deepest recesses of the station in search of vulnerabilities and possible sabotage. Even before that, he had spent his own time studying DS9, peering into as many shadowy corners as he could find—and the station had them in abundance.

And in all that time, until that moment, Blackmer and his team had found nothing.

The security chief reached for his combadge and pressed it. The beeps with which it responded seemed far too cheerful for the circumstances. "Blackmer to Captain Ro," he said.

"Ro here," came the captain's reply. *"Go ahead, Jeff."*

"Captain, I'm down in the lower core, and I just called in a team of specialists," he said. "We've got a major problem. Per your orders, we've been conducting security sweeps throughout the station. I've got an access panel open and I'm looking at a device that clearly doesn't belong here. It's coated in materials that scatter my attempts to scan it."

"Describe the device," she said, her tone serious.

"It's more or less a small, silver box," Blackmer said. "It's affixed to the containment-field generator for one of the reactors. There are characters in relief on the front. I can't read them, but I've been in Starfleet long enough to recognize Andorian writing." The allegation that Lieutenant Commander Douglas had made against Vakell th'Shant occurred to him.

"Andorian?" Ro said, the concern in her voice evident even over the comm channel. *"What does the device look like to you?"*

"Captain," Blackmer said, "it looks like a bomb."

39

Alongside one of her junior officers, T'Jul peered past the console at which they stood and over at the eight Jem'Hadar soldiers captured from *Ren Fejin*. A cadre of Romulan security guards had manacled each of them, then escorted them one at a time from their detention cells. After bringing the soldiers in, the security team remained in the compartment, their weapons armed and ready, ensuring the continued cooperation of their captives.

The eight Jem'Hadar stood at attention, ringing the first detainee who had been accompanied there: Laas. The Changeling's hands had also been bound, though without his ability to adjust his form, he likely posed less of a threat than the soldiers who sought to protect him. None of the prisoners said a word.

"Your time aboard this ship is at an end," T'Jul told the group. "I know that the crews of the two ships we brought here have carried out what could be considered acts of aggression against the Dominion. We intruded on your territory, penetrated your secure facilities, took the nine of you into custody, and essentially ransomed the life of Laas for the equipment we needed."

The Jem'Hadar soldiers said nothing, but they all looked

about the compartment, perhaps searching for weaknesses, for opportunities to escape. The shape-shifter stared down at the platform beneath him. T'Jul could not tell if even a single one of the group listened to what she said.

Wanting to draw their attention, T'Jul walked out from behind the console. She saw some of her own guards tense as she did so, but she also saw at least two of the Jem'Hadar look her way. "I and several others took these actions upon ourselves in an attempt to protect our peoples," she said. "We are not acting on behalf of our governments or in any official capacity." T'Jul doubted that her lie would bear up under scrutiny, but with the crew of *Ren Fejin* having complicated the mission by getting discovered and caught, the commander felt that she needed to provide the praetor and the Romulan Senate—and even the Breen domo—with deniability, no matter how implausible. Of course, considering the source of T'Jul's orders, she realized it could be that neither the praetor nor the Senate even knew about the mission.

"Because it has become critical to help us keep the Federation and its allies in check," T'Jul continued, "we did wish to acquire some of the Dominion's technology. We did not want weaponry, nor did we take it, even though we could have. We also have not harmed a single citizen of the Dominion. We did not confiscate the ketracel-white that the lead Jem'Hadar possessed, and we allowed him to administer it to himself and the others. We have kept you in custody only as long as we've needed to. Rather than leaving you in detention cells, or even killing you, we are now releasing you."

T'Jul waited a beat for any kind of a reaction, but received none. "We are presently orbiting a world outside Dominion space, uninhabited by intelligent life, but habitable," she went on. "We have just transmitted a message back to Overne Three providing the Vorta and the Jem'Hadar with the precise coordinates of where we will be leaving you. On the surface of the planet, you will find emergency rations and a means of liberating yourselves from your manacles."

When she still received no response beyond the apparent

attention of two Jem'Hadar, T'Jul stepped forward again. Several of her security team moved to intercept her, presumably to prevent her from getting too close to their captives, who could no doubt be dangerous even with their hands bound. T'Jul waved the guards away, and then she walked up to the edge of the transporter platform.

"We in these two ships will not return to the Dominion," she said. "Nor will the Romulan Star Empire or the Breen Confederacy, both of which have taken official positions against violating the closed borders of your territory." In reality, T'Jul did not know if either government had taken a stance on the professed isolation of the Dominion, but she reasoned that the Jem'Hadar and the shape-shifter also would not know.

Having said all she intended to say to the nine captives, and most especially to Laas, T'Jul could have ordered the group beamed down to the planet that *Eletrix* orbited. But the commander discovered that she wanted more from the Changeling. She found him arrogant and condescending, but the Dominion had waged a formidable war; T'Jul needed to let Laas know that her people wished to avoid a return to the battlefield against the Founders and their armies, but she also felt that she had to demonstrate her strength.

And so she waited.

Moments passed. T'Jul fixed her gaze on the smooth features of the Changeling's face. In her peripheral vision, she saw members of her security staff glancing at her, and some of the Jem'Hadar as well. The lead Romulan guard spoke her name, perhaps in preparation for trying to move her away from the captives, but while still peering at Laas, she held up a hand to silence the man. She continued to wait.

Eventually, Laas raised his head and looked at her. The instant he did, she turned away and spoke to the officer stationed at the console. "Centurion," she ordered, "signal the bridge to drop the cloak."

The man tapped at his panel. A moment later, he said, "Subcommander Atreev reports that the cloak is down."

"Commence transport," T'Jul said. The man worked his

controls, and behind T'Jul, she heard a familiar whirr as her captives beamed away.

Rather than turn to regard the empty platform, T'Jul looked to the transporter operator and raised an inquiring eyebrow. The centurion nodded his head. "T'Jul to Atreev," she said.

"Atreev here, Commander," said the ship's executive officer.

"Contact the *Ren Fejin* and let them know we're ready to proceed," she told him. "Then cloak the *Eletrix* and take us to warp."

"Right away, Commander," Atreev said.

T'Jul headed quickly to the door without looking around at the transporter platform. She entered the corridor feeling satisfaction at what she and her crew had so far accomplished. The original mission of *Eletrix* in the Gamma Quadrant had, by way of Tomalak, changed considerably, endangering her crew to a far greater extent, but also allowing them to play a greater role in protecting their people.

Now all they had to do was get back to the Empire.

40

People ran.

Lieutenant Sarina Douglas occupied a T-shaped intersection in the docking ring, her phaser on one hip, her tricorder on the other, and both hands busy gesturing and pointing and even pushing as she attempted to direct people toward Deep Space 9's cargo holds. With the station's cramped corridors, dark recesses, and prevalent shadows, it often felt claustrophobic to Douglas, and even small. But with Chief Blackmer's discovery of an explosive device in the lower core, and then—once they knew where to look—other security officers finding another three, the great size of DS9 made itself apparent. Nearly nine hundred crew and fifty-eight hundred civilians put the total number of people aboard just south of seven thousand.

Up ahead, amid the charging throng, Douglas saw two small children, a boy and a girl, racing ahead of a Bolian woman, presumably their mother. Sensing trouble before it happened, the lieutenant watched in horror as the young girl stumbled and fell. The boy continued running, but the woman tried to stop and reach down to help the girl back up. The tide of people pushed past the woman, though, its currents swift and strong, and soon enough she too fell to the deck.

Douglas launched herself forward like a missile. She yelled to the crowd, but to no avail; the sound of scurrying feet, panicked voices, and the computer's looping announcement to evacuate the station buried her words. Douglas struggled forward, leaning into the multitude, pushing along one of the bulkheads as she actually shoved people away from her, trying to forge a path to the fallen woman and girl. She felt sweat running down her face, and only then did she note the rising temperature in the over-full space.

The Bolian boy struck Douglas's leg. She saw the terrified look on his face as she looked down and saw his wide eyes searching the corridor. As he bounded past her, unable to break free of the swarm, she reached down to grab his arm, but her hand missed its target. She lunged instinctively, and her fingertips caught in the fabric of his shirt. Having little choice, she closed her fist and hauled him backward, feeling the shirt tear, but not caring. She heaved him up into her arms, and he clung to her as though trying to keep himself from drowning.

Douglas turned back into the horde, and with her hands around the boy, she put her shoulder down. With the bulkhead to her left, she butted through the masses, until finally she reached the woman and girl, huddling together on the side of the corridor. Douglas pushed around them, turned, and set her back to the running people. She took one hand from the boy and reached to help the woman up. When both the woman and the girl had gotten back to their feet, Douglas moved to transfer the boy into the woman's arms, but he would not let go. She had to reach up and physically turn his head, until at last he saw his mother's face and threw himself into her embrace.

"Go!" Douglas yelled to them, though even she could barely hear the sound of her own voice. Still, the Bolian family moved, the woman clutching the boy in one arm and herding the girl before her with the other. They sped down the corridor and around the corner of the intersection in just seconds, like so much flotsam bobbing down a rushing river.

Douglas followed, returning to her position at the junction. There, the crowd split, moving either left or right along the docking ring. Some people attempted to reverse direction, probably thinking that they had gone the wrong way, or maybe realizing that they had gotten separated from a loved one, but Douglas pushed them forcibly along, bellowing out her instructions that it didn't matter which way they went. She insisted that everybody would get evacuated.

She could only hope that she spoke the truth.

Douglas knew that Captain Ro had ordered all available ships to assist in the mass transfer of people from Deep Space 9 to Bajor. Not wanting to leave the station vulnerable to attack during the exodus, the captain placed *Defiant* on patrol, but she dispatched all six of the station's runabouts to aid in the evacuation effort, and had also enlisted all civilian vessels presently docked. Douglas also knew that the *U.S.S. Canterbury,* posted to the orbit of Bajor during the program that allowed civilian Typhon Pact ships through the wormhole, had also been called in to help. While the half-dozen runabouts could collectively transport between one hundred and two hundred individuals at a time, and the group of civilian vessels perhaps a few hundred more, the *Galaxy*-class *Canterbury* would be able to carry a thousand or more.

I just hope we have enough time, Douglas thought.

Ro Laren leaned in beside Chief Blackmer as two other security officers worked to determine how to remove or disarm the bomb. Other teams, she knew, worked at the other bombs, all of them searching for a solution. At the moment, as the evacuation of the station continued, nothing had yet been attempted, since trying to move, open, or transport the devices might cause them to detonate. Scans failed to penetrate the outer structures of the devices, but traces of revitrite, a known Andorian explosive, had been found on their exteriors.

Ro saw the raised glyphs on the bomb's surface. While she had certainly learned to read some Andorian words during her years in Starfleet, she recognized the writing on the silver box for a different reason. Nearly a year earlier, around the time that Andor had seceded from the Federation, a separatist faction had worked to make that happen. Beyond simply making their arguments or searching for political will among their people, the group had employed terrorist acts to attempt to further their cause.

"The *Treishya*," she read, then backed away from the two officers working over the device, giving them room.

"The group that pushed for secession?" Blackmer asked, following her back.

Ro nodded. She had no idea whether Ensign th'Shant sympathized with the Andorian group, but the accusation Lieutenant Douglas had leveled against him had taken on new meaning. Had the investigation Ro had ordered back then not fully cleared th'Shant, she would have ordered the engineer taken into custody upon the discovery of the first bomb. Likewise, she felt grateful that Blackmer and Douglas had also been exonerated.

"But the *Treishya* achieved their goals when Andor seceded, so why this?" Blackmer asked. "The Andorians haven't declared war on the Federation, and as far as I know, none of them—not even this group—are suggesting that they should."

"I don't know," Ro said. "I think we probably don't know enough about the group's current aims to make that determination. But if this *is* their handiwork, then I suspect that they'll let us know soon enough. Once they—"

"Ops to Captain Ro," called the voice of Colonel Cenn.

Ro took several more steps away from where the security team worked over the bomb, then activated her combadge. "Ro here," she said. "Go ahead."

"The Canterbury *has just left with its third load of evacuees,"* Cenn said. *"They've taken more than three thousand people from the station."*

"Good," Ro said. "How many people does that leave here?"

"All of the crew," Cenn said. *"Several of the civilian ships left without taking anybody aboard, and a few others haven't returned*

once they off-loaded their evacuees. But with the ships that are continuing to help, and some others that have arrived from Bajor, and with the runabouts, we've got about thirteen hundred civilians left on the station."

"So twenty-two hundred total," Ro said.

"*Yes,*" Cenn confirmed.

"What about protecting the wormhole?" Ro asked. "Have we heard back from Starfleet?"

"*Yes,*" Cenn said. "*The* Brisbane *and the* Venture *are the closest ships. They're both on their way, but it'll be at least a day before either of them gets here.*"

"All right," Ro acknowledged. "That's good work, Desca. Keep me informed. Ro out." She looked over at Blackmer. "Jeff, let me know how it's going down here." She started to leave.

"Captain," Blackmer said. "You should think about getting off the station yourself. There's not much more you can do here, and the last thing Starfleet needs is to lose another senior officer."

"I still need a plan to evacuate the crew," Ro said, "as well as strategies for protecting the wormhole, both before and after reinforcements arrive," Ro said. "Once that's done, and once every other person has been removed to safety, then sure, I'll think about leaving."

"*Captain—*"

"Keep me informed, Chief," Ro said, and she turned on her heel and headed for ops.

Kira Nerys brought her hand down hard on the control surface, locking the door that led into the cargo bay. The crowd moving through the docking ring had thinned as people left the station, but if she let any more into the hold, there would be panic when not all of them could board *Xhosa*. Kasidy's ship had already made two runs to Bajor, ferrying a few hundred people each time. Kira had suggested not bothering to dock on their return to DS9, but it turned out that *Xhosa*'s antiquated transporters would have had difficulty beaming over masses of people in a timely fashion. At the same time, evacuation efforts onto other civilian vessels occupied all of the station's transporters.

Kira turned away from the door and toward the hatchway that led into *Xhosa*. There, Kasidy and Luis García Márquez directed people inside, where the rest of Kasidy's crew would send them deeper into the ship, most of them to the freighter's own cargo bays. Kira waited for the last few evacuees to head through the hatch, and as she saw García Márquez dart in after them, she started forward.

She had nearly reached Kasidy when the hold began to brighten. Through a growing white haze of illumination, Kira saw her friend urging her on, motioning her forward with her arms. Kasidy's mouth moved as she clearly called out, but Kira heard nothing. For just a moment, Kira thought that one of the bombs must have detonated, and that she faced the end of her life.

But it's not a bomb, she realized. She felt herself smile as the brilliant light engulfed her, drowning out the rest of her existence. No color reached her eyes, no sound her ears. She had a moment to think that she was about to be handed a gift, and she waited for it to come for her.

And then she was gone.

Kay Eaton walked out of the Arthur Trill Building and onto Broadway in Midtown Manhattan. She finished pulling on her gloves and cinched her long coat tightly closed around her. After yet another impossible day in the offices of *Incredible Tales,* she put her head down and hied along the street. She thought she could use a long soak in a hot bath, with a white landscape of bubbles tickling her chin. She tried to envision herself there, but instead, her mind called up the image of her hands around the skinny neck of Pabst.

"She was *not* the commander of the spaceship," she muttered to herself as she hurried through the rush-hour crowd. "She was the pilot of the *U.S. Temple,* the second-in-command, and he *killed* her."

Although *he* had hired her, although *he* continued to purchase her stories and get her words into print, Douglas Pabst had in some ways become Eaton's enemy. The editor of *Incred-*

ible Tales, Pabst actually had a fair degree of technical, and even artistic, ability, but his slavish devotion to the cowardly sensibilities of the publisher undermined him, and in turn, sabotaged his writers. Mr. Stone paid for the magazine, paid for its bullpen of writers and its one illustrator, but he kept his eyes only on the bottom line. He published science fiction—potentially *visionary* fiction—and yet he displayed no apparent desire, and certainly no courage, to embrace the future.

Eaton had turned in a story last week that she considered one of the best works she had ever written—maybe *the* best thing ever to come out of her typewriter. "Horn and Ivory" moved, filled with action and mystery, with heart and the idea of a greater purpose. Everybody in the office had loved it, even Herbert, who tended not to like much of anything. Even Pabst had offered up his encomium for the story.

But today, he had squelched it. "You can't have a female first officer on a spaceship," he'd said. "Who would believe it?"

What am I supposed to do? she thought in frustration. *Am I supposed to make every woman in every story a damsel in distress? A stewardess? If I can't have the freedom—*

A hand tugged at Eaton's arm. She didn't look around, but pulled away and kept on walking. Only when she heard her name—one of her names—did she stop.

"Miss Hunter?"

Eaton looked back over her shoulder to see an attractive Negro woman standing on the sidewalk, one arm held out in front of her. "You are Miss Hunter, right?" the woman said. "Miss K. C. Hunter?"

"Ye-es," Eaton said, unsure whether she should even speak to the woman. But she looked familiar, and she wore an expression of great sadness. Even before she had said anything but Eaton's pseudonym, she elicited sympathy. "I'm K. C. Hunter," Eaton said.

The woman paced cautiously forward, as though she feared she might spook Eaton and send her darting away. "Hello," she said. "I'm Cassie Johnson." She paused for a second, then chuckled awkwardly. "Cassie," she said. "Kind of like *K. C.*"

"Kind of," Eaton agreed. "Do . . . do I know you?"

"You might have seen me around," Johnson said. "I'm Benny Russell's girl."

"Oh, Benny," Eaton said. "How is he?" Russell had been one of the finest writers Eaton had ever read, and certainly that she'd ever known, but he'd also been deeply tortured. He'd eventually suffered a nervous breakdown and been carted away to an asylum. *How long ago was that?* Eaton wondered. *Two years, maybe?*

"Benny's in trouble," Johnson said. "I'm sorry, Miss Hunter, I know you don't know me, but Benny always spoke so highly of you. I just need somebody to help me help Benny."

"Aren't there doctors at the—" She hesitated, not wanting to use the word *asylum*. "—at the hospital?"

"They've taken him out of that place," Johnson said. "They say he tried to escape."

"So where is he now?"

"They took him to jail," Johnson said, tears forming in her eyes.

"Jail," Eaton echoed. That seemed wrong. Benny had been troubled, but he posed no threat to anybody but himself. So what if he wanted to leave the asylum? Eaton could only imagine how they dealt with him there, considering his treatment at the hands of "polite society." "I think that's terrible, Miss Johnson," she said, "but I don't know what I can do to help."

"I just thought if you could talk to them at the police station," Johnson said, her words coming in a rush. "Make them see that Benny's a good man, just maybe a little sick. He belongs in a place where he can get help, not in jail."

Eaton understood what Johnson was saying, and even agreed, based on what she knew of Benny, but— "I just don't know why the police would listen to me."

"I need *somebody* to talk to them," Johnson said. In her emphasized word, Eaton heard more than what she said. Johnson didn't just need *somebody* to talk to the police; she needed somebody *white*.

"I'm just a . . ." Eaton started to say, and then left her statement unfinished. *I'm just a woman,* she thought, and hated herself for it. *No, I don't hate myself,* she thought. *I hate Pabst and Stone and men like that, and women who think what I just did.*

"All right," Eaton said. "Let's go."

The relief that showed on Johnson's face almost made Eaton cry herself. Johnson grabbed her by the hand and led her back along Broadway. As Eaton ran to keep up, Johnson rounded corners and didn't stop.

Finally, just as Eaton thought she might collapse onto the pavement, her breath coming in deep, noisy gasps, Johnson pulled up in front of a police station. Johnson immediately started up the stone steps, but Eaton reached for her arm and stopped her. "Wait," she said as she tried to catch her breath. "Give me a minute."

Johnson turned and put an arm around Eaton. "Oh, I'm sorry, I'm sorry," she said. "I didn't mean . . . I'm so sorry. Are you all right?"

"Yes," Eaton said between gulps of air. "I'll be fine. I just have to rest a minute." She put her hands on her hips and waited for her breathing to calm. Her coat fell open, but she no longer felt cold in the autumnal air.

Eventually, she said, "My name is Kay."

"What?" Johnson said, obviously confused. "You're not who I thought you were?"

"No, no, I am," Eaton said. "Because I'm a woman, I have to write under a pen name, otherwise the magazine won't publish my work."

"That's ridiculous," Johnson said.

"Of course it is," Eaton said, pleased for the support, if only from a relative stranger. "Anyway, I write under the name K. C. Hunter, but I'm actually Kay Eaton."

"Well, it's nice to officially meet you, Miss Eaton," Johnson said.

Eaton smiled. "If I'm going to help you spring Benny from jail," she said, "maybe you'd better call me Kay."

"Cassie," Johnson said.

"Okay, Cassie. Lead on."

They climbed the stone stairs and entered the police station.

Inside, a tall, well-worn desk sat in the center of one wall. Dingy green tiles lined the floor, and a number of mismatched wooden chairs sat beneath the windows along the front of the room. Several closed doors in the side walls led deeper into the station, their frosted-glass inserts covered by metal grillwork.

Johnson stepped over to the desk and peered up at the uniformed officer who sat behind it. "I'm Cassie Johnson," she said. "I need to talk to somebody about Benny Russell."

Without looking up, the officer said, "Whozzat?"

"Russell, Benny Russell," Johnson said. "He was brought here earlier today."

"Don't know him," the officer said, still not bothering to take his gaze from whatever he looked at on the surface of the desk.

"Look—" Johnson said, but Eaton put a hand on her shoulder and gently guided her back. Eaton herself stepped up to the desk.

"Excuse me, Officer," she said. "My name is Kay Eaton. With whom am I speaking?"

At last, the policeman raised his head. He peered at Eaton with dark eyes. He had an expressionless face and deep-set eyes. For a strange second, Eaton thought she saw his features begin to melt, but then realized it had been a trick of the light. "I'm Sergeant La Dotio," he said. "What can I do for you, ma'am?"

Before Eaton could reply, she saw a streak of motion to her left, followed by a loud thud. She looked in that direction and saw a jagged piece of plaster where it had landed on the floor. "What the—?" she said, but then a second, larger piece fell beside the first.

Eaton looked up. Two frayed holes compromised the dull white ceiling. As Eaton watched, a third piece of plaster came hurtling down and crashed on the floor. Beside her, she heard Johnson yelp.

Eaton felt a tug on her coat sleeve. "Come on," Johnson called to her over a sudden roar that seemed to surround them. "We have to go."

Eaton looked back up in time to see an entire third of the ceiling come plunging down to her left. Beyond it, she saw no sign of the building's second floor. Instead, she saw stars.

And among them, a bright light that moved.

It's the Temple, she thought. *The spaceship from my story.*

"Come on," Johnson screamed, using both hands to try to pull Eaton toward the door. "We have to go now."

Calmly, Eaton peered at the rest of the ceiling, which bowed and appeared as though it might collapse at any moment. She looked down at the dust rising from what had already fallen, and over at Cassie Johnson. And in that instant, Eaton knew that they had to stay, and that somehow, everything would be all right.

And still, Johnson yanked at her arm. "Come on, Miss Eaton!" she yelled. "We have—

—to go," Kasidy called.

Kira blinked, uncertain of her location, either at that moment or in the one preceding. She still felt a tug on her arm. She also heard a voice—Kasidy's voice—and she turned her head to see her friend pulling her toward the hatchway that led to *Xhosa*. Kira tried to focus on Kasidy.

"Come on," Kasidy said. "The ship's full and we have to go."

"No," Kira said, not even loud enough for her to hear the word herself. She cleared her throat, and tried again: "No."

"What?" Kasidy said. "Nerys, let's go."

Running on instinct, Kira quickly took hold of her friend's arm. Kasidy started to duck inside the hatch, but Kira stopped her and said again: "No."

"Nerys, what are you doing?" Kasidy said, her sense of urgency plain. "We have to get off the station."

"Kasidy," she said, "there are still people on the station who need our help." Somehow, though Kira spoke the truth, she knew that it was not the *whole* truth—the *vital* truth. *For now,* she thought, *it'll have to do.*

"Nerys, I want to help people too," Kasidy said, "and we've already gotten people away from here and over to Bajor. But I have a daughter to raise. I just left Rebecca with Jasmine back on Bajor, and I need to get back to her. I can't stay here."

Kira stared deep into Kasidy's eyes. "Yes, you can," she said. "And everything will be all right. I promise."

For the first time, Kasidy hesitated, and so Kira pressed. "People need our help."

Kasidy seemed to think for a few seconds more, then she let out an exasperated breath. She took one step back through the hatch and called out. "Luis, we're done loading out here," she said. "Get the ship going."

Past Kasidy, at the other end of the hatchway, Kira saw *Xhosa*'s acting first mate appear. "Well, then, get inside."

"There are still people who need help here," Kasidy said. Without waiting for a response, she hurried past Kira and down the ramp. García Márquez offered Kira a confused shrug, then reached up inside the ship. The hatches on both *Xhosa* and Deep Space 9 closed.

Kira turned and joined Kasidy at the base of the ramp. "Now what?" Kasidy asked.

"Come on," Kira said, leading the way to the door of the cargo hold, and beyond it, to the rest of Deep Space 9. But even as she ran with her friend to help with the rest of the evacuation, Kira knew that she had no idea what would come next.

41

Jefferson Blackmer flung himself out of the turbolift and raced down the steps into ops. Ahead of him, he saw Captain Ro and Colonel Cenn at the situation table with other officers, clearly monitoring the evacuation and the efforts to disarm or displace the explosive devices.

"I'm getting a peculiar reading not too far from the station," Dalin Slaine said as Blackmer arrived. "It looks almost like a radiation source, but not quite."

"And you don't think it could be a cloaked ship?" Ro asked.

"It doesn't read like any Klingon or Romulan cloak I've ever seen," Slaine said.

"Well, keep an eye on it for now," Ro said. "I don't want to take the *Defiant* away from the wormhole. Once the *Canterbury* is done, we'll have them take a closer look."

Into the pause that followed, Blackmer spoke up. "Captain."

"Chief," Ro said. "We're almost there. The *Canterbury* just started off-loading its latest group of evacuees on Bajor. One more trip back to the station, along with the runabouts and a few of the civilian vessels, and we'll be clear."

"Captain," Blackmer said, "can I speak with you?"

Ro gazed at him, and he could tell that she understood the urgency he felt. She pointed up the other set of stairs. "My office?"

Blackmer followed the captain up, then waited for the doors to close behind them. Ro swung around to the other side of her desk, but she didn't sit. "What is it?" she asked.

"Captain, I've been listening to the bomb techs," he said. "To their estimates of yield and potential damage, and I've been examining the placement of the devices." He reached forward and deposited a padd on her desk. "I don't think they're designed to destroy the station."

"What?" Ro said. "We find four bombs planted in the station's reactor core, and you don't think the intent is to destroy Deep Space Nine?"

"Look at my simulations," he said, pointing to the padd. "If any of the bombs detonate, and if they're as powerful as the bomb techs think, then reactor containment will definitely fail. But even if all four bombs go off, and even if containment fails on all the reactors, there would be time to eject them."

"Provided the explosions don't damage the ejector assemblies," Ro pointed out.

"I thought of that," Blackmer said. "But the bombs were all planted on the opposite side of the reactors from their ejectors." Ro reached down and picked up the padd. As she studied its display, Blackmer said, "Whoever planted the bombs—the *Treishya* or whoever it is—definitely wanted to cripple Deep Space Nine. But it doesn't look like they wanted the massive loss of life that wiping out the station would cause."

"I don't know, Jeff," Ro said skeptically. "It sounds as though you're trying to ascribe benevolent motives to terrorists."

"Believe me, I have no interest in being an apologist for whoever did this," Blackmer said. "But I think we need to understand what they're trying to do if we're to—"

"Ops to Captain Ro," came the anxious voice of Colonel Cenn. *"The wormhole is opening."*

Transitus

In ops, Ro Laren and her crew peered up at the main view-screen, which showed the spinning blue-and-white vortex of the Bajoran wormhole as it wheeled into the visible aspect of its existence. The captain held her breath, her fists tightening, as she waited to see what sort of ship—*whose* ship—would arrive from the Gamma Quadrant. With the explosive devices found aboard the station, as well as the recent interference with transmissions through the communications relay, Ro felt she had good reason to worry just who or what might emerge from the wormhole.

In the center of the dazzling maelstrom, a small, dark shape came into view, its contours curved and uneven. "Magnifying," said Colonel Cenn from the general-services console, and the shape grew to fill the screen. A vessel, its rounded, asymmetrical form distinctly marking it as of Breen origin.

"It's a freighter," Cenn said.

"Its navigational beacon identifies it as the *Ren Fejin,*" Dalin Slaine reported at her tactical station.

Cenn worked his controls. "Records show that it entered the wormhole two and a half months ago," he said.

"Look at the charred areas on its hull," Chief Blackmer said, pointing toward the viewscreen. "It looks like it's been in battle."

Ro initially hadn't seen the burned patches on the Breen ship, but once Blackmer called attention to them, she did. "Why would anybody fire on a civilian vessel with virtually no weaponry?" she asked. "And how would such a vessel survive an attack like that?"

As though in direct response to her question, a spread of narrow blue beams streaked across the viewer. The image on the screen quickly changed, reverting to the previous, more expansive vista. *Defiant* appeared off to the side, slowly approaching the maw of the wormhole and discharging the blue beams from its forward emitters.

"The *Defiant* is projecting a multiphase tachyon detection grid," said Slaine. Since Typhon Pact vessels had first entered the Gamma Quadrant a couple of months earlier, Ro had added

to the list of high-alert procedures a check for cloaked ships—
including phase-cloaked vessels—traveling through the wormhole. Before the discovery of the explosive devices in the lower
core, she had called no such alerts.

On the viewscreen, the Breen freighter passed through the blue
tachyon beams, completely unaffected by them. Seconds passed,
and Ro began to relax as the *Defiant* crew's attempt at detection
revealed nothing. But then the focused particle beams reflected off
a surface that, the instant before, hadn't seemed to be there.

"Shields up!" Ro called out.

"Captain," said Blackmer beside her, "if the bombs should
detonate while the shields are raised—"

"If that cloaked ship fires on us without shields," Ro said,
interrupting the security chief, "the energy discharge to the station could trigger the bombs."

Blackmer said nothing more, and Ro peered over at Dalin
Slaine.

"Shields are up," said the tactical officer.

Prynn Tenmei sat on the bridge of *Defiant,* at the bowed forward console that combined the conn and ops functions. She
kept her eyes focused on the main viewscreen as Lieutenant
Aleco launched a tachyon spread from his position at the tactical
station. The Breen cargo vessel passed through the bright blue
beams without incident, and Tenmei waited for the wormhole
to close so that they could be sure that no cloaked ships had followed from the Gamma Quadrant.

The instant that a tachyon beam bounced off an invisible
surface, Tenmei sent her hands swiftly across her control panel.
Even as Lieutenant Commander Stinson called from the captain's chair for a tractor beam to capture the unknown ship, Tenmei prepared *Defiant* for what might come next. On the viewer,
as the wormhole folded in on itself to a bright speck and disappeared, she saw the tachyon beams replaced by the white rays
of a tractor field. They reached for the target and found it, but
then the entire mass of the invisible ship faded into view, like the
materialization effect of a silent transporter.

A Romulan warbird appeared within the tractor field.

"Evasive!" yelled Stinson, even as twin green streaks leaped toward *Defiant*.

The tractor beam disengaged as the disruptor blasts landed. *Defiant* quaked as Tenmei brought the ship about, anticipating the order for weapons—*"Fire forward phasers!"* called Stinson—but knowing that there wouldn't be time for a weapons lock before the warbird fired again. She turned the ship sharply, wanting to offer its narrower lateral profile as she gained Aleco a few seconds to employ the weapons to their fullest advantage. The helm seemed sluggish, but Tenmei realized that a combination of fear and impatience had heightened her perceptions. *Defiant* moved, and it moved fast, and she thought that the ship might elude the second attack.

It didn't.

Defiant shook violently as another set of disruptors pounded into the hull.

"Shields down to eighty-one percent," said Aleco. "Firing phasers."

Tenmei heard the pulse of the weapons as they discharged, and imagined the deadly, red-tinged yellow beams surging toward the Romulan starship.

"Direct hit on their port wing," said Aleco, but the satisfaction Tenmei heard in those words lasted only until his next one: "Incoming!"

Seconds later, *Defiant* pitched violently to starboard, and Tenmei slammed hard into the side of her console as the inertial dampers faltered before stabilizing again. Amid the cacophony, she heard cries of pain behind her. The overhead lighting died, replaced a few seconds later by the red glow of emergency lights.

"Shields down to sixty-nine percent," called Aleco over the tumult.

"Fire quantum torpedoes!" yelled Stinson.

Tenmei felt the rumble of *Defiant*'s torpedoes as they tore out into space, seeking the hard, green metal of the Romulan warbird. But then the ship bucked again. Tenmei heard a mix of voices issuing orders and shouting reports. Only one word meant anything to her—*"Evasive!"*—and she worked to move *Defiant* out of the line of fire.

When Ro saw the Romulan warbird appear in front of the wormhole, she knew that they had all been deceived: she and her crew, the Federation Council, President Bacco, everybody. If the warbird turned out to be the starship that had accompanied *Enterprise* on the joint mission, then it had clearly left its Starfleet counterpart behind. *Probably in pieces,* Ro thought grimly. If the ship turned out to be a different warbird, then some other Imperial Fleet vessel had illegally stolen into the Gamma Quadrant. Either way, events seemed incompatible with the idea of the Typhon Pact genuinely seeking peace.

"Ready all weapons," Ro said as the Romulan ship exchanged fire with *Defiant.*

"Phasers and quantum torpedoes armed," said Slaine.

"Concentrate on their engines," Ro said. "I want that ship stopped. Fire!"

The station rumbled as weapons launched from up and down the docking pylons. On the ops viewer, Ro watched bright blue packets soar away from DS9 and toward the Romulan warbird, the quantum torpedoes seeking their mark. Golden streaks of phaser fire followed.

They were all intercepted.

Another ship appeared in the line of fire as though out of nowhere, a great silver, teardrop-shaped vessel that Ro recognized at once as a Tzenkethi marauder. The ship shuddered beneath the assault of the station's weapons, its shields flaring, but then brilliant white filaments flashed from a dark recess on the otherwise smooth hull. Deep Space 9 lurched as the plasma cannon landed its salvo.

"Shields down to eighty-seven percent," Slaine called out.

"Target the Tzenkethi's weapons," Ro told her. "Fire at will."

On the screen, the captain saw the station's phasers slice through space, picking out the dark hollow from where the plasma cannon had attacked. A trio of quantum torpedoes followed, causing the Tzenkethi ship's shields to flare even more brightly. In the distance, flashes of blue and yellow and green marked the battlefield of *Defiant* and the Romulan warbird.

"Cenn," Ro said. "Emergency message to the *Canterbury*. I know they're off-loading evacuees, but tell them we're under attack and require the earliest possible assistance."

"Yes, Captain."

Ro watched the plasma-cannon emplacement to see if it would fire again, but instead saw a second section of the Tzenkethi ship's hull retracting, revealing another recess. White fire seared from within, landing another plasma blast on the station. Ro almost went down as DS9 shook, but she grabbed the side of the situation table.

"Shields down to sixty-one percent," Slaine said.

Suddenly, a pair of golden phaser beams rocketed into the Tzenkethi ship, precisely at the location of the second plasma cannon. A second later, Ro saw a runabout dart past. As she watched, it launched a volley of micro-torpedoes.

"Four runabouts have returned from Bajor," Cenn said.

"The marauder's shields are on the verge of overloading," Slaine said.

If we can just hold out until the Canterbury *gets here,* Ro thought. For the moment, it seemed at least a possibility.

But then Lieutenant Commander Candlewood said, "*Another* ship is decloaking." He peered over at Ro from his sciences station. "It's Breen."

Ro couldn't believe it. For months, the Typhon Pact not only had spoken of peace, but had seemingly taken an active role in trying to make it happen. *And now they're attacking us?* she thought.

But she couldn't concern herself with the politics and treachery of it all. *How many people are left on the station? Thirteen hundred civilians, nine hundred crew?* Somehow, she had to keep them safe.

On the main screen, the runabout raced back into view, joined by a second one. Both fired phasers and torpedoes in concert, all of them striking within a small locus on the marauder's hull. Again, the Tzenkethi vessel's shields flared, this time more brightly than ever. Its tapering tip spun around as the ship started to move away. As it swung around, it struck one of the runabouts, carving through its hull with ease. The shattered vessel twisted through space, out of control. It clipped the side of a cargo ship, changed direction, then erupted in a fiery explosion.

And then Deep Space 9 rocked again.

"It's the Breen ship," Slaine said. "Shields down to forty-nine percent."

"Fire on the Breen," Ro said. "And show them to me."

The scene on the main screen changed, bringing the Breen warship into view. An assembly of arcs of different sizes and opposing orientations, the powerful vessel had wasted no time in attacking. Even as DS9's own weapons struck the ship, multiple disruptor bolts lashed out and slammed into the station.

Ro flew from her feet, pain screaming through her body as her arm caught beneath her when she landed on the deck. She cried out, but immediately pushed herself up with her other arm. But the station shook again, and she fell backward.

"Shields at twenty-seven percent," Slaine said.

"Continuous weapons fire," Ro yelled from her place on the deck. "Pound them with every last torpedo."

Ro shifted around on the deck to peer at the main viewer. On it, she watched as phaser beams streaked en masse into the Breen ship, like golden fire raining down upon it. Quantum torpedoes followed, bombarding the hull. Ro saw jets of gas vent from the ship in two different places, signaling ruptures in its hull.

"They've got a hull breach," announced Candlewood. "Make that two."

Like the Tzenkethi ship, the Breen vessel started to move away. "Stop firing only once they're out of range," said Ro, finally climbing to her feet on the unsteady deck. "We need to—"

A roar filled ops, a sound like none Ro had ever heard, and DS9 moved like the surface of a planet during a massive temblor. The captain grabbed for the situation table and held on, bending over it to help her stay on her feet. She didn't know which starship had fired on them, or what weapon they had used, but it seemed miraculous that the station hadn't blasted apart.

"Shields are down," said Slaine.

When the inertial dampers stabilized, Ro peered at the main viewer, expecting to see that the Breen starship had rammed DS9, but instead, she saw that it still moved away. "Who hit us?"

"Nobody," Cenn said, staring down at his console. "One of the bombs detonated. Containment on reactor two has failed."

The faces of the security officers working at that reactor to render the bomb harmless rose in Ro's mind. *Costello. Parks.* They'd been on the station for a long time. And so many other officers had been down in the lower core as well.

"Reactor two will go critical in seven minutes," Cenn said.

"Prepare to eject the reactor," Ro said, and then a terrible thought occurred to her. "Are there any runabouts or civilian ships in the way?"

Candlewood answered from his station. "Scanning," he said. "We've got three runabouts and six civilian vessels in the area, but none of them in the ejection path."

Ro looked to Cenn. "Warn them all." If they ejected the reactor and it should impact a ship—

"Hold on," Ro said. "Cenn, can we use thrusters to turn the station? Use the reactor as a weapon against the Breen or the Tzenkethi ships?"

Cenn shook his head. "Not in the condition we're in," he said. "Shields are gone, we've got—"

Another roar filled ops, and the station quaked again. Ro went sprawling, her injured arm just one of the many pains she felt as she struck the side of a console, then fell to the deck. And still DS9 trembled.

When it stopped, an eerie silence descended around Ro. Then she began to hear small noises: creaks and scrapes, bodies moving slowly on the deck, people groaning in agony. "Cenn?" she called out.

"Here," he said from the vicinity of his console.

Ro hauled herself up on the edge of a workstation and looked across ops to see Cenn climbing to his feet. He leaned heavily on his console and delivered the news that Ro expected.

"Another of the bombs went off," he said. "Reactor three's containment is down."

"Eject both reactors," Ro said. "Do it now."

Cenn worked at his console, and the station bucked with the ejection of the two cores. Ro looked back at the main viewer, wanting to check on the Breen ship. It had moved farther from DS9, and while one of its hull breaches had clearly been sealed, the other still sent a long jet of atmosphere out into space. For the moment, it seemed to—

"Captain," Cenn said, and Ro turned back to look at him. "I've ejected reactor three, but the bomb that took down its containment also damaged the ejection mechanism for reactor two."

"We can't eject the other reactor?" Ro said, unable to keep the shock from her voice. *So much for whoever planted the bombs not wanting to destroy the station,* she thought. Even with everything that had happened, she'd expected somehow to save DS9 and all—or at least most—of the people aboard it.

Cenn shook his head.

Twenty-two hundred people left, Ro thought, horrified.

Unwilling to surrender, she said, "Desca, seal all emergency bulkheads. Route as much power as possible to the structural integrity fields." Cenn went to work immediately.

Peering over at Candlewood, who stood back at his station, Ro said, "John, contact the runabouts. See if—"

His sciences console emitted a familiar tone, and he glanced down at the panel. Ro knew what he would say even before he looked back up at her. "Captain," he said, "the wormhole is opening again."

Seemingly out of nowhere within the river of color and light, the mouth of the wormhole formed, the amorphous construct gyrating to slide the walls that enclosed it into an opening to the stars. On the main viewscreen, a familiar constellation showed directly in its center, shining across the space of the Alpha Quadrant: the Dawn. Then the ship exited the wormhole and entered hell.

Captain Benjamin Sisko jumped up from the command chair and hurried forward, his eyes locked on the viewer. He tried to take it all in and couldn't seem to do so. *Defiant* and a Romulan warbird locked in battle. A Tzenkethi marauder appearing damaged. A Breen warship venting atmosphere. DS9 looking beaten and battered, half of the lights along the docking ring dark. Other, smaller ships moving about . . . runabouts . . . freighters.

Xhosa!

Sisko heard people speaking . . . his crew . . . but their words didn't reach him. *Kasidy's ship,* he thought in desperation. A plume of gas rushed out from one side of *Xhosa* as it tumbled toward the marauder. "Sivadeki," he said, his voice barely audible. "Set course for—"

The Tzenkethi starship reeled around, its tapered end cutting through space. It impacted *Xhosa* amidships. For just a moment, Sisko dared hope that the ship would survive the collision, but then it blew up, sending chunks of its hull spinning off in every direction.

"No!" Sisko cried out. His knees gave out, and he crumpled to the deck. "Kas," he said, his voice dripping with anguish. And she was going to bring— "Rebecca. No."

Sisko felt a hand on his back. He knew people were speaking to him, that his crew was speaking to him, but their voices came to him as though from far away. He couldn't understand them . . . couldn't understand *anything*.

He looked up at the screen again, the scene blurred through his tears. He wiped them away and stared at the viewer, as though his eyes might have lied to him, and if he kept looking, he might see *Xhosa* there, intact and safe.

But Kasidy's ship wasn't there. And still he stared. And hoped. Wanting to take back everything he'd done wrong, all the time he'd wasted.

And then Deep Space 9 exploded.

The story continues in

Star Trek: Typhon Pact
RAISE THE DAWN

Acknowledgments

I first and foremost wish to thank Margaret Clark, without whose influences this book surely would not exist. Margaret's professional editorial skills have always been well complemented by her creativity and intuition, and she served for a long time as a caring steward of the *Star Trek* literary line. I'm also fortunate to be able to call Margaret a friend, with whom I can easily pass an afternoon in a conversation spinning hither and thither, delving into any number of subjects: science, art, history, politics, the woeful state of our mutually beloved but perennially underachieving New York Mets. Thanks for everything, Margaret.

I'd also like to thank Marco Palmieri, who first approached me about contributing to the Typhon Pact storyline. Thanks, too, to Keith R. A. DeCandido, who first introduced the concept of the Murderers' Row lineup of *Trek* adversaries in his novel *A Singular Destiny*. I also appreciate all the great work done by my fellow Pact writers: David Mack, who unmasked the Breen in *Zero Sum Game*; Michael A. Martin, who delved into the Gorn in *Seize the Fire*; and Dayton Ward, who deftly wove a tale of Andorians and Tholians in *Paths of Disharmony*. Not a slacker among them.

I in particular want to single out David Mack, not just for his terrific contribution to the ongoing Typhon Pact saga but also for his understanding in my hour of literary need. In some sense, Dave helped preserve my work in *Rough Beasts of Empire*, *Plagues of Night*, and the forthcoming *Raise the Dawn*—and in some ways, even in *Serpents Among the Ruins*. Mack is a scholar and a gentleman, not to mention a helluva good writer and a stand-up guy.

In writing a novel, an undertaking that requires tremendous amounts of time, energy, and emotion for me, I would be wholly at a loss if not for the wonderful array of people in my life. From the teammates with whom I play baseball, to the women and men of *Halau Hula O Na Lokelani* (also known as the Pasadena Hula Roses), I am fortunate to have a host of positive, interesting, life-affirming folks all around me. As Clarence wrote to George, "Remember *no* man is a failure who has *friends*."

Of course, there are also the people to whom I am closest, and who bolster me every day. Walter Ragan came into my life as a matter of circumstance, but he has shown me nothing but love and support ever since. He is a good man—a Navy man, who served aboard the submarines *Dogfish* and *Grampus*—and I am privileged to have such a good friend.

Anita Smith continues to show me great kindness and support. She is a fun, energetic woman, who also manages to project an enviable tranquillity and peace of mind. I'm very lucky to have her in my life.

Jennifer George impresses me all the time, with her intellect, her sense of humor, her strength, her compassion, her spirit, and the gusto with which she lives her life. Jen is a wonderful woman, and she has recently become, amazingly enough, an Ironman—which does not mean that she's had a sex change. What it does mean is that, to her long list of personal accomplishments, she has now added swimming 2.4 miles, biking 112 miles, and running a full marathon of 26.2 miles—one after the other, all in one day, until the World Triathlon people placed a well-deserved medal around her neck. I am a very proud brother.

Patricia Walenista day after day provides me an exemplar of how to live a meaningful, honorable life. Her intelligence, curiosity, and dedication to the truth are surpassed only by her generosity of spirit. She is a kind, loving, supportive woman. Among the many gifts she has given me through the years, I am ever mindful of two of the most important: she taught me how to read, and to love reading.

Karen Ragan-George wakes up with me every morning and sleeps with me every night, and I am grateful for both of those things. But I am most grateful for the moments between, when I am able to actively share my life with Karen. No one makes me laugh more often or harder. No one understands me more, in matters both great and small. No one else takes my breath away. Beautiful, smart, funny, kind, caring, supportive, artistic—there aren't enough adjectives or superlatives for me to use. All I know is that I am a very fortunate man to have such an incomparable woman by my side. Karen is everything to me.

About the Author

With *Plagues of Night*, DAVID R. GEORGE III returns not only to the world of *Star Trek* but to the ongoing storyline involving the Typhon Pact. David previously contributed to the Pact saga with *Rough Beasts of Empire*, a tale of Romulan politics and deception that also introduced the theretofore unseen Tzenkethi. *Rough Beasts* also added to the continuing post-television *Deep Space Nine* saga, which David visited before in the novels *Twilight* (*Mission: Gamma, Book One*) and *Olympus Descending* (in *Worlds of Deep Space Nine, Volume Three*). He made his first foray into the *DS9* milieu with the novel *The 34th Rule*, co-authored with Quark actor Armin Shimerman.

David also penned the *Crucible* trilogy as part of the fortieth-anniversary celebration of the original *Star Trek*. The three novels utilize the events of the episode "The City on the Edge of Forever" as a means of exploring the series' principal characters. *Provenance of Shadows* follows the life—or lives—of Doctor McCoy through two different timelines. *The Fire and the Rose* delves into the dual, sometimes conflicting natures of Spock. And *The Star to Every Wandering* traces the effects of Edith Keeler's death on Captain Kirk.

In *Serpents Among the Ruins*, David takes readers aboard *Enterprise*-B, under the command of John Harriman, with first officer Demora Sulu. The novel also tells the tale of the Tomed incident, referenced in the *Next Generation* television series. David followed *Serpents* up with another Demora Sulu story, a novella called *Iron and Sacrifice*, which appears in the anthology *Tales from the Captain's Table*.

David wrote an alternate-history *Next Gen* novel, *The Embrace of Cold Architects*, which appears in the anthology *Myriad Universes: Shattered Light*. He also co-wrote the television story for a first-season *Voyager* episode, "Prime Factors." Additionally, David has written more than a dozen articles for *Star Trek Magazine*. His work has appeared on both the *New York Times* and *USA Today* bestseller lists, and his television episode was nominated for a *Sci-Fi Universe* award.

You can chat with David about his writing at facebook.com/ DRGIII.